Chase

VR Tennent

Chase

Copyright © 2024 VR Tennent

Cover art by Kellie's Cover Design

Editing by Cath Lauria and Finishing by Fraser

Published by Frosty Enterprises Ltd

For everyone who put their head above the parapet,
stepped out of their comfort zone,
and did whatever the hell they wanted.

Author Note

Chase is a steamy mafia romance and intended for readers aged
eighteen years and over. It contains sexual scenes, violence,
strong language, and murder.
Chapter fifteen contains physical violence against teenagers.

Chase

Obnoxious. Unwanted. Unhinged.

And obsessed with my brother's girlfriend.

Love was something I never trusted myself to have... until I met her, trouble waiting to happen.

Samantha Coleman rocketed into my life and knocked me sideways. I watched her from the shadows as my obsession grew.

I used my influence to aid her career. I wanted her to have the life she desired, as long as I had control of it.

When danger reared its head, my instinct was to protect her. Step in and maim any villain who posed a threat.

She knew I was always there, and she loved my hidden attention. No longer able to only watch from the sidelines, I finally stepped out into the light.

I wanted her, and she knew it.

Only time will tell if my brother and I can learn to share.

I looked down at this stunning woman bursting with rage. Her blonde hair curled messily in all directions, and her intense blue eyes burned. Her voluptuous breasts were barely contained within the beige trench coat she wore, her long bare legs extending beneath the hem. She was still speaking, but I didn't hear her. All I could think about was the body under the fabric and what I could do to it. How much pleasure I would get from controlling it.

"Don't ever invade my space again, you creep. Who the hell do you think you are?" she snapped.

"My father wouldn't allow Violet to go back to Chicago with that arsehole," I countered grumpily, then crossed my arms over my chest to stop myself from reaching for her. My fingertips ached to touch her fired-up flesh.

"He isn't *allowing* it. He's fucking *arranging* it. Catch up, you absolute idiot," she shot back. "Were you not listening to a word I said?"

A woman had never talked to me like she did.

I always call the shots with women, but this one is different. My Rolex watch, hard-ass attitude, and articulate speech didn't impress her. Wilful eyes surveyed me as if I was a piece of shit on her shoe. When she focused on me, her nose pinched with disgust, but it was her expression that stung most; all I could see was pity.

Regardless, she looked both delectable and fuckable. And in need of a hard spanking. I've been obsessed with her ever since. Thoughts of her smart mouth and delicious figure have consumed my every waking hour. No other woman is of interest, only her. If I don't satisfy this craving soon, I may go insane.

That's why at this moment I'm hidden in the shadowed doorway across from Guilty Pleasures. Samantha hasn't arrived yet, but I'll wait here until she does. Then I'll straighten my suit and walk in like the paying patron I am. Since I met her a matter of weeks ago, all I've wanted to do is force her to submit to me, bend to my will, be mine. I've watched. I've waited. I've craved. Now I'm ready to collect what I'm owed.

The one problem with my plan is this—she's fucking my brother.

I'm not a man who chases a woman. I've never needed to. Normally, they flock to me if I show them a little interest. The only time the game of chase needs to be played is when I compete for her attention with another man—most often my brother, Connor. Since we were teenagers, we loved to go after the same girl, rubbing each other's noses in our success.

Once, our school dance was a hunting ground, and our target was a pretty little brunette whose name I can't even remember. We spent the weeks leading up to the big day romancing our prey. She eventually chose me, and I loved parading her around the school gym hall on that night, much to my brother's disgust. For the majority of the evening we glared at one another, until the girl I won became boring and I left her standing by the drinks table. Connor and I escaped the event with a bottle of vodka in search of more exciting entertainment. We toasted our short competition, then returned to being best friends.

But the rivalry over Samantha is different. Connor seems besotted already, and he has no idea about the desire I have for her. When he speaks to me of their short relationship, there's something in his voice I've never heard before. My sense tells me he cares for her, but my jealousy hopes he doesn't. If my brother is falling for the girl I want, I'm not sure it is a competition I can win. I'm not sure what would be worse—losing the girl or breaking my brother's heart. But then again, if I don't try, her taste will only ever be a mystery, and I'm not sure I can live with that.

The only woman I ever truly wanted before now was *also* one I could never have. She was the wife of one of my closest friends, the only permanent female in our group. Connie and Damon had been teenage sweethearts and were together twenty years when she was cruelly murdered over a year ago. The pain of losing her when she had never been mine was indescribable. It still is.

When the news of her death reached me, I collapsed in the middle of my office, unable to process the information. She was everything a man like me never gets. Both kind and loyal, Damon and her family were her everything. My soul wishes I could experience that kind of love for myself, but my head knows I would never be capable of giving the same.

So, I'll continue to watch the woman I want to experience now from the shadows, understanding that she will never be mine. I'm a man who doesn't deserve love. Most likely, I'm incapable of feeling it. All I feel is the intense need to control and possess something out of my reach, a possession that isn't mine. Yet.

The first time I followed Samantha, it wasn't a planned event. After our initial meeting, I needed to find out more about the bundle of fury who had put me in my place. It had been easy to obtain basic information, my sister being her close friend and having a loose tongue. I'd utilized my contacts to find the rest. Once I had her address, I was able to frequent her apartment, standing outside to catch a glimpse of the elusive Samantha Coleman.

Last week, while staking her out from the dingy café across the street, I witnessed a group of youths urinating in the doorway to her home. That, combined with other unsanitary and disgusting practices I'd seen during my few hours there, led me to decide that this area was not where she should be living. Sure, it was close to her job at the strip club, but if I had my way she wouldn't be there much longer. So, after a few phone calls, I organized her eviction due to fabricated issues with the building. As part of the process, Samantha and one of her roommates were offered an alternative apartment at a reduced rate in a better area. I secured the lease and subsidized the cost during the same phone call. She moves in January.

Unbeknownst to Samantha, she's moving closer to Canary Wharf—where I live. She will live in an apartment partly paid for by me, and I'll ensure that this intriguing woman is safe from the dangers of London, whatever the cost.

CHASE

Once I'd allowed myself to watch for her at her apartment, it had been simple to pick up her trail. Through my contacts at Guilty Pleasures, I was able to access her work schedule. The first night I sat down with a direct view of the pole, she had paused when our eyes met before she lifted her gaze and ignored me. She's been pretending I don't exist ever since.

The problem with becoming obsessed with a woman who has no interest in you is that it feeds the need for the chase. At first, I was unsure if she was comfortable with my presence, but recently, I've learned she is. A few days ago she slowed down when distance opened up between us, almost allowing me to catch up. Then she looked me square in the eye as we boarded the train and smiled broadly. Since that day, I haven't tried to hide. She's enjoying being pursued as much as I'm enjoying the hunt.

The sound of quick, light footsteps disturbs my troubled musings. When I look up, I see her familiar platinum blonde hair and trim, toned body scaling the rickety staircase at the back of the club. Samantha glances over her shoulder before pushing open the door. Our gazes meet and her mouth quirks into a small smile, then she disappears from view behind the fire door.

Her appearance is my cue to go and take my seat, the one I've been occupying for weeks. At the front and center of the stage, I can get the best view of the woman I want to touch but, morally, must try to resist.

Chapter Two

―――◆―――

Guilty Pleasures
Gentlemen's Club, London

Samantha

"The suit is here again," Mia announces. I shrug, trying to act relaxed about the fact that the guy I'm dating's brother appears to be obsessed with me. My roommate pulls her abundance of red waves into a knot and secures it on top of her head with a pin. "That's what, five nights in a row? He's sitting at the front again, with a perfect view of the pole."

"I'm sure he is," I mutter, keeping my attention fixed on myself in the mirror as I apply another coat of bright red lipstick.

"Does he know *you* know that he's following you?"

"I would assume so, considering he's shit at it."

"Does his brother know?"

I turn to face my friend, and she smirks.

"No," I answer bluntly.

"Why would you not tell your boyfriend that his brother is following you?" she says, her lips widening into a grin.

"Connor is not my boyfriend. We're fucking. I don't do relationships, you know that. Who else I'm involved with is none of his business—he agreed to my terms when I accepted his invitation to dinner."

"You're involved with your stalker?" she teases, picking at the open wound. The bizarre enjoyment I am getting out of being followed increases with each day.

"Stalker is a bit far-fetched, don't you think? Stalkers are meant to be dangerous."

"As far as I know, the definition of a stalker is someone who follows you." She lifts her phone from the table beside her and starts tapping at the digits. "Yes, according to the Cambridge English Dictionary, a stalker is someone who illegally follows and watches someone over a period of time." She grins, then adds, "Especially a woman."

"He's not doing anything illegal," I mutter. "He's just...there. Watching." Still sitting at the dressing table, I look into the mirror and my friend's eyes stare straight back at me.

"And that doesn't freak you out? Especially after..."

"No, I mean it did at first. But he's not like him. It actually makes me feel..." I pause, finding it difficult to explain how having a dangerous man following me around the dark streets doesn't bother me like it should. "I feel safe. I just know he won't hurt me."

She pushes her lips together, trying to hide her laughter. Her face is lit up with amusement at my pathetic response.

"And you're enjoying it," she says, teasing. "Two brothers, and both of them want in your panties. And from the color of your cheeks, you wouldn't be against the idea. Dirty bitch."

"I do not—" I begin to protest, and she waves my argument away with a red fingernail.

"Yes you fucking do. Anyway, back to my question. Do you not think the brother you're officially seeing should know about the other one's obsession?"

"No. My situation with Russell is not any of Connor's concern."

"I have a feeling your fuck buddy may have a different opinion than you on that."

"That's his problem, not mine. He knows the situation. Open relationship or none."

"Relationship," she says with a chuckle. "Fuck's sake, Sam. One minute it's fuck buddies and stalkers, and the next you're creating relationships with multiple men."

"Stop twisting my words," I snap.

Mia shrugs her shoulders, then slips the white silk robe covering them off before marching to the dressing room to collect her attire for the evening. I glance in her direction, but she's lost interest in our conversation about my current romantic predicament. Her position is clear—I'm playing two men whether I want to admit it or not. In all honesty, any romance that enters my life always ends up in a mess, so the circumstances should come as no surprise.

After my last long-term partner decided to drag me off stage at the club where I work, I implemented the no-boyfriend rule. For the past twelve months, it's worked well. That was until I met Connor Chase. I allowed myself to be romanced by a man who isn't husband material and lives a life I should stay far away from.

A few weeks ago, a lonely brunette stumbled into the clothes shop I work in to help pay rent. She looked lost, confused, and on her own in the big city. I remembered that feeling well, and my instinct was to help. Little did I know that my small gesture of kindness toward Violet Chase would turn my life upside down by throwing me into a world of dangerous families and domineering men. Sure, working at the strip club has prepared me well, but here we're protected, most of the time. But the world Violet and her brothers live in is a terrifying one, and no one can ever be fully trusted. Not even your closest family.

Guilty Pleasures Gentlemen's Club is one of a select few discreet, members-only establishments in London. From the outside, a passerby wouldn't know it was here. The entrance is a single blue door nestled between a fast food joint and a dry cleaner. There are no signs or prominent details; it looks like a normal entrance to an apartment above the stores on the ground level. But when you push the door open, you're met with a security guard in a tuxedo who only allows you past if you hold the shiny, gold members' card. Those allowed admission must scale a narrow staircase via yet another simple blue door before entering the club.

Inside, a circular stage sits at the center of the room with a pole that extends to the ceiling. Leather armchairs are placed around its edge in pairs, with small glass tables between them. A long, well-stocked bar sits to one side of the room. The whole place screams opulence and wealth, everything trimmed in gold or wrapped in dark velvet. Private booths are scattered around the venue. What happens within these walls stays here. Those who attend are never named, even though we all know who they are.

The men who hold memberships to this club include the most influential and affluent in London. They come here for business and pleasure, and the utmost discretion is guaranteed. When we signed our contract to work, we also signed a non-disclosure agreement. We promised never to discuss who we entertain or what we do for them; information such as that can be dangerous for the patrons if it falls into the wrong hands.

The club itself is owned by a powerful family, the Parkers of Glasgow. Joel Parker, head of the Glasgow mafia, runs a tight ship. He looks after both his staff and clients. We girls are never forced to do something we don't want, but the facilities are here if we choose to provide additional services. Security is tight, and unwanted wandering hands are banned. The no-touch policy is concrete unless an agreement is made in advance, and Joel Parker ensures that rule is enforced with no exceptions.

Last week, a member became overzealous with one of the girls on stage. As she approached the edge, he lunged forward to grab her ankle. Two security guards escorted him from the premises within minutes and his membership was suspended. No discussion, no second chances. If you touch the product without paying, then it's theft, and you are removed, no refunds.

My role within the club changes from day to day. Sometimes I work in the club, usually on the pole, and other times I recruit girls from around London to work here. Our clients attend regularly, and fresh entertainment is always appreciated.

I love my nights performing. The freedom of being on stage and able to express myself is something I've always craved. When I originally moved to the big city, my hopes were immense and unrealistic. In my mind, my feet would be dancing on a Westend stage within days. In reality, it's been six years and, at the age of twenty-seven, I'm running out of time. Perhaps the world of show business isn't for me and I need to consider a career change. I have a niggling craving to work in nursing, but with no qualifications or funds to train, my chances of succeeding are zero, so I may need to accept that my body will have to pay my wages for years to come.

The bright red leotard cuts high over my legs but low across my breasts, which swell within the fabric. My blonde locks are long and straight, stopping halfway down my back. I slip my feet into sky-high black heels, their platform encrusted with diamantes. The music changes outside, and I know there are only a few minutes until I am expected on stage, so I make my way to the club, ready to strut into the center with all eyes on me.

My colleague finishes her set, dismounting from the pole before waving and blowing kisses to the crowd. Men holler like schoolboys, and she beams at them. I roll my eyes. As much as I love performing, I hate the sleazeballs who gawk. Their eyes on my body make my skin crawl—most of them, anyway. There are a few whose attention I enjoy. No one touches me, though. Those days have passed, and I won't be giving anyone a private performance for cash.

The familiar beat fills the air, and I take my cue to step out of the shadows. The whistles begin as they do every night after I climb onto the stage and cross the sleek, black-tiled floor. My hands rise above my head, and I spin three hundred and sixty degrees, keeping my chin up and focusing on the mirrors covering the walls behind the men.

My fingers wrap around the stainless steel, followed by my leg. I spin again, then launch into the routine I know so well. Lost in the music, the watchers become irrelevant. The stares fade into the shadows, no more than a hum in the air.

My body vibrates to the beat as my skin slides over the slick metal. Every movement is on point, my heels hitting the floor before rising immediately to fly again. I pull myself higher into the air, wrapping a leg firmly around the bar, then allowing my body to fall backward, leaving me upside down and spinning slowly. I extend my arms and free leg dramatically, and my hair touches the floor with gravity pulling at the tips.

The final beats of the tune sound, and I know it's time for my dismount. Clutching the pole, I release my leg. I stretch lengthways, every muscle tensing to maintain the shape, then raise my ankles high to resemble an L-shape. I slowly walk through the air before lowering myself inch by inch to rest on the floor. With a flick of my hair, the music changes to the recognizable transition piece between dancers, and I stand to enjoy the audience's appreciation.

I walk to the front of the stage to take my bow. As I bend, crossing my legs and opening my arms wide, I'm momentarily frozen to the spot as my eyes lock with the man in front of me.

Russell Chase sits in the middle chair, as he has every time I've performed since the first time he appeared weeks ago. He's dark-haired, handsome, and an absolute asshole, but hell I find him attractive. He's bigger than his brother, Connor, and the opposite of him in personality. But put them side by side, and there's no doubt they're related. Both are gorgeous, wealthy, masculine, and oh so fucking dangerous. They are the light, and I am the moth. There's no doubt in my mind I'll get burned—or worse, incinerated—if the current situation continues: dating one brother while being stalked by the other. The solution is to walk away; the temptation is to sample both delicacies if the offer arises.

Dark eyes watch me retreat from the stage as he sits, wide-legged, sipping an amber drink. His hand drops to his crotch as his gaze holds mine, and he blatantly readjusts his cock, then smirks. A gasp catches in my throat, but I will my features to remain impassive. He can't know he affects me. I won't have a man like that think I want him. His ego doesn't need any nurturing; I'm sure there's a never-ending queue of featherbrained women willing to make him feel good.

When I reach the door to the dressing rooms, I turn to have a final glance at the crowd. Russell is gone, which is no surprise. I know exactly where he'll be; this won't be the last time I see him this evening. His presence will surround me until I enter the safety of my apartment, and up until then, he'll watch.

My journey home isn't long, at least not for now. A short walk to the tube station, two stops, then five minutes through the dark streets on the other side and I'll be there. I pull my black winter jacket around me as I step out through the rear entrance of the club onto the old, iron staircase. My heavy boots cause the metal to trill as I descend. It's cold, and a thin sheet of ice covers the ground. My sole slips, and as I grab the freezing handrail, the structure wobbles with the movement. For all the money spent inside the club, the outside needs extreme mainte-nance, but part of me believes that omission is deliberate —— a way to keep prying eyes off of what's inside.

His familiar shadowed figure stands in the same betting shop doorway as it has every time I have walked home recently. He should make me nervous, and the first time he was here, he did. But I know this man isn't like any of the other men I've met. He gives me a sense of peace with his presence. His bizarre obsession with me feels right.

I stroll past him, less than three feet between us, but keep my eyes focused in front, refusing to give him any attention. He steps out behind me, his dull footsteps echoing in the silent night. I keep walking, each stride deliberate and steady.

I skip down the steps at the tube station when the announcer advises the next train is approaching the platform. My toes land on the solid yellow line, the station quiet with only a handful of people milling around. I glance to my left, and Russell steps up to the line at the next door along. He doesn't look at me, but I see a dark smile on his lips. He enjoys this, him following and me knowing damn fine he's there.

We both step onto the train in synchronization, the doors opening and closing with equal precision. I stand in the center of the train and hold the red pole. He mirrors my movement, walking toward me and grabbing the same pole, his hand a fraction above mine. We don't look at each other, but I can hear his breathing, measured and throaty. I inhale deep to steady my nerves, and the strong aroma of cinnamon and male fills my nostrils. Fuck, he smells as good as he looks.

My stop approaches; he recedes, then steps out the next door in time with me once more. We've played the same game for days. The first night he followed me I was nervous but not terrified, then as each night passed it became perversely normal for him to be here. A naughty pleasure I craved.

The final part of my journey is short, only a few minutes walk to my apartment. After exiting the tube station, I turn down a small alleyway, reducing the time further. Russell is still behind me, possibly a hundred feet away. The sound of him is clear, but the scent of him sadly absent.

I'm passing a rear entrance to an office block when I become aware that we're not alone in the alleyway. Two men step out to block my path. Both are tall, with long beards and shaved heads. The clothes they wear are dirty and covered in rips and stains. It's hard to put an age on them, with it being dark and them unkempt, but I would guess they are in their fifties.

"All right, sweetheart?" the one on the right says. "Aren't you a pretty little thing? Got any cash?"

"No, move out my fucking way, arsehole." I reply, then step to the side before trying to walk around him. His hand flies out to connect with the wall to stop me from passing.

He leans in, his nose inches from mine. "Nasty little bitch, give us what we want and we won't hurt you."

"Piss off," I snarl, then drop my hand into my coat pocket in search of the small pen knife I carry for situations such as this.

"Money," the other bastard orders, reaching forward to grab my wrist.

The sound of a man clearing his throat causes both of them to move their focus from me, and I take the opportunity to wield my knife, swiping at the first man's arm. I catch his hand with the blade, and he snaps it away. I push past him and run.

When I get to the end of the alleyway, I turn back briefly. Russell has one man pinned against the brick wall by his throat, while the other asshole lays on the ground motionless. Russell's arm retracts, then a balled fist hits his captive squarely in the stomach. He glances in my direction, smiles and salutes, then continues his assault. I take that as my cue to escape home.

After pushing open my bedroom door, I throw myself onto my already messed-up bed; I didn't bother straightening the sheets this morning. As I hit the soft cotton, my phone beeps, and I pull it out of my pocket. A message from an unknown number blinks back at me on the screen.

> *Threats terminated. I'll always have your back, Trouble. Fuck, you look good wielding a knife. I love a lady with claws.*

CHAPTER THREE

---◆◇◆---

Connor's Apartment, The Level

Connor

My best friend stands opposite me in my kitchen as I stir the soup prepared by our shared housekeeper in the pot. His dark eyes move around my living area, taking in the details of my preparations for my date with Samantha tonight.

"Who did you say you were seeing?" Harrison asks. He walks over to the vase of red roses placed between the two settings on my glass dining room table. He touches one of the buds and glances in my direction.

"None of your business."

"Is it serious?"

"It's never serious," I mutter back, not looking at him. "But the more effort I make, the better rewarded I'll be. Women like flowers. It encourages them to spread their legs."

"True," he agrees, "but you never normally have to go to this extent to get laid." I scowl at him, then refocus on not burning the French onion soup. Mrs. D would kill me. She's busy finishing cleaning my bedroom in case I get lucky. I hope tonight is the night I do. Samantha made it clear we wouldn't be fucking until she said so, and hell, she's making me work for it. It's been six weeks of torture, me romancing, and her holding out. I've barely touched her ass through her jeans.

Harrison continues wandering around my home. He's been both my brother and I's best friend since we were children. When he was eight years old, we found him dumped in a ditch. My father took him under his wing, supporting his education while he was in the care system. Now the three of us own a law firm in Canary Wharf, all of us flying high, earning thousands each day, and living as neighbors in our fortress in the sky.

Russell, the oldest, owns the penthouse and often reminds us he's in charge—not that either of us listens. Harrison and I have apartments on the second-highest floor alongside our private boardroom. These two floors are known as The Level and are off-limits to anyone but those invited. Up here is our safe haven, away from the chaos of London and the dark world we work in.

"How's my sister?" I ask him, trying to divert the conversation away from my love life and back to his.

"She's fine. Full of hormones." He chuckles and shakes his head. "This morning, she told me that I should go out on the balcony and look down because that's where I'd be headed if I left my socks on the living room floor again. She said once she moves in full time, it won't be happening or I'll be looking for another roommate."

My sister, Violet, has been the love of Harrison's life since they were kids. After disappearing for thirteen years, she appeared back in London this summer, heartbroken and pregnant with her long-term lover's baby, a man who she's now discovered was married the whole time. My friend has stepped up to be both a dependable partner for her and father-to-be for the baby. Finally, both of them are with who they always should have been if outside elements hadn't gotten in the way. I love to see them both so happy.

"Anyway, who is it you're seeing?" he prompts again.

"It's none of your business," I repeat. The last thing I want Violet to know is that I'm trying to seduce her best friend. She knows we speak, but I don't want her unsolicited advice or opinions. Or worse, Violet speaking to Samantha on my behalf. Russell knows, but I tell him everything—he's a true brother. Hot-headed, sure, and sometimes insane, but he is the man I trust with my darkest secrets.

When I told him I was dating Samantha, he assumed it was casual sex. I never corrected him. Any sexual conquest always has been, but I know deep down this is different. However, she refuses to make it exclusive, insisting she never commits to anyone. She wants to remain independent with her options open. In the past, this would have been a dealbreaker for me, but to have her, I would agree to anything. My balls are firmly lodged in her grasp—metaphorically anyway. I wish they were physically.

"As you're not forthcoming with any information," Harrison says, "I'll be going. Your sister will come looking for me if I don't reappear soon."

"Yeah, fuck off. Keep that explosive bomb of hormones in your apartment." He laughs, then waves as he leaves through my front door. Harrison is like another brother, and I hope one day to be able to call him one.

My attention returns to the soup as our elderly housekeeper appears. "Everything is ready, Mr. Chase," she tells me. Mrs. D is an absolute diamond and maintains the whole two floors of The Level. She's like a mother to us, ensuring our homes are clean and food fresh as we go about our busy lives. "Is there anything else you need before I leave?"

"No, Mrs. D. You're an angel, as always."

"Well, I hope the young lady appreciates all the effort you have gone to." She holds my gaze for a moment, her eyes dancing with mischief. "I get the feeling this one is rather special."

"I think so," I admit, relieved at having someone to confide in. "This is something I've never felt before."

"What is?"

"This feeling. It's like..." I trail off, not knowing how to explain the constant need for Samantha. The constant craving

23

to have her with me. "In a matter of weeks, she has me thinking of her in every waking moment. I open my eyes and she's there; when I close them, she appears in my dreams." The older woman chuckles. "What's so funny?"

"That, my boy," she whispers, walking over to me and reaching up to touch my cheek, "is what it feels like to fall in love."

"Love?" I scoff dramatically, all the while knowing she's right.

"Yes." She smiles softly. "You may be a successful man in your thirties, Connor, but this is the first time for you. I see it in your eyes. This girl is special, so don't mess it up. Go all in. You deserve to be loved." Wrinkled fingers pinch my cheek, then she rises on tiptoe and presses her lips to my skin "Have a wonderful night," she says before leaving.

Thirty minutes later, I'm in my bedroom adjusting my hair again in the mirror when the alarm sounds that my front door has opened. I stalk through to my open-plan living space to find Russell escorting Samantha into my home.

"Look what I found on the street," he says sarcastically. I narrow my eyes at him, and he cocks his head to one side before beaming. "I think this is your lost property."

"I'm no one's property," Samantha snaps. My focus drops to my brother's hand on the small of her back. My body tenses, annoyed by the contact. Fucking asshole always has to overstep the mark.

"Stop touching my girlfriend," I tell him. He raises both hands in mock surrender and takes a deliberate step to the side as his grin widens further. My brother knows how to push my buttons, and trying to take what's mine is one of the ways he enjoys doing it.

"Girlfriend?" he questions, turning to Samantha who flushes as he stares. She bites her lip, and an uneasy feeling skims my skin. She's affected by him; I can see it blatant and natural. "I thought your relationship was only sex. Girlfriend is a level up from fuck buddy."

"We haven't had sex," Samantha says, hostile, and I wince. Fuck, he'll never let me live this down. I've been implying that she's explosive between the sheets. His face lights up but abruptly darkens as she strolls to my side, throws the handbag she's carrying on the floor, then wraps her arms around my neck.

She looks incredible wearing a figure-hugging winter coat, the zipper lowered and exposing the swell of her breasts. Long, slender legs protrude from the hem before dainty feet are encased in strappy black heels. Her toenails are painted scarlet, a hint of the fun that is no doubt underneath her clothes. Azure eyes lock on to mine, and she says sexily, "But I have a feeling that situation will be changing tonight."

Lost in her gaze, I only hear the sound of rushed footsteps and my front door slamming closed as my brother leaves. Choke on that, sucker.

***

Samantha

Connor wraps his arms around my waist, big hands splaying over my ass and pulling me to him. His cock hardens against my stomach, and I smile against his lips. The door vibrates loudly after being thumped closed.

"Are you going to let me touch you tonight?" he asks, his voice soft but filled with hope. The smell of mint hits my nostrils from freshly brushed teeth.

"You're already touching me." Our lips connect briefly before he pulls back.

"You're such a fucking tease. I want to feel what's underneath this." His strong fingers squeeze my ass through my jacket. I wriggle from his grip, then step back from him. His pupils dilate slightly as I lift one hand to my zipper, pinch it between my fingers, and lower it slowly.

There's the sound of metal on metal as it glides down my body. My jacket opens, exposing the barely-there bra and thong underneath. "Fuck," he hisses, his eyes flicking upward as his hand runs through his hair. A naughty smile plays on his lips when he returns to focus on me. "What sort of dress code is this?"

I open the jacket fully and slip it off my shoulders, letting it fall into a puddle on the floor. Then, I lift my hands into the air and spin in front of him so he gets the full effect of my sheer underwear. I spent ages ensuring that no pesky hair would be found when he was down there. When my eyes return to his on the completion of my rotation, we stare at each other for a beat.

"The dress code of a woman who wants to make a man feel oh so fucking good," I whisper.

"A man? Or your man?" he asks, raising an eyebrow.

"The man standing right here, right now. You deserve a reward after your exemplary behavior these past few weeks."

"If this is the prize for behaving myself," he mutters, stepping forward and taking hold of my hips. "I'll join the fucking Boy Scouts." I laugh, the sheer joy of being in his presence consuming me. Connor Chase makes me so happy; he's the ultimate morally gray Prince Charming, deadly but swoon-worthy.

"But..." I lift a single finger to his lips while biting my own, trying to hide the threatening smile. "Before I reward you, I need to eat. You want me in tip-top shape for our first time." His hands take both of mine and drop to waist level. Our eyes are locked. I can't bear to look away from his beautiful brown ones.

"I'll give you whatever you want," he says fiercely, "if it means I'm going to be able to do all the things I've been dreaming about tonight."

"I didn't say you would be doing anything," I tell him. "You'll take what you're given." He opens his mouth to protest, and I glance over his shoulder at the liquid bubbling over a pot on the stove. "I think you need to get back in the kitchen." He follows my line of sight, then lets go of my hands before almost sprinting to remove the pot from the heat.

"Fuck, Mrs. D will kill me if it's ruined."

I move round to stand behind him, then slide my hands around his waist as he stirs the soup in the pot. The feel of denim beneath my fingers heightens my libido, and my stomach flips, I press my body against his back and slide one leg between his so my thigh touches his ass.

"If you've burned my meal, Mr. Chase," I purr, "what would have been a reward this evening, may have to morph into a punishment." Placing my lips against his perfectly white shirt, I press firmly, then nip taut skin through the soft fabric. When I pull back, a smudge of red stains the pristine surface. "Whoops," I say with a giggle. "I've messed up your shirt with my lipstick. We may have to take turns punishing each other."

"Fuck this," he growls, spinning to face me. "You're pushing my limits on being a gentleman."

"I didn't say you were a gentleman," I shoot back, cocking my head to the side and widening my eyes. "I said you were well-behaved. And good boys deserve a reward."

"And I am fucking claiming it." He turns back briefly and flicks the switch on the stove, then grabs my ass lifting me in one motion up onto his waist. My legs and arms wrap around him as he walks across his kitchen to sit me on the island.

The surface is an expanse of cool black granite. As he releases my body and steps away, I place my hands behind me and shake my hair. Strong fingers come to my knees and encourage my legs wide, exposing the see-through scrap of material covering my pussy.

"You look incredible," he says, the lilt of arousal clear in his tone.

"What about dinner?"

"I'm skipping straight to dessert." He takes one of my ankles in each hand, encouraging them upwards until my knees are bent and heels are balanced on the worktop. "Lie down," he orders firmly, and I push myself backward then lower myself, my hair splaying across the dark surface.

Connor stands between my legs and looks down at me, lying in the middle of his counter with my legs wide. He places a hand on either side of my waist before lowering his lips to my stomach and pressing gently just above my belly button. He repeats the process slowly, each time moving his lips fractionally farther down. Strong hands move under my legs and lift them onto his shoulders.

He glances up at me. "Raise your hands above your head," he says. "You look perfectly laid out, like a final meal. If I were on death row, you would be my last request." I do as he asks, and hungry eyes run over my skin. "Now, stay like that while I get to know the part of you I've been dying to meet."

"I was rewarding you," I protest.

"If I do a good job, you can pay me back later. The only sound I want to hear now is your moans. It's rude to interrupt someone while they're eating."

Chapter Four

Russell's Penthouse, The Level

Russell

Fury. That's all I feel at this moment. My bastard brother is downstairs with the woman I want, and jealousy and rage consume every inch of my body. She knew what she was doing when she walked across the room and draped herself over him. It was deliberate, and a direct goad. A statement that she isn't mine to have.

But if I can't have her, I'll make damn sure he can't either. Our whole lives have been like this, brothers so close but always confrontational. That fact isn't going to change now.

As I sit in my penthouse, looking over the London rooftops, my mind wanders to what they're doing only a floor below me. Perhaps now they are sitting down to dinner. A meal my brother has put a lot of effort into, or Mrs. D has. No doubt, Connor will have given her a single rose and taken her by the hand before offering her a chair. He'll sweet talk her, only the way he can.

Though my brother and I are both ruthless, Connor does a better job of hiding the jagged edges. My faults are stark and undeniable. They burst from me when I least expect it, all the parts of myself I hate. And every poor bastard I meet knows it.

My mind fills with images of him wining and dining with her. They hold hands across the table as they discuss nonsense, both of them pretending tonight isn't purely a fuck fest, that this is somehow dating like adults. But I know my brother, and I've had plenty of girls like Samantha. Neither of those backgrounds merge into meaningful relationships. From the small interaction I saw tonight, it's obvious there was chemistry. However, incompatible liquids should never mix; they cause explosions, which result in casualties or worse.

Unable to shake the painful images from my mind, I stand abruptly then walk over to the drink cabinet and pour myself another glass of whiskey. I watch the amber liquid splash into the heavy crystal glass, then immediately lift it to my lips, downing it in one swallow. As I go to pour another, I give in to the niggling urge. I place the glass back down on the wooden surface and make my way to my balcony, pushing open the sliding door and stepping out into the cold winter air. The sharpness bites through the thin black t-shirt I am wearing, but I ignore the stabbing reality of my actions.

The ladder between my apartment and my brother's below are only meant to be used in emergencies, and then only if absolutely necessary. They were installed after the building was constructed outside of standard regulations. But living the life we do, we always ensure we have an escape route. As dangerous as it sounds, ladders at the top of a skyscraper may offer a safer route than being cornered by an enemy.

I stand, grasping the freezing chrome handrail as I look down on the lights of the city, trying to twist the current situation into a conceivable emergency. I can't. It doesn't matter which spin I place on it right now, there's no sane reason for me to descend from the fifty-eighth to the fifty-seventh floor hanging onto the outside of the building, but I won't rest until I see what is happening. If I see her with him, perhaps the visual reality will curb my growing obsession.

I step up onto the barrier, swing my leg over the rail, and place a foot on the cold metal. When my body is fully on the outside of the balcony, I brave a glance down and my stomach flips. Fuck, this is high up. My mind briefly wanders to what would happen if I let go. How high up *am* I? I've never thought to check. Thinking back on my knowledge of buildings, I know each floor is around ten to twelve feet tall. As I make the calculation, I slowly start to descend the rungs, pushing the soles of my shoes against the slick grips.

Seven hundred—right now I should be around seven hundred feet in the air. If I were to fall, there would be none of me left. I'd be unrecognizable, merely a disgusting splatter on the pavement below. Plenty of people would celebrate the loss of me, very few would mourn. I know I'm not liked by most.

After what feels like an eternity, my foot hits the top of the handrail of Connor's apartment. Nervous of being seen, I slide off the ladder quickly and move to stand behind the half-closed curtain covering the glass sliding doors. His living space, like all of the apartments in this building, is open plan, and I have a direct view of the kitchen. My rage, which had subsided slightly as I scaled the skyscraper and calculated the distance between myself and death, reappears with full force.

Samantha is laid out on top of the modern kitchen island, her knees bent and open wide. Long slender legs are hooked over Connor's shoulders, and ankle-breaking black heels dangle down his back. She looks to be wearing only a minute bra—I can see her plump nipples erect beneath the sheer fabric. Waves of blonde hair I've imagined wrapping around my fingers lie across the dark surface. My brother's face is buried between her legs, his expression hidden by her thigh, but his tense body and firm fingers gripping her ass tell me he's enjoying himself.

His subject's eyes are closed, but I watch on as she arches her back from the worktop, thrusting her pussy upwards farther into his face. His fingers tighten and plump flesh spills around the edges of his grip, the skin turning a beautiful shade of pink.

He pulls her closer and she slides fractionally toward the edge, deeper onto his tongue.

I watch on in awe, disgusted with myself but unable to tear my eyes away. Samantha writhes underneath my brother's touch, completely lost in the moment. Her chin lifts and her eyes open, her stunning body spasming before my eyes. The unmistakable sight of a woman reaching orgasm plays out before me. I can't hear the moan that escapes her lips, but I don't need to. I know it is one of pleasure. My brother rises from his position, wiping at his lips with his hand. They smile manically at one another, and Samantha's focus moves toward where I stand.

Unknowingly, I have moved out into the open. I'm caught standing like a schoolboy with his nose pressed against the glass watching a forbidden scene play out before me.

She doesn't flinch; she merely stares back impassively as if I'm not there. I take the opportunity to step once again behind the curtain, out of view. Momentarily, I consider that she didn't see me, even though I know she did. There was no scream of terror—she just looked at me like all the times she has as I watched her dance, with nothing but pity and disdain in her gaze. Having swerved an awkward conversation or beating from my brother, I take the chance to leave, scurrying back to my penthouse the way I came.

***

CHASE

The Level Boardroom

Connor strolls into the boardroom the following morning like the cat that got the cream. Sadly, I watched as he drank, and the reality increased my anger, which hasn't dissipated since last night. He's dressed in his sweats while I sit in my full suit, ready to leave immediately after this meeting to head to our office in Canary Wharf.

We use the boardroom on the same floor as Connor and Harrison's apartment for meetings that can't be conducted in the office. Perhaps the information being discussed is highly sensitive, or it most likely concerns a case that isn't officially on our law firm's books. We meet here with men who support our *other* business dealings, the ones that can't be discussed out in the open.

"Day off?" I snap as Connor walks over to make a coffee at the machine.

"Coffee?" he replies, glancing over his shoulder. "You sound as if you need it."

"No."

"No, thank you," he corrects me. "Fuck Russ, who twisted your panties this morning?"

"You," I mutter. "This is meant to be a business meeting, and you're here dressed as if you're lounging on the sofa scratching your cock."

"Fuck off." He lifts his mug from the machine, then walks over to sit down opposite me. The large glass boardroom table

35

stretches out between us. "I'll get ready once we've had this shitshow of a meeting, whatever it's about."

"Still got company?" I probe, unable to keep my questions at bay. The desperation to know whether Samantha stayed the night is fierce.

"No, she went home," he says with a scowl, and I relax fractionally. Not staying over means things haven't progressed beyond fucking. Once she spends the night, my position could become more complicated. Not that it isn't already.

"Did your tongue action not satisfy her?" The words pass between my lips before I can stop them. His eyes narrow, but he says nothing. His response tells me that Samantha never told him about my snooping. My confidence rises a fraction with his lack of knowledge, so I revert to my old ways. "Maybe she needs a real man to make her cunt drip."

He shoots to his feet and storms around the table until he stands above me. "Stand the fuck up," he snarls.

"No." His fingers take hold of my shirt collar and pull me to my feet. "What's up, brother? Have I struck a nerve? Was your piece not satisfied with your performance?" We stand in the boardroom, nose to nose as he pulls me toward him. "Unsatisfied women have wandering eyes...and arses."

My brother pulls harder on my clothes then pushes me back a few steps. Being taller and bigger than him, I could stop the motion if I wanted to, but I allow him his caveman moment.

"Never speak of Samantha like some cheap slut again," he barks. "You're not fit to lick her boots."

"Possessive already, brother. She must be good in bed. That's if you got the chance to find out. The little bitch has been holding out on you from what she said last night." I keep goading him, unsettled by his reaction to my comments. It's clear he cares, which makes my position even more precarious. If I am going to pursue Samantha, I need to know what I am getting into.

He laughs out loud and then rolls his eyes. "You're still a fucking teenager, Russ. You've no idea what it feels like to be with a real woman. One you fucking want." We stare at each other, and his eyes narrow. "Yes brother, I want to make her mine. Permanently. Do you have a problem with that?"

I force a shrug from my body to deflect his suspicion, but the uneasy sensation in my belly magnifies.

"No, it's your life. If you want to be chained to one woman, it's your cock that will miss out. Has she agreed to your request for exclusivity?"

"I haven't asked her yet," he says. "But I am confident she's not sleeping with anyone else. She has too much respect for herself to be putting it around."

"Maybe," I mutter, pulling his fingers from my shirt collar. "I suppose you'll find out. Probably best to head down to the sexual health clinic and get checked out, though. You never know what vermin chicks could be riddled with." I don't see his fist coming—the sharp crack to my jaw takes me by surprise, and I stagger backward.

"I said shut the fuck up."

Just then, the boardroom door opens, and Harrison walks in already dressed for the office. "Morning, boys," he says, jovially. All these happy bastards in love are doing my head in. "Shit, am I interrupting a Chase brothers' debate?"

"No debate," Connor responds as I rub at my chin. "Russ knows exactly where I stand."

"That's going to bruise, you arsehole."

"Just don't check yourself out in the mirror for a few days," Connor shoots back. "Then you won't need to stress about your good looks."

"I'm due in court," I say, petulantly. He shrugs, turns, and walks back to finish making his coffee, completely unruffled by the fact he will have marked my face.

Harrison looks between us, not speaking but assessing the situation. He's watched many of our arguments since we were teenagers, so our disagreeing won't come as a surprise. He's also ripped us apart before we tore limbs from each other in the past.

"How was your night?" he asks Connor, but before he can answer, the private elevator to the boardroom sounds, alerting us to the other members of our little vigilante band's arrival.

"Thank fuck, saved by the bell. At least I won't need to listen to your lovey-dovey bullshit," I mutter. Connor frowns, but then all our attention moves to Damon and Hunter entering the room.

"Morning," they call in unison.

"Mine is two sugar and milk," Hunter adds in Connor's direction. He's stirring his drink in the mug. "And give me one of those cute biscuits on the side." Connor flips him the bird, but takes a second cup from the shelf to do as he's told.

Hunter Devane and Damon McKinney couldn't be more different. Hunter is the head of the Irish mafia in London, and Chief Constable Damon McKinney is on his payroll. They're friends and should-be enemies, but both are key players within our little team. Our band of five works together in the shadows to bring some justice in cases where legal routes won't obtain it. Together, we've taken down and disposed of an array of criminals who caused unnecessary pain to the people of London. Being called here today means there's yet another task to investigate, and finding justice may require blurred lines and sharp knives.

Hunter strolls over to the boardroom table and pulls out one of the black leather chairs. He places a booted foot on the smooth material, then rolls up the leg of his dark jeans to expose three knives strapped to his calf.

"For fuck sake, Devane," Harrison mutters. "Take your feet off the furniture. Dirty arsehole. Mrs. D just cleaned in here yesterday."

"Just getting my breakfast," he replies, pulling a small knife from its resting place. He drops his foot back on to the floor before dusting at the mark on the chair lazily with a hand before sitting down. Connor places Hunter's coffee beside him then goes to take his own chair.

In the center of the table is a huge basket of fresh fruit. Mrs. D is an angel at keeping us fed and clean. Damon appears at my side, grabbing my shoulder in welcome. We watch on as the knife between Hunter's fingers flies across the table and spears a plump, red apple. He leans forward, lifting it with the handle of the knife. He spins three hundred sixty degrees in his seat, then takes a bite out of the soft flesh.

"Okay," Hunter says, gesturing with his free hand. "Does someone want to tell me why we are here?"

The remaining men take their seats, and all eyes move to Harrison, who called this meeting late last night. Harry tends to be the point of information when it comes to cases or new justices needing to be served. His background as an orphan has given him a kind heart and the drive to right wrongs, but his skills as a lawyer make him dangerous to anyone who stands in his way.

"Organs," Harrison says.

"Organs?" Connor questions. "As in the musical instrument played in a church?"

"No, you fuckwit," I snap, annoyed by my brother's stupidity. This fucking woman has gone to his brain and he's dreaming of musical notes and hearts. "I assume you mean organs from the body?"

"Yes," Harrison confirms. "There's a growing black market for organs within London. Demand is increasing, and there are questionable practices in place at a few hospitals."

"And you have come by this information how?" Damon probes. "There hasn't been anything passed by my desk in an official capacity, and I am not aware of any chat in the station regarding black market organ sales."

"A client of the law firm brought it to my attention. His mother sadly passed away last week. She had not permitted her organs to be donated. When the family visited her for one last time, a nurse mentioned the selfless gift of organ donation his mother had made. The loose-lipped nurse went on to say a woman had received her heart, which had in turn saved her life.

"The information, which I assume was told in an attempt to comfort my client on the loss of his mother, shocked him, because his mother had always believed the body should not be tampered with upon death. He requested to see her medical records, and then came to me to be sure there wasn't any organ donation request he was unaware of. After scouring through the records, it's clear that donating her organs was against his mother's wishes."

"And the reason the police haven't been informed?" Damon asks sharply.

"My client is well known to your lot, and he doesn't want to attract any unwanted attention," Harrison tells him. All the men in the room chuckle and nod. That's the general situation with most of our law firm's clients. They pay us to defend them for a reason, and we charge what we do because we're bloody good at it.

"My lot," Damon says with an eye roll. "The way things are going, I won't be part of the boys in blue for much longer." Hunter slaps his hands on the table and all eyes snap to him.

"About fucking time, McKinney. You need to come fully to the dark side. I told you, you always have a job with me."

"Maybe. Can we get back to the information?" Damon says, diverting the conversation back to the task at hand and away from his complex career choices.

"Anyway," Harrison continues. "The client in question asked me to do some research, and after a few calls it turns out that his isn't the only family who have found their deceased loved ones' organs gone against their wishes. The hospitals in question are claiming paperwork issues, but my gut tells me there's more to it."

"Okay, so what do you need from us?" I ask.

"Nothing at the moment, maybe just keep your ears to the ground. But if you could do some digging at the station, McKinney?" Damon nods. "And Devane, maybe ask some of your men on the ground if they've heard of any organs being sold?"

"Sold?" Connor interrupts. "How do we know they've been sold?"

"We don't," Harrison says. "But what I know from the little research I've done is that these transplants aren't on the organ procurement or transplantation register anywhere in the government records I can access, nationally or internationally. There's no trace of where these organs have gone on any legal medical database. The only details are at the hospital level, which seems to keep its data to itself, and are scarce from what I could find in general."

"Fuck, so you're telling me that some maniac is selling hearts, lungs, and kidneys from dead people then sticking them in half-dead people," I mutter, my stomach churning at the images of dirty operating rooms and backstreet doctors flitting through my mind.

"Perhaps," Harrison says, "But we won't know until we find out who's removing them, and who's receiving them."

Hunter claps his hands and rubs them together. His eyes are wild. Anything related to blood and gore is his thing. The small knife he used to skewer the apple now balances on the tip of his finger. He throws it high in the air. It circles, then drops back down, and he catches it nimbly between his fingers and grins.

"Well, when we find the bastards stealing poor grannies' organs, I'll be happy to cut out theirs and give them to more needy individuals."

Chapter Five

Chase, Chase and Waite
Law Firm, Canary Wharf

Connor

Russell storms around the main office. He strides between the desks of our team members snarling at people as he passes. He's always been an asshole, but today is one of his worst days ever. I know my brother, and he acts like a jerk when he hurts. What's hurting him, however, is the real question.

Unable to watch any more carnage, I rise and go to open my office door. Harrison isn't here; he's in court all day. His calming influence is missed. The three of us run the law firm together, but he's the best manager. I keep to myself, preferring to pore over files rather than discuss issues between staff members. Russell is the loose cannon and has caused more than one employment tribunal against the firm.

"Russ, can I have a word?" I call.

"No, I'm busy." Intense eyes barely glance in my direction before returning to focus on our poor accounts clerk, who's on the receiving end of his wrath.

"Russ, now." My voice is raised higher than before, the tone sharp. He pauses mid-scream then turns to face me, his face contorting in irritation. "Now," I repeat.

Before my eyes, he transforms further into a sulky teenager, slamming his hand down on the clerk's desk then storming across the office floor. He goes to push past me, one suited shoulder colliding with the other. I step back to allow him entry, and he grunts what could be a "thank you." After he starts pacing around my office, I close the door and return to sit at my desk.

I watch my brother stalk in circles, every so often stopping to look at one of the pieces of artwork on the walls. He spends a few minutes studying a contemporary abstract that hangs center stage on the longest wall.

What interested me about the painting was the bizarre mix of colors and outlines, which allowed different viewers to see a variety of subjects. To some it's merely shapes and tone, for others, there's a battle scene with horses and knights. For me it's also an investment and, hopefully, profit. Artwork has held value for centuries, and that won't change now. It's somewhere I feel safe lodging my money.

"I never know what you see in this shit," Russell says, his eyes still fixed on the painting. "A toddler could draw better."

"I see dollar bills, brother. Long-term security. My man tells me this artist is one to watch. It made sense to buy now rather than in a year when his notoriety grows more."

"Is your art expert a magician as well? It would take a miracle to make this crap worth anything. What did you pay for it?" he asks, finally breaking his stare and turning to face me.

"You don't want to know."

"Tell me. Make my day better."

I shrug and lean back on my chair. Russell is tense—that much is obvious—but then again, he always is. My brother is always one sentence away from detonation, no matter how well his day is going.

"Five hundred."

"Well," he says, "for five hundred pounds it's worth the risk, I suppose."

"No, brother. Five hundred thousand." The familiar flare of shock washes over his face, his eyeballs bulging from their sockets as his hands ball into fists.

"You spent five hundred thousand pounds on *that*." He gestures over his shoulder with his chin. "Have you undergone a lobotomy I wasn't aware of?"

One syllable at a time, I tell him, "It is an investment."

"You would be better throwing cash on a roulette wheel."

"Maybe, but then again, I could be sitting on the next Picasso." He grunts non-committally, then returns to staring at the blocks of color. "Are you going to tell me what's bothering you, or do I have to guess?"

"I'm fine," he says, "just fed up being surrounded by fuckwits and love-drunk idiots." I snigger, and he spins to face me once more. His eyes narrow. "You being one of them."

"Am I a fuckwit or a love-drunk idiot? Please tell."

"Both. What did you want, or did you call me here for your entertainment?" He moves to sit on the opposite chair, then leans back to mirror my pose. It doesn't escape me how alike we are, though I am not sure Russ sees it. Our mannerisms often mimic one another, something I notice again as I maintain my calm state. Meanwhile, my brother misses small things daily in his constant state of fury.

"I wondered what your thoughts were on this supposed organ theft Waite has uncovered. Interesting, no?"

"There will always be a crime when there's money to be made," he says. "People's desperation to survive makes sustaining life a lucrative business."

"True, but I wonder how the donors are chosen and then matched with the recipients." His focus moves around my office, and I hear his foot hitting the floor in a slow rhythm as he thinks. "The majority of major organs need to be transplanted within a matter of hours. It's a delicate operation to manage legally, never mind under the radar."

"No doubt we will be dragged into this shit whether we want to be or not," he says at last. "So, how was your romantic evening?" His question surprises me after his shitty attitude earlier.

"Enjoyable."

"I bet." He squares his shoulders and his mouth twists in the way it always does before he offends someone. "I mean, she is a professional sex worker, so she's bound to know the best ways to milk a cock."

"You disgusting bastard. She dances."

"Now," he continues, "but maybe you should ask the stunning Samantha what she offered as extras in the past." His eyes widen, and I grind my teeth in a pathetic attempt to hold my temper.

"We all have a past, Russ. We've all done things we regret. It's how we look to the future that matters. Samantha has ambition and career goals."

"To do what? She's yet another failed Westend wannabe according to Violet."

I won't comment on his knowledge, but I file away the fact that he has been discussing my soon-to-be girlfriend with our sister.

"She wants to be a nurse. She has been looking at options to return to study," I tell him, and his mouth snaps closed. Shock flutters over his features before he rearranges them again to become inexpressive. "Her dream of working in theatre may have fallen flat, but she knows where she wants to be now. And her long-term goal isn't to be a pole dancer."

"And she told you this?"

"Yes."

"She'd look hot in a nurse's uniform," he says, and I pick up the blue spikey stress ball sitting on my desk to launch it at him. It bounces off his forehead, and he laughs. The charged atmosphere disappears with the sound—I love to see him smile when he's relaxed. It's sadly all too infrequent.

Even though my brother is an asshole, I love him and he loves me. We have watched each other's back since we were kids, but with Russell being the oldest, it was always him who bore the brunt of our father's wrath. That's something I'll never forget or take for granted. My brother took a beating more than once for me, and I know, if he felt he needed to, he would do it again now.

"You're such a jackass."

"But you love me," he says. I don't answer him, but we grin at each other for a moment. "Are you seeing her again tonight?"

"No, she's working."

"Ah, the complications of dating a career woman. Well, brother, the chat was great, but I need to return to my station."

"Don't fire anyone," I say, and he shrugs. "I mean it. The team is working well, and we don't need any reruns of your previous dismissals."

"If the bastards will do their work and not eat my lunch in the process, then we won't have a problem." My mind flits back to the afternoon I found him clearing someone's desk because they had eaten his sandwich. "It's a simple request."

"Stick to the process, Russ."

"Why should I when I have Waite to sort it out? He loves a difficult case to fight. I like to keep him on his toes by creating some myself." With that final statement, he walks out of my office, slamming the door as he leaves. My prized artwork rattles on the walls, and a signed copy of Stephen King's *The Shining* crashes to the floor. It falls open on a familiar page, and the quote about always being the caretaker blinks back at me.

Yes, Mr. King, and don't I fucking know it.

My mind wanders back to the night before, my first taste of Samantha. Hell, it had been amazing. She was sweeter than I could ever imagine. After my unexpected meal on my kitchen island when she arrived barely dressed, we moved to my bedroom. It had been explosive from start to finish. Her body had molded around my fingers as if she was made for me. As I grazed her thighs with my fingertips, she'd spread her legs further. My lips touching her skin caused a tingle of electricity to pass between us.

When I took her the first time, she was beneath me. Her blonde hair spilled over my black satin sheets. Still wearing her see-through bra, I'd released her tits from the cups. The wire pushed them higher, erect nipples begging me to suck them. I'd taken the first one between my teeth gently, then run my tongue around the tip. Her back arched, pussy touching my cock still contained in my boxers.

"Please," she'd whimpered, impatient.

"Not yet." I'd tightened my grip on her nipple, my teeth biting into the soft flesh. She pushed harder against me, then wrapped her hands around my neck. I'd removed them one by one, pinning them down on the pillows on either side of her head. "I said, not yet. When I tell you no, I mean it."

"Can I not persuade you?" Her wrists flexed beneath my grip, and I responded by pushing them further into the goose feather. The dark satin gave way as smooth flesh sunk into the fabric. "I need you to fuck me now."

"No. There's something you need to learn if this is going to be a regular event." She blinked up at me with bright blue eyes, her fierce expression morphed into curiosity. "When I fuck, I like to be in control. As this is our first time, I've been gentle."

"Why? I'm a big girl. Tell me what you want to do to me." Her lips widened to expose perfect white teeth. I tightened the grip on her left wrist.

"I want to tie this to that." My eyes moved deliberately to the left-hand bedpost. Her line of vision followed mine. "Then I want to do the same to this one over here." I transferred the pressure to her right wrist before moving my focus to the right-hand bedpost. Her breasts rose into the air as a breath caught in her throat.

"Are you nasty in the bedroom, Mr. Chase?" she teased, and I smiled to myself.

"Nasty? No. Demanding? One hundred percent. When you allow me to do what I want to do to you, Sam, I want you to enjoy it. I want to be able to secure you, and use your body for my pleasure while you crumble under me." Her breathing, which was getting louder with my words, deepened further.

With my left hand, I skimmed her skin then placed my palm over her pussy. "Are you wet thinking of what it would feel like for me to have complete control of you?"

"Yes," she hissed between her teeth. "I want it now."

"No, our first time needs to be like this. But one night soon, I'll tie you up, spread your legs, and fuck you until you can't walk. Now, close your eyes." The blue orbs I'd been fixated on disappeared. I quickly freed my cock and moved the scrap of material dividing us to the side, then slid between swollen, wet lips.

Her pussy opened enough to let me in, but her walls held on tightly. She groaned with my entry, immediately flexing, her hips wanting more. "You're on birth control?" I whispered, dropping my lips to her ear.

"Uh huh," she confirmed, eyes still closed.

"Good, because I never want to fuck you with anything between us. You feel so fucking good, Sam." Her eyes opened, and she smiled the most dazzling smile.

"Move," she said, deliberately mouthing the word. "I want to feel what it's like to be fucked by a gentleman."

"A gentleman, you say. I doubt you will call me that after you can't walk tomorrow."

Sex has mostly been pleasurable for me. I could count on one hand how many times I've not enjoyed the feel of a woman. Over the years, though, I've never had a serious relationship. Sure, some girls hung around for a while, but I was never sure if they were there for me or my wallet. My experience has been that as time passes, expectations increase. The restaurants have to get more expensive, the trips more luxurious, and the gifts more frequent. When the time inevitably comes that I feel more like an ATM than a man, I tend to end the connection.

Samantha, however, emits an alien vibe—one I am unfamiliar with. When we are together, her attention is never fixed on the label on my suit jacket or the color of my credit card. When she talks to me, she looks me dead in the eye, her focus never wavering from the words coming from my lips. She listens and responds with sensible points or an amusing quip.

The conversations we've had over these few short weeks have been mind-blowing. Not because of the content, but because of the interaction. The fact is, she listens to what I say. She's interested in my opinions on topics that may seem unimportant to most. She seems happy for me to discuss my latest artwork purchase or the new horror novel I'm engrossed in. We touch on my work and my role within the law firm, where I fit into the puzzle of Chase, Chase, and Waite. We speak about my ongoing issues with the family dynamic between my criminal father and Violet.

Russell's never-ending issues and toxic temperament seem to be a recurring theme. I've told her stories of our childhood, the good and the bad. We discuss whatever pops into our heads at the moment, whether it's complex or a random news report we see in the newspaper as we pass by the store.

In return, she's given me a small glimpse into who she is, though her information is guarded. She talks of her childhood fondly. Her parents still live on the coast somewhere in a small cottage by the sea. She speaks to them often but hasn't visited in a while due to her work commitments and lack of funds. London is an expensive place to live when you're trying to make ends meet. What would be pocket change to me is a week's wages to her, and that's a fact I'm highly aware of.

She's talked of her disappointment over how her career has progressed. The bright lights she craved so badly have dulled in her eyes. I can see it. For all her buckets of sass and independence, Samantha Coleman is lost in some ways. She's stuck somewhere between wanting a better life and being forced to work to pay for the one she has.

There's a lot I don't know about her, and I know if I wanted to, I have the connections to find out. In the past, I would have, but what I have with Sam is different. There's a trust there I've never felt before and deep down, I truly believe I'll find everything I need to know when the time feels right for her.

CHAPTER SIX

Samantha and Mia's Apartment, London

Samantha

Connor Chase can fuck. The man knows how to please a woman. Last night was all the evidence I needed to prove it. He put every ounce of effort into my pleasure, and I have every intention of enjoying round two as soon as possible. He was dominant but gentle, his promises for our future meetings thrilling. The dull ache between my legs throbs for my attention, reminding me of where he was.

Fuck, I can still feel him. The sensation of my body wrapped around him is fresh in my mind.

Once he slid inside me, he filled every inch until I came around his cock. Holding my wrists firmly on the pillows, his thrusts became more urgent. As I strained against his touch, he pushed harder; the soft purple bruise on my left wrist tells me he got carried away. It was a taste of the lover he could be.

He's sworn this was the first of many pleasurable experiences, but I suspect what he has in mind could push the limits of my control. He wants me completely at his mercy, and my body available for him to do as he pleases. The idea is as terrifying as it is exhilarating. The one thing Connor has in his favor, that most men I've been involved with don't, is I trust him. I'm playing with a gentleman in public, but a deviant between the sheets. The thought makes my heart race but my pussy ache, both parts of my body straining for more contact with him.

My striptease in the middle of his kitchen hadn't been planned, but Russell had pushed my buttons earlier in the evening. The bastard has this amazing talent of being a complete and utter asshole every time he opens his mouth. His bad mood and shitty personality are somehow intriguing, though. My infatuation with terrible men started as a teenager and never stopped. If they're stitched out of red flags I'm all in, and both Chase brothers have more than plenty, albeit in different ways.

I had been leaving my apartment yesterday evening when I stepped out onto the cold pavement and directly into Russell's chest. Strong hands grabbed my shoulders and gently directed me backward. When I glanced up, his intense brown eyes stared back.

"You have an appointment this evening I believe, Trouble," he said casually, then released me from his grip. "Please allow me to escort you to my brother's home." He had lifted one hand into the air and waved it in a grand gesture as he bowed.

My focus moved to the sleek black sports car sitting at the curb—the number plate CH4SE didn't attempt to hide who it belonged to. The alloy wheels glinted under the low street-light, each one with too many spokes to count. In the center was a black badge with his surname elegantly embossed across the middle in silver. It screamed wealth, self-assured male, and idiotic superiority. It was pathetically mesmerizing.

"No thanks," I replied, walking past him in the direction of the tube station. He reached for my elbow, and I pulled it from his grip. Spinning to face him, my hands gravitated to my hips. "What the hell do you *want*?" He flashed me a sexy smile, and I attempted to return a grimace. This man I hardly knew, but felt bizarrely connected to, was causing sensations of lust to run through me that I didn't want to be feeling. Guilt stabbed violently, reminding me I was on my way to meet his brother.

"Merely to escort a lady to her appointment. We wouldn't want you to run into any issues like the other evening. It was lucky I happened to be there; those thieving bastards in the alleyway weren't going to give up easily. Perhaps you could even call me your knight in shining armor."

"Knight in shining armor, more like the devil in the shadows," I replied with a laugh. "Every time I turn around, you're there. I can look after myself." He stepped forward, his hand reaching for mine but retracting. "What do you want, Russell?" I repeated. "What you're doing makes no sense; I'm seeing your brother."

"I know," he whispered, his eyes dropping away. "But I can't get you out of my mind. I need to know you're okay. The thought of you walking these streets on your own is unsettling."

"I don't walk the streets!" I hissed, offended. "I'm not a fucking hooker."

"That's not what I meant, and you bloody know it." His expression, which had softened briefly, hardened once more. He narrowed his eyes, then a smirk appeared on his lips. "But you used to cater to very specific needs from what I hear. I know all about your past, Trouble. You are a woman of many talents."

"Stop calling me that!" I snapped, furious with myself for the thrill that ran through me with the pet name. "My name is Samantha. Actually, Miss Coleman, and make sure you use it."

"I will endeavor to use it in the future, Miss Coleman," he said, his words blunt but rolling off his tongue like silk. His fingers lifted unexpectedly toward my face, and I stepped away. His face contorted, and he lowered his hand to his side. "What the fuck? I was reaching for your cheek. Did you think..."

"It's not your fucking cheek to touch," I shot back, embarrassed by the small indication of fear I allowed him to see. I've lost count of the number of men who thought striking a woman was appropriate. "Keep your hands to yourself."

His focus never left my face, but he allowed the moment to pass with no further questions. "Is it my brother's?"

"Is what your brother's?"

"Your cheek. Does it belong to him?"

"No, I'm no one's. All this..." I opened my hands wide. "Is mine and only mine to do with as I please."

"Well, I want to make sure this delectable self-owned property gets to its destination in one piece." He gestured to his car once again. "Let me take you to The Level. Connor will appreciate my chivalrous ways. It's not something many people see."

I laughed out loud then, and his eyebrows drew together in confusion.

"Does a gentleman stalk a lady? Because you know that is what this is, right?" The confusion marring his features didn't subside. "You being everywhere I am is stalking, you understand that? Being a lawyer, I would assume this was covered within your degree. You know, between what is right and what is wrong."

"I'm not stalking you. I'm looking out for you," he challenged.

"You tell yourself that. Now, I need to go. I have a date."

"Yes, I know," he muttered, clearly annoyed. His obvious jealousy of my relationship with his brother was perversely enjoyable. The man likes people to think he has a heart of stone and is an asshole through and through, but my senses tell me he's putting up a façade. Russell Chase isn't as brave or nasty as he likes to appear. Underneath it all, a confused teenage boy is screaming to get out, aching to be loved—he just isn't sure how.

"I'll see you later, no doubt," I told him, then turned to walk away.

"Please..." he pleaded. "Let me drive you." I ignored him and continued to walk in the direction of the station. It only took a matter of minutes to arrive at the steps, and as I descended, I was aware of a large form walking on the other side of the dividing handrail.

"Are you leaving your car there?" I asked him, and he grunted a barely audible sound. "You're a braver man than me."

"It's insured."

"Well, I hope your deductible isn't too high." I glanced in his direction. "Because I would bet that there will be no wheels on it by the time you return. You're on the wrong side of the walkway, by the way," I added, now keeping my eyes fixed straight ahead. "People will think you're a dickhead."

"That fact isn't up for debate; I *am* a dickhead." His confession caused my lips to quirk briefly, then I rearranged my features, not wanting him to know he made me smile. "But this dickhead is too busy stalking his prey to care."

"So now you *are* a stalker..."

"Stalking as in the verb, not the noun."

"Smart-ass," I teased, and he chuckled.

We arrived at the platform, both of us coming to stop at the thick yellow line marking the edge. He stood close enough that if I'd reached out an inch, our little fingers could link easily. The situation was completely different from every other time we had boarded the train together these past weeks. This time, we stepped through the same open doors in synchronization. We both grabbed the central pole, his hand sitting fractionally above mine. Our journey was made in silence, the carriage relatively quiet. There was only us and a handful of others to begin with, but with each stop, more travelers climbed aboard and filled the space around us quickly.

With every addition, our bodies moved closer to each other, the reduced space causing us to move in the other's direction until my breasts connected with his sleeve after we swept around a corner. I moved to turn away, and his hand shot out to grab my hip.

"No," he whispered. "If this is the only way I can get close enough to touch you, Trouble, allow me to enjoy it."

"What do you want from me?" I said, my voice low but pained. "This is wrong. You can't pursue your brother's..." I trailed off, not knowing how to describe myself.

"My brother's what?" he prompted. "Girlfriend? Partner? Fuck buddy?"

"Friend."

"Ah," he said. "So Connor is in the friend zone. That's good to know. Well, if that's the case, then the game is on." His hand, still sitting on my hip, squeezed gently, and my stomach flipped against my wishes. Heat coated my cheeks. "You like me touching you, Trouble, don't you?"

"My name is Samantha."

"But to me, Miss Coleman, you are nothing but fucking trouble. What would it take for me to move into your friend zone too? I could keep my brother company in there."

"I'll show you the fucking friend zone," I muttered, pissed by his ability to flit from asshole to jovial idiot by the second.

Before he could reply, our stop appeared, and I moved out of his grasp then exited the carriage as quickly as possible. His heavy footsteps appeared behind me within moments, so I ducked into the ladies bathroom. I was flustered by his honesty but more so by my body's reaction to him. When I looked in the mirror, all I saw were flushed cheeks, and all I could feel was my heart beating heavily in my chest. That was when my sanity snapped, and I decided to make damn sure which brother knew I was seeing him tonight.

In the middle of the underground public bathroom, I shrugged out of my winter coat and wriggled out of the classy black dress I was wearing. An older lady dressed as if trekking to the North Pole hissed audibly behind me. I glared at her before resuming to stuff my dress in my handbag and put my jacket back on.

When I returned to the platform, Russell was leaning against the wall, tapping at his phone screen. I strode past him, close enough to ensure he heard the clip of my heels on the concrete. He glanced up and moved to walk beside me.

"Five feet," I said sharply.

"What?"

"Five feet behind. If you're going to persist with this stupid stalking fetish, at least attempt to mimic the real thing."

Mia rattling my bedroom door interrupts the memory, and before I can shout to her to come in, she bursts into my room. In one hand she's carrying a bottle of champagne. In the other, she holds two glasses. Clamped under her chin is a small, brown, rectangular envelope.

"These," she screeches, waving the bottle in the air, "were left outside our door just now. This is for you." She leans forward, awkwardly offering me the letter with her chin.

"Who left them?"

"I don't know. The doorbell rang, but by the time I got there, whoever it was was gone."

I pluck the letter from its place and stare at the typed name and address. The postmark in the top left-hand corner tells me it's from a private hospital I've never stepped foot in, one of those places only people with money go.

From what I've read, it was bought by an American investment company around five years ago, one with its fingers in many pies in the UK. My research told me that other companies under its ownership included advertising and drug manufacturing. I remember ruling out applying for a position here because I wanted to work and train directly within the National Health Service. I didn't want to be a pawn in a conglomerate operation.

Wishful thinking, now that I reminisce of what I hoped would happen. A year since starting my investigation into becoming a nurse, I'm still dancing at the club after sending multiple applications to colleges, universities, and traineeships. Maybe I need to be more realistic about the opportunities within this career path too. Beggars can't be choosers after all.

"Are you waiting on test results or something?" Mia prompts, gesturing at the name—Varley Medical.

"Even if I was, it wouldn't be from there."

"What is it then?" she continues, squinting at the envelope as if somehow she can read through the paper.

"I don't know."

"Well, bloody open it." Mia places the two glasses down on my bedside cabinet, then pops the cork on the champagne. "We need to know whether we're celebrating or commiserating."

I slide my thumbnail under the flap, slowly lifting the paper from the glue. It pops open, and I pull the mysterious letter into the light. Once unfolded, I stare at the text in complete confusion.

Varley Medical,
London,
E1 8JH
dr.rivera@varley.com

Dear Miss Coleman,

I am delighted to inform you that you have been awarded an offer of employment to undertake your Adult Nursing (BSc) at Varley Medical, London. Your course, which predominantly includes on-the-job training, will require study at home and in a university setting from September 2023.

Until then, you will gain valuable experience within my ward as a nursing assistant.

Being a private hospital, we can support a flexible work pattern.

If you wish to accept this offer of employment or require further details, please reply to the email address above, so we can confirm your start date for January.

Kind Regards

Dr. Josephine Rivera

Varley Medical

London

"You didn't tell me you'd applied for a trainee nursing position," Mia stammers. "Since when did you want to wipe old people's asses?"

"There's a lot more to nursing than that, but that *is* most likely where I would begin." I stare at the piece of paper that could change my life, and it all seems too good to be true. "I didn't apply for anything recently. The last time I applied was months ago, and I can't remember completing anything for Varley Medical. I know I didn't."

"You must have," she cries. "Maybe after a few cocktails and you've forgotten?"

"Maybe, or..." My thoughts move to the only person I've discussed my desire to be a nurse with. The person in recent weeks who's listened as I spoke. Would Connor be influential enough to negotiate an offer of employment and training in an industry I have no qualifications to work in? It seems the only plausible reason.

"Or what?" Mia prompts.

"Nothing. It must be a scam. Even if it isn't, there's no way I can afford the tuition. I'll call them tomorrow and let them know. Someone is probably trying to rip-off students for fees."

Mia unplugs my phone from its resting place beside my bed and passes it to me. "Call now. It might not be a con. That letter looks legit. There is a watermark." She hands me a glass of champagne, takes her own, then leaves my bedroom, calling over her shoulder, "Once you've spoken to them, let me know whether the occasion is a happy one."

I watch her leave, then dial the number at the top of the letter. I'm one hundred percent certain it's a scam.

***

Russell

Sitting at my desk in my office, I lean back in my chair with my phone at my ear. The woman on the other end purrs and chirps like she has a thousand times before. Dr. Josephine Rivera and I have a history. Our sexual relationship is now over, but I've helped her out enough to know I can call in a favor.

"Thanks again for sorting that out, Josie. Samantha will be delighted with the traineeship offer. I'll have the full amount transferred as agreed today."

"Who is this girl, Russ? She must be special if you're actively helping her pursue a career."

"Just a woman needing a break in life," I reply. "And I'm fortunate enough to be able to help."

CHAPTER SEVEN

The Level Boardroom

2nd Jan 2023

Russell

"Happy New Year!" Hunter announces as he steps out of the elevator and into the boardroom.

"What is there to be fucking happy about?" Damon snaps. It's ten thirty in the morning and he's nursing his second whiskey of the day.

"Oh, I don't know, the blue skies, the birds singing." Hunter gestures to the windows which look out onto the gray London rooftops. "It's the start of a new three hundred sixty-five-day book. What do you plan to write?"

Harrison, Connor, and I listen to the ridiculous conversation with interest. Hunter knows damn well that Damon is in a bad mood, and he knows why. Damon is also one hundred percent responsible for landing himself in this situation. My sympathy is non-existent.

"My obituary, and it's the second of January so it's three hundred sixty-four pages now," Damon mutters grumpily.

"Emma left," I say by way of pointless explanation. "You were an absolute dickhead, so the woman you were getting a second chance with left. Don't take your bad attitude out on us."

"It was a mutual decision."

"Are you trying to tell me you wanted her to go?" I ask sarcastically.

Earlier, when we all arrived in the boardroom, Connor had distributed coffees like he had been in recent weeks. His constant good mood has made him more generous. Each time we meet, he takes it upon himself to ensure everyone has a drink in their hand, whether that be alcoholic or not. Damon had recounted the argument in his home the previous day that resulted in his nanny leaving her position. My friend has been struggling to move on from the death of his wife eighteen months ago. He finally seemed happy, but then his and his new love's pasts crashed together, sending the whole relationship into turmoil.

"It was best she did," he replies quietly, his eyes focused on the cold drink between his fingers. He lifts the glass to his lips and drains the final drops. "After the fiasco at the restaurant opening, there was no going back. A relationship with her wasn't an option."

"You're a fucking coward," I tell him, furious with him for being an obstinate fool. His focus snaps to me, and he narrows his eyes. "Coward," I repeat the word loudly, emphasizing both syllables.

"Perhaps, but I am better to be a lonely coward than responsible for the death of another woman. Emma is better off without me."

"And what about her daughter?" I prompt, focusing on the detail that I know will provoke a reaction. Emma was also Damon and his late wife's surrogate. For months, he's struggled with the concept of who the child's mother is. I know guilt when I see it, and my friend is riddled.

"Emma never wanted children," he states, then turns away. "Can we move the conversation on? If I'd have known today was a debrief on my failed relationships, I would have stayed home."

"Not an option," Hunter interjects. "You work for me now; you go where I tell you." Damon resigned from the police force yesterday after things became too complicated at a New Year's Eve event. Everything collided at once, resulting in the lost and broken man drinking whiskey at the boardroom table before noon this morning.

Harrison clears his throat. He's sitting beside my brother on the opposite side of the table from Damon and myself. Hunter walks over and sits on Damon's other side. I see him reach over and squeeze our friend's shoulder in sympathy. My annoyance wavers a fraction as understanding flits through my mind on his position. Within two years, he was widowed, became a father, found love again, lost his career, and fought against men determined to break him.

My friend is lost and confused, but he can't see how lucky he is. Damon has always had love. From a teenage boy when he met his wife, to finding the same again after her death. He has what so many of us around this table, most likely all of us, desire: a home with a woman who adores us and small feet at our table. Although I may never have admitted to wanting such things out loud, deep down, having someone to call mine and a dependent or two to call me "Daddy" is the ultimate dream.

"Perhaps we should give McKinney a break," Connor suggests, and I roll my eyes. My fucking brother, the mouthpiece of common sense. "It's been a tough few days. All we need to confirm is that the issues of the other night are terminated."

"And to congratulate me for not dying," I say, petulantly. I barely remember falling to the floor after our enemies slipped a sedative into my drink to divert our attention, but the aftereffects weren't at all fun. "I was the one they drugged."

"Yes, Russ," he replies with a sigh. "You're here. We can all see that the drug they gave you as a distraction didn't cause your exit from Earth." My brother's dark eyes focus on me, and he smirks. "I would have preferred it if it had been a longer-lasting sedative. A few days' peace from your nonsense would have been a good start to 2023."

"Fuck off. You would be lost without me," I tell him.

"Yeah, but hell, I'd be a lot less stressed."

"Anyway," Harrison interrupts, "if we can get onto actual business, some of us have other places to be." His eyes move to the door that leads to the hallway. My sister will be in their apartment, fully eight months pregnant and no doubt waiting for him. "I can confirm that the threats to Damon and his family are now incarcerated and awaiting trial."

"That's it?" Hunter says.

"On that detail, it's all that needs to be said." He looks at Damon sitting quietly and sipping yet another drink. "I'll update you all as things progress."

"What else do we need to know?" Connor asks. His expression has changed from his normal calm manner to annoyance. I suspect he's questioning whether he needed to come here today, probably like the rest of us.

Harrison pours himself a glass of water from the clear, pristine jug beside him. We all settle in our seats, waiting for the rest of the update. Casually, I wonder how things have ended with him pretty much being in charge. Growing up, I was the oldest and always the one leading our group. But over the last few years, Harrison has become more confident in his ability.

Until my sister reappeared, this was a major issue for me. I was pathetically jealous of both his success in court and his ability to manage people and situations. My relationship with the man I considered my best friend other than my brother was in tatters, and it was all due to my pigheadedness. In recent weeks, we've moved forward, and although my failure stings,

I'm coming to understand that that's on me. I can't hold my friend accountable for my shortcomings.

"Remember that a few weeks ago," Harrison begins, "it was brought to my attention that organs were being removed from patients against their wishes. My client, whose mother was a victim of this supposed mistake, has asked questions but is getting no further explanation beyond what was said previously. He contacted me yesterday to let me know it's happened again."

"To the same family?" I ask, doubting whether the same error could happen twice. He shakes his head, then picks up his phone from the table before tapping the screen.

"No, but it *is* a friend of my client's family. The error occurred in the same hospital on the same ward. The gentleman passed away, and his organs were removed from his body against the express wishes on his medical documents."

"When did this happen?"

"Two days after my client's mother's passing. The families have been associates for decades, and it was a conversation at a New Year's Eve party that brought the similarities to light. Both are looking to sue for damages."

"I find it hard to believe that a mistake like this could be made twice. Are you able to give us details of the hospital in question and the doctor involved?"

"It's a high-end private medical center in Mayfair called Harbridges. Very exclusive membership with eye-watering fees which makes the confusion even more surprising. The man who runs it, Dr. Oliver Winslow, is well-known in inner circles and is a highly sought-after physician," Harrison says. "The center is part of a group of private medical establishments in the city."

"And what was the doctor's explanation for the confusion?" Connor asks.

"Paperwork irregularities. The doctor provided a document allegedly signed by the patient during their treatment permitting organ donation in the event of their death." Harrison hits another button on his phone, and a document appears on the large screen on the wall. It was a completed organ donation enrolment form.

"What are we looking at?" Damon asks.

"The supposed document that both donors signed before their treatment. This is the evidence presented by the hospital to prove that the removal of the organs was within the client's wishes. The families are disputing them. Neither patient ever agreed to be registered on the organ donor list prior to completing this form."

"So what are we saying?" Hunter interjects. "That paperwork is being forged within the hospital to allow the removal of organs from unsuspecting patients?"

"I'm not convinced they're forged," Harrison says. "My client confirmed the signature is similar to his mother's. But I do suspect patients are being forced to complete the paperwork when their health declines to the point where the medical staff believe they won't survive."

We sit around the boardroom table, attempting to absorb what this information could possibly mean. There are so many variables and unconfirmable details. Documents signed by patients that directly challenge what their families thought they knew are certainly suspicious, but we all know that people keep secrets; they'll say one thing and do another. Could it simply be a perverse chance that two people changed their minds in the same hospital and decided to donate their organs to save someone else?

The idea seems unlikely but can't be discounted. A lot of the families our law firm works for are large and wealthy. The members are kept close, and a lot of pressure is exerted to submit to family norms. If organ donation was something not approved of, it would be unlikely that any family member would be registered. This would support the idea that members who had the opportunity to register, and wanted to, might take the chance while in a medical setting to change their position.

"We need to find out who completes the organ donation forms in the hospitals and at what point the suggestion is made," I say.

"There's a specific team member allocated to the task as far as I'm aware," Harrison advises. "It was the same administration staff signature on both documents. Perhaps it would be worth a chat, but I feel we need to understand the extent of the issue first. How many patients are changing their stance in their final days?"

"If we're aware of two," Connor adds, "I have no doubt there will be more."

"That's something I agree with you on," Hunter says, pushing himself up to stand. "Is there anything else Damon or I need to know? Because we have some business to attend to."

"What kind of business?" Damon asks, rising to join him.

"I'm going to knock some fucking sense into you. We're going to the gym. You can pulverize me, and I'll kick your ass until you sort this depressive attitude out."

Damon rolls his eyes. Neither man waits to hear if anything else needs to be discussed before heading to the elevator and leaving. I assume both men need to let off some steam.

Harrison follows their lead, making his own excuses for getting back to our sister. Christmas in general has been tough. We had dangerous altercations on both Boxing Day and New Year's. The earlier one was due to Violet's ex rearing his head again. Most of our little group is finishing the festive season with extra bruises and a few near misses in our lives. I hope this year will be less eventful.

"Can you imagine?" Connor says randomly before walking over the fridge, collecting two beers and coming back to sit beside me. He passes me one followed by the bottle opener in his hand. I snap the cap, then he does the same and takes a drink.

"You'll need to give me an idea of what to imagine. Naked woman, booming bank accounts, crushing my opponent in the courtroom? Any of those tend to be of a high priority."

76

"No, you fuckwit. Do you ever think of anyone but yourself?" he mutters, taking another swig. All the fucking time, though he doesn't know it. I've stepped in the way of danger to protect both him and my sister since we were kids. He wouldn't believe me if he truly knew how many times a belt had cracked my skin on his behalf. So I shrug my shoulders and maintain my asshole persona. "What if it was one of our family who this happened to? Was Mother's sister not treated at Harbridges?"

"I don't remember, but she *did* die in hospital. It could have been there. But she was an organ donor, we all are."

"I know," he huffs. "But imagine how we would feel if we weren't. If someone cut our family open, or us!" His voice rises with anger. "The audacity. The butchery. I'd be furious."

"Brother, I'd hunt them fucking down and remove their organs one by one with a blunt knife, ensuring they were alive as long as possible to witness it. They better pray not to inflict such evil on someone we care for or it will be the last thing they do." Connor leans forward, lifting a hand and squeezing it into a fist. I copy his actions, and we bump knuckles. It is something we've done since we were kids. "I got you, Bro. Always."

Chapter Eight

—◦—

Connor's Apartment, The Level

Samantha

I wake to an empty bedroom. Connor has disappeared, but the distinct smell of him is still fresh on the dark silk. Lifting my arms, I stretch, then wiggle my toes to ensure all parts of my body are still in one piece after last night. As we've come to know each other better, our sex sessions have become more adventurous. When Connor says he wants you immobile to do with as he pleases, he means it.

The bedroom door opens, swinging backward and bouncing off the wall. Connor stands bollock naked in the doorway holding a tray. His deep brown eyes dance as he walks across the room; his cock hangs softened between his legs, but there's no mistaking the familiar swell starting as he comes closer.

"Morning, Nurse Coleman," he says with a dazzling grin. "Can I interest you in some sustenance before your first day at work?"

"I've got a long way to go before I become a qualified nurse," I tell him, pushing myself up to sit. He places the tray onto my lap, full of freshly made scrambled eggs and toast waiting to be eaten alongside a steaming latte. "It's merely orientation anyway."

"It's day one of your new career. This is an important milestone. Eat." He sits down on the edge of the bed, watching me intently as I lift the first forkful of eggs to my mouth. "How are you feeling?"

"Terrified. It's one hell of a career change."

"You'll be amazing. And I can't wait to see you in your new uniform." He reaches forward and runs deft fingers from my earlobe to the base of my throat. "I'm glad you decided to stop dancing," he admits.

"Why?" I ask, unsure what he's going to say.

"Because the only man I want you to dance for is me." His admission surprises me. He's never given me any indication my work at Guilty Pleasures made him uncomfortable. I place my fork back onto the plate, then turn in his direction to give him my full attention. He looks down at his hands, twisting his fingers together, clearly uncomfortable.

"Were you jealous, Mr. Chase?" I tease gently, all the while feeling guilty. Connor is unaware that Russell follows me. He also doesn't know that he watched me dance at the club. And I am one hundred percent confident he would have a coronary if he knew his brother had watched us have sex.

Russell may have stopped speaking to me, but his presence never leaves. He's my silent shadow, always watching, waiting, and clearing any threat from my path. Occasionally, a message from an unknown number will pop onto my screen. It can vary from a warning about my safety to complimenting what I wear. But I know it's him—he's the only man ever to call me Trouble.

My relationship with Connor, if you can call it that, has progressed so naturally, it's kind of unnerving. In the past, men have made demands of me, but Connor doesn't. We discuss our schedules and plan time together which suits us both. He adds a relaxed calm to my life I didn't know I needed.

His apartment has grown on me, too. At first, I found the lavish decoration and expensive content mildly disconcerting. The thought of smashing a drinking glass which cost three figures to replace was eye-watering. However, we've broken more than a few during dinner when he decides he can't wait any longer to have me, and Connor doesn't seem to care how much damage is caused as long as I'm willing to be his.

What I've discovered about him is that, although he's quiet, control is something Connor doesn't like to give up. He has a subtle but domineering quality that's hard to say no to, and in all honesty, I wouldn't want to. My willingness to give my body to him has surprised me more than anything as our relationship has developed. For once in my life, I want someone else to be in charge while I enjoy the ride.

Connor stands, then strides over to the huge walk-in wardrobe set to the right-hand side. He disappears from view, and I focus on eating my breakfast. The layout inside his closet is insane, suit after suit and shirt after shirt hanging precisely in their designated position. It's the exact opposite of my clothing, which lays discarded on my bedroom floor or over the ironing board waiting to be smoothed out.

On my first overnight, I'd woken around three and stumbled out of bed naked in search of his ensuite. A wrong turn had landed me in the center of his dressing area. After flicking on the light, I'd stood with my jaw hanging open as I surveyed the insane wealth surrounding me. Beyond the suits and shirts, there were designer shoes, watches, and cufflinks. It was more of a store than a personal dressing area.

Connor appeared after waking and finding me gone. He had watched from the doorway, his expression nervous. When our eyes met, I tried to smile, but I believe it must have been more of a frown as sadness flitted over his features.

"Everything okay?" he'd asked.

"Sure," I murmured, embarrassed at being caught snooping. "I was just trying to get to the bathroom."

"Next door along." He sighed softly. "Come back to bed, please. I miss you."

"Your life is so different from mine. I can't imagine what it must feel like to have all this," I'd said as he went to turn away.

He paused, then twisted back to face me. I gestured at the racks of clothing and items laid out on shelves.

"They're only clothes, Sam. Inanimate objects with little value beyond a price tag."

"It's not only the clothes..." I'd trailed off, nervous to show any insecurity. He stepped into the closet, taking my hand and encouraging me to sit on the small velvet bench in the center. He lowered beside me, then wrapped a strong arm around my shoulders, pulling me to him.

"What else is bothering you?"

"I'm not the kind of girl you normally date," I said simply.

"I don't normally date, but I'm pleased that you've accepted we are." He smiled, then pressed a small kiss on my forehead. "I was beginning to think you were just using me for your selfish pleasure."

"You don't date," I scoffed, but I laughed at his comment. The way he fucks me, I'd be forgiven for thinking *I'm* the one being used. But hell, I enjoy it. "I don't believe that."

"It's true," he shot back, his eyes narrowing with irritation. "It's been a few years since I actively dated. The women I've met in the past were incompatible with me, and I gave up trying."

"And you think we are compatible?" He frowned again, clearly confused by my question. "A girl from the streets and a top-notch lawyer."

"You're not from the streets. A little white cottage next to the sea with hard-working parents does not constitute that. Stop talking shit about yourself." He wrapped me a fraction tighter in his arm. "And just because you've had to work in less savory industries doesn't reflect who you are. Sometimes we have to do things to survive."

"Less savory." I giggled. "I think you mean sex work."

"And it's in the past, and this is your future. What happened back then doesn't define who you are now, but it helped you become the most incredible woman today." He leaned in a little closer, his warm breath tickled my lips. I'd blinked at him, stunned by his compliment. "If you haven't noticed, I think you're fucking awesome."

Connor reappearing fully dressed interrupts my recollection. He walks back over to the bed and sits down once more. In his crisp white shirt and dark trousers, he looks every inch the lawyer as he carries his suit jacket over one arm. The silver ribbon on a small black box in his hand glints in the morning light.

"What's it?" I ask as he passes it to me. Then, he lifts the tray from my knees and places it on the bedside table.

"You won't know until you open it. It's a gift, that's the idea. It's a surprise."

"Smart ass," I mutter and pull the lid from the plain little box. Inside is soft pink tissue paper wrapped around a small object. I pull the little parcel from its resting place and unwrap it to find a lanyard. The most stunning lanyard I've ever seen.

The material is woven strands of gold, black, and silver. Above the clip where you would attach your identification are five small silver charms. I hold it up and stare at what should be a simple functional item, but there is so much more to it.

"I figured you would need one of these for your name badge," he says quietly, and my eyes flick to him before returning to the little charms. "Each one means something. I thought it would be a good reminder for you about how far you've come to get here."

"It's beautiful," I whisper, my emotion surfacing unexpectedly. "Did you pick all these?"

He nods. "The cottage for your childhood. The high-heel for your time dancing. The heart because it was your kind heart that led you to me after you helped Violet." He pauses, allowing me a moment to digest his explanation. "The law scales is for me because I want you to know I support you even on the toughest days. And finally, the stethoscope because medicine is where your future lies."

"You're so thoughtful," I murmur, then turn and take his face in my hands. "I love it. Thank you." Our lips connect, and I push my tongue into his mouth. His hands move to my hair, and he starts to climb up on the bed as his bedroom door flies open. "Raincheck," I whisper.

"Bestie! Today is the day!" Violet's shriek resonates off the walls. She waddles into the middle of the room, her nine-month-pregnant bump leading the way. Her brother, who has me pinned below him, groans then climbs off the bed. I pull the duvet up over my breasts.

"Timing, Vi," he says, grumpily. "Your timing, as always, sucks."

"Yes, I'm a cock block. Now, go away. Let me help my friend here get ready for her first day as a nurse." She stops directly in front of him; he towers over her small frame. Delicate hands with perfectly painted pink nails land on her hips and she cocks her head to the side. "Go."

"This is my bedroom. You weren't allowed in it when we were kids, and the same rules apply as adults. Actually, how did you get in here?"

"Harry gave me his key." She dangles the little bundle millimeters from his nose. He lifts a hand to snatch them, and she pulls it away to her side.

"Gave you it or did you take it without asking?"

She shrugs, not confirming or denying anything. Then her future husband's voice—they're due to be married in a matter of weeks—sounds from the hallway.

"Vi, are you in here?" Harrison appears, and I pull the covers further around myself. "Where the fuck are my keys?" She spins the little bundle on her finger and smiles at him. He tries to look aggravated but chuckles, then walks over and wraps his arms around her before dropping a kiss on her nose. "You are such a pain in my ass."

"Always," she replies, biting her lip. "How did you find me?"

"You left every fucking door open. It wasn't a hard trail to follow. Did you find what you were looking for?"

"I did," she says, turning and gesturing to me, still naked in bed.

"This is my fucking bedroom," Connor states, his words sharp. "No one should be in here unless invited. You two are the worst fucking neighbors."

"It could be worse," Harrison suggests with a grin. "You could live on the same floor as Russell. Come on. Let us go get a coffee and leave these ladies to it." Connor's attention moves to me and I smile, encouraging him to go.

"I'll see you before I leave," I tell him. "My train isn't until eight-thirty."

"I've delayed my nine o'clock," he replies. "I'll drive you." Before I can respond, he turns and follows Harrison from the bedroom. I watch him leave, my heart fluttering in my chest.

"Oh my word, I love the fact you are dating my brother," Violet says excitedly, then sits down on the edge of the bed. "I mean, we'll be sister-in-laws!"

"Calm down, it's early days. We haven't put a definition on what this is. And I won't be walking down any aisle any time soon."

"Except the contraception one," she suggests with a smile. "Come on, let's get you ready for your big day."

***

Connor takes my hand as we step into the elevator outside his apartment. He hits the button for the underground parking lot, but the glass box that looks out over the city begins to rise toward the penthouse.

"Wrong button?" I say with a smile.

"Russ must have called it before we got in." My heart sinks slightly. It's been such a lovely morning, and I'm so looking forward to the first day of my new career. The last person I want to come face to face with is Russell. As my relationship with Connor grows, my awareness of his brother does, too.

Within an hour of handing my notice into Guilty Pleasures, my phone had lit up with an anonymous message.

> I'll miss you. You were my favorite part of the week.

My fingers lift to the charms on my new lanyard, patiently hanging around my neck for my ID card. "I love this, by the way. Thank you."

"You're welcome," Connor replies, leaning down to kiss my cheek.

The doors open, and Russell steps into the small space with no more than a grunt of acknowledgment. Mrs. D, their shared housekeeper, waves manically behind him to us all. She smiles wildly, and I can't help but wave back. Connor blows her a kiss, then the doors close and the elevator starts its descent.

"Garage?" Russell says.

"I assume you're asking if we are going to the garage," his brother retorts, and they scowl at one another.

"Well, I need my fucking car to get to the office for our nine o'clock." He emphasizes the word "our;" clearly, he knows Connor won't be in the office then.

"That meeting is delayed until ten. I'm taking Sam to her first day at the hospital."

Russell's focus comes to me. Dark, dangerous eyes move from the top of my head down my body then back up to my lips. My eyes move between the brothers, similar but different, and both oh-so sexy. Naughtily, my mind paints a picture of what it would be like to have both of them.

"Not the nurse's uniform I had in mind," Russell says. "The ones I like have suspender belts and crotchless underwear. The kind of nurses that get you into *trouble*." The pet name he uses for me rolls off his tongue, and my insides tighten.

"Piss off, Russ," Connor mutters. "You don't always have to be the arsehole. Wishing Sam luck on her first day would be the normal human reaction." I reach for his hand and link our fingers together, uneasy with the current situation. Connor seems oblivious to the fact Russell is eyeing me like a cat does a mouse.

"Good luck, Trouble. I hope you have a wonderful first day in your new employment." My mind almost explodes as he calls me Trouble in front of his brother within the tiny enclosed space. Connor stiffens beside me but doesn't comment. I've noticed he can hold his tongue and assess a situation before reacting.

Thankfully, the buzzer pings when we reach our destination, and the doors open. Russell turns around and stalks out into the parking garage. Connor and I look on as he climbs into his car and drives away.

CHAPTER NINE

***

Varley Medical, London

Samantha

My new place of work is a modern, purpose-built facility in the center of the city. The outside of the square building is covered in large, smooth white panels and reflective silver windows. At the entrance, signified by a canopy and two large marble pillars, sit two highly polished ambulances painted in white and red. The words "PRIVATE AMBULANCE" are boldly printed down the side. Perfectly designed planters filled with green foliage are strategically placed around the edge of the pavement, almost creating a barrier between passersby and the hospital.

We pull into the underground car park, and I duck instinctively as we pass under the height restriction barrier. Connor's vehicle is nothing like Russell's low, sporty one. He drives a colossal off-road Jeep, one you have to climb up two steps to get in. The front and rear are protected by thick metal bars, which sit in stark contrast to the bright red paint.

Today was my first time seeing his car. Living in the city, anytime we have had plans, we've called a taxi or simply walked where we needed to go. What I'm sitting in now is the complete opposite of what I expected Connor Chase's car to look like. For a quiet, unassuming man in so many ways, what he drives makes a statement on the road.

The red and white striped barrier lifts, and we drive into the best-lit parking garage I've ever seen. Each space has a small light above it indicating if it's available or not.

"There's a space there," I say, pointing to a place between two small cars.

"No, we want two spaces together." His eyes keep scanning as he drives slowly up and down each line of parked cars.

"You're one of those arseholes, aren't you?" He stops the car and turns to face me. I stare straight back at him, trying to keep my face blank which is difficult considering all I want to do when I look at him is smile.

"What arseholes?" he asks, raising an eyebrow. His shirt sits open at the collar, the soft material skims over muscle that I am getting to know so well. He holds my focus with strong, direct eye contact.

"The ones that park over two spaces like they're driving a fucking army tank." He laughs, his face lighting up in amusement. I smile goofily back at him.

"Yes, that's exactly what I'm going to do."

After a few minutes, we find what he is looking for—two parking spaces side by side. Connor reverses into the gap, ensuring he covers the center of the spot, minimizing the risk of his car being hit accidentally by another driver. When he's happy with our position, he turns off the engine and removes the key.

"You ready?" he asks, cocking his head to one side and smiling. I sit in the passenger seat, my nerves rising by the second. My hands, which are twisted in my lap, sweat lightly. This is potentially the most nerve-wracking day of my whole life.

"As ready as I'll ever be," I tell him, then push open my door before stepping out. Connor gets out as well, then walks around to meet me. I shrug the small backpack I have over my shoulder, then touch the charms on my lanyard, ensuring they are still there. It's crazy how important small pieces of metal can become so quickly. His eyes follow the movement of my hand, and he wraps his fingers around mine.

"I am one hundred percent with you today," he says softly. "You've got this." Then he encourages me toward the elevator to the floors above.

We reach the doors, and he takes both my hands, pulling my body forward against his and wrapping my arms around his waist. I blink up at him as he gazes back. "This is your stop." He leans down and kisses me, strong and domineering. His tongue pushes into my mouth, sweeping across every surface. His hands lift, and he cups my face, holding me to him, not letting go until he's completely satisfied.

"Um...are you trying to make me horny before my first day?" I ask, digging my nails into his ass. His cock is hard against my stomach, so I push a little harder against him, lowering one hand to cup his balls through his suit trousers.

"No, I just didn't want you to forget me in your new life. But you have that effect on me—one look at you and I get a boner."

"I could never forget you," I whisper, placing my lips at the base of his throat. He moans gently above me, a distinctly male sound. "I'll see you and your boner later?"

"Call me when you're finished, and I'll come to collect you."

"No need. I'll get the underground."

He waves away my comment with a scowl. "It wasn't a request; it was a statement. I will pick you up. I want to hear all about your first day, and I don't want any interruptions. Violet has something planned for us all this evening to celebrate. Once we get back to The Level, I probably won't get near you until she's bled every detail from you."

I laugh out loud, but the expression on his face tells me he's serious. And he's probably right; Violet can be demanding when I am in her company. Having lacked female friendship in her life for so long, she gets carried away when we're together and forgets that anyone else is there.

"Okay, I'll call you," I relent, sensing that allowing him to do this is important to him.

"Good," he says, leaning in for a final kiss. "Then once we've been sociable tonight at my sister's fucking party, I'll take you to bed to celebrate properly."

"I can't wait."

His hand reaches out, pressing the call button for the elevator. The doors immediately open, surprising us both. I step inside, and he stands back, his eyes not leaving mine until we can't see each other anymore. Clutching my lanyard, the elevator rises, and I smile at myself in the mirrored wall. Here I am, walking into a new job, having recently moved into a better apartment with Mia, and tonight going back to the most amazing man. It's astounding how life can change in a matter of months to something completely unexpected.

The numbers on the display count up slowly from minus one to level four, where I've been told to go. After what feels like an eternity, the elevator stops, and the sleek stainless steel doors open into a reception space. It's surprisingly quiet, not like the publicly funded hospitals I've been in before, which all seem to be crammed with never-ending lines of patients. There are only two ladies in the waiting room, both sitting on large leather sofas and reading glossy magazines.

Taking a breath to steady my nerves, I start my walk across the pristine white marble floor to the desk on the opposite side of the room. A gentleman there sits on a large leather chair. He presses his lips together in a painful smile as I approach.

"Good morning, welcome to Varley Medical. How can I help you today, ma'am?" he says professionally. My eyes focus on the navy Varley Medical logo prominent on his pale pink shirt before holding his gaze.

"I'm Samantha Coleman. I was to report here on my first day. I have an appointment with Dr. Rivera."

"Ah yes, the new trainee. I'm Bryan, and I run the reception desk on this floor." He stands then offers me his hand. We shake, and his grip is surprisingly firm. He looks older than me, possibly in his mid-forties, with waved blond hair that flops over his forehead and bright-blue eyes. "Welcome to the team. If you follow me, I will take you through to meet the doctor."

Bryan moves to the side of his desk and gestures toward a corridor at the far end of the reception area. He walks in that direction, and I scurry after him. The passageway is lined with stark white doors that blend into the walls painted an identical color. Each one has a silver plaque with black writing detailing the name of the person who owns it or what the purpose of the room is. At the very last door on the right-hand side, he stops and raps, alerting the occupant to our presence.

"Come in," a shrill voice trills. Bryan pushes open the obstruction and leads me inside.

"Dr. Rivera," he says formally. "Your new trainee is here. Samantha Coleman."

"You're late," she snaps frostily. Confused, I glance at my watch, I'm ten minutes early. "Leave us, Bryan. I will call you when and if I decide Samantha needs a tour of the facilities." My escort gulps involuntarily; his eyes tell me he's wary of his boss, and my initial impression isn't great either. With almost a bow, he leaves.

"Good morning, Dr. Rivera," I say politely. "I want to thank you for the opportunity…"

"Yes, yes, take a seat. If you will be working in my department, I need to know who I've hired." She leans back in her highbacked red velvet chair and tents her fingers in front of her. Most likely in her early forties, she's a slim woman with overly taut skin and a bundle of jet-black hair twisted precisely on top of her head. Her features are sharp and her eyes dark; I'm unsure if she would ever be able to look happy.

I wander over and sit down on the small gray standard chair opposite her, then place my bag on the floor. She surveys me curiously, taking in my basic appearance in my winter coat and leggings. I will my feet to stay steady and keep my shoes on the ground. The last thing I want to do is annoy her with inane nervous foot tapping.

"You certainly have friends in high places," she says. "No qualifications relevant to working in the medical sector, and yet you've managed to secure a fully funded training placement."

I balk at the directness of her words. The source of the funding and indeed the job offer is still surprising, I was told it was a previous scholarship application that had been reassessed. My suspicions lead to Connor, but anytime I've broached the subject he has denied any knowledge, insisting it must be the scholarship. When Violet questioned how I was able to give up work and focus on my new career on a trainee's salary, I told her

I had come into an inheritance. It felt the easier option than her going all investigator on me.

"The offer was as much of a surprise to me as anyone," I reply. "But I'm delighted to have the opportunity, and will work hard both in the hospital and on my studies."

"You'll have to." Her eyes narrow beyond a degree I think humanly possible to see, but the furious look on her face tells me she can see me just fine. "I don't like line skippers or people who think they are entitled to a leg up. If you're going to stay here, you need to prove you have the ability."

"Yes, ma'am." It's all I can think to say. Part of me wants to tell the ignorant bitch to fuck off, while the other wants to worship at her feet. This is the opportunity I've been waiting for to move toward a life somewhat more normal. I can't screw it up.

"Good. If you work hard and keep your mouth shut, we will get on just fine." She moves to put her elbows on the surface, grinding her teeth before speaking which makes her even more unlikeable. "From now on, you will shadow a senior nurse on her duties. I have allocated Barbara to be your mentor; you will meet her today and your work rotation will mirror hers. Your university classes don't commence until September, so until then, please be advised this is a probationary period."

"Thank you." She doesn't respond in kind, merely continues the information dump.

"Today, you will get a tour of the entire hospital, though you'll be based on this floor with me primarily. Initially, you'll be focused on the basic daily care of patients."

I go to open my mouth to ask what her specialization is, then decide against it. Not knowing may put another black mark against my name, and it's obvious from her attitude I already have one. I plan to look her up later. "Any questions, please direct them first to Barbara. Then if she can't answer your query, come to me."

"Yes, ma'am."

"Good," she says, then presses the button on the intercom. She doesn't speak, merely sits back once more. "Bryan will come and take you on a tour of the hospital now. You're dismissed."

"Yes, ma'am," I repeat like a fucking schoolgirl speaking to the principal. Internally I wince, hating myself for it but knowing I need to keep this woman on my side. "I look forward to working with you Dr. Rivera." I stand and offer her my hand. She takes it, surprising me—I expected her to ignore the gesture. Her fine bones wrap around my palm, and she squeezes firmly.

"I do too, Samantha. You certainly are a bolt out of the blue." My perplexed look amuses her, and she sniggers. "Mystery job offers and money from unexpected places...one must ask themselves what you've done to gain such support."

"It was a surprise to me too," I mumble, and she raises an eyebrow cynically.

"Now," she says, her tone harsh. "We both know that's a fib." Her door opens, and we both look at a flustered Bryan standing in the doorway. He waits silently as she glares at him. "Knock, Bryan. It's basic manners." He gabbles an apology of sorts, and she waves me away. I retreat from her office, then scurry into the hallway behind Bryan.

"You survived," he says with a chuckle.

"Barely."

He laughs out loud this time. His timid expression softens, and he morphs from an uptight employee to someone who looks more friendly.

"She is challenging." He runs his left hand through his hair; there is no wedding ring on his finger. "But she keeps a roof over mine and the kid's heads." I notice he doesn't mention a partner, and I don't ask. Too many times my big mouth has landed me in difficult conversations.

"How many kids do you have?"

"Four," he replies, and I gasp. "Yeah, it's expensive. Come on, this way. It will be break-time now anyway, and all the girls should be in the staff room."

At the opposite end of the corridor is the door marked "Staff Room." Inside is a group of four women dressed in nursing uniforms sitting around a table drinking mugs of tea and eating chocolate biscuits. It strikes me as amusingly characteristic, and the kind of situation you see on TV sitcoms.

"Morning ladies," Bryan says, announcing our entry. "May I introduce the new victim of floor four?" They laugh then turn, all eyes landing on me. Four nurses, all older, all wiser, assessing their new recruit.

"What's your bra size?" one woman shouts. I see from her name badge she's called Stella. With her head of gray curls and granny-like appearance, it's the last question I would ever expect she would ask.

"Um...thirty-two E."

"Jeez, love, I'd hate to be carrying those melons around all day. Does your back not hurt?" I blink at her completely confounded by the direction of the conversation. "And your panties? What size are they?"

"Ten."

"Well, we all know what assets you have, don't we Samantha? Bryan, if I catch you staring at her tits, you'll get a clip around the ear."

"Tits aren't my thing," he informs her, and she grins.

"They must have been in the past. You have four kids."

"Yeah, but I was always an ass-man." They all burst out laughing, and an even older woman takes pity on me, standing and walking over to take my hands.

"Ignore them," she tells me kindly. "Stella, go and collect Samantha's uniform. What is your shoe size, dear?"

"Seven."

"Two of everything so she has plenty." Stella stands, leaving the room in search of what I assume will be my clothing while at work. "I'm Barbara, I'll be your mentor here. Anything at all, you ask. We want you to love this career as much as we do." She pulls a card from the pocket of her white, wide-leg trousers. "These are my contact details. Now come and sit down, have some tea, and pop those in your phone."

We walk over to the table together and, after sitting down, she pours steaming hot tea into a mug for me, then begins to introduce my new colleagues.

***

The day passes in a whirl of information and laughter. After Stella brought me my new uniform and I changed, Bryan gave me a two-hour tour of the hospital. There's not an inch of Varley Medical I haven't seen, including the morgue. I suspect he was enjoying being away from his desk and the wrath of Dr. Rivera.

He tells me all about his previously married life and his new one as a single father to four boys. His ex-wife now lives overseas with her new billionaire husband, who sends pennies in child support each month. Anytime Bryan has challenged the payments, he comes up against expensive lawyers and oodles of paperwork.

"She put me off women for life," he told me. "Just upped and fucked off. But I have my boys, and that's all that matters. They're happy."

"What ages are they?" I ask, my brain trying to compute the logistics of it all.

"Four, twelve, thirteen, and seventeen. I'm not sure what I'll do when Peter leaves for university next summer. He helps with the childcare of the others when I'm working."

"It must be difficult; do you not have family who can help?"

"Sadly not. My mother passed away, and my father is in permanent care. Her family has never been interested, so it's just me and the boys." He smiled softly. "But I like it that way."

"And no special someone on the horizon? Woman? Man?" I continued probing, my curiosity getting the better of me.

"Oh, I like you," he said, turning and placing his hands on his hips. "You're a little terrier. You'll get all the gossip. But make sure you keep me up to date with anything juicy."

"Sorry," I muttered, annoyed with myself thinking I'd overstepped.

"Don't be. I can see we'll have a lot of fun. But no, there is no special someone. I've had no time to even investigate that part of my life. Maybe in the future..." His voice faded, and the look in his eye became wistful. "There's someone out there for everyone, we can only hope we find them."

As I'm stuffing the last of my uniform into my backpack, my memory of Bryan's words sends my thoughts to Connor and what we have. We may not have known each other long, but what we have is special. I know that. However, in the back of my mind, there's a niggling worry that something is missing and I need it to complete the puzzle. What it is, I'm frightened to consider, as my suspicions are not a place I want to go.

I texted Connor twenty minutes ago to say I was ready to be collected. When I walk out into the underground car park, I'm surprised to see a low black sportscar sitting waiting and not the bright-red jeep. My gaze moves to the man leaning against the driver's door dressed in a sharp suit and talking on his phone.

Russell's eyes meet mine, and he smiles; my stomach tightens the way it always fucking does, and my heart sinks. I will my body not to respond to him but like a treacherous whore, a heat warms my cheeks.

"Taxi for Nurse Coleman," he says, stepping forward, lowering his phone, and inclining a fraction.

"Where is Connor?" I ask him, and he glowers.

"Stuck at the office. He asked me to come to pick you up. Apparently, getting the tube isn't an option today. This is an important day it seems."

"It's okay. I imagine you're busy. I'll get the tube." I turn to walk toward the pedestrian exit, but he reaches for my arm, stopping me mid-step.

"No, I am here to collect you on my brother's request. You'll come with me." My uncertainty around him dissipates with his instruction. I spin to face him, pulling my arm from his grip.

"You do not fucking tell me what to do. I'm taking the underground."

"Okay, I won't tell you." I turn to walk away again, only to find myself lifted around the waist and carried around to the passenger door. He holds me steady, strong arms wrapped around my waist so my back is firmly against his chest. I kick my feet wildly, my heel hitting his shin. "Ouch," he grumbles, pulling open the door and then placing me back on my feet. "Get in."

"No."

"Get in, or I'll throw you in myself," he warns. I take a step, and he moves in the same direction, holding me prisoner between his body and the open car door. I glare at him, and he grins. "You look even better mad."

"I'm dating your brother," I remind him.

"I know, but there is no harm in looking," he says. "You undress me plenty with those baby blues."

"In your dreams." He leans down, placing his lips to my ear. His scent of cinnamon fills my nostrils, and my body tenses. I don't want to want him; I don't even like him. But fuck, he calls to me.

"Trouble, you are the star of my wet dreams. I may not be able to touch you, but it won't stop me fucking you with my eyes. Now, get in the fucking car so I can deliver you to your boyfriend."

Irritated but beaten, I climb into the passenger seat. He closes the door and locks the car until he walks around to the other side. I pull the handle, but the door doesn't unclick. The asshole has me trapped. After opening the driver's door, he shrugs out of his suit jacket then throws it onto the tiny rear seat before getting in. I watch him fold himself into the car, his firm, toned body molding to the seat.

"How was your first day?" he asks casually, starting the engine as if we had had no disagreement and I'm here because I want to be.

"Good," I reply. "I met my colleagues and the doctor I'll be working for."

"Josephine Rivera," he says, and I nod, surprised by his knowledge. "How is the feisty bitch?" He chuckles as we pull out of the parking lot into the cold dark January evening.

"You know her?"

"I sure do. And she is as much trouble as you are."

Chapter Ten

The Level Boardroom

Connor

As I stand looking out over the city, I check my watch again. Half past seven. Russell was meant to collect Samantha at six o'clock then drive straight here. It should have taken thirty minutes at most. My bastard brother has once again changed the plan and is doing his own fucking thing. Namely, yanking my chain. His jibes and taunts have become more frequent in recent weeks, both in and out of the office. It's becoming harder to keep my mouth closed.

"Where the hell are they?" I mutter, starting to pace again. Harrison walks up behind me and places his hand on my shoulder. I stop then turn to face him. Violet, who has been sitting at the table eating raisins by the handful, stands and waddles out of the room, but not before kissing her future husband's cheek. Raisins have been her third-trimester craving; every time I've seen her, she's had a bag in her hand.

"They'll be here," Harrison assures me, his voice calm. "Perhaps they've been caught up in traffic." He passes me the glass of whiskey in his hand. "Have a drink. What's making you so prickly?"

"He likes her," I state, the worry that's been eating away at me surfacing. Russell has always been an open book in my eyes; I can tell by his behavior how he feels about someone. To most people, he's a pain in the ass. My brother likes to upset those around him before they have the chance to do the same to him. But with Samantha, although he's rude and obnoxious, there's a softness in his eyes that I've only seen with family. And one thing I know about my brother is when he decides he wants something, nothing stands in his way. I can only hope that his sights aren't set firmly on what's mine.

"Russell always wants what he can't have. How many women have you two played this game over?" My friend eyes me knowingly; he's seen this dozens of times before with Russell and I competing for the same girl, even if one of us is already dating her. "Are you and Sam doing well? From what Violet says, she's into you."

"My sister and her big mouth discussing my private life." He laughs but nods in agreement. "This is different. I don't want this to be a competition. I couldn't bear to lose her."

Harrison cocks his head to the side, his shrewd eyes running over my face. He doesn't speak, just leaves empty air for my words. It's a mannerism he has perfected both in and out of the courtroom: the ability to make someone uncomfortable enough to tell him what's on their mind. "I like this girl. What we have feels…" The emptiness opens up again, and my heart fills with fear at the thought of losing her.

"Feels what?" he prompts.

"Real." We both stand staring at each other, and he smiles kindly. "She's the first woman I've been with who isn't interested in my credit card. There are no expectations from her of fancy dinners or expensive gifts. I think she likes me for, well, me."

"So, what are you worried about? It sounds like the perfect basis for a relationship."

I shrug, not knowing what to say. The thought of saying my biggest insecurities out loud is unpleasant. Unnerved, I walk back over to the floor-to-ceiling windows that look out over London. It's dark now, so the lights of the city spread out across the blackness. Cars still weave through the streets; it's silent in our fortress up here, but I know outside the city is bustling.

"I think she likes him too," I admit, not looking at my friend. "Though I don't think she knows it." He wanders over to stand beside me, and we both stare out into the dark.

"Are you psychic?" He asks with mild sarcasm.

"No, just a realist." Harrison glances at me, concern clear on his features. "You and I both know that it's obvious when two people like each other. And I see how she responds to him when he's being an ass. She glows."

"Why would you ask him to collect her from work then, if you're concerned about an attraction between them?"

I take another sip of my drink, knowing my answer will probably make no sense to my friend. Russell is a non-negotiable part of my life. My big brother has looked out for me since day one. He's a necessary thorn in my side.

"Because he's my brother. I trust him with my life. He's the first man I would call in any situation, good or bad. I needed help, so I asked him." Harrison nods fractionally, but his face tells me he doesn't agree. "And if there *is* something between them, am I not better knowing now than in a year?"

Just then, the sound of laughter bursts through the door, and we both turn to find Russell and Samantha walking into the room. Her face is lit up as he tells her what I assume is a joke. She looks stunning, relaxed, and at ease. But what's more disconcerting is Russell; there's a natural happiness there I haven't seen in years, not since we were kids. Samantha reaches out and slaps his arm.

"You are such an arsehole," she teases.

"Guilty as charged," he agrees, then bows dramatically. My jealousy spikes, and I feel the fury mixed with insecurity build in my chest to a bursting point. My fists clench at my sides. It's taking all my composure not to storm across the room and punch my brother in the face.

"I'll leave you to it," Harrison says under his breath, then walks toward the door.

"Where are you going, Waite?" Russell shouts. "This is a celebration!"

"I'll go get your sister," he tells him without as much as a glance in his direction, then exits through the doorway the happy couple just appeared from.

Samantha meets my gaze, and her stunning smile widens. It does nothing to calm me. I only become more furious that time with him has made her this happy. She looks fucking radiant.

"Where the fuck have you been?" I snap at Russell, and his cheerfulness evaporates.

"Collecting your girlfriend from her work like you asked me to."

"And it took you almost two hours to get here. Where have you been?" He pauses, and his expression tells me I'm not going to like the next words out of his mouth.

"A hotel," he says with a smirk. "Trouble and I hired one of those rooms by the hour." Samantha freezes at his words, paling as he wraps an arm around her. "I was the best you ever had, wasn't I?"

His eyebrows raise, silently goading a reaction. I notice once again he's using Trouble as an endearment toward her. Russell only names people he likes, and it's clear he's taken more than a liking to my girl.

"Russell, did your mother never tell you lying is bad?" Samantha says once she seems to regain some composure. "We went to a bar for a drink."

"You were meant to come straight back here."

Russell shrugs, and Samantha steps out of his embrace. She walks over to me, lifting her hand to my cheek. She looks at me with concern—her fingertips graze my skin tenderly. "I'm here now," she says. "I'm sorry. We thought there was time." She rises on tiptoe and presses soft lips to mine. "Let me make it up to you." The sound of the door slamming within seconds once again signals Russell's exit. We both turn to look, and he's gone.

Samantha blinks up through dark lashes, her blue eyes sparkle under the light. She's still dressed in her uniform with a heavy winter coat over the top. "I'm sorry," she says again. "Russell said we weren't supposed to be here until seven-thirty."

"I'm sure he did," I mutter.

"What is that supposed to mean?"

"Russell has always been difficult. We've talked about this before." I stop speaking, unsure about how much of my insecurities to divulge. "He likes to make life challenging for others." She doesn't say anything, but her body tenses under my touch. She bites her lip as if trying to stop herself from talking. "I got stuck at the office because he booked a meeting in my calendar. He knew I was planning to pick you up, and the jackass put a fly in the ointment."

"Why would he do that?" she asks quietly. We look at each other for a beat, then her eyes drop away.

"He knew tonight was important, and as always, it all has to be about him."

"I'm here now," she says again. "And I'm here with you."

"But for how long?"

Her face twists uneasily. We've skirted around the topic of what this is and where our relationship is going, but Samantha never wants to plan too far ahead. She tells me that every time something good happens, it gets blown to pieces by life. So, for now, she just wants to enjoy what we have and not put a label on it.

I like labels, and I like to know where I stand, but to have her I'm willing to wait. I just hope my waiting for her doesn't ultimately mean I lose her to him.

***

Samantha

Connor's eyes run over my face for what feels like the millionth time since I arrived minutes ago, as if in search of the truth. These past weeks with him have been some of the best of my life, and I hate to see him upset due to my actions.

"Listen, it was a misunderstanding," I suggest, knowing full well it wasn't. "I'm going to go and freshen up." I rise on tiptoe to kiss him. He accepts my lips, but there isn't the enthusiasm behind the act that normally exists. "I'll be back in a moment," I whisper, closing my eyes and willing the tears behind my lids not to fall. Connor is always so loving, but today there's a wall between us, and deep down I know why.

I rush to his apartment, opening the door with the entry card he gave me last week. Once in the safety of his bedroom, I pull my phone out of my pocket and do something I haven't done before. I text the unknown number in my contacts. The one I receive the odd complimentary texts from.

> Did you do that deliberately?

What?

> Delay me returning from work. Tell me that we didn't need to be here until 7:30.

Yes.

> Why?

Because I wanted to spend some time with you, Trouble. Watching you from afar isn't always enough.

I stare at the answer on my screen. No excuses, no half-truths. I asked the question, and Russell answered me honestly. My phone beeps again, alerting me to a second message.

I enjoyed myself. And if you're being honest, you did too.

Not wanting to confirm or deny his statement, I switch my phone off then place it on the bedside table to be dealt with later. I move to sit at the dressing table that appeared in Connor's bedroom last week, complete with a huge mirror surrounded by lights.

When I asked Connor about the delivery, he told me I needed somewhere comfortable which was my space to get ready when I stayed here. He wants me to stay often. On the same day, he cleared out one of the sections of his huge walk-in closet for me too. It had been a step forward in our short relationship; things were beginning to feel grown up. I knew I should tell him about Russell's communication with me, and the fact he still appears when I least expect him to—not speaking to or approaching me, but there watching as I leave work or in the mornings when I arrive.

As I look at myself and take in my bedraggled appearance, it's clear the busy day I've had has taken its toll. My eyes are tired, and my hair droops messily down around my face. The terrible, unflattering uniform is already marked with the little interaction I had with patients as I was introduced to the wards. I lift the white top over my head and throw it onto the floor as the door opens.

Connor walks in; he's still looking fresh and sharp even after a day at the office. His eyes widen as he sees me sitting on the stool in my bra. "I thought you'd got lost," he says, walking over and placing his hands on my shoulders. Strong fingers sit on my collarbone, and I feel the warmth from his palms seep into my skin.

"Sorry, I was taking a moment. Are Violet and Harrison waiting?" He shakes his head and intense eyes meet mine in the mirror. He flexes his fingers against my skin and this feeling of happiness I'm becoming used to flutters in my chest.

"No, I told them I'd let them know when you were ready to celebrate. Are you tired?"

"A little."

"Come," he says, moving to my side and extending his hand toward me. "You need a shower, and it will help wake you up." He smiles sexily. "And I'll do my best to arouse your energy too." He tugs at my hand and I stand.

"I'm sorry about tonight. You were upset, and I didn't like it. I didn't like that I caused you pain," I confess; the guilt has been growing since his altercation with his brother in the boardroom.

Connor takes a step toward me, keeping hold of my fingers. Beautiful dark eyes hold mine as his free hand lifts to my face and moves a pesky stray hair from my eyes. I swallow, overwhelmed by the charge between us. There's no doubt in my mind I truly care for this gorgeous, selfless man. He only needs to trace my skin and it buzzes beneath his touch with need.

"It wasn't your fault," he says, his voice kind but inviting no argument. "It was my idiot brother playing games like he always does."

I want to tell him that isn't true. I want to tell him that I am guilty by complicity. I should tell him his brother has made it clear he likes me with both his words and actions, but I'm terrified of the result. If I admit I've gone along with Russell's absurd ploys, then I need to acknowledge I've enjoyed them.

"Connor..."

He places a single finger on my lips to stop me from speaking.

"Shh, I don't want any more apologies. The last thing I want to be thinking about is Russell and his reckless ideas. Tonight is all about you. I'm sorry your welcome home wasn't a pleasant one." His second hand drops, intertwining his fingers with mine. He pulls me toward him, wrapping my arms around his waist like he has dozens of times before. "And I'm going to make it up to you starting right now."

"No, Connor, I'm going to make amends for worrying you first." His cock is hard against my stomach, his intentions of how we can improve the evening obvious. My hands move to his ass, and I pull him hard against me. I look up at him as he stares down, his focus unwavering from my face. My heart skips as the silent desire passes between us. He needs to know I want him, and I must show him how much. "Kiss me."

Without speaking, he leans down and warm lips lock over mine. At first, our kiss is gentle, each of us reminding the other of why we're both standing here in his bedroom. Why for the first time in years either of us are considering more than a fucking-only situation. Even though we haven't discussed in-depth what we are, there's no doubt that we have progressed from friends with benefits to a couple, and I need to start treating our relationship as such. Allowing this ridiculous situation with Russell to continue isn't an option. If I want to make a go of things with Connor, that needs to end.

Our kiss becomes more passionate with each stroke of our tongues. He lifts a hand, grabbing my chin and securing my mouth on his. When I try to pull back a fraction his grip tightens, and his second arm wraps around my waist, holding me fast. His tongue dives deeper, claiming each corner in my mouth. When he finally releases me, sharp teeth nip my lip as he retracts.

"What do you have in mind?" he asks, cocking his head to the side.

"For what?"

"What are you going to do to make it up to me? That hour and a half I didn't know where you were was torture." He tries to look serious, but I can see the unwanted smile playing on his lips.

"I'm going to suck your dick," I tell him frankly, and he laughs. "Is that suitable recompense?" He shrugs but starts unbuttoning his shirt.

"Depends how far I can stuff my cock down your throat." Once his shirt hangs open, he unfastens each cuff. "And if you'll swallow," he adds as I slip his shirt from his shoulders; it glides down his arms before falling to the floor. His smooth, toned body glistens under the soft bedroom light.

"I want to taste every last drop you'll give me," I whisper, my nipples hardening beneath the lace.

"Good, because once I've fucked this pretty mouth, I want to taste myself on your lips. I'll fill you so full that you'll be relishing me for days." I drop to my knees, my hands moving to his belt. "Take your bra off," he orders. "I want to see those tits bounce as I fuck your mouth."

Quickly, I remove my bra, throwing it to the side, then return to removing his clothes and boxers. He slips out of his socks, resulting in him standing before me naked in the center of the room. I'm on my knees, his cock level with my eyes.

"Open," he orders, and my jaw responds immediately. He slips his dick between my teeth. "Suck. Feel me filling your mouth, and think about how that will feel fucking your pussy once we're done here." He thrusts, and I run my tongue around him each time he recedes.

When he pauses, I take the opportunity to play with the tip while reaching out to cup his balls. His hands move to my hair, twisting the strands between his fingers until almost the point of pain. A low moan sounds above me, so I increase the pace of my tongue, flicking and circling before running it down his length to his balls.

I take him in my mouth once more, applying pressure to his ass with greedy fingers and encouraging him to push deeper. His hips move in long deep strokes, and I savor the length of him moving in and out my mouth. His knees bend slightly, then one hand roams reaching toward my chest; it grabs at my breast, taking a strong grip. I wince, but mumble a moan incoherently and dig my nails into his skin. He responds by increasing the speed of his cock between my lips.

The tip of his dick connects with the back of my throat as we both get lost in the moment. He pushes harder, and I hold him as tight to me as I can to encourage him to keep going. His cock jerks, and hot, salty cum coats my tastebuds. He moves to withdraw, but I hold on tight, continuing to suck every last drop from him. Deft fingers play gently with my hair, and I'm aware of his focus on me when I peek up. We gaze at one another as I use my tongue to clean him, the emotion running between us palpable. It's as if tonight is the beginning of something more. An understanding that this is it.

Once done, he encourages me to stand then removes my remaining clothes. As he leads me to the bathroom, we don't speak—we don't need to.

The large walk-in shower sits at the back of the room. Connor releases me, then moves to turn on the rainfall. Steam immediately floats from the head, and he adjusts the knobs before checking with his hand for the perfect temperature.

His hand reaches for mine, then he pulls the band from my contained hair with the other. He guides me under the flow of warm water. At first, he stands back, allowing the stream to run over my body. I wipe the water from my eyes. Wet strands fall over my shoulders, and Connor reaches for the shampoo bottle. I step forward out of the water as he squirts a blob of creamy liquid into his palm.

"Turn around," he says softly, and I do as he asks. "Keep your feet steady."

His hands land in my hair, and he begins to wash, twisting and folding my locks, then massaging my scalp. White suds flow down my body to land on the natural stone we both stand on. He steps forward so that his chest is hard against my back, and we both are under the flow of water. The unmistakable sensation of his cock hardening again touches my ass.

"You see that bar?" He points to the solid silver bar bolted to the shower tray. My mind wonders if it was installed for the purpose of having sex in the shower, but I don't ask. "I want you to bend over, spread your legs, and hold on. Do you understand?"

"Yes."

"Yes, what?" he growls, then nips my earlobe between his teeth.

"Yes, sir." The name pops from my mouth on impulse, and we both freeze. After a moment he chuckles.

"I was hoping for please, but if you want to call me sir, I am happy to answer to that name. Now bend."

"Yes, sir." I do as he says, bending from my waist and widening my stance. My fingers grip the slick silver pole. Connor places a hand on each ass cheek, squeezing hard then rubbing softly as the pain becomes almost unbearable.

I feel something touch my entrance. When he slams himself inside, I realize there's to be no warm-up; he takes me hard and fast, stretching me wide in one thrust. My stomach tightens as my pussy strains to accommodate him. He gives me no time to prepare before pulling back and slamming in again. I wobble, letting go with one hand.

"I said fucking hold on," he snarls, grabbing my waist tighter and slamming into me again. I hold tight, bent over in his shower, and let him fuck me as if it's the last time he ever will. My orgasm builds, that familiar vibration starting from deep within and pulsating until I can't contain it. I bend my knees and adjust my stance to ensure the tip of his cock hits the sweet spot. My pussy contracts hard as my orgasm hits.

"Fuck yes," he shouts. "That's my girl. Don't you fucking let me go. Hold on until I tell you we're done."

He continues to pound, sliding deep, hitting hard over and over again as I lose control, my body going limp in his arms. He rides me through every convulsion, my stomach contracting harder with each surge of pleasure. He holds himself deep inside as his cock jerks and he finds his high. Strong hands move up my body, finding my breasts and playing gently with my nipples as we stand together in the shower. I'm bent over, still filled with him, as the warm water runs down my back and over my shoulders.

"Stand up," he says as he withdraws. He turns me to face him and steps back out of the stream of water. He picks up the shampoo once more and washes my hair again, then rinses the suds from the strands. After he grabs the conditioner, he guides me out of the water then massages the cream into my scalp. I look up at him, mesmerized by the care in each action. No one has ever made me feel as wanted as I do at this moment.

Reaching up, he lifts the shower head from its resting place then removes the lotion from my hair. Before moving to concentrate on my body, he applies soap to each area slowly, taking care to clean me thoroughly before rinsing the remnants away. Each time he meets my gaze, we smile at one another tenderly. Right now, this feels so fucking real. I would let Connor Chase look after me for a lifetime.

After the shower, he brings me a massive fluffy towel, wrapping it around my shoulders. I wander back to the dressing table, sit down, and start to brush my hair. Connor disappears into the dressing area and appears a few minutes later redressed.

"You changed?" I say. "They'll know we had sex."

"And?" He replies with a glance at his watch. "We've been gone forty-five minutes. I don't think even Violet is dozy enough to think we were only in here talking." He walks over and drops a kiss on my forehead. "You finish getting ready, and I'll go tell them we are ready to celebrate your first day at work.

"Okay. I won't be long."

"Take your time. You are the leading lady tonight." He leaves his bedroom, and as I hear the front door click closed, I collect my cell and switch it back on. Four messages waiting, all of them from Russell. Without looking, I type out the one I need to send.

> This stops today. I care for your brother. I want to be with him. Stop following me,

stop contacting me. Keep your distance. If you don't, I'll tell him.

Chapter Eleven

—◆—

Varley Medical, London

March 2023

Russell

It turns out that following someone when they don't know you're there is an extremely satisfying pastime. Tailing Samantha when she knew of my presence and observing the guilt on her face as she enjoyed it was fun. However, knowing where she is and all the small tasks she completes each day without her knowledge is even more gratifying. According to her, I was a terrible stalker, and for her pleasure I was. But now, watching her is purely for myself, and I'll be sure to relish every last moment.

When her message popped up on my screen back in January, I was furious. Her rejection had stung worse than any other before. It was my understanding that we had an unspoken agreement between us, that there was a connection to be enjoyed even though we weren't able to act on it physically.

I saw the way her nipples budded under her clothes as she passed me in the street. The way her breathing hitched when I was close enough she could feel my breath on her skin. How her steps became slower as I fell out of her view with a glance over her shoulder. She wanted me there, and even if she hated the fact, she knew it.

Over these past months shadowing her, spying even, I've learned a lot about Samantha Coleman. When someone doesn't know you're in their presence, their guard is down and they act as the person they are, not the person they think they should be. I know how she likes her tea, the way she leaves her socks beside the washing basket in Connor's dressing room rather than in it, and how she loves when her pussy is filled with thick fingers while her clit is sucked. The noise she makes as she orgasms is angelic, and the way she likes to sink her teeth into my brother's flesh makes me wish it was me.

What started as infatuation has become a senseless obsession, a need to know where she is and what she's doing. And even though I've hidden in the darkness these past months, I know it will soon be time to step into the light. I need her to know I'm here. She needs to know that although she told me no, I continue to ensure she's safe.

The private hospital is quiet like always today. I'm sitting on a bench on the other side of the street from the entrance waiting for Samantha to appear after her shift. It was easy to obtain her work schedule from Josephine Rivera; she owes me far more than a single job offer.

Varley Medical is a place for the rich and famous. It is *not* the sort of place you can attend on a normal private health insurance package. To obtain an appointment you must already be registered with the center itself. If your name isn't on the list, you're not getting in. My family has been treated here since we were children; it was a stipulation of my fathers as he prioritized privacy and security. This past year has shown me exactly why.

Edward Chase, my father, is currently incarcerated by Her Majesty's Prison Service for charges including fraud, drug dealing, and murder. It turns out it wasn't only our family he ruled with a brutal dictatorship, it was his whole business empire. I had known since I was a teenager that my father's world was dangerous. I saw enough men beaten, and took plenty myself, to understand we weren't normal. But the revelations that came out once Violet returned from Chicago shocked even me. My father is evil to the bone.

My mother was left destitute after the government froze all assets in my father's name. Earlier this year, she moved into an apartment within the same building where my siblings and I live. Our housekeeper, Mrs. D, has become a good support to her and is probably the first female friend she's had since childhood. Then there's the added benefit that she is now a grandmother, and I in turn am an uncle.

Violet gave birth to a beautiful baby girl a matter of weeks ago, and my mother loves being there to help. Evie has become her pride and joy and given her a true purpose while we navigate this time of uncertainty. It turns out my mother was as trapped by my father as we all were, but now she's free. It's wonderful to see her grow.

What could be considered an ambulance swings rapidly into the parking bay at the front of the hospital, causing me to glance up when it smashes a plant pot. It's a white van with a high roof, and there are painted red stripes along the side with the words "private ambulance" written in bold black letters. Two men dressed head to toe in black jump out and run up the steps into the building. They return minutes later carrying what looks like a white cooler. I watch as they slide open the side door of the vehicle and one man steps in holding the box.

Inside the ambulance isn't like you would expect. There's no bed or cupboards holding supplies. It's simply an empty van with nothing to suggest any sort of medical work is undertaken inside. My interest gets the better of me, and I stand then cross the street as they close the door. The driver gets in, and I step in front of the vehicle as he switches on the engine.

"Mate," he shouts out of the open window, "out the fucking way."

"A question, if you don't mind."

"I do mind. We have a time-sensitive delivery. Get out of the way."

"It will only take a moment," I continue, walking around to the driver's window. "What goods are you carrying? And do you have an I.D. for the company you're working for? I notice there are no details on the vehicle."

"Who's asking?"

I pull my business card from my inside pocket and pass it to him. He squints at the writing, and I wonder if his eyesight is adequate to be driving. As I look over the vehicle, its dilapidated condition becomes more apparent; the panel edges are speckled with rust, and the front tire is worn to the point of unusable.

"It strikes me as unusual that an ambulance would have no interior fixings or access from the cab to the rear compartment," I say, signaling behind him. His colleague rattles on the metal, and the man I'm speaking to barks at him to be quiet.

"This is a stand-in vehicle," he tells me. "It was being refurbished, but my ambulance is off the road so they gave me this one to transport organs."

"Ah, so that's what is in the box." I lean into the window a fraction. "I love gore. Do tell me, is it a heart or kidney in that box? And where are you taking it?"

"Patient confidentiality," he snaps, then pushes the gear lever into drive. "Back off, Mr. Chase. We must be going." The van starts to move, and I step back. As he leaves the parking area I take a picture of the number plate. This will require more investigation later, but first, I have someone to visit. I turn and walk into the hospital—if Samantha won't come to me, I'll go to her. I'm done waiting.

After taking the elevator to the fourth floor, I step out into the familiar reception area. Bryan, who runs the desk, is sitting in his usual position, shuffling papers and talking on the phone. As I cross the shiny tiles, he looks up and smiles brightly.

"Mr. Chase," he says. "How can I help you today?"

"Is Josie in?" I ask casually. "She isn't expecting me, but it would be good to catch up." He lifts the telephone receiver to his ear and stabs at a button I can't see.

"Dr. Rivera." The squabbling of a pissed-off woman can be heard as he addresses her. "I know, I'm sorry to interrupt, but Mr. Chase is here to see you." The irrational screeching stops, and Bryan replaces the handset.

"Just go through," he says.

"Thanks, Bryan. She doesn't change."

He chuckles but doesn't respond. I would expect he's too fond of his job to do so. With a wave, I wander off in the direction of the office I know well for both business and pleasure.

Josephine is waiting for me when I arrive, standing in the doorway and leaning casually against the frame. She's wearing a fitted black dress that finishes just above her knee; the neckline dips low, exposing the swell of her breasts. Wide red lips smile brazenly as I drop my hand to her hip then kiss her cheek.

"Business or pleasure?" she purrs, and I laugh.

"Always business, Josie. You know that."

She pouts dramatically. "That never used to be a rule." Her hands move to her hips and she straightens. "We had some fun times over this desk."

"Yes, we did. But then you returned to your ex-husband. The one I fleeced for two million pounds in your divorce settlement," I remind her.

She giggles like a schoolgirl, then slaps at my shoulder. "Spoilsport."

"I'm saving your husband from paying you for a second divorce."

Josephine totters across her office then throws herself down on her chair before crossing one leg over the other. I close the door and take the seat opposite.

"So, what can I do for you?"

"I'm here to make sure my money is being well spent," I tell her. "How is Samantha getting on? It's been a few months."

"Are you and her fucking?" she asks, her nose pinching in annoyance.

"No."

"So why pay for her education and not tell her?" She raises her eyebrows and narrows dark, suspicious eyes.

"Think of me as Robin Hood."

She laughs out loud then shakes her head. "Robin Fucking Hood, my arse. I'll tell you what," she says, then taps her lips with a long thin finger. "You can ask her yourself." She presses the call button to Bryan before I can stop her and asks him to send in Sam. I glare at her, but she shrugs my mood away. A few minutes later, there's a knock at the door.

"Come in," Josephine calls, and I hear the door creak open.

"You wanted to see me, Dr. Rivera."

"Yes, Samantha. Do come in." There is the sound of the door closing, and soft footsteps across the office in my direction. The hairs on the back of my neck stand on end as I keep my eyes focused on the bitch on the other side of the desk. "Your funder is here for an update on your progress." My body freezes as the information I wanted to be kept secret is blurted out into the open.

"Excuse me?" Samantha says, clearly shocked. Knowing I must face this straight on, I stand and turn to face her. She's staring at me with an expression that could convey either happiness or horror. She looks naturally stunning with no makeup, hair high in a ponytail, even while wearing a shapeless uniform. This woman makes my body yearn whenever she gets within ten feet of me. It's disconcerting.

"Mr. Chase here funded your whole program." I glance at the doctor who's gesturing at me. "And now he wants to know he didn't waste his money."

"Oh..." Samantha stammers, her expression morphing to complete confusion. I wonder how she's going to navigate the situation, if she'll acknowledge that we know one another or not and how well.

"Are you not going to say 'thank you'?" Josephine snaps, then walks around her desk to stand beside me and lays a hand on my arm. Samantha stiffens, and I get a ridiculous kick from the idea that she could be jealous of another woman touching me.

The three of us stand in the office in what resembles a stand-off. Every person waiting for someone else to make a move. Finally, Samantha clears her throat and takes a step forward, then extends a hand. I take it—our bodies connect, and I swear a bolt of electricity passes between us.

"Thank you, Mr. Chase," Samantha says formally. "I appreciate your investment in my career." She squares her shoulders, and her eyes lock with mine.

"You're very welcome, Miss Coleman," I reply, releasing her hand. "Do ensure you take full advantage of the opportunity. I wouldn't want you to get into any *trouble*."

***

Samantha

My worst fear has been confirmed—it was Russell who paid for this opportunity. It was he who arranged for me to follow my ambition into nursing. The idea had crossed my mind on a few occasions, but I'd dismissed the notion as ridiculous.

I was wrong.

We face off in the middle of my boss's office after being introduced as if strangers. Dr. Rivera's focus moves between us assessing the situation, and with each second that passes, her mood darkens.

"Have you found your training so far, interesting?" Russell asks, breaking the silence.

"Very. Dr. Rivera is an extremely knowledgeable professional, and my fellow nursing team have taken great care to show me the ropes."

"Ropes?" he replies with a cheeky smile, visibly relaxing. "Are your rope tying skills improving?"

"It's a figure of speech," I shoot back with a scowl.

"Nurse Coleman, watch your manners," the doctor warns, moving closer to Russell. She raises her fine-boned hand and places it up onto his shoulder. I don't like it. "Mr. Chase is a good friend of mine. I won't have a staff member disrespect him."

"No disrespect intended." I take a breath, trying to steady my nerves at the unexpected situation I've found myself in after a long day on my feet. Russell takes a small step away from the doctor, and her hand drops to her side. She frowns fractionally before readjusting her features. I wonder what relationship they've had in the past and if it was a romantic connection or purely business. Her mannerisms indicate something personal, but he shows no sign of there being more than a business connection.

"It's fine, Miss Coleman," Russell says, maintaining the façade. "But I would suggest you stick to nursing rather than teaching the English language. Adages are not professional in the workplace."

"My apologies, Mr. Chase." His eyes blacken as I use his surname. "I will be sure to remove adages, catchphrases, and general slang from my working day vocabulary."

"Good to hear. Well, thank you, Miss Coleman, you can go," he says dismissively, then turns to the doctor. I stand like a lemon, pissed off by his arrogance. When I don't move immediately, his focus returns to me. "You can go." He mouths each word dramatically and my irritation rises to another level, but I turn and walk out of the room, biting my tongue.

Back out in the reception area, Bryan is busy banging on his keyboard. As I approach, he looks up and smiles. These past few months, he's become someone I feel comfortable being around. I love hearing all the crazy stories about his kids and his unreliable ex.

"So, how did your date go?" I ask him, and he grimaces. His usually happy demeanor disappears with my question, and I kick myself for asking. "From your expression I would say not great."

"Dating apps suck," he says, his expression becoming more sad. "The guy was an idiot." He stops typing, then picks up his phone and opens the app he has been using to search for potential partners. He opens the messaging service and passes the handset to me.

Message after message from some guy called Colin who Bryan has met once for a quick coffee, fills the screen. Lines of text declaring his undying love and begging him to give him another chance.

"Oh, you attracted a loose cannon," I mutter. "Did you sleep with him?"

"No," he spits. "We barely made it past the coffee, and not for the right reasons. All he talked about was some online game he plays constantly and his long list of previous sexual conquests."

"There are always going to be duds in the dating pool," I tell him, trying to be supportive. My heart aches for him. He was so looking forward to stepping out into the world of dating again and investigating his new-found interest in men. "The next one could be a keeper." He hisses through his teeth but doesn't respond to my comment. "It was your first time back dating; give yourself a chance."

"Sam, I have four kids and no money. The last thing I need to waste time on is men worse than my ex-wife. Maybe I'm better off single." He restarts typing, and I continue to flick through the app on his phone, hoping to find something positive to suggest.

My eyes land on a handsome man with dark hair, hazel eyes, and the most gorgeous smile. "What about him?" I say, turning the phone in my friend's direction. He glances up then shakes his head. "Why not? His name is Tom. He's forty-two and works as a vet. Nevermind the fact that he's hot. If you're going to explore your sexuality, Bryan, at least do it with someone you want to rip the clothes off."

"Look at him," he replies sadly, not looking at me. "Why would he be interested in me?"

I stare at my beautiful friend, and my sadness for his situation grows. His ex-wife ripped him to pieces and left him with very little confidence. Even though I've never met her, I hate her. How she could do wrong to such a kind man I will never understand.

"Because you're beautiful," I tell him, walking around to the other side of his desk and wrapping my arms around him. "Bryan, any man would be lucky to have you. You're a catch. Never forget it."

"I'm not sure potential suiters would agree that a broke single dad to four reprobates constitutes a catch."

"Then they're idiots. You, my friend, are gorgeous both inside and out. You deserve to be happy. Don't settle, he's out there. Keep looking, and enjoy the search." I kiss his cheek before releasing him. He smiles up at me.

"Thanks, Sam. You're not so bad yourself. Anyway, what did Casanova want with you?" he asks, raising an eyebrow.

"Who?"

"The hot lawyer. He's quite a ladies' man from what I hear, and I know for a fact he and our good doctor bumped uglies for a while." He runs a hand through his hair then grins.

"How do you know that?" I ask, my nosiness getting the better of me.

"I saw them," Bryan says with a chuckle. "Her bent over the desk, dress over her head, and him balls deep. Fuck, I wish he was into men."

"She's too old for him" I mutter, my cheeks flushing.

135

"I'd imagine it's perspective. When he's fucking her doggy style, her pussy will look the same as a twenty-two-year-old."

"Rude, dickhead. Not a vision I want, my boss's pussy." Bryan shrugs and goes back to typing furiously.

I haven't told anyone here much about my private life, and I've never mentioned Connor. It's something I want to keep to myself. Most of my work colleagues are low on funds, and sick of treating the rich and famous who spend fifty-pound notes like penny coins. Telling them I had a millionaire boyfriend didn't seem like a sensible course of action. Now, if Connor insists on picking me up at work, we meet around the corner.

"The heart was collected by those two idiots again," Bryan tells me, interrupting my thoughts. "I don't like them."

"Me neither. I mean, I'd have thought an organ transportation service would be more professional. Was any paperwork signed this time?" Bryan shakes his head. "Do we know where they were taking the organ?"

"No, Dr. Rivera says she handles all the paperwork before removing the organ. We don't need to concern ourselves with that."

"Does that not strike you as..." I trail off when I hear the click of high heels on the tiles. The doctor and Russell appear; they completely ignore us and walk to the elevator. I watch as he presses the button and when the doors open, she embraces him warmly and kisses his cheek. An unwanted emotion stabs my chest, one I don't want to admit I feel when it comes to him. One I have no right to be feeling. Jealousy.

I wait until Russell steps into the elevator. Dr. Rivera watches the doors close, her eyes fixed on him. Once he has disappeared, she turns and stalks back to her office again without so much as a glance.

"That organ transporter," I say to Bryan, returning to the previous conversation. "Something doesn't sit right with it."

"Sam," he says kindly. "Take my advice. Keep your nose out of this. Do your job and learn, but don't start questioning processes within this department. The doctor isn't someone you want to make an enemy of. She's one of those people where her bite *is* actually worse than her bark. Don't get bitten."

"That's how bad behavior continues," I mutter.

"What?" he snaps, pouting as if offended. "What do you mean bad behavior?"

"People get away with shit because others turn a blind eye. I'm telling you, Bryan, there's something fishy going on. And I want to know what."

"We're small prawns. Don't get involved."

"It's pawns, Bryan," I say, then turn and walk away to finish my shift.

***

That evening, Connor and I are sprawled on the huge velvet corner sofa in his apartment. We've just eaten a banquet of Chinese takeout, and my stomach feels fit to burst. He sits pushed back into the corner as I lie with my head on his lap. Deft fingers play with my hair as we watch a predictable rom-com on his huge television.

"I like this," I whisper then close my eyes, enjoying the gentle strokes on my skin.

"The situation, or us in general?" His fingers move lower to my breast, and he plays with my nipple through the fabric of my tank top. It hardens under his touch.

"All of it." I push myself up and move to straddle him, placing my hands on either side of his head. "I love everything about us."

"Everything?" He raises an eyebrow. "Elaborate, please. I could do with having my ego massaged."

"I'll do more than massage your ego." I wriggle off the sofa and drop to my knees between his legs. My hands move to the waistband of the gray jogging bottoms he's wearing, and I tug impatiently. He lifts his hips to allow the material to slip over his ass, and his cock springs free. "Commando, I like it."

"Noted. I will throw all my boxers away and walk around commando from now on. Your pleasure is my number one priority." I laugh, and his eyes lock with mine. They glint with the need of a man who knows what's coming next.

"First of all, I love how we laugh," I tell him, and he smiles. "Second, I love the way you kiss me every time I arrive here."

"You like that?"

"Yeah, it feels coupley." My cheeks heat, embarrassed by the admission.

"Coupley? I'm not sure that's a word in the English dictionary," he teases.

"Do not question my language skills. Not after..."

"After what?" he asks, confused.

"Nothing," I say quickly, not wanting to think or tell him about Russell's nonsense today. "Third, my favorite thing about us is the way you don't demand my time. The way you don't demand sex from me. What we have feels...complicit."

"Sex should always be consensual, Sam," he says softly, stroking my cheek. "And both participants need to get what they want from it."

"Don't get me wrong," I add hastily. "I love it when you're bossy, but I know with you if I say no, you'll understand. You make me feel safe."

"You always have a choice with me. And if I ever lay my hands on the bastard who didn't give you one, I'll fucking end him." He holds my focus firm, then raises both eyebrows. "Who is he?" I shake my head, not wanting to discuss this with him. "I want a name."

"It doesn't matter, it's in the past," I murmur, placing my hands on his knees and dropping my gaze between his feet. The last thing I want to discuss with him is my overly controlling ex who believed my body was his property.

"Of course it matters. Your reaction is the only evidence I need that it matters. I *will* find him," he says, confidently. "And when I do, he'll wish he wasn't fucking born." I glance up to see honest, intense eyes staring back, and my fear of the past seems to disintegrate. This man...I believe every word from his lips. He's everything I don't deserve. He's got me, and I, in return, want to give him my soul.

"I adore you," I whisper, never breaking our focus.

"And I worship you, but right now, I want you to suck my dick." I giggle, taken aback by the unexpected request, absurd in the tense moment but appreciated. "Take those pretty pink lips and wrap them around my cock. I want to be balls deep in your throat before I sink myself in your pussy."

"Yes, sir," I say with a smile and salute him. As I go to take him in my mouth, his hand touches my head.

"Wait, first I want you naked." I blink up at him, and he signals for me to stand. "Strip." I gape at him, and he smiles sexily as he sits on his sofa with his cock standing tall against his toned stomach and his jogging bottoms around his ankles. He'd been topless when I returned from work, and I wasn't complaining.

"You want me to dance?"

"No, I want you fucking naked. Take your clothes off, get on your knees, and suck my dick until I shoot my load down your throat."

"Yes, sir," I reply sexily, then lift my top over my head and slide out of the shorts I'm wearing. His eyes drop to my bare pussy. "Oops, I'm commando too. It's fate."

"Get over here," he growls, and I drop to my knees once more then take him fully in my mouth. He hisses as I give him no time to prepare, sucking greedily on his thick cock. He fills my mouth, and I push him further, wanting to take him as far as I can. His hands move to my hair; strong fingers twist the strands pulling on my scalp. I'm mid-suck when I'm interrupted by a furious voice. It takes me a moment to realize it's coming from Connor.

"What the fuck do you think you're doing?" he shouts, livid. When I look up, I see Russell standing in the apartment watching us. He looks at his brother, then at me, before returning his attention to Connor and smirks.

"Enjoying the porn show," he says casually.

"Too far, Russ," Connor snarls, jumping to his feet. His body connects with mine, and I'm thrown onto my backside. My breasts jiggle, and Russell's eyes widen further. "Sam, put your clothes on." Connor wrestles with his joggers, trying to pull them hastily up from his ankles as I reach for anything to cover myself.

Once dressed, Connor stalks toward his brother then grabs his shirt by the collar. He's dressed the same way he was when I saw him earlier at the hospital. "How the fuck did you get in here?" Connor shouts, his usual calm manner obliterated. "And how much whiskey have you drank? You fucking stink." Russell's eyes flit to the balcony. "Tell me you didn't."

"I did."

"You climbed down the outside of the building to get in here. Why not use the fucking door?" Russell shrugs, his gaze roaming the room, looking everywhere but at his younger brother. "Russ, have you done this before?"

"No comment."

"No comment? Seriously, I've caught you snooping on me and my girlfriend, and that's all you fucking have to say." Russell shrugs again, and the fury radiating from Connor increases to a furnace. "Fuck Russ, *have* you done this before?"

Russell looks directly at him, his eyebrows drawn together, then his eyes dance with mischief. "More than once," he says casually. "You two can certainly put on a show."

I watch as Connor pushes Russell hard in the chest. He stumbles backward and Connor hits him again before manhandling him out onto the balcony. They wrestle for a few minutes, a suited body wrapping around a bare one. Russell throws a punch, and it connects with Connor's nose. Blood spurts from his nostrils instantly.

"Stop," I shriek, running to the doorway as the two men lose control. I try to get between them, and Russell draws back and aims at his brother. He misses as Connor steps to the side. Russell stumbles forward, his large body connecting with mine. I fall to the ground, throwing my hands down to save myself as the tears start to fall. Both men freeze, and four concerned eyes fall on me.

"Too fucking far," Connor growls. "Fuck off back to your own apartment the way you came." He pushes him toward the ladder, pinning him against the railing.

Russell grabs for the rung and pulls himself upwards so he is balanced between the ladder and balcony. He swings a foot in Connor's direction, connecting with his abdomen. On instinct,

Connor deflects the blow and pushes him hard on the thighs. Russell wobbles. His palms grip the cool metal, then release. The next few seconds happen in slow motion—I watch in horror as he falls then disappears behind the barrier and out of sight.

CHAPTER TWELVE

Connor's Apartment, The Level

Connor

"Russ!" I scream, leaning as far over the barrier as I can. My terrified fingers grasp the freezing metal rail. "Russ! Fuck! Answer me." Samantha appears at my side and places a soft hand on my shoulder. "Russ!"

"He fell, Connor, we need to alert the authorities," she says, her voice frighteningly calm. "We need to call an ambulance."

"No, he'll be fine. I'll call the reception desk, speak to Matthew. I can't have killed my brother. I can't have." The plead spills from me, desperation taking hold for it to be true. My brother...I pushed my brother off my balcony. I murdered him.

No, he has to be alive.

"It was an accident," she calls to my back as I spin and run into my apartment. I grab my phone and hit the direct dial to Matthew, the head of security for the building.

"Mr. Chase," he answers formally. "How can I—"

"It's my brother," I blurt out, the shock of what happened moments ago developing into sheer terror. I've murdered my brother. The longer the fact runs through my head, the more real it becomes. I've killed a member of my family in rage. The man I love most in this world. "He fell from my balcony. He's…"

"Understood, Mr. Chase," Matthew replies, maintaining his professionalism even though I've just told him my brother has fallen from over fifty stories to his death.

"Please, you need to go outside, you need to find him. Help him."

"Mr. Chase, I'm walking outside the building now. Please stay on the line." I listen as Matthew's heavy boots sound off the pavement as he walks the perimeter of the building. Time passes but he doesn't speak.

"What's happening? Do you have a flashlight?" I finally demand.

"Yes, I have a flashlight and the street is well lit. There's no sign of him, sir," he says. "Your brother hasn't fallen to ground level."

"Well, where the fuck is he then?" My mind whirls with every bizarre possibility, but how many options are there when you fall from a skyscraper in the middle of the night? "Check again and any neighboring areas that he could have fallen into. We need to find him. I need my brother." Any thread of sanity has disappeared; my voice is booming and deranged as I shout. "I need my brother," I repeat, anger breaking into emotion. When I lift my hand to my face, my fingers meet wet skin. I swipe at the fucking tears streaming from my eyes.

"Mr. Chase, please remain calm. We'll find him. I'll come to your apartment now, and we'll organize a search of the building."

"Thank you, Matthew." My horror at the thought of Russell being splattered across the cold dark streets eases a fraction, but it's quickly replaced by the fear of the unknown. Just because he never fell the full distance, doesn't mean he is alive.

As I stand in the center of my apartment, I drop my head into my hands. I'm at a complete loss as to how to handle this insane situation. The chances of Russell surviving are zero.

Just then, Samantha walks in through the door followed by Harrison and Violet. I never even heard her leave. In my sister's arms is her young daughter swaddled in a blanket. She passes Evie to her husband and runs to me, wrapping her arms around my waist.

"It will be okay," she says fiercely, her face buried into my chest. I hold my little sister and allow myself to sob for a moment. "Sam says it was an accident. This isn't your fault, Connor. We'll find him."

"He's dead," I reply, broken. The hope that this isn't the case has utterly disappeared. "No one could survive a fall like that, no one. Not even our bonehead brother."

Another knock at the door announces Matthew and two further security staff arriving. Sam appears at my side and links her fingers through mine. Her hand feels strong under my touch. She maintains an aura of stillness, which I'm not sure is due to fear or shock. She squeezes my hand softly. I flex my fingers, a silent thank you for her support as I try to pull myself together. My first venture into love could end with me going to prison and losing my brother. Love is the gateway to life going wrong.

"Good evening, Mr. Chase, Miss Coleman," Matthew says, acknowledging us, then he turns to my sister and Harrison. "Mr. and Mrs. Waite."

"Good evening, Matthew," Harrison says, stepping forward in a clear indication that he's taking control of the situation. Violet clings to him as their daughter sleeps soundly in his arms. Tears run down my sister's cheeks as she tries to control the wail behind her lips. "There's been an incident this evening, and we're unsure of the outcome." Matthew listens intently, his two men standing silently behind. "Russell was climbing on the exterior ladder back to his apartment and fell."

"He didn't hit ground level, sir," Matthew advises. "I checked myself." Harrison mutters something I can't hear. It strikes me as odd how methodically the whole situation is being handled.

147

Nothing feels out of control except for me. "We'll start a sweep of the whole building immediately."

"Keep me informed, Matthew. We'll go to the penthouse and check he isn't there. If he has managed to gain entry via another balcony, he may just have gone home." Matthew nods, but the look that passes between them is one of complete disillusion. "Violet, take Samantha to our apartment," Harrison says as Matthew and his team leave.

"No, I want to help," Samantha counters, and Harrison scowls. "This is my fault."

I take her in my arms and kiss her forehead. I hold her to me, willing her not to feel any guilt about what has happened. Of all the people in my apartment this evening, Sam is the least to blame. "Of course it isn't. Russell shouldn't have been on the ladder. I shouldn't have pushed him. This isn't your fault," I tell her firmly.

"Connor," she whispers, blinking up at me. "You have no idea how wrong you are." I stare back at her, perplexed by the comment. Before I can ask more, Violet comes over and encourages her to follow.

"Come with me," Violet says, tugging on Sam's hand which is frozen on my back. I feel Violet begin to prize her fingers from my skin. "Sam, we can't do anything to help. Come with Evie and me; we'll put her to bed, and by then the boys will have an update."

"No," she snarls. "I'm going to look as well. Take Evie home, Violet." Sam releases me, then storms toward the door wearing only her tank and shorts.

"You've no shoes on," Violet calls behind her.

"I don't care." She slams the door as she disappears.

Harrison walks over to his wife and passes her their daughter. "You go home, Vi." He kisses her softly on the lips, and she begins to cry again. "Evie needs her bed. We'll find him. I'll send Sam to you once she calms down. I love you."

I watch the interaction between my best friend and my little sister with what can only be described as gratitude. If today turns out as bad as I think it will, tonight Violet could lose both her brothers.

"You ready?" Harrison says, his astute eyes landing on me. "You better put some clothes on." I glance at myself in the large mirror that hangs on the wall. I'm still dressed in only my gray jogging bottoms. A dirty t-shirt lies over a chair in the corner where I dumped it earlier. I quickly grab it and pull it on.

"As ready as I'll ever be," I tell him.

"Go home, Vi," he reminds his wife. "I'll let you know as soon as there is any news." I follow him out of my apartment and toward the penthouse.

Our trip to Russell's home is made in silence. There's no front door as such; the elevator opens directly into his living space. The only means of access is with a specific entry card, of which I have a spare on my keys.

"I'm not sure what to do," I say to Harrison as we step out into the apartment. Everything is in it's position as it normally is. Russell likes his home orderly, even though he's a nightmare in the office with leaving crap around.

"Me neither," he replies, his eyes moving around the open plan space. "Russ, are you here?" No one responds. The apartment is deathly silent. "Check all the rooms. If he somehow came back here injured, then he may have passed out."

"Should we not call the police?" I ask, looking to my friend for advice.

"And say what? That you pushed your brother off a building? All that would happen is you'll get locked up and my wife will lose her family." My normally calm friend loses control a fraction. "What the fuck happened?"

"He was watching."

Harrison focuses on me, clearly confused. "What do you mean he was watching?"

I take a breath, trying to steel myself to tell my friend about what transpired tonight. "Connor! Fucking tell me what's going on. I can't help you otherwise."

I am about to start speaking again when the sound of footsteps distracts me. I turn to see Hunter and Damon walking across the room. I look from Harrison to them and back.

"I called them," he says, inviting no argument. "We all need to be here."

"Have you called your boys in blue?" I snap at Damon as he comes to my side.

"Fuck off, Chase," he mutters. "I'm no longer a member of that team. You fucking know it. We're here to help."

"Is someone going to tell us what happened?" Hunter asks, for once an expression of fear on his features. His question is simple and to the point, no familiar asshole comments in sight. "Waite said Russell fell from your balcony. What was he doing?"

"Connor was just about to tell me," Harrison interrupts. "Tell us all."

"He was watching," I begin, the anger that my brother was spying on us mixed with misery at the outcome.

"Watching what?" Damon asks.

"Samantha and me on the sofa having sex." My three friends stare at me dumbfounded. "We were..." I pause, unsure of how much information to divulge. Figuring this may be my last night as a free man, I decide to be open and honest with the men I trust most in this world. The only man missing is my brother. "She was on her knees sucking my dick when I looked up and saw him standing there watching her. It was like he was transfixed."

"What the actual fuck..." Hunter mutters. "He was a peeping tom?"

"Yes, and in true Russell fashion, he made a sarcastic comment. I lost it." Shame starts to invade my chest as the memory of what I did to my brother comes clear in my mind. I close my eyes, reliving the scene in real time. "I pulled up my joggers and confronted him, then pushed him out onto the balcony. We wrestled, and he hit Samantha in the face by accident. I manhandled him back up to the ladder." The wetness seeps from my eyes again, more tears falling with each fact laid bare. "He went for me again, and I reacted by pushing his legs. Then he fell into the blackness, he was gone."

Damon looks at me, concern and terror marring his face. His focus moves from me to each man in the room. "We need to figure out why he was outside your apartment and where he could have landed when he fell," he says almost to himself.

"He never hit the ground directly outside the building," Harrison advises. "Matthew and his team have been scouring the surrounding area. They're now starting door-to-door balcony checks within the building."

"Where is Samantha?" Hunter asks. "And Violet?"

"Samantha went to look for him herself. Violet is at home with the baby," I say.

"Call your girlfriend and tell her to get her ass up here," Hunter says. "This is fucking weird. She must know something." I pull my phone from my pocket, and her cell rings out. I immediately redial, and then there's a buzz on the penthouse intercom. Harrison walks over to answer it, and Samantha's trembling voice can be heard from the speaker.

"Let me in," she whispers in clear pain. "I've just got on the elevator." The sound of its approach buzzes, and Harrison hits the allow entry button. The doors open, and Samantha runs into my arms.

"They can't find him," she wails. "We've been walking up and down the streets, checking basement stairways. There's no sign of him."

"You've been outside like this," I say, squeezing the bare skin at her midsection. Her naked feet look almost blue against the dark wood floor. "You're freezing." I look around the room for something to wrap her in. Finding nothing, I hold her tighter to my torso, willing some heat to pass between us.

"I'll get a blanket," Damon says, walking off in the direction of the spare bedroom. I hear the door creak open, then the words, "Holy fucking hell."

"What is it? Is it him?" Harrison shouts, running in the direction of Damon's outburst. We all follow swiftly. Samantha's hand is locked in mine as we step into the bedroom. Everyone comes to a stop in synchronization. We all stand in the doorway with our jaws hanging open.

"What the actual fuck," Hunter grunts out.

"Oh…" Samantha says under her breath. "I mean, I knew…" She trails off as I focus on her.

"You knew what?" I hiss, my stare moving from her to the hundreds of photographs pinned to the walls of the room. "What the hell did you know and didn't bother to tell me?"

"That he…" Her eyes widen as I take a step toward her but drop her hand. I lean down, unblinking, and she cowers slightly.

"What?" I repeat, demanding information as every possible perverse scenario pops into my head. "Were you fucking him? Is this some sort of sick joke the two of you are playing?"

"No!" she stammers, reaching for me. I step back out of reach.

"Samantha," Harrison interrupts, his tone clear and firm. "Tell us what you know about all this." He waves his hand, signalling the insanity around us.

"He was following me," she says quietly, her eyes fixed on the floor. "He has been for a while."

"Since when?" I growl, furious at Russell for his behavior and with her for not telling me. I'm at a complete loss from the fact that this has been going on and I didn't know. The room is lined with images of her, candid snaps of her everyday life. My brother has seen so much more of her routine than I have.

"Last year." The words are barely audible as the fact catches in her throat. "Since I met him, the same night I met you."

"That's fucking months!" I shout, throwing my hands in the air and storming up to the photos on the wall. "So these?" I start pulling images from their resting place, tearing them up, and throwing them on the perfectly made bed. "You knew he was taking every one of these, and you never thought to tell me? You didn't think I deserved to know that my brother was obsessed with my girlfriend?"

"Of course I did," she says, walking toward me. "I didn't know about the photos. It all started with him following me home from the club, and he intervened once when I was attacked."

"You were attacked?" I yell. "Was I not man enough to know this? What is this, Sam? Did you get off knowing two brothers were into you?"

"No, it's just..."

"Did you love the attention? Was that more important than your feelings for me? More important than our relationship?" I turn to face her once again, shredded images of her scattered on the bed and around my feet. "How could you not tell me? My brother, who I trust with my life, was stalking you, and you didn't think to say."

"Of course I did, but he's so important to you. I didn't want to be the reason you fell out." Her face twists in despair. Both of us stand gaping at the other with no idea where to go from here. "He didn't hurt me. He was just there."

"How often?" I continue, wanting but not wanting to know the details. My brain throws every interaction between her and my brother in my face as a memory. The small gestures, the smiles I noticed and ignored. "How often did he follow you? What did he do exactly?"

"It started at the club, I told you that," she whispers, her voice broken and cheeks now stained with tears. She sits down on the bed and throws her head into her hands, sobbing into her fingers. "It started when he came to watch me dance, not long after I came to tell you about Violet being held prisoner by your father. The next thing I knew, every shift he was there. He would wait outside the rear entrance, then follow me home. We rarely spoke except on a few occasions."

"What else?" The other men in the room stand silently, but I know they are taking in every last detail.

"Then after he collected me from work in January, and we were late back here." She stops speaking and looks up, and I glare back at her.

"The night you went drinking instead of coming here from work. Are you telling me you knowingly socialized with him even when you knew he was obsessed with you?" The unbelievable scenario is mindblowing. My brother has been stalking my girlfriend, and she seems to have fucking enjoyed it.

"Yes," she admits, her face reddened beyond anything I've ever seen before. "But I told him to stop after that night. I told him to stop following and contacting me."

"How did he contact you?" I ask, clinging to the new piece of information.

"By message from an unknown phone."

"Did you contact him?"

"No," she replies firmly. "I never encouraged him, but I will admit to enjoying the attention. It was nice to feel wanted."

"You don't think I want you?" I stammer, shocked and even more furious. "These last months, have I not proven I want you?"

"Yes, but that's not what I mean..."

"Well, fucking enlighten me, because if you're wanting an unhinged, obsessive arsehole, you picked the wrong fucking brother." She reaches for my hand, and I push it away. "Don't touch me."

"I didn't do anything," she wails again. I hate the sound of her pained voice—all I want to do is make her happy. All I've wanted to do these past months was build an amazing life together.

"You did!" I counter. "Omission is still a lie, Samantha. Not telling me what the fuck was going on is still untruthful. Your actions are more eye-opening than what you say."

"I didn't want to cause you trouble."

"Well, while you were not causing trouble." I lift my hands to form speech quotations on the word trouble. "You were enjoying my brother's attention."

She falls silent, her eyes dropping away. I expect her to cry again, but she doesn't. After a few moments, her gaze lifts and fierce blue eyes hold mine. She stands and straightens her shoulders.

"Is it too much to ask for understanding? Could you possibly entertain the idea that by not telling you perhaps I was protecting you?"

"Protecting me?" I scoff. "How does lying protect me?"

"I didn't want to be the one who wrecked your relationship with the man you put on a pedestal. The man you think the sun shines from every fucking day. I didn't want to be that girl." Her hands ball into fists, and she looks from me to the other men then back to me. "Maybe I thought I could handle it? I knew he wouldn't hurt me. He would never do that to you, never mind me."

I blink, unsure how to respond as her words start to make an insane kind of sense. Nothing about this situation or our lives, in general, is normal, so why would this be any different? Of course my brother and I would be obsessed with the same girl. Russell and I have always fought over everything while patting each other on the back.

What hurts most is that deep down I knew there was something, but this I wasn't expecting.

"Russell loves you, Connor, you're the most important person in his world." She deflates slightly as the height of our argument starts to dispel. "Part of me wondered if he was looking out for me because he knew I was important to you."

"Important to me?" I repeat back. "Samantha, I'm in love with you." She swallows visibly, taken aback by my admission. "But this is a lot to take in—you, him, and everything that's gone on behind my back."

"I'm sorry," she says, reaching for me again. "How can I—" Her words are interrupted by the elevator sounding, and we charge back through to the living area.

Matthew stands in front of the open doors. He smiles broadly before saying, "We found him, and he's alive."

CHAPTER THIRTEEN

Varley Medical, London

Samantha

Connor paces up and down the corridor for the hundredth time. Russell is having his injuries assessed by Dr. Rivera. She banished us all from the room. I sit on the blue leather chair in the hallway and watch him stress over and over about what happened—how it was him who caused his brother to fall to near death.

After Matthew appeared at the penthouse, he told us that Russell had been found and they were waiting on an ambulance and the fire department. Unbelievably, Russell had merely dropped five stories onto the sun lounger on an extended balcony of an apartment on the fifty-second floor. During his descent, he'd apparently hit his head on a railing and knocked himself unconscious. The rattan material of the lounger had broken his fall.

His suspected injuries, according to the paramedics, were concussion and a broken leg. I'd blinked at Connor in shock when he relayed what he was told in the ambulance. I had followed behind in a car with Violet and Harrison. Mrs. D was called in the middle of the night to take care of Evie.

"Only Russell Chase could fall from the fifty-seventh floor and not die," Hunter says with a chuckle to no one in particular.

"We don't know for sure what his injuries are," Connor snaps back. "It could be more serious."

"Nah, that balloon has enough hot air in him to cushion any fall. He'll be fine." Hunter stands, then walks over and grabs Connor's shoulder. "You didn't kill your brother, my friend. Stop beating yourself up and be thankful for how tonight ended."

Violet sits beside me, holding my hand. Connor hasn't touched me since we arrived here. He's been deliberately moving out of my way. The other men are scattered in seats in the corridor, talking between themselves quietly, all of us impatiently waiting for any news of what is happening. Finally, the doctor steps out of the treatment room.

Dr. Rivera walks up to Connor and embraces him warmly. He hasn't mentioned knowing her beyond pleasantries since I worked here. "He's going to be fine," she says with a small smile.

"A displaced fracture to his left tibia and moderate concussion. Minor injuries considering what happened."

"Can I see him?" Connor asks, hope obvious in his voice. The doctor smiles again kindly. The woman in front of me is far removed from the dragon I'm used to working for. Her usual persona is cold and sharp as she orders us around the ward, criticizing any small perceived flaw.

"Yes, he's sleeping though, and you'll need to be quiet. The fracture in his leg can't be set and put in plaster until the swelling reduces. We conducted an MRI scan for any damage to the brain, and there is some minor inflammation, which is expected with this type of injury. But all in all, I'm not concerned there will be any lasting harm."

"Excellent," Connor says, his mood lightening. "Please, can my sister come in too, Doctor?" She looks at Violet still holding my hand; her focus then lands on me and her eyebrows lift in surprise.

"Trainee Nurse Coleman," she says. She emphasizes the word trainee. "What are you doing here?"

I look up, and her eyes narrow. "I was at the apartment when the fall occurred," I tell her.

"Mr. Chase's apartment?" she questions. Her expression darkens further as I nod. "And what would you be doing there?"

My hackles rise with the query—this woman grates on me more each day with her jibes and prods for information, while she remains guarded and aloof.

Violet stands and encourages me to follow. She walks forward, closer to Connor, and passes my hand over. He takes it and then pulls me beside him, wrapping an arm around my waist. The terror I'd felt that he may want to end things subsides slightly as our bodies connect. His close proximity is calming; the smell of him fills my nostrils, and the anxiousness which had risen in my chest moments ago softens.

"Samantha is my brother's fiancée," Violet announces firmly, and Connor's eyes shoot in my direction.

"We're all extremely excited regarding the upcoming wedding," she continues, smiling wide at the doctor. "I'm going to be Sam's bridesmaid. We haven't decided on a color scheme yet." Connor clears his throat, attempting to stop his sister from veering into a story about our fictional upcoming nuptials. I stand quietly beside him, holding his hand and unsure what the status between us is. Violet ignores him. "I was thinking sky-blue, maybe with a hint of mint-green. What do you think?" She turns to me and beams.

"It sounds lovely," I say, trying to appear confident but failing miserably.

"What a curious situation," the doctor muses, looking at Connor. He stares back at her and straightens his shoulders.

"Please explain that comment." His grip tightens on my waist.

"It's nothing of importance. Go see your brother," she says, waving in the direction of Russell's room.

"With all due respect, Doctor, I would appreciate clarity on what was just said. Why would my being engaged to Samantha be curious?"

Dr. Rivera looks from him to me, then back to Connor. Violet shuffles impatiently from foot to foot. I hold my breath, willing her not to say what I'm terrified will pass through her vile lips.

"Well, I'm perplexed as Samantha never mentioned knowing the Chase family, never mind being engaged to one of you." She pauses, and a horrid smile appears, the one her staff know means our days are about to become more complex. "But it does explain why our education fees have been covered."

"That was a bursary," Connor says, confused.

"No, Mr. Chase. Samantha's full fees were paid by your brother."

No one speaks, but silent inquiries fill the air with each moment that passes.

"Excuse me," Connor stutters eventually, letting go of my waist. His face screws up as if in pain, and those beautiful eyes normally full of fun wither before me. My heart aches knowing I've done this. My inability to tell him what has been going on has made the impact so much worse than it needed to be. This fact will hurt him more than any other revealed tonight. My sense tells me that my time with Connor Chase ends here.

"Your brother, Russell, paid Miss Coleman's course in full and provided living expenses toward her bursary. There was no bursary for a trainee nursing associate position from a previous application. Samantha obtained a placement here purely on his request," the doctor confirms brusquely in her most professional tone.

"Did you know about this?" Connor spits, turning to face me. "What the fuck has been going on behind my back, Sam?"

"I only found out recently myself," I whisper. So many facts have been blown out into the open in a matter of hours. All the silent issues of these past months that I've been trying to bury are facing me and need to be dealt with.

"Go home," he tells me, turning away. I reach for him, but he shrugs my hand away. The doctor watches on, obvious amusement flickering in her eyes.

"I want to support you," I tell him. Connor walks toward Russell's door, while Violet stands motionless between us, unsure what to say or do. The other men stand, then Hunter comes to my side and takes my elbow. Harrison collects his wife and leads her nearer her brother's room, encouraging her away from the altercation. "Connor..." I call to his back.

"Go home," he repeats, not sparing a glance.

"Brother," Violet says softly. The lilt of her voice is calmer than I've ever heard. The siblings face one another, and he shakes his head.

"No, Violet. I can't deal with this." Their conversation is only half-spoken but I know much unsaid dialogue is passing between them. "It's too much. All of it is too much. More complications that I don't need in my life."

"Don't do something you'll regret in a few days. Samantha wasn't the one obsessed," she reminds him. My beautiful friend glances over, her expression sad. She had been so excited when Connor and I became official. My relationship with him has been one of the most real experiences of my life, and I ruined it. Guilt rears its head, stabbing deep in my chest because of my untruths to both of them.

"Please go home, Samantha. I don't need your support. I'll call you later," Connor says quietly, still not looking in my direction. He sighs softly, his desolation clear. "We can...actually, I don't know what we can do. But I do know I don't want you here right now."

Damon appears on my other side and mimics Hunter's hold. "It's time to go home," Damon says firmly. "I'll drive you." I shrug them off, but both tighten their grip. "It's not a choice. Connor has asked that you leave."

"And I can do so under my own power," I snap, furious at multiple men trying to tell me what to do.

"He may have asked you to go," Hunter continues the conversation, "but that doesn't mean he wants you to roam around London on your own. We'll ensure you get home safe."

"She's a big girl," Dr. Rivera interrupts. "With what's transpired tonight, it's clear Samantha is perfectly capable of looking after herself." She giggles, then covers ruby-red lips with a hand, feigning embarrassment. "Engaged to one brother while rinsing the other for money. That's quite the talent you have. The thing is, bad behavior tends to bite you on the ass after a while, and tonight you have been well and truly ravaged."

"What is your problem?" I hiss, losing the little control I was maintaining. "Since I arrived in this department, you've made it quite clear you hate me. Do tell me, Doctor, what exactly did I do to offend you?"

"You got this traineeship through connections, not talent," she replies instantly. "And I fucking hate people who get where they are without deserving it. I'll see you in the morning. Don't be late for your shift." I glance up at the digital clock on the wall; three in the morning and I start work at seven. "I suggest you get some sleep, because it's going to be a busy day." With that, she follows the others into Russell's room. I watch them disappear with a large, dangerous man attached to each elbow.

Once the door is closed and the others are out of sight, I pull at my arms again. "Let me go," I mutter. "Fuck's sake, I'm not going anywhere. If you want to escort me home, I couldn't care less." Both men release my elbows, then Hunter takes the lead, walking in the direction of the elevator. I follow with Damon behind me like a wall at my back, close enough that if I move out of line he can grab me.

The doors open as we approach. The compartment is empty, and we all step inside in the same order as we leave the reception area. Neither of my companions speaks during our descent to the parking garage below; they act as if they don't know I exist. The doors reopen, and we step out into the deserted garage, where only a handful of cars are scattered around. One large

SUV sits in a space in the far corner of the basement. Damon leads us in its direction.

Everything about this car screams underworld, from the black paintwork to dark tints on the windows. I am surprised when a man steps out of the driver's side. He's big, most likely in his thirties and sporting an array of tattoos.

"Greyson," Hunter says in a brusk form of welcome.

"Boss," he replies with a nod. "Where to?"

"If you can take Miss Samantha home, then drop McKinney. Where is Annie?" Hunter asks as if only just remembering Damon has a daughter. His nanny, who also became his lover, left him a matter of months ago when he was a complete and utter asshole with her. She disappeared to Scotland. They should be together, but neither seems willing to drop the stubbornness and reach out, according to Violet, anyway. My friend is a fountain of gossip and keeps me entertained with Harrison, her brothers, and their friend's stories.

"Her grandparents have her," he says casually.

"Really?" Greyson interjects.

"Yes. It's a work in progress but when I called them needing childcare, they were keen to help."

"It takes a village to raise a child," Hunter mutters, waving his hand around as if signaling to thousands of invisible people surrounding him.

"How would you know? You don't have any," Damon counters.

"Perhaps not biological, but I've taken plenty under my wing."

"I don't think bad boys from young offenders programs count, Boss," Greyson says. "It's not what the proverb means."

"Maybe not," Hunter replies with a shrug. "But I see you all as my children, under my supervision and protection." He holds his arms wide, steps back, and looks to the ceiling. "May I always be able to provide you and many others with employment, shelter, and a prosperous future."

"Are you for fucking real?" I snarl, stunned by his ego. Hunter's focus shoots to me, his head immediately straightening. He's a slim man; he doesn't have the bulk or strength of the other two. His long dark hair is scraped back into a bun, but there's a sophistication to him that comes across as natural. Violet says of all the men who frequent The Level, he's the most deadly.

"I'm always fucking real," he says, his tone calm but icy. "Do enlighten me as to what you find fake?"

"It was a figure of speech."

His head cocks to one side as astute eyes run over my face. "I liked you the first time we met back in September when you squared up to Russell. You have potential, Miss Samantha, if you're ever looking for employment…"

I laugh out loud. "What? And become one of your minions, the men you have surrounding you to do your dirty work? No, thank you."

He steps toward me; Damon tenses at my side and Greyson moves a step closer, both of them readying themselves in case shit kicks off.

"Don't worry, boys," Hunter says, his eyes flicking between them then back to me. "This one is too precious to good friends, and I can see the appeal." His hand lifts, his fingers grabbing my chin. "How I would love to cut out that smart-ass tongue, though. A mute, feisty little demon would be easier to manage."

I don't think—my knee lifts on impulse and connects directly with his balls. He lets go of my chin, stumbling backward, his hands over his crown jewels. The other men glance at each other and burst into laughter while their boss hops around the parking garage.

"Don't ever touch me or any woman without her consent," I warn, my eyes moving between all three of them as all their mouths drop open. "You bastards may think you're big and brave. You may think you're in control of the fucking world. But know that your guns and dangerous reputations don't scare me."

"Maybe they should," Hunter shoots back. I walk forward so I'm within inches of *supposedly* the most dangerous man in London. After blowing out firmly through my nose, I allow my eyes to move from his face down his body, pausing on his cock still covered by his hands.

"I'm not the one standing in the middle of a parking garage after three in the morning holding my privates," I tell him. "All of you fuck off. I'm going home, and I'll take the night bus."

With that, I turn and walk forcefully away from the three men, leaving the basement without looking back.

CHAPTER FOURTEEN

Varley Medical, London

Russell

Fuck, my head hurts. I lift a hand to my skull and my finger-tips meet soft fabric. With my eyes firmly closed, I lean back into the pillow which isn't my own—it's too hard. I wiggle my neck in an attempt to release some tension, but it doesn't work. A spasm holds my muscles taut.

"Where the hell am I?" I mutter, not wanting to open my eyes and face the day. The events of last night are blurred, a mess of static images in my mind that I can't organize into a coherent order.

"Varley Medical," a familiar voice replies unexpectedly. I freeze, unsure what to say. "You can look at me. It's your leg that's broken, not your eye sockets." Hesitantly, I crack open my right eye. The bright strip light is harsh against the darkness of my lids. "Do you have a headache?" the voice says sharply.

"Everywhere aches," I reply, and Josie giggles. I attempt to now open both eyes, blinking to give myself time to adjust to the light. It's a painful but necessary task.

"That's not surprising. Most men who fall off a building would be a splatter of bones and flesh on the pavement. But not you, Russell Chase, no—you manage to land on a deckchair and merely break your leg. In all, it's quite remarkable."

Once I manage to focus, I see her sitting on a dark blue chair beside my bed, dressed casually in simple jeans and a black, long-sleeved t-shirt. Her hair is pulled high into a ponytail and secured with a bright red band. One leg is flung over the other, and long fingers drum on her knee. There's no doubt she is a striking woman, but my previous attraction to her has vanished. My desire for any woman other than Samantha ended the night I met her.

"What on earth were you doing climbing up the outside of the building anyway?" she asks, uncrossing her legs and leaning forward.

"That is none of your business, Josie." Pain sears through my skull and my vision blurs. I need to speak to Connor; from what little I remember, I well and truly fucked up. The only clear image I have is him and the look of disgust on his face when he saw me in his apartment. "Is my brother here?"

"He went home once he knew you weren't going to die." She stands, then brushes down the front of her jeans with her palms, removing invisible dust. Her facial expression tells me she's unhappy at my lack of explanation. "This is my day off. I only came in to see you were all right."

"And I appreciate that, but I don't remember fully what happened. How did I get here? And what's wrong with me?"

"I told you, you fell off your building and broke your leg. A displaced tibia to be precise, so expect to be six weeks before bearing weight and fully ten weeks before walking normally." Pieces of my recollection start to fit into place, and my argument with Connor becomes more vivid. "You also have a mild concussion, but there should be no long lasting effects. You at least know who I am."

"I could never forget you, Josie," I say.

She places a hand on my arm lying on the bed. Her skin is surprisingly cold against mine. "As much as I would like to believe that, you've forgotten me."

"You're married," I remind her, not for the first time. "I don't want to talk about our friends-with-benefits arrangement, it's in the past."

She *tsks* through her teeth but squeezes my arm gently. "I miss you," she whispers, sullenly. The sternness in her eyes dwindles and for a moment, the strong, independent woman I know looks uncertain.

"We're still friends," I assure her. "But I don't sleep with married women. I told you that when you chose to go back to him." She swallows visibly, and her mouth opens as if to speak then recloses. "That decision marked the end of our sexual relationship."

"It wasn't even a relationship," she murmurs before turning away, then lifts her hand to wipe at her eye.

"Not a long-term one, but we both knew that. We agreed, Josie. This isn't about me or the fact we ended," I say, taking a stab in the dark at what could be wrong. We've been friends for years, since I met her freshly out of law school and she needed representation for motoring offenses. Ever since, Josephine Rivera has floated in and out of my life when it suits both her and me. "What's going on? I know when you're hiding something."

"Nothing," she says, then her pager beeps. She glances down at the message. "I need to go. The organ transport team will be here in ten minutes. I have a kidney for a patient being removed as we speak."

"I thought it was your day off," I ask, confused.

"My colleague, Dr. Winslow, is performing the surgery, but I like to oversee the dispatch of the organs." Her eyes are fixed on the doorway, and she shuffles from foot to foot, clearly keen to be on her way. "I'll send a nurse in to help you get comfortable."

"Okay, I'll see you later. Assuming I'm still here."

She glances over and smiles softly. "I'm keeping you in for a few days for observation."

"Is that not extreme for a broken leg?"

"But you also had a bump to the head, and head injuries no matter how minor are something I take extremely seriously. Especially when it comes to the people I..." She trails off, and I see a flush at the base of her neck and behind her ears. She clears her throat before continuing. "When it comes to people I care about." I watch as she leaves the room without looking back.

Left on my own, I try to wriggle up to sit and immediately regret the movement as my leg almost snaps in two. Instead, I lie staring at the blank white ceiling, watching the fan spin around at the center of the room.

My remembrances of the night before begin to merge more fluidly. I recall being in my apartment drinking whiskey, then scaling the ladder as I've done dozens of times these past weeks. Samantha and Connor had been once again having fun on the sofa, and with the sliding doors to the balcony cracked open a fraction I could hear the conversation between them.

She had been on her knees with his dick in her mouth when I'd heard the words I dreaded. "I fucking love you," Connor said so quietly it was barely audible, but there was no doubt in my mind what the phrase was. My sanity snapped, and I stalked into the room, standing over them as she worked on him. His hands were in her hair as he encouraged her to take all of him. I remember my brother looking up at me, and his eyes popping wide. Then the whole of hell let loose.

The door opens, disturbing my memories, and Samantha walks in. She's dressed in her pale blue nursing uniform, which hangs shapeless from her curves. Wide, nervous eyes meet mine, and I see her take a breath before approaching the bed.

"Good afternoon, Mr. Chase," she says professionally. "Would you like to sit up?"

"Please, Trouble." She stills, then picks up the handset from its casing on the bed and presses buttons. The back lifts, sitting me up more, and she plumps the pillows around me then moves to my broken leg, ensuring it's elevated a fraction.

"Are you in any pain?" she asks, continuing to poke and prod at the bedding.

"A little."

"It's not a surprise," she whispers. "You gave us all a fright." She looks up, and all I can see in those beautiful eyes I've been lost in for weeks is pain. When I examine her more closely, it's clear she's exhausted with smudges beneath her eyes. "Do you remember what happened?"

"Yes, most of it. I fucked up, I'm sorry," I say, surprising both myself and her.

"We've both fucked up. This, whatever it is, has been wrong, and it was unforgivable for us to not tell him." She picks up a jug of water sitting on my bedside table, then pours a small glass before handing it to me. "Drink."

I lift the glass to my lips and take a sip. The water is refreshing on my dry tongue. I go to take another, and Samantha pinches the glass from my fingers.

"Slow, small sips," she advises firmly.

"I'm surprised you're willing to talk to me."

"I work here, I don't have a choice," she says. "Dr. Rivera has assigned you as one of my patients. So if you need anything, press the bell." She signals to the small button with the image of a nurse on it attached to my bed. For a few minutes, she moves around the room, arranging and rearranging small items.

"You're stalling."

She pauses on my accusation, then walks back to the bed and sits on the chair beside me. "Why?" she asks, folding her arms across her chest.

"Why what? That's an open, ambiguous question. If you want an answer from me then you'll need to be more specific."

"Why me? Why scale the side of a building? Why is your spare room covered in my photos?" I blink at her, stunned by her knowledge of the archive in my home. She cocks her head to the side, and her eyes narrow. The uncertain atmosphere of earlier changes to a more intense one. "I asked you to stop back in January, and you didn't. I need to know what your end game was."

"I didn't have one, " I answer honestly. "I've never felt this way about anyone before. I didn't know how to handle it."

"You don't know me," she mutters, crossing her arms over her chest. A sigh escapes her lips as she leans back in the chair and closes her eyes for a moment.

"But I want to." It strikes me as odd she hasn't mentioned Connor; they were together when this whole fiasco started. "Is my brother coming to visit?"

She reopens her eyes and focuses on me, her expression turning morbid. "I wouldn't know. I've not spoken to him since he asked me to leave last night." Her truth sits between us, and uneasiness flutters over my skin. Tired eyes fill with tears. She places her elbows on her knees, drops her head into her hands, and sobs.

"Trouble," I whisper, panicked by her emotion. Her tears run freely onto her fingers, seeping through the gaps between them. I try to reach for her hand, but she's out of my grasp. Watching her hurt is the most painful situation I've ever witnessed. Knowing I caused the pain is unbearable. "Tell me what he said."

"It doesn't matter, it's over. I ruined it. We were both happy, and because of me and my stupidity, we won't get to explore where things would have gone."

The unfamiliar sensation of guilt which had been creeping up on me slaps me square in the face. I look at this beautiful woman who made my brother happy and realize that my selfish actions have ruined what could have been for them.

"I'm sorry," I whisper almost under my breath, and her eyes rise to meet mine. "You were mesmerizing the first moment I met you, and I couldn't let you go. Watching you seemed the solution to my jealousy. I hate what you have with him, but I also love seeing my brother happy." We stare at one another for a few minutes. The insanity of these past months is all running at full speed through my head.

"What do you want from me?" she says.

"Your attention." The words are pathetic said out loud, but they are sadly true. "Most women would run a mile if a man followed them or watched them have sex."

She swallows as her cheeks flush. Her eyes move around the room, looking everywhere but at me. She takes a deep breath as if steeling herself to speak. "I care about Connor, this isn't fair on him. No matter how excited or flattered I was that you wanted me, I should have put my relationship with him first, and now, I don't know if I can fix it." She sighs softly as her tears start once more. "He won't even return my calls."

"Because I was coming to speak to both of you," Connor's voice says unexpectedly from the doorway. I gape at him as he walks across the room then leans down to hug me.

"I hate you, you fucking bastard," he says as he embraces me. I wrap my hands around his back as we hold one another in the way we have since we were kids whenever we survived a dangerous situation. "But I'm relieved you're alive."

"You won't be for much longer," I mutter, and he pulls back scowling. "You threw me off a fucking balcony."

"No, I deflected your foot as you tried to kick me, and you're such a weakling you couldn't hold on."

"It was attempted murder," I continue to jibe. "Maybe I'll get McKinney to arrest you."

"He's not even in the police force now, you fuckwit."

Samantha clears her throat, bringing both our attention to her. She rises from the chair. "I'll go and let you both catch up."

"No," Connor says frankly. "I wanted to talk to both of you. I need to know what has been going on and where I stand in this mess."

"I'm not sure what..." Samantha begins, but I hold up my hand to cut her off.

"I'm in love with your girlfriend," I tell my brother. "Completely and utterly besotted since the night we met her last year." I pause for a moment, allowing the honesty to sink into everyone in the room. "When I couldn't have her, I did the next best thing."

"And went bat-shit stalker crazy?" he says, rolling his eyes.

"Pretty much. One night at the club led to another, then the next thing I know, I was following her."

"Have you slept together?" he asks, bluntly.

"No!" Samantha shrieks, shocked by the question. "Nothing ever happened. I promise. It was just a silly infatuation."

"Yours or his?" Connor continues, and her mouth drops open a fraction. "Yours or his?" he repeats, his dark eyes locked on hers and not letting go. She stands frozen to the spot under his stare.

"Both of us," she whispers, and the embarrassment at her truth coats her cheeks immediately.

"I thought so," Connor says, his voice low but firm. "Are you interested in pursuing a relationship with him?" Samantha shakes her head, but my brother's face tells me he doesn't believe her.

"Have you slept together?" he asks again. I recognize his tactics in his queries as he tries to extract the truth from the person he's speaking to. For once, I sit quietly and let the scenario play out before me. I'm unsure where he's going with this.

"No," she says again. "I told you that. The only person I'm sleeping with is you."

"I think you should," Connor says, shocking us both.

"What?" Samantha snaps. "You think I should sleep with your brother?"

"Yes."

"Why? Now you're finished with me, he can have your cast-offs? Is that what the plan is?" She turns to walk toward the door. My brother walks after her and reaches to place a hand on her shoulder. She stops under his touch but keeps her eyes facing forward. Her whole body is tense as she waits for him to speak.

"I'll never willingly be done with you," he says tenderly. "But I can't move forward in our relationship unless I am sure there's nothing between you two. I want you both to investigate what's there, but I want you to come back to me, Sam. Then I want to make you my wife."

His suggestion sits in the air, suspended in a haze of shock. No one speaks, all of us contemplating what this may look like. Connor turns to face me.

"We've dated the same girl before," he says, and I nod.

"It's not the same thing, and you know it. Before it was the fun of the chase, this is different," I have to point out.

181

"It is," he says. "And that's why I need to be sure she wants me." He speaks as though she isn't in the room with us. "I couldn't live with myself if I walked away from the best thing that's ever happened to me. But I also don't want to move forward wondering if she's going to leave me for you."

"I stalked her," I admit, and my brother smirks.

"You've always been an unhinged maniac, Russ." He lifts a hand and rubs his forehead. "But the fact Sam never told me, and she enjoyed it, tells me that perhaps she's unhinged in her own way too."

Samantha steps up beside him, reaching for his hand then withdrawing, uncertain of his reaction. Her eyes run over his face then flit to me. "Can I still see you?" she asks him. He lifts a hand to her chin, running his thumb over her bottom lip.

"This is the only way I'll allow you to," he says. "If you don't agree to this, we're finished. I can't live my life worrying about a desire you have. I want you to see both of us, then decide who it is you want."

"Like a competition," I shout. "And the winner gets all the pussy."

Connor laughs, then kisses Samantha in front of me. My hackles rise with his open affection. Game on, brother.

"And if that's my competitor," he says, gesturing in my direction. "I've got this won hands down. But you need to sample the bacon to know when it's the prime meat between your thighs."

CHAPTER FIFTEEN

The Chase Family Home, Kensington

Twenty years earlier...

Connor

White powder everywhere. Mountains of it scattered across the work surfaces and bar stools in our kitchen. Violet is standing on the other side of the island, mixing an unknown substance in a bowl. Her dark curls, still unbrushed since this morning, are unruly around her shoulders. My little sister looks up and smiles when she hears my footsteps. Almost thirteen now, she's growing up fast but still has a childlike demeanor. Her wide brown eyes dance as she continues to stir whatever she is making.

"Does Mum know you're in here?" I ask. The closer to the mayhem I get, the more apparent the destruction is.

"No, I'm making surprise pancakes. Want one?" I shake my head as my gaze runs over the array of pots, pans, and glasses lying out amongst the food debris. A pack of chocolate chips lies scattered within the mounds of flour. The dark buttons have smashed against the granite worksurface.

"Does anyone know you're in here?"

"You do," she says brightly, and my heart sinks. Our father runs our home with an iron fist, and he doesn't enjoy cute family moments or surprises. The older I become, the more I've discovered the man he is: a dangerous one with little control over his temper.

"That's not what I meant. Where's Mum?" She shrugs indifferently and starts to spoon some of the mixture onto a tray covered with silver foil. I watch as she lifts what looks like a ladle, sweeping it over the counter before lobbing the gloopy mess onto the tray. Liquid drizzles onto the granite and starts to mix with the flour, creating a mulch. "Should you not move the tray closer to the bowl?"

"I'll tidy it up once I'm done. Do you think Dad will like them?" she says sweetly, her eyes firmly set on her task. When I don't reply she glances up, hopeful, then her face falls as she takes in my expression.

"The Martins are due to arrive any minute, Violet. You were meant to be dressed and ready to greet them."

Her eyes run over me taking in my freshly pressed white shirt and black slacks. "Oh..." she mumbles, then drops the bowl she's holding onto the counter. The ladle bounces off the top then disappears behind the unit. More beige mixture flies into the air and lands all over the kitchen floor. Violet squeaks, stepping backward fast. "Shit!"

"Violet Chase!" our father's voice roars from the hallway. I hear brusk footsteps, then he appears in the kitchen. "That language is not appropriate, and will not be tolerated in this house." A big man, he fills the doorway as he stands surveying the scene confronting him in his modern, sleek kitchen. His chestnut eyes lock onto Violet, who's clutching the countertop. She widens similar ones to him as he glares at her.

"I'm sorry, sir," she begins. The words tumble out rapidly. "I was trying..."

"Yes, Violet. You are very trying," he says, eerily quiet as he steps forward in her direction. Already dressed in his suit, he looks the epitome of the successful businessman, which he is. "What is all this?" he asks, waving a hand at the mess.

"Pancakes," she whispers.

"Speak up!" With every foot closer he gets to his daughter, the more she withers beneath his stare. She steps backward as he rounds the kitchen island to put them on the same side as each other.

"I was trying to make pancakes for us all," she repeats, a fraction louder with a clear note of terror in her words.

"And did you have permission to make pancakes?" His question is rhetorical; I know he knows she didn't. I also know the best thing to do at this point of a conversation with my father is to stay quiet and shake your head, but Violet always has something to say, and today that will most likely land her in hot water.

"No, but..."

"But nothing," he roars. "You took items and ingredients from my kitchen, paid for by me, and did not ask permission. That makes you no better than a common thief."

"No," she shrieks as he lunges and grabs her arm. "I was trying—"

"I don't give a fuck what you were trying to do. You're my daughter, living under my roof. Until that fact changes, you will not take anything that I consider mine without permission." Violet starts to cry, tears seeping from her eyes as sobs catch in her throat. "Save your tears, Violet. Today, you will learn about punishment and how it is dispensed."

"Sir," I shout, wanting to divert the attention from her to me. "I understand you feel—"

"Stop talking now, boy," he growls. "Or you'll end up receiving the same punishment that your sister is about to experience." He lets go of Violet's arm, and her hand snaps to the pale flesh marked red where he seized her. His hands move to his belt, and he begins to unfasten the buckle. Violet wails, and a violent hand strikes her hard across the face. She falls to the floor, then my father returns to removing his belt.

"The Martins," I say into the tense abyss. "They'll be here soon. Surely her punishment can wait." My father turns to face me, wrapping his belt around one hand then slapping his palm with the loose strap.

"Do you think I will allow the appearance of some wannabe friends to stop justice when it needs to be served?" He raises his eyebrows, and I shake my head. Just then, a staff member, one of his guards, appears in the doorway.

"Sir, your guests are here. Mrs. Chase is waiting for you in the library."

"Send them away," my father snaps. "I'm no longer feeling sociable."

"Yes, sir," the man replies, expressionless, before disappearing back from where he came.

The first blow comes down unexpectedly; Violet's shriek alerts me to what is happening. I dash around the counter, putting myself between my sister and the belt. It catches my back as I turn away in an attempt to lessen the blow. The leather comes down again, harder than the last. The pain sears across my skin as my little sister cowers below me.

"Move," my father roars. "You will both receive twenty lashes, no exceptions, for disrespecting my home and my rules." He stands above us, glaring down. I look up at the man meant to keep us safe, and my heart breaks again as it has a thousand times before. His lack of regard for us as his children is soul-destroying. He takes the rule of being seen and not heard to the next level.

Rough hands grab me, pulling me to my feet. Strong fingers bite into my flesh through the material of my shirt. He lifts me, my feet parting from the ground momentarily before he spins me to face the counter.

"Hands there," he snarls, tapping the granite with his belt. "You too, Violet." My sister scrambles up beside me and mimics my pose. Her fingers visibly shake, and I place a hand over hers. "My children are exactly that. *Mine.* You will act as I tell you to, speak when you're spoken to, and only partake in other activities when you have my express permission."

"I was only trying to make you a surprise," Violet sobs as she clutches the ledge. "I wanted to make you happy."

Our father laughs, loud and nasty. "Happy? Violet, you have been incapable of that every year you've had on this planet. You're here because your mother wanted another child. When you turned out to be a girl, I should have thrown you in the Thames."

I squeeze her fingers in solidarity; when the tyrant who runs our home is furious, only venom passes his lips. It's at times like this that I know he hates us. We're nothing but property he must maintain. On some days, he's kind and considerate, wanting to discuss our futures and hopes. But every up is met with a faster downward spiral where he knocks us straight back to reality.

I glance over my shoulder as the belt is lifted high into the air. I turn back and screw my eyes closed, but the blow never comes. The sound of a chair being knocked across the room causes Violet and I to spin to see the commotion. Russell has my father by the collar, and he pushes him backward toward the door. Our father thrashes at him with the strap, and my brother takes the blows to his side as if they don't connect.

"Never touch my brother and sister, you evil bastard," Russell roars in the older man's face. In his late teens and with a keen interest in working out, my brother is strong. He pushes firmly as our father steps backward across the tiles. When they reach the door, they both stop.

"Are you quite finished, Russell?" our father asks, calm and collected. My brother, however, looks fit to burst. Redness emanates over his face and fiercely across the back of his neck.

"No," he snaps back, leaning in closer. "You're nothing but a fucking bully. Leave them alone, they're kids." He pulls at the shirt in his grasp, shaking the man before him.

"And my boy, are you now a man?" The question is laden with threats. "Are you willing to take punishment like a man for your outburst?" Russell's eyes flick to us still standing at the counter.

"If you spare them," he says quietly, "you can take your wrath out on me."

Chapter Sixteen

Varley Medical, London

Samantha

The hospital is quiet on a Sunday night; there are only myself and one other staff member on our floor. Bryan sits at his computer typing away, attempting to catch up on basic administration before the new week starts. He was off unexpectedly last week as one of his sons became ill. The doctor insisted he make up the lost hours or take a cut to his paycheck.

I'm moving between each patient's room when he calls me over to his desk. "Can you take these to the doctor?" he asks. "Please, every time I've seen her today she's moaned about me being off last week. I can't take any more whining. Four kids whine enough, I don't need to hear it at work from a supposed adult." He looks up and flutters his eyelashes dramatically. "You know you're my favorite."

"Bullshit. I bet you tell all the girls that." I stand directly in front of his desk and place my hands on my hips.

"Sam, you know you are the only nurse on this floor I would consider fucking." He smiles broadly. "I would even consider letting you wear a strap and fuck me." I hold out a hand, trying to stop the laughter hissing through my teeth. On the most boring days, Bryan lightens up the ward to no end.

"But I wouldn't consider allowing you to," I tell him. "Once you tasted this delicacy..." I wiggle my hips dramatically and place both hands on my breasts as they jiggle, before holding out my hand again. "You would never go back to cock. Not that you've had any."

His cheeks color slightly. His lack of a love life has been a hot topic of conversation in the staffroom. Various ladies have offered to set him up with their sons, friends, nephews, friends of cousins, and any other gay man they know. Bryan has declined all offers.

"I'm worried," he says softly. "What if..."

"What if what?" I remain standing in front of him, hand extended like a lemon waiting for both the paperwork and his words. "Spit it out."

"What if I don't like it?"

"Fucking a man?" I ask. "If you don't like ass sex, just go back to shagging women. Or stick with blowjobs. There are lots of ways to have sex. Whatever makes you happy."

"But what if the reality doesn't live up to the fantasy? It's one thing jerking off to pictures on the internet. It's another to have a man in my bed."

"You need to find a man willing to *get* in your bed first. Stop worrying about what hasn't happened." Bryan shakes his head and widens his eyes as I speak. I ignore him. He's hearing this whether he wants to or not." You deserve to live your life too. Are you going to give me that paperwork, or do you want to go see the dragon yourself?"

"The dragon is standing directly behind you, Nurse," my boss says over my shoulder, and I inwardly detonate. Shit. I scowl at my friend, who shrugs his shoulders and gives me a look telling me he tried to warn me. "I'll collect my own documents, Bryan." She steps forward and plucks the wad of papers from his hand. "Come and see me when your shift ends, Nurse Coleman. We have some issues to discuss, both personally and professionally." Without another word, she turns and stalks off toward her office.

The sun begins to rise, the orange beam cracking through the blinds of the windows. Finally, my shift is coming to an end. A look at my watch tells me it's six in the morning. Other than my run-in with Dr. Rivera, the night was relatively uneventful. However, that will no doubt change as I still have to visit her in her office before finishing.

Russell has been asleep since I arrived, and when I checked in on him a few minutes ago, before my shift finished, he was still dead to the world. As I approached his bedside, he had mumbled something incoherent. I'd allowed myself a few moments to gaze at him while he couldn't stare back.

Connor's suggestion that I date both of them came completely out of the blue. Since he proposed the trial period, I haven't spoken to either of them about it. The idea that I need to sample what Russell has to offer to be sure that it's Connor I want feels wrong in so many ways, especially since our relationship feels so right. But then again, if I was truly settled on a future with him, would I be developing these insane feelings for his brother at all?

I told them both that I needed a few days to consider the proposition. There are a lot of variables to consider when entering into what is essentially a love triangle, but perhaps I'm already part of one. The difference now is that all parties are aware of the situation. On one hand, I feel elated with the opportunity to explore the possibilities; on the other, I worry about the risk and, ultimately, my final decision.

As I muse over my situation, I make my way to Dr. Rivera's office as I was instructed to do. She's known to spend the night in the hospital on occasion, so it wasn't a surprise she requested to see me. As I approach her door, light streams through a small crack creating a line on the dark hallway floor. There's a rumbling of voices which I assume is a television, but upon getting closer, I realize that it's multiple people having a conversation.

"Doctor, we had an agreement," a man's voice says gruffly. "And per that agreement, my boss can change the parameters as he sees fit."

"I can't do any more than I am," the doctor responds, her tone wavering with insecurity. "People are already asking questions. There aren't enough patients who are registered as organ donors for me to meet your demand. I've had to start removing organs from non-registered sources. The lack of paperwork is a daily risk to us all."

"That isn't our problem. You have a debt to pay, and this is how you chose to pay it."

What in the actual fuck have I walked into? All thought of interrupting the meeting evaporates. Organ theft happening under the noses of dozens of medics. The idea is as horrifying as it is absurd. I need to learn more about what is going on. This can't be true even though everything I am hearing tells me it is.

Deciding that standing in the center of the hallway isn't the safest place to be, given what's clearly an unsavory business meeting is taking place, I move to the side and into an adjacent room. Standing beside the wall with the door opened a fraction, I can still hear the conversation and even see the man facing the doctor's desk.

From the back, he looks like any other businessman. He's tall, well over six feet, with short neat hair and a crisp dark suit. Broad-shouldered, his muscles strain against the smooth material, filling every inch of the garment. With him standing in front of her desk, I can just make her out behind him. He leans down, placing his hands on the surface.

"We need more regular shipments," he growls. "Find a way to make it happen or we'll begin to take payment by other means. Whatever means necessary. You're running out of time, Doctor." A low chuckle sounds from his huge frame. "Find the goods, or I'll start bringing you donors."

"That isn't possible," she hisses, panicked. "I can't just start cutting organs out of random people."

He moves out of view, and the doctor follows him moments later. Unable to help myself, I step out of the room and move closer to the doorway to get a better look. With my body to one side hidden behind the wall, I peer in; another two men I didn't see earlier stand on either side of the doctor, each around a foot away from her. As large if not larger than their boss, they wear similar tight suits with crisp shirts. Each one has matching tattoos protruding from the collar that spike up toward smoothly shaved heads. Their arms are crossed over their chests in a way that makes them appear formidable.

The man in charge makes a small signal with one hand, and each man moves toward her and places a hand on her shoulder. Their fingers sit over the plain white t-shirt she's wearing, and the material bunches beneath the pressure. Her eyes widen, a display of the fear coursing through her in the moment.

I watch in horror as the man to her right pulls a short knife from his waistband. He places the tip behind her left ear and holds the weapon steady. Dr. Rivera swallows as all the color drains from her already pale face.

"Is there a problem, Doctor?" the man controlling the situation asks.

"No," she whispers, clearly terrified.

"Good, I'm delighted we have an understanding." The goon drops the knife away, but not before nicking her skin. A small droplet of blood runs down her flesh. "So the updated conditions of our arrangement are this: we'll provide you with the required organs each day and the timescale required. It's then up to you to find suitable donors. Once the operation is scheduled, I'll arrange for the collection team to visit. Between yourself and Winslow, this should be more than possible."

The doctor sits frozen in her chair listening to what are practically impossible demands. With each word, the desolation she's feeling becomes more clear, and she withers before my eyes. The man reminds her again how this is the payment for a past debt; I wonder how she got herself in this situation, and ultimately what I can do to help her...or if I should get involved at all.

"When do you need the next shipment?" she asks quietly. The little fight I saw in her when I stumbled across the scene gone.

"Tomorrow," he tells her. "Do you have a suitable candidate?"

"There will be one," she says sadly. "I have a couple of patients in their final days with organs suited for donation."

"Ensure one of them checks out tomorrow." He straightens then turns unexpectedly, and I step backward in an attempt not to be seen. I don't see the small trash can behind me and my foot collides with the woven metal. It bounces noisily across the corridor.

Panicked, I take off at a run back toward the reception area. I'm aware of a flood of light behind me as the door to the doctor's office opens. There's the sound of heavy footsteps, and I duck into the first available room, not looking to see who the occupant is. I click the door closed and stand behind it with my ear to the cool plastic.

"This is an unexpected surprise," a warm, masculine voice says from behind me.

"Shhh," I hiss with a glance over my shoulder, and Russell frowns back.

"You storm into my room at six in the morning, and I'm the one who has to be quiet?" I flip the lock on the door closed, then turn to face him. "What do you have in mind, Trouble? Because I'm not fit for any acrobatics." He gestures to his broken leg which has now been set in plaster. "But if you want to get on top, I'm sure I could withstand the pain to experience the pleasure."

The door handle flexes, and I spin to face it then walk backward, my eyes fixed on the moving metal. My heart begins to race as I replay the events in the doctor's office. Unsaid threats and violence laced every word during the brutal scene, so many unspoken and unknown dangers that she was terrified of.

The back of my knees hit the bed, and I sit down on the mattress, eyes still fixed on the door. The person attempting to enter seems to have moved on, but no part of me wants to go back outside this room. I am sitting halfway down the bed;

Russell lies behind me. A warm hand connects with my hip, and I glance at him. His expression is quizzical, concerned.

"What happened, Trouble?" he asks, softer than I've ever heard him speak. "You look like you've seen a ghost."

"Not a ghost, a crime lord," I whisper, and his eyebrows draw together in confusion. I place my hand over his as the heat drains from my body. Icy coolness spreads through every inch of me as panic sets in. My mind swims with so many unanswered questions, yet the discrepancies I've witnessed in the hospital since starting my job are suddenly more understandable. The missing paperwork, the confusion from families over their loved ones' requests to be organ donors...

"Trouble," he prompts, then the handle rattles again. His focus moves to the door, and he wriggles in the bed before hissing through his teeth as pain no doubt surges from his leg. "What did you see?"

"Dr. Rivera," I whisper. "I think she's selling organs."

His expression darkens a fraction, but there's no hint of surprise there. Astute eyes run over my face as he watches my every move. Uncertainty flickers in my chest, an internal debate as to whether this is information I can trust him with. I know he has a history with the doctor over many years. The connection I have with him is only a matter of months and hasn't gone beyond simple fascination. It's fleeting in comparison.

"What did you see?" he asks firmly.

"They'll be coming. They heard me outside the office."

"Tell me what you saw, Trouble," he prompts, his tone even softer.

"Three men," I begin, but then the door unlocks. I jump to my feet and move to the sink in the corner, pretending to fill a small basin with water. The door opens, and Bryan steps into the room; his focus moves from me to Russell then back again.

"Everything okay?" he asks.

"Yes, all good. I am just going to freshen Mr. Chase up then I'll be heading off." Bryan glances at his watch, a clear sign he knows my requirement to be here is over. "I thought you'd gone home," I add.

"Just about to, I was going to walk you to the station." Russell tenses, and he openly glares at my friend. "I'll wait for you." Bryan turns and walks away without acknowledging my patient's existence. He leaves the door open, and I place the basin back in the sink then walk over, reclose the door, and return to stand at the bedside.

"There were three men," I start my story again. "They were threatening the doctor, telling her she needs to provide organs to order or they'll begin bringing her donors to operate on. She has a debt of some kind to pay. They had a knife, and they cut her."

"Where?" he asks, sharp.

"Behind her ear. It was a warning. They mentioned another name, Winslow, I think." He narrows his eyes as if searching his mind for when he heard that before. "Do you know him?"

"No, but it's familiar. I need to think. And where were you when all this was happening?"

"Outside her office."

"So you're telling me," he says, his voice low like a grumbling in his chest. "That you saw three large dangerous men with knives threatening Josie." Annoyance bites as he uses her first name, the familiarity between them unsettling. I don't like to think of her with him. "And instead of getting the fuck out of there, you stood around and listened to their conversation."

I blink at him, startled that out of what I just told him, that me staying within earshot of the incident is what he's focused on. He reaches for my hand, his fingertips skimming my knuckles. I slip my hand into his, and strong fingers grasp tight. We stare at one another and unexpected emotions rise to the surface of my mind. The terror of the past minutes is coming to a head.

"Trouble," he says. "Never fucking take a risk like that again. If you find yourself in the path of danger, you get the fuck out of there. Do you understand me? You risk your life for no one."

"Is that what you would do?" His beautiful brown eyes soften, and he gifts me with a small smile. "Would you save yourself before anyone else?"

"I am selfish enough to do that, yes."

I drop my eyes away and let go of his hand. It falls to the bed, palm open. I walk over to the windows which look out onto the city. The busy morning bustle is underway, and everyone is going about their daily lives.

"I don't believe you," I tell him. "Under all that bravado, I know there's a gentle soul desperate to get out." He chuckles, and I turn back to face him. He shakes his head, but hesitation flits across his features, and my heart aches for him. Russell can't see in himself what I do, that underneath the asshole is a man who cares.

"You have me all wrong, Trouble. Gentle isn't a word in my vocabulary."

"Then why do you care what happens to me? I'm not your concern."

"You were my concern from the minute I laid eyes on you in the boardroom months ago," he says honestly. "Whether you accept it or not, whether it was what you wanted, as soon as you landed in my life, you became my concern."

"I am not yours," I tell him frankly. However, the previous feelings I've experienced when a man tried to claim ownership of me don't surface. The automatic reaction to dispute their claim, to be my own person, and insist that I am no one's isn't there. Deep down, the idea of being his is pleasurable. Having someone that obsessed as my guardian is the type of joy I never expected to experience—a man who would look out for me, even when I wasn't sharing his bed.

"Yes you are, Trouble. And you're about to learn exactly what it means to be the property of a Chase brother."

Chapter Seventeen

The Level, Canary Wharf

Connor

Russell had been in the hospital for a week when Dr. Rivera decided he could return home. The time spent inside seemed extreme, but with the events that led up to his admission, his not being here had been a welcome relief. Samantha is off work today, and we'll go to Varley Medical together to bring him back to The Level. She was unsure when I suggested we do this, but as this situation will be our new standard for a while, we need to try to normalize it as much as possible.

I truly believe the only way to get this girl is to allow her the space to choose me. If life has taught me anything, it's that when you push so hard the image becomes blurred, you often lose what you want. In any aspect, when you start to hold too tight, people automatically pull away. It's a defense mechanism. We as humans are prey, so when we feel threatened, our instinct is to run. The last thing in this world I want is Samantha to run from me, so if giving her this time to consider what she desires means she will be mine in the end, it's a sacrifice I'm willing to make.

The morning after Russell fell from the roof, I sat at my kitchen counter with my coffee and considered everything that had happened, both the night before and in the months previous to it. I'd missed all the red flags. My brother is someone I know possibly even better than myself; it hadn't gone unnoticed that he was acting different. The time gaps where I didn't know where he was, I accept now—I didn't ask because I didn't want to know.

There was a relief in learning his interest in Samantha was an obsession that hadn't gone beyond him watching and her enjoying the attention. Strangely, it had shown a sort of respect for me, which I didn't expect. It was like they were feeding a need without acting on it. Taking what they could, while not overstepping an invisible line.

That morning, my apartment was empty without her. She had been spending more time in my home, and I was becoming used to the company—the familiarity of having her here either waiting for me when I returned from the office, or her slipping into my bed in the middle of the night. I'd questioned how I wanted to tackle the revelations of her and my brother. Did I want to draw a line and move on? Did I want to walk away but demand they stay apart? Or did I cut ties with my brother and her?

Every option that flitted through my mind seemed wrong. Each situation was one I couldn't see myself living. As hurt as I was that she could want someone other than me, my need for her was greater. I had to find an alternative solution. One which meant I could keep her, but not trap her. One where I didn't ultimately lose my best friend, the man who has protected me his whole life. The man I truly want to see happier than anyone in the world.

The sad reality is that I had to accept that what could make him happy is also the one thing essential to me: Samantha.

***

Damon had appeared unexpectedly the morning after Russell fell, knocking at ten a.m. When I opened the door, he gave me a sympathetic smile and then asked to come in. I stayed mute but allowed him entry in answer, and he stepped into my home. We wandered through to the living space, and I fired up the coffee machine as he took a seat at my table opposite where my own mug sat.

"How are you?" he asked simply. I didn't answer immediately, focused on my task of pulling a mug and the necessary items from the cupboard. Even though I didn't meet his gaze, I knew he was staring at me with intense eyes, willing me to speak.

"Confused," I said eventually.

"That's understandable." I braved a glance in his direction. I'd expected to see pity, but all that was apparent on his features was concern. My friend, who was dealing with his own struggles in his relationship, had shown up today for me because he was troubled over how last night transpired. "I would imagine the whole fiasco would be a shock." I laughed out loud, and he raised an eyebrow and smirked.

"Understatement of the century," I told him.

The coffee machine signaled it was ready to use, and I placed the mug under the tap. The hot, dark beverage spilled into the cup, and the rich aroma filled my nostrils. I breathed deeply, enjoying the simple pleasure. After it was done, I lifted the mug and the plate with sugar, milk, and a small biscuit I'd prepared. I never used to have biscuits in the house, but Samantha loves a little treat with her hot drinks. They became a necessary purchase on my shopping list.

The doubt flickered again, the hurt that she might not want me. And how much I'd miss her if it ended here.

I moved to the table, placing Damon's drink in front of him then returning to my seat. My half-drunk coffee sat where I left it, and I wrapped my fingers around the handle but didn't take a sip. We sat in silence for a few minutes as he added the sugar and milk, then stirred his drink with the small silver spoon I left on the plate.

Although I consider Damon a friend, and a close one—he is a man I trust with my life—our relationship has always been more toward business than friendship. He's much closer with

Harrison than Russell or myself, which isn't surprising considering I've always had my brother to lean on. It made me wonder why he was here.

"I'm surprised you're here," I said, trying to open up some dialogue. "I'd have thought you'd be at home with Annie."

"Mrs. D is on babysitting duty," he replied. "Annie hasn't been sleeping as well since..." He paused, and his eyes dropped to the biscuit he was now unwrapping. He looked to compose himself by taking a deep breath before continuing with what he was going to say. "Annie hasn't slept well these past months since Emma left. Mrs. D told me not to come home too early and risk waking her. So I slept in Harrison's spare room."

"Did you get any sleep in that mad house?" I asked with a chuckle. My niece, Evie, doesn't sleep at all. My sister is forever complaining about being exhausted.

"Very little, but at least it's not my baby that kept me up." He sighed. "I should be going home to a smiley little girl, at least. She's a fiend after a bad night. Who knew a one-year-old could be so testing."

"I am pretty sure testing their parents is in the contract when they're born."

The conversation continued loosely around the children for a while—his daughter and my little niece, who came into our lives a matter of weeks ago and whom we're all crazy about. It was relaxing speaking to someone who knew the situation I am in but wasn't tightly connected to the confusion.

"How are you really?" he said, taking the opportunity to bring the focus to me during a lull in our conversation.

"I told you, confused."

"Last night you were ending things," he said, and I shrugged. "Is that what you want? Do you feel cheated?" I shook my head. Of all the things I felt, the last of them was cheated in any way. At the end of the day, it was me who had experienced Samantha fully, not my brother.

"I lashed out. I panicked."

He picked up his mug and drank deep before placing it back down on the table.

"I can offer you some sort of explanation," he suggested, surprising me. "Well, not an explanation per se, but perhaps a different perspective on what's happened."

"Please do." I sat back in my chair, interested in what he had to say. A pep talk hadn't been something I was expecting when he appeared. I assumed he'd been sent to check on me by my sister; now it seemed he was here under his own steam.

"It's possible to care about and be in love with two people at the same time." The statement was candid and to the point. Internally, I winced with the directness. The harsh reality that love isn't always like in the storybooks. "I am."

"With all due respect, it's not the same situation."

"No, but there are similarities. But because I'm an idiot, I've ended up on my own. Emma left because I refused to let go of the past. Actions and reactions always have consequences. In my situation, I was the one in the middle between a future I could have and the past I once had. I acted irrationally, struggling with the guilt and morality of it all."

"Do you not think you could fix things with Emma?"

He sighed, his chest rising and falling in defeat. The stubbornness that got him here showed through the cracks. "I doubt she would want to. What I am saying is, Samantha was devastated last night with both the thought of hurting you, and losing you. She cares, Connor, a lot. And I heard you tell her you love her. Those words weren't said frivolously. Don't let a snap decision risk what you have. Don't make the same mistake I have. It's a lonely place to be."

"What if she leaves? What if she chooses him?" The real fear surfaced again, the idea that she would prefer my brother over me. The niggling worry that Russell will be able to provide what she needs more than I can, that in some way they're more suited. My self-doubt screams at me to end it now and not leave myself open to the devastation of being the one not chosen.

"Then you will know she isn't the right girl for you." He finished his drink and rose from his chair. "All I am saying is, investigate every avenue before you throw away what could be. Have the conversation." He walked around my table, and I stood to face him. His hand shot out and grabbed mine, shaking it firmly, before he pulled me into a hug. "You're one of the most genuine men I know. You deserve happiness but that doesn't come with an instruction manual. If you suspect this girl is the one, do what you can to keep her."

CHASE

***

Another knock at the door interrupts the memory of my conversation with Damon and, ultimately, why I decided to suggest Samantha see both of us. I walk over and open it to find her on the other side. We haven't spent much time together this week; she's stayed in her apartment while I stayed in mine. Apart from brief messages and catching up for coffee one day, I haven't seen her since the discussion in Russell's hospital room.

"Hi," she says, her cheeks turning the most stunning shade of pink.

"You're early." Her face falls at my reaction, and I chastise myself for being an ass.

"I can go. We could meet at the hospital." She moves to turn away, and I reach for her hand. Our fingers connect, and she stills but doesn't look at me. The pain those two simple words inflicted emanates from her. She's taken my statement as a rejection.

"No, I'm sorry. I just wasn't expecting it to be you. You have a key, why didn't you use it?" Her head pivots in my direction, causing the blonde hair I love wrapped in my fingers to sway. Dressed simply in jeans and a long-sleeved red top, she's every inch the girl next door—the woman I could see spending my life with. A delicate hand slips into her pocket and pulls out my key; she offers it to me.

"I'm not sure it's appropriate that I have access to your home," she says sadly. "After everything I've done, you have every right to draw back or away completely."

"I meant what I said," I tell her. "I want this to work, but I won't beg you to be with me. You have to make that decision on your own." I wrap my hand around hers, and in this moment, it feels as though the key that she's holding is the key to my heart as well. I squeeze her fingers closed so her skin encases the cool metal. "Keep it. I want you to be here when you want to be."

We stand on either side of the threshold to my home, my hand holding hers and a key that signifies what could be between us. Only a week ago, our relationship was incredibly simple in my eyes, and moving forward in a way I expect it does for those who live normal lives. Now, we're navigating something completely different, neither of us knowing fully where this will end up.

"I've missed you," she says, shyly.

"I've missed you too." My fingers tighten, and I pull her to me, holding her against my chest. She wraps her arms around my back and begins to cry, low, soft sobs as she buries her face into my shirt.

"I'm so sorry," she gasps out as she comes up for breath. "This insanity doesn't mean I don't love you. I don't want you thinking that." I place my hands on her shoulders, pushing so I can look down at the woman who holds my heart in her hands, and I try with all my might to smile. Her pain is something I can't bear.

"Sam, I may not understand what you feel, because the way I feel about you leaves no room for someone else." She bites her lip nervously, but I need to be honest. "What I've suggested is a temporary measure. This is me giving you a chance to explore what you want. It isn't permission for you to sample any desire for years to come."

"I would never..."

I lift a finger to her lips to stop her from speaking. "Perhaps not, but the only reason I ever suggested this was because I love you, and I want you to be mine forever. I love my brother too, and if you're meant for him, then I want you both to be happy." I pull her to me again, resting my chin on the top of her head. "But as much as I love him, I hope your heart lands firmly with me."

She starts to cry again, and I maneuver her into my apartment, still holding her to me before sitting on the sofa beside her. I wrap my arm around her shoulders, and she leans in against my chest.

"How do you see this working?" she asks, not looking at me. She moves to sit forward on her chair, placing her hands on her knees and playing with the material of her jeans. There's a small rip. She pulls at the threads viciously, tugging until the gap widens.

"I don't know," I answer honestly. "I hope we will find some kind of natural rhythm. That our relationship will continue to move forward while you explore what you think is missing." I place my hand on the small of her back, and she breathes deep, her body expanding and contracting. The bones of her spine protrude through her top, and I note she's lost weight in this past week.

"I never said our relationship was missing anything," she mumbles into her fingers.

"Perhaps not in our relationship, but in your life, maybe." She sits up leaning against my palm, and I drum on her back in an attempt to console her. "Sam, I don't need anything but you. But we're all different, and you have to find what you need."

"I want you," she tells me, turning to face me and then climbing up onto my lap. Her lips crash into mine as the tears that have continued to fall wet my cheeks. Her hands move to my hair, pulling me to her as she explores my mouth. "I've missed this so fucking much."

"Me too," I whisper against wet salty lips. "Me too." Now, I need to pray she wants me enough to stay once all the options are on the table.

CHAPTER EIGHTEEN

Connor's Apartment, The Level

Samantha

This man is everything. He offers a future I never believed I could have—one filled with love and hope. After everything that's happened, he's willing to give me a chance to figure out what I truly want. Sitting on his lap, I lay my head on his shoulder as he plays with a strand of my hair.

"How long until we need to leave to collect, Russell?" I ask him, and he smiles.

"Not long enough for what you're thinking." His lips touch mine momentarily. "It's been a week since you were in my bed; I want to savor every touch. We aren't rushing it."

"But…" I protest, and his teeth nip my ear.

"No," he says, firmly. "Do you understand? No."

"Yes, sir." His cock pulsates beneath my ass, and I shuffle to create a little friction. He groans, but strong hands lift me to my feet.

"No," he repeats as his hard dick strains against the material of his jeans. He stands, then takes my face in his hands to kiss me again. "Every part of me wants to fuck you right now, but we have places to be. And you need to eat."

"Eat?" I question, cocking my head to the side as I glimpse up at him.

"Yes, eat." His hands move to my waist, and he flexes his fingers. "You've lost weight this past week. It's not good. Before we go to the hospital, I'll make you something."

"I already had breakfast," I tell him, waving away his concerns.

"Maybe today." His fingers grab my chin, tilting my head back so I look up at him. "But you've not been eating every day, have you? Otherwise," the hand on my waist pinches my skin, "you wouldn't have lost any weight."

"I haven't been hungry," I whisper, sullen at being scolded. "It's been stressful." He takes my hand, then leads me to the kitchen island before lifting me onto the counter. I open my knees, and he stands between my legs. Memories of our past encounters here flit through my mind, and my mouth dries in anticipation of what could happen next. I wrap my legs around his waist, pulling him to me.

"Not today," he warns, stepping back and encouraging my legs to release him. "You need real food." I watch as he moves around the kitchen and starts to pull items from the shelves. Three eggs, a bottle of milk, baking soda, and flour are laid out on the counter one by one. He ducks out of sight, then appears once more with a bowl and a whisk. "Pancakes?"

"Sure, whatever is easiest. Can I help?" He signals to a cupboard behind me, and I jump down from the counter. "What do you need?"

"The scale, please," he says, and I open the door, my eyes searching for the requested equipment. I spot it on the lowest shelf and have to bend to collect the machine. "Nice ass." I giggle at the unexpected compliment, but when I straighten, I pretend to scowl in annoyance. "It's true," he says, "you have a lovely ass."

"Thanks," I mutter before walking over and placing the scale on the counter beside him. He hands me the bag of flour. Before I lose my bravado, and while spirits seem high, there's something else I need to come clean about. I had considered contacting him to tell him about the conversation I'd overheard, but I hadn't had the nerve with everything going on. "Connor," I say, and he meets my eye. "I need to tell you something. The other night when I was at the hospital, there was an incident."

"I know," he says. "Russ told me." Taken aback, I gawk at him. "You honestly didn't think he wouldn't. Your safety is a priority for both of us. We can all discuss what happened later, and you can both fill me in on the details. One hundred grams of flour," he orders, gesturing to the bag in my hand. "Stop thinking about it right now; let's just enjoy being you and me." He flashes me an encouraging smile. "Criminals and dubious situations will always be there. They can wait until we enjoy our pancakes."

"How many pancakes are you making?" I ask, relieved by his reaction to my withholding yet more information from him. He glances at me.

"I don't know, but it's the only recipe I have. Normally I get ten or something."

"I won't eat ten pancakes!"

He laughs, then bumps my hip with his. "It's the only recipe I have," he repeats. "Don't worry, I'll eat some."

"You did go to school?" He turns to face me, then places both hands on his hips, leaning forward so our noses touch. "You know how to divide by two? That way, you would make fewer."

Without a word, he pinches some flour from the bag I'm holding then flicks it upwards. The powder floats into the air, landing over us. When I look down, my top is covered. My eyes snap up to his. I take the bag in my hands and shake the open end at him. Flour flies everywhere, covering him from head to toe.

"Oh, you're in trouble," he says menacingly and steps toward me. I dash around to the other side of the island. We stare at one another across the counter. "Do you think this." He taps the obstruction with one hand. "Will stop me taking what's mine?"

I bite my lip to hide my smile, reveling in the fact he called me his.

"You'll have to catch me first," I tell him, then make a run for the bedroom. As I burst through the door, I quickly attempt to slam it shut, but strong hands stop its progress barely inches from closing. I stand on the other side, both hands pressed up against the wood. Connor pushes on the other side, and it cracks open a fraction more.

The pressure relents for a moment before being applied more forcefully. I step back as the door gives way. "Am I getting closer to catching you?" he says, chuckling. At a standoff, we both lean against the barrier between us. I know if he wanted to, he could push his way in here, but he doesn't. He enjoys this game as much as I do.

"No." I release the door, kick off my shoes, and run for the bed, jumping onto the center as he stumbles through. He looks up at me, bouncing up and down on the middle of his huge bed, freshly made with navy silk sheets. The flour scattered over my hair floats down, coating the material. With each jump, bits of it are thrown into the air. He stands shaking his head, clearly amused, before climbing up to join me.

We bounce together, up and down, as if we are children enjoying the forbidden. He leans down and grabs a pillow, then slaps me playfully with it on the backside. I grab the other, and the next thing I know, we're play fighting like teenage girls, smacking each other all over with the soft weapons. My pillow gives way first, exploding messily across the room. Feathers join the floating flour.

Connor grins manically at me, and I return a similar gesture. After the second pillow detonates, we both collapse onto the mattress, breathing heavily as if we've just completed three rounds of boxing. We lie side by side amongst the mess we created, staring at the ceiling. He links his fingers through mine.

"Don't you love it," he says. "When life feels what I expect it feels like for normal people?"

"Normal people? Are you not human?"

He laughs but squeezes my fingers. "You know what I mean. Like if I was a school teacher and you were a nurse. If we were everyday people who worked the nine-to-five, saved to buy a house, and life was completed by a pension and a couple of kids."

"You want kids?" I ask him.

He turns to face me, propping himself up on one elbow. Shrewd clear eyes run over my face, and he takes a breath before speaking. Uncertainty flits over his features for a second.

"With you, that would be my ultimate achievement." My mouth drops open momentarily stunned by his honesty. His free hand comes to my cheek, wiping at a tear I didn't know was falling. "The only future I see is with you. We may not have known each other long, but I have no doubt you're mine."

"I don't want to disappoint you," I whisper, choked with emotion.

"The only way you'll do that is by not giving us a chance at being happy." He pushes himself from the bed, standing abruptly. The moment which had started jovial turned serious. "We better get tidied up and go," he says. "Russell will be waiting for us. I'll make you a sandwich, it will be quicker than pancakes." He disappears in the direction of the kitchen, and I sit up only to be faced with my reflection in the mirror.

The woman looking back at me is far removed from the one of last year. A new career, new hopes, and new relationships, all thanks to a random meeting with Violet in a clothes shop. That life event had knocked the course of my life at a right angle. Things are becoming ever more complicated between suspected criminal activities within the hospital and my complex love life. Once Russell returns to The Level, changes will have to be made if we're to fully investigate the possibility of being together and what our crazy feelings mean.

My focus moves to the open door, where I can hear Connor rummaging in the kitchen. I do wonder if he regrets his suggestion, or if he's as comfortable as he makes out he is. The next few weeks will be life-changing once again, either in a good way or a detrimental one. I can only hope that when the time comes, I make the right decision.

***

Connor takes my hand as we exit the elevator on the fourth floor of Varley Medical. He guides me across the tiles and past Bryan sitting at his desk. "Hi, Sam," he calls to my retreating back; I glance over Connor's shoulder and wave with my free hand. There's the click of heels coming toward us and as we round the corner, we're met head-on by Dr. Rivera.

"Good afternoon, Mr. Chase," she says, holding out her hand. He ignores the gesture and her eyes move to me. "And Samantha," she adds, her face pinching in displeasure. "Russell will be able to be discharged in a few minutes. We are just waiting for his medication to be delivered from the pharmacy."

"I called ahead," Connor snaps, his tone sharper than I've ever heard it. "Why is everything not ready as I requested?" He narrows his eyes, and she recoils under his glower. "We are busy people, doctor. I don't appreciate incompetence." Her jaw drops, and I clear my throat to hide a laugh. Connor tugs at my hand, and we walk past her toward Russell's room.

Connor taps on the door and pushes it open without waiting to be invited. Russell is sitting on the edge of the bed, dressed in a hooded top and shorts. His cast leg sits awkwardly with his heel on the floor. In each hand, he holds a crutch. He places the ends on the floor and pushes himself up to stand before his focus moves to us. As his eyes lock with my gaze, my stomach flips.

Connor leads me toward him, then lets go of my hand before leaning down and collecting the already-packed sports bag that sits at his feet. "Have you got everything?" Connor asks him, ignoring the charged energy in the room.

"I have now," his brother replies, his eyes still focused on me. I wither slightly under his stare. "I can't wait to get home and start exploring this." He moves toward me, placing a crutch on either side of my body. He's bigger than Connor; his huge frame blocks my view of his brother. Russell leans down and kisses my cheek gently. My body heats with the simple gesture, and my nipples harden instantly, poking through the material of my top. His eyes drop to my chest and he smirks. "Right answer, Trouble. I can see you're as pleased to see me as I am you."

Connor moves to our side, coming back into view. His expression is hard to read; I can't tell if it's his brother's actions that have made him uncomfortable or my reaction. "Let's go," he says quietly before walking in the direction of the exit.

"After you," Russell tells me, gesturing for me to follow. I turn and trace Connor's path. When we reach the reception area, Connor is at the desk talking to Bryan. As I get closer, it becomes apparent he's complaining about the fact Russell's medication wasn't ready when we arrived. I walk over and place a soothing hand on his arm. He glances at me, then goes back to sounding off at poor Bryan about incompetence.

"You have it now," I point out, tapping the white bag in his hand.

"That's not the point," he mutters. Russell whistles loudly across the space, and we both turn to face him. He's standing by the elevator, one crutch poised across the doors to stop them from closing.

"Come on," he calls. "Let's get out of this fucking place." Connor sighs, then relents before taking my hand, leading me away from Bryan and toward the unknown we're about to experience back at The Level.

CHAPTER NINETEEN

---◆---

Russell's Penthouse, The Level

Russell

My home looks identical to how I left it over a week ago. The bottle of whiskey I was drinking sits next to my unwashed glass on the table. My plate sits on the counter with remnants of the fast food that was my dinner the night I fell. Annoyed, my eyes scan the room for any indication that Mrs. D has been able to undertake her normal duties.

"Has Mrs. D been off work?" I ask Connor as he walks over to pick up the hub that controls the penthouse. He presses a few buttons and the blinds open. The spring sunshine pours into the room, highlighting the dust covering the glossy black surfaces of my furniture.

"No," he replies. "She refused to work up here."

"Why? That's what I pay her for."

He looks up, holding my focus with a blank stare. "Her words were, 'I won't be working for Mr. Chase until he can prove he isn't a manipulative, unhinged character.'" The stern look on his face flickers as he struggles to bury his amusement. "'I had been told not to clean the spare bedroom as it was being used for highly confidential work. If I had known it was the headquarters for his stalking enterprise, I would have informed you.'" My brother mimics our housekeeper's cadence and tone perfectly. "She's not happy with you," he adds, so I don't doubt her stance.

"I gathered as much."

"She also said she won't be setting foot back in this apartment until the ridiculous shrine in the bedroom is removed and it's been cleaned by someone else. She's seemingly too old to deal with a week's worth of stale male."

"I've not fucking been here," I mutter. "Maybe it's time to find a new housekeeper."

"Good luck with that," Connor tells me. "Your reputation precedes you."

I ignore the comment. He's right. There would be no way I could replace Mrs. D with someone else. She's the timepiece that keeps my home running smoothly—all of our homes. I don't know how she does it, but I suspect she may have magical capabilities.

"I'll apologize," I tell him. He raises an eyebrow. "Today," I add.

"Good."

Samantha hovers at the edge of the room, twisting her fingers together nervously. She coughs gently, moving both of our attention to her. She looks endearing, dressed casually in a simple T-shirt and jeans. Her hair is wrapped up on top of her head and secured with an overly large black clip, but stray strands fall around her face. She has this perfectly imperfect look nailed.

"You look good in here, Trouble," I tell her, and her cheeks flush red. I love how a simple compliment affects her. Even when I was following her months ago and she knew I was there but didn't acknowledge my presence, I enjoyed how a single look would cause her skin to color and how I could obtain a reaction with my proximity.

"She looks better in my apartment," Connor interjects before taking advantage of the fact he can walk easily and strolling across to her side. He places a hand on her waist then leans down to peck her cheek. Her skin, which was the shade of tomato, turns beetroot. She drops her eyes away from both of us, clearly uncomfortable with the complex situation of having two men fighting over her.

"This isn't fair," she mumbles to her feet. "I'm not sure how this is supposed to play out."

"Neither are we," he says. "But if we're both going to be seeing you for the foreseeable future, then we better figure it out."

"Shall we set up a schedule?" I suggest, and Samantha giggles nervously, quickly placing a delicate hand over her mouth. When she drops it away, her plump lips spread into the most mesmerizing smile. My heart, already beating hard with the reality of her being in my home, increases its rhythm. The muscle strains against my breastbone. I take a breath to steady my nerves, unsettled by her amusement.

"She isn't a piece of meat," Connor scolds. "I think we should leave it up to Sam who she sees when. I mean, I certainly know her better than you do." He turns to face me, and cocks his head to the side. The look in his eyes is one he uses when he tries to pick a fight. It's been the same since he was a small boy trying to steal my toys; this time I'm stealing his. "You have some catching up to do."

"That's enough," Samantha warns. "Either both of you start behaving, or I'll see neither. I was perfectly happy single." She places a hand on my brother's arm, her fingers flexing against his shirt. Her touch causes him to stand slightly taller, and he visibly puffs his chest out in silent victory. I scowl openly, and he responds to my grimace with a grin.

Deciding not to take his open challenge lying down, I hop over to Samantha's opposite side. The gesture that had been smooth in my head is made incredibly difficult by the clanging of the crutches off the floor. After what seems an age, I arrive at her side. I stand close enough to her that I'm in her space but not touching her. My brother bristles beside us; I ignore him. He started this crazy public competition.

"Trouble," I say, my voice low. "You couldn't stay away from me if you wanted to." Her breath audibly catches in her throat, her body tensing more with each word. "And you fucking know it. If I didn't have this fucking cast on, things could move much faster, but I'm sure we can improvise."

Connor's face darkens, but he doesn't say anything. We've fought over the same girl before; competition doesn't scare us. But we both know this girl is different, and losing will mean giving up the opportunity to have a relationship that could last.

"You started this, brother," I tell him as his focus locks with mine. He steps into my space, and I straighten as much as I can, hindered by my crutches. He leans forward and narrows his eyes.

"No, you started it by coming after my girl," he says fiercely. "The only reason I suggested this was so when she realizes what an arsehole you are, she'll come back to me." A self-assured smile appears on his lips, and he chuckles softly as he glances at Sam then returns his focus to me. "You always fuck up, Russ. Normally, I do my best to dig you out of the hole you create. This time, I'm fucking banking on you getting buried."

"Don't be an arsehole," I say, lifting one crutch and tapping him on the shoulder. His eyes follow the movement, before his head snaps back to its original position. "This time I have every intention of getting it right."

Samantha steps between us, laying a hand on both our chests. She sighs softly before shaking her head. "Perhaps this isn't such a good idea," she says. "I don't want to be the reason there are issues between you."

"There have always been issues," Connor counters, never averting his eyes from mine. "I love and hate my brother in the same measure; he's my best friend and my worst enemy. I want him to be happy, but I also want to fucking bury him."

"The feeling is mutual."

"Perhaps this isn't the best way to nurture your relationship," she suggests. "Blood is thicker than water; it would be best if I walked away." She drops her hands, and sheer panic surges through my body. The thought of not getting the opportunity to investigate what could be isn't something I am willing to accept. Her lithe frame takes a decisive step backward. "I'm going home," she says, and my brother and I reach for her in synchronization. Our hands wrap around a different wrist, and we all freeze.

The three of us stand in the center of my penthouse, Samantha in the middle but connected to both of us. "All I want is for you to be sure of our future," my brother says dejectedly. "My solution to your feelings may be unconventional, but it makes sense. You need to figure out what you want. You both do." He huffs gently, a sign that the altercation between us is passing. "I love both of you. And if you can't be happy with me, there isn't another man I'd trust to look after you better than my brother would."

"Thank you," I tell him, taken aback by his kind words. His eyes move to meet mine, and we stare at each other like we have so many times before, since we were kids. My brother and I, although we've had our issues, always had a unique understanding of each other. "I wouldn't be doing this if I didn't believe what Trouble and I have is special."

"You don't know yet," he says. "All you've both experienced is lust and infatuation, and it takes a lot more than that to create a meaningful relationship. I can only hope the candle burns out and you can both move past it. But if you don't, I know I gave myself every chance to be with the girl I should be."

"Same," I agree, releasing Samantha's wrist and extending my hand in the direction of my brother. He takes it and we shake firmly. "May love succeed, and we both find exactly what is meant for us."

"I know what's meant for me," he replies. "There is no doubt in my mind that Samantha Coleman is for me. You have to accept that too."

"And what about me?" Samantha snaps.

"You," Connor says, his voice barely audible, "need to understand that no matter who you end up with, you will always be looked after by one of us. The life you used to have is gone, and now you are firmly part of the Chase family."

"This is ridiculous," she mutters. "If any more testosterone starts flying around this room, I'll turn into a fucking man myself. There is no guarantee I'll end up with either of you." Connor and I laugh, and her face skews in annoyance.

"Do you believe that, Trouble?" I ask between the sniggers. "Everyone in this room knows you're here to stay; it's with whom that is the question. That body of yours calls to me like a siren. I can feel your need from here. And I've seen how you react to my brother when he fucks you." Connor stiffens, his manner—which had relaxed a fraction—hardening once more.

"Don't be a smart ass," she grumbles but doesn't try to debate my statement. She knows she can't.

"And don't you swear," I tease. "It doesn't suit those pretty lips." She steps forward , placing a hand on our chests once more. The tension in the room increases yet again as we all stand within inches of each other.

"This is insane. You two may think you call the shots." Her body expands and contracts as she breathes, her breasts rising and falling tantalizingly. Four eyes drop to her chest, watching intently before returning to her face. "But one thing hasn't changed, and it never will—no man tells me what to do. If you both want to be with me, you better learn that now, or you'll be looking for another woman to warm your beds."

"Noted," Connor mutters, nodding in acceptance.

"And you?" she prompts in my direction.

"Understood, ma'am. Let the games begin."

CHAPTER TWENTY

———◆———

Russell's Penthouse, The Level

Samantha

The tense atmosphere dissipates slightly, and I drop my hands from both brother's chests. How two men can be so alike but dissimilar takes my breath away. They offer comparable but completely different things. Connor is strong and stable; he treats me with kindness and respect while ravishing my body in the bedroom. Russell has an intense persona that makes my hair stand on end within a few feet of him. He's so in control but unhinged; life with him would never be boring. Both men leave me with no doubt of being wanted, but they show it in very different ways.

"Shall we discuss the situation at the hospital?" Connor suggests in his usual calm manner. Russell nods, then starts to limp toward the sofas. We watch as he cautiously lowers himself down and discards his crutches on the floor. I walk over and pull the small footrest to where he sits, then carefully lift his injured leg so it's resting elevated.

"Thanks, Trouble," he says, and I feel the excitement those words create bubble in my chest. "I'm fucking lucky to have a professional nurse at my disposal."

"My rates will need to be agreed upon," I tease, and he flashes me a cheeky smile. When either of these men focus on me, my awareness of anyone else in the room disappears. I find myself acting naturally as if it was only the man I'm looking at and myself.

"Do you want to be paid in cash or pleasure?"

Connor, clearing his throat, breaks the moment. He joins us at the sofas, taking my hand and guiding me to the one opposite his brother. We sit together, and he wraps an arm around my shoulders.

"Russell and I have discussed the situation at the hospital," Connor begins, and I stiffen slightly. The idea of them discussing me and my work is an uncomfortable one. "We think you should quit."

"No," I snap, instantly annoyed by his meddling.

"Sam, it's dangerous. I won't have you put yourself in harm's way." His grip tightens, and he pulls me hard against his body. "I can't lose you. If the last week hasn't proven that, I don't know what will."

"I'm already involved," I tell him. "Me being on the inside legitimately could be a benefit. Don't disregard the possibility out of fear." Russell doesn't contribute; he sits quietly, listening to our opinions. I focus on him, and he stares back impassively. "Is this your honest opinion? Or are you agreeing to keep the peace?" I ask him.

"When have I ever done anything to keep the peace?" he answers with a shrug.

"So you think I should leave the job and training you paid for?"

"I can afford to lose the money, Trouble. There's plenty more to fund a placement elsewhere if required." His lips quirk into a small smile. My heart strains a little; the knowledge he funded this opportunity still astounds me. "Though I'd much prefer if you specialized in nursing me privately."

"Not going to happen," I mutter, pissed at them for ganging up on me but grateful that they're both here with me.

"However," he says, "I did also say that you were a big girl capable of making her own decisions, and I wasn't confident that you would leave on our suggestion."

"You were right." He chuckles softly, then his eyes move to his brother and he raises an eyebrow in jest.

"Told you so," Russell goads.

"It was worth a try," Connor replies with a sigh. "So what's the plan, then?"

I unwrap myself from his arm and sit forward. I move my focus between them before putting forward my proposal, one I know neither of them will appreciate.

"What if I gain information and pass it to you?" I say, my voice steady although my heart starts to race.

"No," Connor snaps.

"There has to be information at the hospital. In her office. We need to find out what is going on and stop this insanity now."

"Law enforcement does, you don't."

I glare at Connor, and he does the same right back. Overprotective asshole.

"I'm involved in this, Connor, whether you like it or not. My place of work, my boss, is wrapped up in something dangerous. She was being threatened by mobsters under my nose. I can't stand by and let this pass over my head as if nothing is happening."

I push myself up to stand, then walk over to the half-drunk bottle of whiskey, lifting it from the table. The two men watch as I unscrew the cap, place the glass on my lips, and drink. Russell extends a hand in my direction. I move to him, pass him the bottle, and he does the same before offering it to his brother. Connor leans forward and accepts the bottle before taking his swig.

"What if someone innocent gets hurt?" I say.

"Like you, you mean?" Connor shoots back. "You're innocent in all this. You accepted a job offer, nothing more. I won't have you hurt." He pauses before adding, "Or worse." He sits back in his chair, lifting a single hand and running it through his dark hair. The sound leaving his lips is somewhere between a sigh of inevitability and a groan of annoyance.

"She's going to do this, with or without us," Russell tells his brother as if I'm not there. They look at each other with the kind of understanding only siblings have. Silent words pass between them, a full discussion from simple expressions and gestures. "We're beaten. Nurse Coleman has our arses whipped into submission."

His explanation makes me giggle, and they both glance over. My mouth dries as two of the most stunning men I've ever known look at me as if they want to rip my panties off. What makes my stomach flip is the knowledge that they do, and I'm going to get the opportunity to experience both of them.

"We're going to have to support this hair-brained scheme, aren't we?" Connor says to his brother with a knowing look.

"For the sake of having our dicks sucked, I think so." I freeze on the crude statement, waiting for the fire to ignite and the uncomfortable atmosphere between them to return. Surprisingly, it doesn't. Connor laughs, then shakes his head. A genuine lightness appears on his face, and I relax a little.

"You're such an arsehole," he mutters, then his eyes move back to me. "Information gathering only, Sam. No idiotic attempts at stopping anything when you're at the hospital on your own. Tell us everything. Every move, every operation, every person who enters that bloody place that makes you unsure." He swallows as if trying to contain words he doesn't want to say. "If you risk yourself, I will come down there and drag you out myself."

"Yes, sir," I reply in a low whisper, and his pupils dilate. Casually, I step toward him, then lean down and place my lips on his cheek. His hand lifts to mine, warm skin wrapping around my fingers and squeezing gently. I turn, then move to his brother before repeating the same gesture. Russell, however, cups my cheek, running his thumb a fraction below my eye. The duplicated affection feels absurdly normal. No one flinches, and there's no obvious sign of discomfort.

When I rise, I'm aware of Connor standing. He walks to my side and places his hand on the small of my back. "I'm going to go back to my apartment," he says. "Give you both time to settle in up here. I'll see you later?" The simple statement is asked as a question.

"Sure," I tell him with a small smile. He leans down to peck my lips then turns to his brother and extends a hand. The two men shake firmly.

"I'm trusting you with what I cherish most in this world because it's what she wants. Don't fucking screw it up. Hurt her, and I will make good on all those promises I've made to kill you." I wait for Russell's witty retort or open teasing. It doesn't come.

"Understood," he replies sincerely. Connor nods, then leaves. I'm left standing in the center of the penthouse with the man I shouldn't want but have permission to have.

As the door clicks closed, Russell sighs dramatically. "Well, that was a little awkward," he says. "Hopefully, this stuff will get easier. So, what do you want to do, Trouble?"

"Um..."

"I'd offer you rampant sex or to go dancing, but I'm kind of hindered just now." He gestures to his cast. "But I'm sure I can manage to give you a tour of my home." He leans down and collects his crutches from the floor; strong fingers wrap around the handles after sliding his arms into the grips. I bend and gently help him lift his cast leg from its resting place before he pushes himself up. He towers above me as I stand in front of him. "I meant it when I said you look good in here."

The energy in the room increases a notch as we stare at one another. We've been in close proximity before, but today is different. Today is day one of a new us, a time beginning when we can discover what this truly is. Whether what Russell and I have is simple lust or if the feelings that scream to be acknowledged are more than that. If there's a possibility to care for and, ultimately, love two men.

But that possibility doesn't change the sad reality that, one day, they will want me to choose.

Russell hops to my left and then moves toward the open-plan kitchen area, which is similar to his brother's but bigger. More work surfaces, cupboards, and machines are laid out and ready to use. "Do you like to cook?" I ask him.

"No, I just like to look as if I do. This is Mrs. D's domain. She prepares everything so I only have to warm it up. Other than that, I live on telephone orders."

"That's unhealthy," I scold. He stops and then turns to face me. "Fast food isn't a sustainable diet."

"I didn't say it was fast food." He reaches for a drawer and pulls it open. Inside, there's a pile of restaurant menus. He lifts the bundle out then holds it in my direction. "Have a look through those and tell me what you want to eat. They all deliver." I take them from him and start to scan through the array of cuisine on offer from high-end restaurants around the city.

"But these aren't delivery menus," I question.

"No, they're restaurant menus, but for certain clients they'll make a special effort." He flashes me a cheeky smile. "I am one of those clients, and now, you are too." Butterflies flutter in my chest as he refers to me as being part of all this. That what he has, somehow I'm now part of.

"This one," I say. I place all the menus on the counter and push a simple Italian option toward him. Some of the others had descriptions that made no sense to me, so I decided to go for what I knew. "I'd be happy with pizza."

"Good choice; I'll organize it." He pulls his phone from his pocket before tapping the screen and raising it to his ear.

"Are you not going to ask me what I like?"

"I know how you like your pizza, Trouble."

I cross my arms over my chest and narrow my eyes at him for his presumptuousness. I listen on as he tells the person at the end of the line the exact way I like my pizza: with extra cheese and a double portion of pineapple. He orders a few accompaniments, then disconnects the call.

"How do you know that?" I ask him, trying to keep my tone a fraction pissed. Secretly, I am happy that he notices the small things.

"You would be amazed by what I know," he says, stepping toward me and placing a crutch on either side of my body. He stands insanely close, then warm lips meet mine in the middle of his kitchen. His kiss is gentle, our lips intertwining before our mouths open and tongues begin to explore new territory. One crutch falls to the floor, and he pulls me to him but winces in pain with the sharp movement.

"Be careful," I whisper against his lips. "You're injured."

"It's okay, Trouble. I'm fucking a nurse." I laugh out loud and he smiles goofily. His manner and expression are miles away from the grumpy, obstinate lawyer I met months ago, the man who appeared to hate everyone and only want to cause distress.

"You will be, but it won't be anytime soon. We need to ensure you're healing properly first."

"Trouble, it's my leg that's broken, not my cock. He's still in perfect working order." His hand drops to my ass and pulls me forward forcefully so my stomach is tight against his swelling dick. My arousal heightens as the tension between us morphs into need. This man, whom I've kept at a distance for months, is here, and he wants me. "Let me show you the bedroom," he whispers, dropping his lips to my ear. His warm breath tickles my skin, then his mouth lowers further and he places a single kiss on my neck. "This way."

He releases me, wobbling backward, then moves in the direction of the bedrooms. He pushes open the first door, which opens wide into the biggest bedroom I've ever seen.

In the center is a super king-sized bed draped in red and black satin. The headboard extends up the wall in black velvet, stitched intricately in glittering red thread. A large matching sofa sits to one side with a low black glass table. On the far wall, there are floor-to-ceiling windows offering a view for miles over London.

He gestures for me to enter and as I walk into the room, the door clicks closed behind me. I move to the windows, looking out at the roof garden which sits on top of the apartment below on the other side. He appears behind me, standing close enough I can feel him. His hand reaches past and connects with a small silver panel on the glass, and it slides open, allowing access to the garden. I gasp at the movement, and Russell chuckles.

"This is my favorite place," he says quietly. "I can't wait to share it with you." We both step out into the cold London evening; the skies are darkening as the sun disappears for another day.

The roof garden runs down the full length of the apartment before disappearing around the corner. Russell heads in that direction, weaving between the perfectly pruned plants and modern statues that decorate the area and provide a zen-like quality. Hidden at the rear, I'm stunned to find a small infinity pool. Only around five meters long and perhaps three wide, it's located on the edge of the building. But what's most breathtaking is the glass wall that encases it, meaning when in use, you can swim to the perimeter and look out over the city.

"Do you like to swim?" he asks, his voice quiet but hopeful.

"Yes, but surely at this time of year, it's a bit cold."

"Trouble, in what world do you think I wouldn't have a heated pool? We can use this at all times of the year. You just tell me how hot you like it, and I'll make it happen." His words are laden with sexual innuendo, and I giggle like a schoolgirl.

"Are we still talking about the swimming pool?" I ask.

"Perhaps, as I do plan to fuck you in it once I have this bloody thing off." He signals to his cast. My mind whirls as naughty thoughts of him taking me against that glass wall flit through my head. My nipples harden beneath my top in excitement. One thick finger flicks the bud through the material, and he smirks. "Those nipples of yours are better than words; one look at them, and I know exactly what you're thinking. And they're telling me you like that idea."

Chapter Twenty-One

---◆◆◆---

Varley Medical, London

Samantha

Bryan sits at his desk typing away furiously. He stares at his screen as if the world depends on his work, normally relaxed demeanor nowhere to be seen. The jovial fun we have day to day is absent.

My shift started an hour ago, and it's been relatively quiet. At six in the morning, patients are starting to wake up and the day is only just beginning. The routine of getting people woken, fed, and washed is becoming second nature to me. In some ways, it's my favorite part of the day. The seemingly pointless conversations I have with them become important. When someone chooses to tell me about their life, I take time to listen. Them sharing their stories deserves my time, and beyond the care I can give to their health, simply being interested can be a far better medicine.

"Everything okay?" I ask, wandering up to Bryan's station.

"Not really," he mutters back.

"You're in early today."

"I need to take some time off later this week. Peter is having some issues, and I need to be there to support him," he says evasively. "I can't afford to lose any wages, though. Things are difficult enough." He doesn't look up from his screen, but the man I'm looking at is clearly terrified, the fear emanating from him obvious. His body shakes when the temperature in the room is well below sweat level. Every muscle quivers as he pounds on his keyboard.

"Anything I can help with?" I ask, keeping my voice soft. I'm trying to convey sympathy without being condescending.

"No, I don't want to talk about it," he states sharply. I take that as my cue to move on. Bryan has never silenced a chat with me before. We've become firm friends since January. I see him as my sidekick in the world of Varley Medical, always available with a listening ear and kind words. Today, I will let his reluctance to lean on me go, but whatever the issue, it will be readdressed, and if I can help him I will.

Just then, Dr. Rivera appears as the elevator doors open. Beside her is a young woman, most likely in her twenties, with jet-black hair and wearing clothes that look to have seen better days. She walks across the reception area a few steps behind the doctor, not speaking. Her hands are clasped in front of her, fingers knitted together nervously.

I watch them disappear from view around the corner, toward the doctor's office. Something doesn't sit right, and I decide this could be my opportunity to gather some information. Without a word, I follow their path but on arrival at the office, the door is firmly closed, which is unusual. Sensing defeat, I turn and make my way to the next patient I need to see.

An hour later, I'm called to the doctor's office. When I arrive, she's sitting in her chair as she does every day—with an air of superiority. The young woman lies on the couch reserved for difficult conversations. Her thin body is huddled in one corner as her head rests on the armrest. I'm unsure if she's sleeping, as her eyes are closed, but she's silent. No gentle snores can be heard.

"Nurse Coleman," Dr. Rivera says professionally as I step into the room. "I need you to undertake some private duties before your shift ends. But please do not discuss them with the other members of staff; it's highly confidential circumstances." Unsure what to say, I try to stop my jaw from opening at the unexpected request. Of all the people in the department I thought she would ask for help, the last one would be me. "Do you understand?" she prompts when I don't answer.

"Yes, doctor."

"The young lady on my sofa is a last-minute donor for our patient requiring a kidney transplant in room 400. Lord Woodward. As you are aware, our patient is in a critical condition and we're in the final days of him being suitable for a transplant." I listen on, confused. I've heard this man being talked about between the nurses; he is on palliative care. Until now, there was no indication a transplant was forthcoming, or that he was a candidate for one. "I'll be conducting the operation within the next few days, once the blood and antibody tests have been completed."

"Where did she come from?" I ask, perplexed and uncertain. Everything about this screams wrongdoing.

"The girl is the niece of our client." Her use of the word "client" causes my hackles to rise. Client has connotations of payment being the primary focus, while patient evokes a more caring outlook. "She's come here under her own wishes. Her family is unaware, as none of them were willing to donate to their elderly uncle. Lord Woodward has no living children. This girl is his last hope of survival."

"And she's his niece?" I say, skeptically. Every fiber of my being tells me this woman is no more that man's family than I am.

"That's what I said, isn't it?" She narrows her eyes, and the look of disdain I have become so familiar with flits over her features. "Do remember, nurse, you are the last one at the door of this department. If you choose to be awkward, I have every capability of terminating your employment. I will also ensure you never work in private medicine again."

My instinct is to retaliate to her threat, but I remind myself of my purpose for being here. This obscene situation could be my opportunity to learn more about what's going on in the ward. I look at the young woman resting on the sofa and know damn well she's no niece of the man lying in room four hundred who's spent his time here pressing the nurse's call button every ten minutes.

"Understood, doctor," I say through gritted teeth. "What exactly would you like me to do?" She visibly relaxes on my agreement, and I congratulate myself on keeping my mouth shut. She lifts a tattered piece of paper from her desk and waves it at me.

"Take this," she says, "and get Bryan to check her into room 402." I stare at the scrap of paper, the blurred photocopy of a passport. The woman on the sofa's picture gazes back at me. Her name is noted as Lauren Woodward, and she's detailed as being twenty-four years old, according to her date of birth.

"Where is the original document?" I question. My limited experience in the department tells me that all donors need to be identity checked before admittance. The strangeness of the situation only gets more warped.

"I've seen it," the doctor snaps. "Just do as you're told, nurse. I am in charge here." She pauses, taking a deep breath before continuing her instruction. "Once she's logged onto the system, come back and escort her to her room. Ensure she showers and is made comfortable. I will visit her later this morning to conduct the required tests. No food or drink until I advise she's able to."

"Yes, doctor. Would she like to visit her uncle?"

"No, he's not to know she is here. He would be more likely to reject the donation. We don't want to risk more delay on his surgery. I gave this young lady my word I would respect her privacy, and you need to as well."

With the questionable identification in my hands, I return to Bryan's desk. He glances up, and his pained expression softens a little. "I'm sorry," he says. "I shouldn't have spoken to you the way I did earlier."

"It's okay. I know what it can feel like to have numerous pressures and no obvious relief." I walk around to stand beside him and place my hand on his shoulder. "If you need help, don't hesitate to ask. I may be able to."

"Thanks, Sam." He places his fingers over mine. "It's nice to feel I have a friend in here. What can I do for you?" I pass him the pathetic paperwork, and he stares at it.

"Can you check this patient into room 402?"

"Sure, what is she in for?"

"She's a kidney donor."

"Where are the authorization paperwork and health checks?" he asks, confused, and I shrug.

"The doctor said these were ongoing. She's seen the relevant paperwork. I was only given this and told to check her in." He grumbles something I can't hear. "What was that?"

"Nothing. Where is she now?"

"In the office with Dr. Rivera." His look tells me this isn't the answer he was looking for. "She's the recipient's niece, apparently."

"Neither of us believe that." He exhales dramatically. "Things are getting stranger by the day in this place. But we must do as we are told. The dragon has me by the balls, Sam. I can't risk losing this job, and my pay is way above anything else I could get." His questioning of the circumstances makes me want to tell him what I know, our suspicions on the organ theft and sale circuit. But Bryan is in deep; he's been at Varley Medical for years and was aware of discrepancies long before I joined the team. I keep my mouth shut. "I'll process this." He gestures at the paper. "You go sort out the poor woman."

"Thanks, Bryan," I say, then return to the doctor's office.

When I arrive back, the woman supposedly called Lauren is sitting up, staring blankly at the wall. She doesn't turn when I open the door. The doctor is reading an academic paper regarding heart transplants at her desk.

"The room is ready," I announce, and the doctors eyes flick to me. She nods but doesn't speak. "Bryan was asking about the authorization form."

"Tell him I will drop it on his desk later," she responds curtly.

"Yes, doctor." I move in front of my newest patient, stepping into her line of sight. Blank eyes flick up. "Would you like to come with me?" She rises without a word. At this proximity, she looks even more scraggy than before. Her eyes are swollen red from hours of crying. The dark, baggy clothes hang off her limp frame, each item clearly worn at the edges. "Do you have a bag?" I ask, and she shakes her head.

"You'll need to organize some essentials for Lauren, nurse," Dr. Rivera interjects. "She arrived here in somewhat of a hurry."

A multitude of questions sit on my tongue, wanting to challenge my boss, but I know this is my opportunity to earn a little trust. If I shut this down now, I may jeopardize what we could learn about the wider operation going on. Against my morals, I merely nod, then signal for Lauren to follow me. We leave the office, her walking slightly behind at my shoulder.

Her room is only a minute away, and when I open the door, the smell of bleach hits my nostrils will full force. I immediately go over and open the windows the tiny portion they allow. "The cleaners have been liberal with the chemicals," I say jovially, trying to strike up a thread of conversation. "The fresh air should clear the smell soon."

"At least it's clean," she replies, wistfully. Her tired eyes roam over the blank space. "Can I sleep? It's been a while since..." Her words trail off, and a soft pink coats her cheeks. "I've not had much rest, the worry with my uncle's condition, you see."

"That's understandable," I tell her, not believing a word. "Where did you say you live?"

"In the city, not far from him."

"And his own children weren't able to donate?" I ask, taking a chance to confirm my suspicions.

"No," she replies instantly. "They weren't a suitable blood type." The effort it takes to maintain a neutral expression is unbearable. Surely, if this were the Lord's niece, she would know he had no children. I refrain from pointing this out.

"They'll be grateful to you then, when they discover your selflessness."

"Perhaps. Will you excuse me nurse? I really need to rest."

"Of course." I smile the most genuine smile I can muster. "Have a shower first. The bathroom is just through here; there's shampoo, conditioner, and body wash. Towels are there as well. I'll place some nightwear on the bed for your return."

"Thank you," she says, almost under her breath. The façade cracks slightly as her voice breaks.

"You get sorted, and I'll pop in later when I have any updates."

***

My shift ends while most of my colleagues are taking lunch. Early shift is a blessing; I get to finish my day at work and still have hours in the afternoon and evening to enjoy. Bryan left long ago and on my way out, I saunter past his desk in hope of snagging what I need. Lauren's passport image stares back at me. Quickly, I pull my phone from my pocket and snap a photo, then make my way to the elevator.

On my descent, I look at the young woman who I'm obligated to care for, all the while wondering what I can do to help. I flick to my contacts, then swipe between the two men I need to tell about the revelations of the day. They're next to each other in my contact list, as I listed them by their surname first. Unsure what to do, I create a group chat with the three of us, then send the photo of what I believe is forged identification.

Russell immediately responds with a shoulder-shrug emoji. At the top of the screen, the word, typing, flashes then his response pops onto the screen.

> *Sorry Trouble, not my type. And with my leg, I don't think I'm capable of a three-some yet.*

I laugh out loud; the woman who joined me in the compartment from the floor below frowns at me. "Sorry, my boyfriend is being a clown," I tell her before realizing how I described him. *Boyfriend.* Just then, Connor responds, the concern clear from his text.

> *What do you need? I'm here.*

Two brothers, so different in so many ways. Both make my heart ache with want and my pussy with need. How will I ever choose? Will this crazy situation ever be resolved without someone's heart being broken? The deeper we get, the less I feel it's possible. But, I know I can't walk away. We've gone too far.

I type back a quick message, explaining I need information on this patient. Connor immediately fires back.

> *Come to our office, not over text.*

Russell is then marked as typing, and I dread what will pop up on my screen. Will he be serious or say something to rile his brother? It's doubtful that he could allow a moment to pass without ruffling feathers.

Come to my office first. I miss you more.

As I step out onto the busy London afternoon, the messages between the two continue to ping in my pocket. With each glance at my screen, the conversation gets more ridiculous. The Chase brothers have the ability to bicker in any situation, it seems. Momentarily, I regret creating a group chat, but I can't help but smile when they challenge each other to convince me to see them first using only emoji.

Russell proceeds to send an up arrow then twenty aubergine emoji in a row followed by a hot face and a huge smiley. Connor, however, sends only three—a diamond ring, a couple, and a baby. The chat goes dead, and I stride toward the office unsure what the hell I'm walking into.

Chapter
Twenty-Two

Chase, Chase, and Waite
Law Offices, Canary Wharf

Connor

She arrives and my heart all but stops. Samantha has never been to our offices, but seeing her step out of the elevator onto our floor makes me so fucking happy. She's been on my mind since this morning, since she left my bed to head to work in the early hours. Every day I spend with her makes me even more certain she's the girl for me.

Last night, she had reappeared at my apartment two hours after I left her with my brother. So many questions had been on my tongue, leaving me desperate for answers. I'd been too nervous to ask any. She walked into my living room as I'd lounged on the sofa pretending to watch television. The expression on her face was wary; I told myself this was as strange for her as it was for me. I was the one that instigated the damn situation, after all.

I'd stood, walked over to her, then placed my hands on her elbows as she gazed upwards. Her lips had quirked up a fraction, and she sighed softly. "You hungry?" I asked, and she shook her head.

"No, Russ ordered takeout." Her casual explanation stung a little, but the natural cadence of her voice relaxed with the detail. I tried to keep my face impassive but wanted to show interest, trying to provide some assurance that I was okay with this.

"Where from?"

She'd cocked her head to one side as her eyes ran over my face, the way she does when she is assessing how someone will react to a situation. I see similarities between us in that sense. Samantha, for all she's strong willed, isn't impulsive. She can watch a scenario unfold and react accordingly. For me, I find an independent self-assured woman incredibly attractive, and my girl is both those things.

"An Italian place. We had pizza."

"Any dessert?"

Her eyes narrowed, an uneasy look darkening her pretty features. "Are you asking me what I think you are?" she said, her tone irritated. She stepped backward out of my embrace, and I reprimanded myself for the indirect question. Samantha appreciates honesty and privacy. Whether she slept with my brother is none of my business while we navigate this part of our relationship.

"Yes," I answered, embarrassed. "Sorry, I won't ask for information on what you do with him again. It's not my concern."

"We didn't," she told me, her face softening with my apology. "Russell and I are only getting to know one another, and he has a broken leg." She flashed me an encouraging smile, but it didn't last. "But Connor, I'm not sure you'll be able to handle when things do progress. It worries me."

"I don't want to think about it," I admitted, furious that I allowed myself to feel jealous over a situation I had created. "But I know this is what we need to happen for you to be sure about us."

"Then don't think about it," she said. "Not when I'm here with you. Come, let me show you just how much I want you." She held out her hand. I took it, and she led me through to my bedroom.

When we arrived in the center, she let go and disappeared into the dressing area. I stood like a spare part in the middle of my bedroom, unsure what was going on. A few minutes later, Sam reappeared dressed in nothing but her red thigh-high boots, holding some of my favorite sexual aids in her hand. Her blonde hair was loose, the waves sitting softly against her shoulders. Those eyes I love more than anything danced with excitement.

She strolled toward me, placing one foot deliberately in front of the other, her breasts perky but swinging free with each step.

I swallowed the instinct to grab her, throw her on the bed, and ravish her right in the moment. The items in her hands told me she expected a far more thorough experience. She offered me the black leather spreader bar and smiled sexily. I watched as she then lifted the black silk eye mask and tied it expertly across her eyes.

"Do as you wish, sir," she murmured, offering me her wrists.

"Fuck, you'll be the death of me." She giggled, and my already hard cock strained in my boxers.

"Tell me exactly what you're going to do, sir. I want every last detail." I smiled to myself as I looked at the most beautiful girl in the world standing in my bedroom, blindfolded in sky-high boots, telling me to do as I wish and talk her through it. "Every last detail," she repeated.

I reached for her fingers, interlinking her hand with mine.

"The summary of the situation is—"

"I don't want a summary, sir. I want the full extended version." I laughed out loud at that, and she grinned. "Fuck me, and tell me exactly how you're going to do it. I want to know how I make you feel. What you see when you see me."

"I see perfection," I whispered fiercely, stepping forward and placing my free hand on her cheek. "I see pure fucking perfection. Every part of you fits seamlessly with me." I'd kissed her then, taking her mouth hard. When I withdrew, she lifted her chin upward, straining her neck and reaching for my lips, which hovered millimeters above her. Our breaths mixed as we exhaled, the excitement causing us both to breathe deeper. "Bed," I ordered, moving to put my hand on her back.

She submitted to my touch, stepping to the edge of the bed, her knees connecting with the silk. "Climb up and crawl into the center. I want you on your hands and knees."

"Yes, sir," she said, a breath catching in her throat. Her nipples sat hard on plump breasts as they swung with her movement. I walked to my bedside table and took the final two pieces of equipment I needed from the drawer. When I looked back to the bed, she had done as I instructed. Samantha was in the center on all fours, legs spread, naked except for red leather.

"Are you ready?" I asked her, and she tittered in response. "I'll take that as a yes." I took the spreader bar and connected a cuff to each ankle. The dark leather sat heavy on the soft sheets between her legs. "I want you wide," I told her, reaching and adjusting the bar to spread her more. "Drop to your elbows." She did as she was told, and the pussy I love to sink inside came into even better view.

"I'm going to bind your wrists behind you back," I said, and she moaned quietly. "Give me your hands." She moved both arms to her back so her shoulders lay against the bed sheet. Her head was turned to one side, the eye mask still securely in place. I wrapped the length of silk in my hand around one wrist, then the other, securing her firmly. "Do you know how good you look like this?"

"What do I look like?" she whispered, breathless. "Tell me."

"My perfect home," I told her. Still dressed, I moved to her side and climbed up beside her. Wrapping her hair around my fingers, I tugged softly. "These are my reins for you. I love it when you're bent over like now, and I pull your head back as I go deep. The way your throat extends under my touch."

Releasing the strands, I dropped my fingers to her lips; I played softly with the plump pink skin. "This mouth makes me want to kiss you until I can no longer breathe. I love your wit and independence. I love the fact you know who you are and what you want." She didn't reply, just listened intently to each word as my focus moved down her body over her back.

"Your body feels incredible. The way you wrap yourself around me as we sit on the sofa as much as when you tense under my touch. How you mimic my movements naturally when we come together." My hand arrived at her ass, and I moved to between her legs, crouching behind her.

"But this," I said, "this part of you shows me exactly how you feel." With a single finger, I touched her lips, which were already damp. "The way your body prepares itself for me lets me know you want me inside you."

"Always," she muttered as I slid my finger home. The slick walls of her pussy sucked hard, and my cock throbbed in my boxers again. I pulsed my finger gently inside, teasing both her and me about what was to come before withdrawing. I moved off the bed.

"What are you doing?" she asked, needy. "I want to imagine it."

"Undressing. I'm unbuttoning my shirt. First the cuffs, now the front." She groaned again. "Now, I'm removing my belt." I deliberately clicked the buckle so she could hear the metal undoing, then pulled it roughly from my jeans so the leather scraped against the denim before it clattered onto the floor.

"Tell me when you're naked," she said, panting.

"I'm naked," I confirmed as I removed my final clothes.

"What are you going to do now?" Her voice pleaded for information. She loves when I talk her through sex—it heightens the excitement as we both wait for the next sensation. I lowered myself behind her, lining my lips up at her entrance.

"I'm going to drive you insane before I fuck you hard." I took her thighs in my hands, then firmly pulled her back onto my face. My tongue sought her clit, and I worked the magic button hard and relentlessly. Flicking the spot, I felt her tense in my arms. As I played, I was aware of the wetness of her lips increasing, her body readying itself to be taken. She pushed back, greedy for more. I was happy to oblige.

I moved to her entrance, pushing my tongue deep to taste everything she gave me. My left hand found her clit, and I circled the spot with a soft finger as I drank, lapping up her arousal as if it was the elixir of life.

"You're going to come for me," I told her. "You're going to soak my face." I pushed a fraction harder on her clit, my tongue focused on her already wet lips. "Drown me in you, I'll die a happy man."

"Connor," she murmured. "It's too much. I can't."

"Let go, Sam. You can and you will. Show me how much you want my cock. Show me what's waiting for me in that pretty pussy, how wet and ready you are. Let me taste all of you first. Then I'll fill you up with all of me." I increased the speed on her clit, swirling fast as it swelled beneath my fingertip. "You're not getting any cock until you're a good girl and come for me."

She released then, the sweet liquid running from her onto my tongue. "Good girl," I whispered between laps, then rose to my knees.

Taking her hips in my hands, I lined my rock-hard dick up and slid in smoothly. We moaned in unison as we came together, her perfect body opening. Soft walls encased my cock, though I could feel the remaining vibrations of her orgasm still flowing. I worked my hips slow to start, thrusting and withdrawing, enjoying the heaven my earlier foreplay created. I looked down, enjoying the visual perks. Her wide and restrained, and for now, all mine to do with as I pleased.

"You like this?" I asked as I finished another long, slow thrust. "I'm going to get faster. I'm going to ride this stunning pussy until you come around my cock, and I want to hear how fucking good it feels. I want you to scream." She groaned with the increased rhythm. "Louder," I ordered, squeezing an asscheek firmly so she wailed. I took that as my cue to go quicker and harder. I slammed inside her, my cock desperate to shoot its load and fill her with me, mark her body as mine with my cum.

"Connor," she screamed as I pounded.

"It's not Connor," I told her. "In here, it's sir." She vibrated under my touch as I held tight, pushing harder, the sense of orgasm getting closer. Her legs twitched and the bar rattled as it stopped her from gaining any relief from the building sensation.

"Sir," she spat out. "More, please." I grabbed a portion of her hair, pulling her head back and extending that sexy-as-hell neck. My hips worked faster, knowing she was mine and below me until I allowed her not to be. Until I released her from her current state.

"I want to fuck you while you orgasm," I told her. "Come for me, and I'll ride you through it. Please me, give me what I want." As if on instruction, her pussy gripped my cock, crushing me blissfully. I kept going, pushing more as she crumbled around me, the noise from her a twisted combination of ecstasy and relief. Her body soaked my cock and balls as I finally let go deep inside her, shooting every last drop into the woman that would be one hundred percent mine, whether she knew it yet or not.

Last night, I realized no matter what—Samantha is the one thing in my life I wasn't willing to lose. Her being mine forever isn't a debatable outcome; whatever happens, I have to win.

Samantha stands in the doorway of my office, leaning against the frame and refocusing my attention from the night before. "Can I help you, miss?" I call across. She shrugs before stepping into the room.

"I'm here to see a man about a promise he made," she says.

"What promise would that be?"

"A diamond ring, a happily ever after, and the pitter-patter of tiny feet."

My heart skips as she quotes my emoji message back to me. Deep down, I know Russell will be seething that I sent something so heartfelt, but I wanted to play my hand boldly. No matter what happens, I don't want her to think long-term wasn't my plan.

"I'm aware of the potential contract," I confirm as she walks toward my desk. I push my chair back, and she slides between me and the surface before jumping up to sit before me. "Are you in need of some advice?"

"No," she says, leaning forward, her eyes holding mine. "All I need is a little time to sort my shit out so I don't let you down."

CHAPTER
TWENTY-THREE

Chase, Chase, and Waite
Law Offices, Canary Wharf

Russell

I stuff the unwanted letter from my father into my desk drawer. The three pages will go unread. All I needed to see was his opening line in his handwriting— *I'm dying. I need you, son*—to know I wasn't interested in its contents.

He's the last person I ever want to help. Locked up is where he needs to be, whether he's dying or not. I hope he rots in a jail cell until he departs this earth. I will never know why he felt it necessary to contact me now. He can't be stupid enough to think I would care after all the evil he did to my siblings and me.

His terminal diagnosis is something I'll keep to myself. Everyone else he's hurt doesn't need to know. No one's heartstrings will be pulled on because of my loose tongue. I look forward to notifying everyone of his death when it occurs.

Samantha arrived ten minutes ago; I saw her on the camera leaving the elevator. She didn't come to my office first, and now I'm pissed. Grabbing my crutches, I maneuver myself from my desk to search for her, though I fucking know where she'll be, and the fact she picked to see him first is infuriating.

Connor's office door is ajar, but I hear the unmistakable laughter from across the office. Limping toward the sound, I push open the door with my crutch. It swings backward and clatters off the white wall. I hope it leaves a dent.

"You were to come to my office first," I say, my tone conveying my annoyed attitude. Samantha sits on my brother's desk as he leans back in his chair, staring at her. She glances over her shoulder and rolls her eyes.

"I decided not to," she says with a smirk. "You don't always get everything you want. That's a lesson you need to learn."

"I *do* always get what I want, Trouble." Her eyes narrow, but a sexy smile plays on her lips. "And I'm the one with the broken leg, so why am I hobbling across the office to meet you both?"

"You shouldn't be back at work," she shoots back. "It's too soon."

"I told him that," Connor adds.

"Don't fucking gang up on me," I mutter, pissed off by their tag-teaming. "All I would have done at home was sit with my laptop anyway. At least here I have company."

"But you're terrible company," Connor tells me. Samantha jumps down, then leans over to kiss him on the forehead before turning to me. She saunters across the office insanely slowly before arriving at my side.

"Oh, I don't know," she says. "I reckon you can be pretty good company." She rises on tiptoe and places her lips on my cheek. It feels so fucking good. "Come and sit down, and I'll tell you what happened at the hospital today." She touches my elbow, directing me to the desk.

"I think this would be a better conversation to have with the others at The Level," Connor suggests as I take my first step. "So we can all try to figure out what the hell is going on. I'll call the others."

Connor pushes his chair back and stands before walking around to the other side of his desk. He lifts the keys from the small bowl on the side table, throwing them up in the air before catching them in his palm. He walks past Sam and me in the direction of the door.

"Are you both coming?" he calls over his shoulder. "I'll drive."

"Well, it's not as if I can fucking drive," I call to his retreating back. Samantha giggles, and it's the sweetest sound.

"You two are dreadful siblings," she tells me. "Can you have a conversation and not try to annoy the other?"

"Trouble, we have spent over thirty years perfecting our relationship. Why would we change it when it works so beautifully?"

"Are you both coming?" Connor repeats from the doorway. "Come on, let's go." Samantha shakes her head but moves toward the door. Connor holds his hand out to her, and she takes it. "You hold onto your crutches, brother. I'll make sure our girl is okay."

"Once I'm back to normal," I tell him, "I'll kick your ass for taking advantage of my lack of mobility." Samantha passes by him and moves out of view. My brother takes the opportunity to stick his tongue out like a schoolboy before turning away. When I reach the door, he has wrapped an arm around her waist and is guiding her toward the elevators. I limp behind them, thinking of all the ways I can make him pay in the future.

The elevator opens, and the two of them step inside. As I go to join them, the doors begin to close. "Hold the elevator," I shout, but they continue to slide. When I reach the threshold, I attempt to thrust one crutch between the doors but miss. My last view is my brother placing his hand on Samantha's face and dropping his lips to hers as they disappear behind the metal.

Infuriated by his teasing, I hit the button to call the elevator aggressively with the rubber stopper on the bottom of my crutch. The band around it lights up orange, but the numbers continue to descend, stopping at the basement. I watch impatiently as the numbers begin to rise again. Eventually, the doors open, and I'm surprised to see Sam standing in the compart-ment. She smiles shyly, then bites her lip.

"I'm here to collect my patient," she says, and my cock stirs in my suit. Fuck, I wish I was in a state to fuck her right here in the elevator.

"I'll be raising a complaint with your boss," I tell her, and her cheeks color. "Leaving an immobile man alone to disap-pear with your boyfriend isn't very professional." I step into the space with her, and the doors close. "But maybe you can convince me not to report you."

"And how can I do that?"

"By making me fucking happy later on."

We stare at each other as the elevator drops to the garage level. I half expect to see Connor waiting for us when we arrive, but he's already in his car and has pulled it closer to where we are. Samantha walks at my pace as we make our way toward him, then she opens the passenger door. I climb in beside my brother, but it's difficult due to the height.

"This is a shit-mobile," I mumble, annoyed, as Samantha takes my crutches.

"No, you're just damaged goods," Connor retorts.

"Stop it," Samantha hisses. "You two are unbelievable. Can we manage a short drive with no bickering? You're like a pair of pathetic teenage boys." My brother and I glance at each other, and Connor shrugs. "Honestly, if I have to listen to another 'my dick is bigger than your dick'-type debate. I'll leave you both to it."

She slams my door closed and scrambles into the rear seat, throwing my crutches on the floor.

"We've been told off," Connor says, and we laugh.

"But there isn't a snowball's chance in hell that we'll ever stop," I say. "Riling you up is one of my favorite pastimes."

"And don't I fucking know it."

Connor slides the stick into gear, and we pull out of the underground parking garage into the busy London traffic. Our apartments are around the corner, so it takes only minutes to arrive at The Level. Once we've parked again in an underground parking area, we all clamber out of the vehicle and make our way to the elevator that directly accesses the boardroom.

"Everyone should be there," Connor tells us. "I messaged them, and they were there anyway with Harrison. Hunter has a legal issue."

"When doesn't he," I say as the doors open for us to find our friends already placed around the table, waiting for us. Harrison, Damon, and Hunter sit sipping on beer bottles and chatting amongst themselves as we enter the room.

"Good afternoon, lovers," Hunter calls across, and I scowl at him. He grins, completely unruffled by my expression. Connor leads Samantha to a chair on the far side of the table then takes the seat beside her. I limp over and sit on her other side. Harrison passes each of us a beer before taking his seat.

"So," Damon says. "There are some updates regarding the organ theft we need to be aware of?"

"Yes," Samantha tells him. "There were some developments at work. I think people are being brought to her to have their organs removed."

"Well, that's how organ donation works," Damon says grumpily. "One person gives their organs to another."

"Yes, but this girl said she was a family member and isn't," Samantha shoots back. "She was thin and dirty. All she wanted to do was sleep. I'm telling you now, something isn't right." Damon frowns but doesn't respond.

I place my hand on Samantha's thigh in support, and her eyes flick to me. She smiles softly in thanks. Looking down, I see my brother has done the same thing. His hand sits on her opposite thigh. We sit together, connected by this beautiful woman between us. Both of us touching her, and her completing us.

"We have a problem," Connor says, and I know what he's going to say before he does. "Samantha is working in a department which we suspect is harvesting stolen organs to order. She's putting herself in danger to gain information." My brother doesn't look at me. He's taking the opportunity to put his opinion on the table before anyone else gets the chance.

"That isn't a problem," I say casually. "Having eyes on the inside will be beneficial."

"I am not putting her in danger," Connor states, as he straightens in his seat. Harrison sits, not speaking but watching every man in the room's reaction. "I want her to quit. She shouldn't be working in a department where we know there's a potential danger."

"I'm sitting fucking beside you," Samantha snaps. "Don't talk about me as if I'm not here."

"I won't have you endangering yourself," he says, his head snapping around to face her. "You need to quit."

"She doesn't have to," I counter. "It isn't your position to tell her what to do. And we don't know the whole situation with the organ retrieval or sale."

"I don't give a fuck," Connor says petulantly. He takes her hands in his. "I want you to quit."

"No," she says, "Russell is right. This isn't your choice. And if we're wrong about the criminal elements of this, I don't want to give up on a career I love. My training is going well."

Connor's fist smashes down on the glass table; it vibrates beneath the impact. He closes his eyes then throws his head back before pushing himself out of his seat and storms around the room.

I don't know why he's surprised by her rebuke; we already had the same discussion in the penthouse, and her response was identical. Maybe he was looking for support from the others but looking at them. it isn't forthcoming. They know as well as me how beneficial her being there could be for us in stopping this.

"We'll protect her," Hunter tells him.

I watch my brother crumble as the thoughts of what could go wrong hit him. The panic on his features is something I've not seen since we were kids, when my father decided to distribute punishment on one of us and made the other watch.

"How can we?" he shoots back. "We have no real idea what's going on. But from experience, we all know that there is no corruption without evidence. And the little we have indicates something much bigger. Where there's lawbreaking, there's danger, and anyone close is at risk." He stops at Sam's chair and kneels beside her. His gaze moves around the room, hesitating on each of us. "More than one of us in here has lost someone, temporarily or permanently, to our enemies."

Harrison stands and walks over to him, then places a hand on his shoulder. The men look at each other. Silent acknowledgment passes between them as to what his words mean.

"Violet came back," Harrison says softly. "We won. She's here and safe with us."

"But Connie wasn't so lucky," Connor replies, glancing at Damon, who swallows. "She lost her life because of the man she loved."

"That's harsh," I snap at my brother. "You can't blame McKinney for her death. The only people responsible are the man who ordered the hit and the bastard who pulled the trigger."

"It's okay. I feel responsible," Damon mutters, and my sympathy grows again. I used to hold him responsible too, until I accepted that no matter what we do, our loved ones don't deserve to pay the price for our actions. That said, we cannot control the choices of others—evil people do evil things. They take revenge in the most devastating ways. We can only hope the good we do outweighs the bad we create, and in the end, the results are something we can live with. I hope my friend can learn to do so.

"You shouldn't," I tell him. "Villains will always be malicious. And we'll continue to fight it."

"All I am saying is." Connor's focus moves back to the woman whose hands he's now holding. "I don't want you to be unnecessarily put in harm's way. I couldn't bear it if you're hurt in all this. Now that we're aware of the situation, we can get involved. But my involvement will put a target on your back as my partner." My skin prickles with the word "partner." He has never referred to anyone in that way.

Sam stills, then takes a deep breath. "I'm already in the middle," she says. "And I'm more than capable of looking after myself. Let me help you all."

Hunter stands and walks around to join us all, only leaving Damon on the opposite side of the table. "Stand up," he says to Samantha, and she glances at me. I nod, unsure where he is going with this, but I trust him enough to allow it. Sam rises, Connor following and standing at her side. "How do we know you aren't involved, nurse?" She blinks at him, startled by the accusation. Connor opens his mouth to protest, and Hunter raises his hand sharply to silence him.

We all watch in shock as Samantha suddenly drops to her knees, arms covering her face. Connor and I glance at one another, then he lowers himself down beside her, taking her hands and encouraging her to rise.

"Hunter wasn't going to hit you," he tells her. I push myself up as well to join them.

"Maybe *he* wasn't," I say. "But I want to know who fucking *has* hit you."

"It doesn't matter," she whispers, her eyes firmly fixed on the floor. I reach out and touch her elbow, and wary eyes flick to me.

"Yes, it fucking does. I want a name. All this other shit can wait." She pauses again, uncertainty painted blatantly on her face. "Trouble..." I warn. "I want his—"

"*We* want his," Connor corrects me.

"Name. Now," my brother and I demand in unison. We glance at one another and smile. In this situation, we're one hundred percent together. Our words hit the air perfectly in sync. Samantha's shoulders sag; she knows we won't give this up without a name.

"Jasper," she replies quietly. "Jasper Hastings."

CHAPTER
TWENTY-FOUR

Westminster Financial Solutions, City of London

Connor

Russell and I sit in my car opposite the accountancy firm Samantha's ex-boyfriend owns. Jasper Hastings is well known in the London financial district, having grown his business from nothing over the past ten years. I've met him occasionally at various charity events. He's always the man dripping in women and waving one hundred pound notes at the auction.

Once Samantha relented and offered up the name of the bastard who'd hit her, my brother and I made a silent agreement to teach him a lesson. It turned out Hastings was a regular at Guilty Pleasures and had taken a liking to Sam. That admiration quickly turned to obsession when she agreed to go on a few dates with him. The locations were always private, and their relationship a secret. He explained the requirement away with wanting to maintain his privacy.

After six months of dating, he demanded she stop dancing. He wanted her to move into an apartment provided by him and be his on-call girlfriend—not that he took her anywhere. She told us she was forever seeing him in pictures at events, but she was never invited. When she refused, he began to apply pressure.

First, he threatened to cut contact with her. I smiled to myself when she described his threat. Sam isn't a lady who succumbs to intimidation. She told him he knew where the door was.

Then he tried the emotion card. Begging her to think of him and his feelings. How it felt for him while she danced for other men. He seemed to forget the fact that it was in the club where he met her. She described how he would turn up at her door with dozens of roses and throw himself onto his knees. She refused to quit every damn time.

He grew bored and impatient after around a month of flitting between these tactics. Jasper Hastings is a man used to getting what he wants. The first time he raised his hand to her was after a Saturday night performance, when he'd arrived to collect her after a show.

She had met him at the rear entrance to the club. He stood at the bottom of the rickety staircase waiting for her with a warm smile on his lips but ice in his heart. When she reached the bottom, he asked her, "Did you quit?" And when she gave an unsatisfactory answer, he dragged her from the last step to his car by her hair, throwing her onto the back seat before climbing in after and beating her.

My fury grew as she relived the incident before Russell and myself. She described in detail how he had pinned her down by straddling her, then held her wrists above her head in his left hand. His weight on her mid-section had kept her immobile as he struck her over and over. Her front tooth was broken in the vile incident. The following morning, she woke in his bed with black eyes, staring into the face of a private dentist employed to fix the injuries he inflicted.

The cycle continued for months, Sam not relenting to his demands and him responding with abuse. It wasn't until her friend Mia noticed bruises that it was brought to the security team's attention at Guilty Pleasures. Hastings stormed into the club one night and pulled Sam from the stage. He'd been swiftly removed and warned physically never to return or contact her again.

We were surprised to hear he gave up so easily after his altercation with the team, but men like Jasper Hastings are cowards. They thrive on the pain of those they consider weaker than themselves. Sam, no doubt, was a conquest he desired to break, and the more she pushed back, the more he needed to control her.

When my brother and I discussed what happened after Sam had gone home, we both agreed that justice hadn't been served. It was our job to ensure that the necessary punishment was distributed. Hastings deserves to pay, not only for the hell he put Sam through, but for every other woman he had hurt in his lifetime. I could guarantee that he'd merely have moved on to someone else. The only way to stop a bully is to take their power away.

So now, three days after she gave us the name we requested, we're sitting outside the bastard's place of work waiting for him. Harrison and Hunter are in the deep underground tunnels beneath the pavement, setting the stage for what we consider true justice. Damon unexpectedly left for Aviemore in Scotland yesterday after accepting the only way to be happy is to swallow his pride and apologize to the woman whose heart he broke. That brings our little band of vigilantes down to four, but we all have enough thirst for justice to make up for a lack in numbers.

"When did Blake say their meeting ends?" Russell asks me, clearly impatient to get on with the job. Another benefit of our position in this world is the people we meet and the ties we create.

Marshall Blake is an independent righter of wrongs. An influential businessman who spends his time monitoring the London sex industry after his sister was murdered, he was more than happy to help us set up Hastings. He knew Sam from Guilty Pleasures, so he immediately arranged a meeting with our target when he became aware of the situation.

"Eight," I tell him for the umpteenth time. "He'll message me when they head for the elevator." Just then, my phone pings, and the message we have been waiting for pops on the screen.

> *It's on. On street in five minutes. No one else.*

My hand rests on the handgun sitting on my leg. Russell's eyes flick to me, then the gun.

"How far are we going to go, brother?" he asks, his voice low and ominous.

"It depends on his responses to my questions, but if we have to..." I trail off, not needing to say the last words in the sentence. In my mind, there's no doubt that Hastings will die tonight. He'll disappear and never be found. He'll pay for what he did to my girl and be stopped from doing it to anyone else in the future. Russell nods, and I see a flicker of excitement on his face.

"Good," he says. "I'm glad we're on the same page."

Just then, the door opens across the street, and two men in suits enter the dark London night. I recognize Blake as he takes the other man's hand and shakes it firmly. He turns and walks away, striding purposely, carrying a neat leather briefcase. Hastings watches him go, then moves toward a dark sports car at the curb.

I start the engine and swing across the road, pulling in front of the vehicle as he climbs in. He pauses, glancing up as I open the driver's door.

"Well, if it isn't Connor Chase," he says jovially. He moves toward me, reaching out one hand to shake mine. "What brings you here? You certainly know how to make an entrance." He gestures to my car blocking his.

"Business," I reply shortly as Russell clambers out the passenger door. He pulls himself up on his crutches and makes his way around the cars to stand behind Hastings.

"Jeez, what happened to you?" Hastings asks my brother.

"Complications with a ladder."

"Ouch," he says, returning his focus to me. His eyes widen when he sees the gun in my hand pointing at his stomach. "What the fuck?"

"Get in our car," I say simply.

"Will I, fuck!" He goes to move, and Russell's gun slides into his back. He freezes.

"I suggest you do as he says," my brother says menacingly.

"Do you honestly think you'll get away with this?" Hastings snarls.

"I am one hundred percent sure we'll get away with this. Now, get in the fucking car."

London is home to an extensive underground system that goes far beyond the active railway. Beneath the streets are miles of disused tunnels and tube stations. Some places haven't been seen by the human eye for decades. It's here that we're free to dispense our toughest justice. This is where we take the men who deserve never to see the light of day again. And that's where Hastings will be ended too.

Mayfair is around two miles from Westminster. It's one of London's most influential areas, and home to the rich and famous. We weave through the evening traffic, taking a route past Buckingham Palace. The building stands proudly in the now-illuminated evening skies.

Russell sits in the rear of my car; our captive is in the passenger seat with my brother's gun pressed to the back of his chair. Once he climbed into the vehicle, I secured his wrists with cable ties then attached them to his belt. He gives the impression of a schoolboy waiting patiently for his class to start which, in a way, he is. But it's a lesson he won't receive twice.

"Wave to the king," I suggest as we pass the palace. His furious eyes flick to mine, and he scowls. "It may be your last chance."

"I would if my hands weren't attached to my dick," he snarls. I grin back at him.

"Push me, and I'll staple them to it." He visibly winces as no doubt the image of his hands being nailed to his privates flits through his mind.

"What the fuck do you idiots want?" We haven't told him why he's here. I wanted to leave him to sweat for a while. With no explanation, we took his phone from his pocket then started on our journey.

"You'll find out in good time," Russell says, eerily soft. "Not far now."

The red brick building comes into view, sporting an inconspicuous gray door against the stone. Down Street Tube Station hasn't operated since 1932, when it was closed after only twenty-five years of service. Residents in areas such as Mayfair don't ride on the underground. In recent years, it's been adapted for tourism in the form of tours of the disused passageways and rooms. It has an interesting history, with parts of it being used at headquarters for Winston Churchill during the Second World War.

I draw up in front of the building as Hunter and Harrison step out of the archway on the other side of the mini-mart next door. Both are dressed smartly in chic suits and sharp white shirts. Hunter holds a bundle of keys in one hand as he approaches my window, an excited smile on his lips. I press the button to lower the glass, and he leans down to speak to me. His eyes lock onto my passenger.

"Good evening, Mr. Hastings," he drawls. "Thank you for joining us."

"It's not as if I had a fucking choice." Hunter shrugs as the passenger door opens and Harrison stabs our captive in the arm with a needle. His eyes pop wide as he realizes what's happening, but within moments, I see the darkness fall over his eyes, and he passes out.

"Good job, Waite," Hunter tells his accomplice. Harrison grins, obviously proud of himself. He loves all this undercover bullshit. "Now, let's get him inside before he wakes up. Come on, Russ."

Russell starts to clamber out of the car. Hunter walks around to the passenger side and helps Harrison extract Hastings, throwing an arm around each of their necks as if he has just had too much to drink.

"You go park somewhere," Harrison says, "then meet us downstairs." Both my car doors slam, and I watch them all disappear through the inconspicuous gray door and out of sight.

I find a parking spot farther down the street between a vintage red Mini and a luxurious black Bentley. After reversing my jeep into the space, I sit momentarily, considering what will happen tonight. Yes, I've dispensed justice before. I've heard men scream and beg for their lives. But never has it seemed more important to make one pay as it does now. I want to hear every cut of his flesh, every break of his bones. Not only do I want to watch and listen, but I need to partake. I rarely get involved in the actual violence, leaving it to the men who always enjoy it. But tonight, I will fucking enjoy every slash.

After climbing out of the car, I slam my door closed then walk down the street toward the station entrance. On stepping through, I find a dark, narrow staircase. A simple white sign on the wall tells me there are one hundred and three steps to descend. As I step down, old white and red tiles line the walls. In the distance, I hear trains passing on nearby tracks beneath the city streets, the sound of metal scraping over metal loud and clear.

On reaching the bottom of the stairs, the noise of the train subsides and I can hear voices from further along the corridor. I find them in a small room. My friends stand in a circle with our prisoner in the center. In the corner is an old metal bathtub from a time long gone. Hunter's focus moves to me as I step in to join them.

"Interesting place, isn't it?" he says casually. "Hard to believe people practically lived down here during the war. Churchill probably washed his balls in that bath."

"How did you get access?" I ask him.

"Someone I know is a tour guide. It felt the most fitting place for this." There are dozens of abandoned tunnels and stations around London. We've used many over the years, but this is our first time in Down St. He turns to Hastings, who's now awake and standing in the center. "I would imagine many of your arsehole friends live in Mayfair."

"I fucking live in Mayfair," he growls back.

"And you'll die here," Russell tells him. "Your blood will seep into the ground deep below the pavement you have walked."

"If you've brought me here to kill me, fucking get on with it." His voice is wavering despite his words. "But before you do, I want to know why."

I chuckle under my breath as I am reminded we haven't told him the why of the situation. He's in the dark.

"Samantha." My word is blunt and clear.

"Who?" His lips twist into a smirk. "I don't know any tart by that name."

"Watch your mouth," I snap, stepping forward into his space. Our eyes lock, and we glare at each other. "The woman you beat to a pulp in the back of your car."

"Which one?" he goads. His vile features are highlighted in the murky tunnels, and the only light sources are pathetically dim wall sconces. "Some little whores love it rough. The way their skin marks is..." He trails off, then rolls his eyes dramatically. "Fucking perfect." My fist connects with his chin hard, and he stumbles backward.

"Let's see if your skin marks so prettily." I land another blow on the same spot.

"You need to get to the gym, Chase. That will barely leave a bruise." He tries to smile nastily, but his lips barely widen, as if frozen.

"Is there water down here?" I ask Hunter, ignoring the asshole in front of me, wanting to focus on what pain I can inflict next. He signals to a small tap on the wall, a black bucket placed beneath. Harrison moves toward it. We all watch him fill the dirty, disused tub one bucket at a time. My attention turns back to Hastings. "You will regret ever laying a hand on her. These last hours of your life will pass so slowly, you'll be praying for death."

Russell stands to one side, leaning against the wall, balanced on his crutches. He rocks slightly as if uncomfortable. "You okay?" I ask him, and he shrugs. "How the fuck did you get down those stairs?"

"With difficulty," he replies, deadpan. "But it will be fucking worth it to see this bastard die."

"I'm surprised you're here," Hastings says to my brother. "Your reputation precedes you. You're no angel."

"I don't proclaim to be." Russell limps toward him. "But I never have or will lay a finger on a lady."

"Don't knock it until you've tried it. Men like us love to see fear in others. Whether that is physical or mental." He grins disgustingly, leaning forward into Russell's face. His body turns and bumps my brother's shoulder with his. The movement is awkward due to his hands still being tied. It mimics the gesture of friends. "You and me are cut from the same cloth."

My brother turns away, not reacting impulsively as I expect him to. A few moments later, the crutch connects with Hastings's skull. Russell raises the metal tube again, then brings it down hard on his face. Blood spurts from his nose, splattering his shirt then running liberally over his lips. He drops to his knees but continues to smile. Harrison continues to fill the tub as if nothing has happened.

"Say that again," Russell snarls.

"Men. Like. Us," Hastings repeats.

This time, it's me who loses control. I grab Hastings by the collar, pushing him forcefully to the bathtub. Turning the bastard away from me, I kick him hard at the back of his knees and he drops to the floor. Clutching the back of his shirt collar, I push his head down into the freezing water. With his hands still tied to his belt, he flails his shoulders but can't fight me off. Hunter appears on the other side to apply more pressure. We hold him under the water for thirty seconds. Russell counts in the background, then we pull him from the water. Hastings gasps for breath.

"Men like you," I say furiously. "Only pathetic cowards mistreat women."

Hunter pushes his head forward, and I follow. We hold him longer this time, forcing the air from his body and allowing the water to invade his lungs before releasing him again.

"You won't die by drowning," Hunter tells him. "That's a death too easy for a bastard. This is stage one in an exit from this earth so beautiful, and you'll be your own audience at every stage." My friend's eyes move to me. "Again, and this time for one minute. I find any longer than that, they can die by accident. I have too much fun planned for that to happen."

CHAPTER TWENTY-FIVE

---◄◦►---

Down St. Abandoned
Underground Station,
Mayfair

Russell

I watch in both horror and awe as my brother holds Hastings under the water level. When he and Hunter pull him out, the bastard gasps violently in a vain attempt to fill his dying lungs with air. Once he seems to settle again, they thrust him back below the water. It's the cruelest method when conducting any torture—giving your victim a false sense that the ordeal is over only to reenact the brutality. The process is exhausting and exhilarating for all concerned, whether a participant or spectator.

Harrison approaches Connor from behind and taps him on the shoulder. My brother's focus flits to him briefly. He releases his grip on Hastings. "Enough," Harrison says firmly. "You don't want to kill him too soon." Hunter sighs dramatically but pulls his victim from the water again.

"Spoilsport," he says cheekily. He lets go of the man he's holding, who falls forward onto the edge of the bath, his shoulders colliding with the metal before he collapses to the floor. "We should stick with water. I don't think our friend enjoys it. His body vibrates wonderfully with fear." Hastings doesn't speak; he shakes his head viciously, trying to clear the water from his ears and face as he lies in a heap.

"Lie him flat on his back," I suggest, then reach for a dirty rag lying over a metal rail on the wall. It was probably white at one point; now, it's a morbid gray speckled with black. Heaven knows how long it's been down here. Hunter and Connor maneuver Hastings onto his back. "Fill the bucket, Waite." Harrison goes back to the tap and twists open the faucet.

I hobble over then drop my crutches onto the floor, offering the dirty rag to my brother. "Pull that over his face," I tell him, then turn to Hunter. "Pin him down." My friend moves to kneel on our captive's chest. "Pass me the bucket." Harrison walks over, passing me the now full bucket. "I'm going to enjoy this." I tip the water over the dirty rag, and it soaks it immediately. I keep the stream of water constant as Hastings kicks his legs in panic. "Sometimes, the oldest torture techniques are the best; prepare yourself, you arsehole, because you will experience many tonight."

Slowly, we refill the bucket and I pour the water over Hastings's face. As time passes, he fights less. His will to survive ebbing from his body as the reality of what's happening to him sets in. I imagine his mouth gawping beneath the disgusting fabric only to be met with more liquid.

Once he stills, we remove it and pull him up to sit. He's limp, and I wonder if we have gone too far already. But then, he coughs aggressively, throwing himself forward from the waist. His face is filthy, covered in remnants of dirty water. Hunter grabs him by the collar, pulls him up to stand, then pushes him to a wooden spindle chair which seems strategically located in the corner of the room. Hastings collapses onto the seat.

Another train passes the station, but we can't see it. The noise is loud behind the wall. The clatter fills the space, and everyone stops speaking. Once it subsides, Hunter pulls his knife from his belt and walks toward Hastings, who looks up with tired, beaten eyes.

My friend spins the knife between his fingers, then lowers it swiftly and opens our captive's suit jacket and shirt at the shoulders, exposing flesh. He does the same on the opposite side, then pulls both lots of material down his arms so they bunch at his still-tied hands. "Perfect," he mutters before driving the blade into his shoulder. Hastings wails in pain, and Hunter pulls the knife from his body then turns and passes it to Connor. "Your turn, Chase. Use him as a fucking pin cushion."

Connor takes the blade, looks at me, and I nod in encouragement. It would be typical for me to take part in the rough justice we distribute. I'm not embarrassed to admit I find a thrill in physically punishing someone who deserves it. But Connor rarely gets involved. He's the one who stands back and allows others to take the lead. But today, it's obvious he wants to be the one who inflicts the pain.

The knife cuts into the flesh at the top of each arm over and over again. Eventually, Hastings's body gives the impression that his arms are hanging, almost detached.

"Stand," Connor barks, and Hastings wobbles to his feet. "Follow me." We all look at each other, unsure of where he's going with this. My brother walks out into the passageway and heads toward the noise of yet another train. At the bottom of the corridor is a modern sign with an arrow, telling us the Piccadilly line is to our left.

"I thought the tunnels weren't used," I asked, signaling to the sign.

"Those were installed for contractors," Hunter explains. "So they don't get lost."

We follow the arrow and are met with a metal grate that looks onto the in-use trainline. Connor is leading the way, with Hastings behind him. Connor stops, and his eyes run over the obstruction. His foot lifts, and he kicks it violently. It only causes it to wobble. I look to Hunter and Harrison. They both shrug, then my eyes land on an old bench sitting to the side of the corridor. The two men not related to me by blood read my thoughts and go to lift it.

"Out of the way," I tell my brother, who places his hand on our captive's chest, pushing him out of the way as the bench connects with the metal. It bends but doesn't give way until the fourth hit. One side pops open, and between us, we're able to bend it out of the way.

Hastings turns and tries to scurry off down the corridor. The fact he can still walk is amazing, but prey will always fight until they accept they're beaten, even if the odds are stacked against them.

Connor strides behind him then grabs his collar, pulling him back to the tracks. He spins the bastard to face him, pushing him so his heels are only millimeters from the line. The sound of a train approaching echoes up the tunnel. Connor smiles menacingly at the man he holds. He grabs the top one of his arms and squeezes. Hastings yells in pain as the previously inflicted wounds strain with movement.

"Stop," he pleads. "Please don't kill me."

"Too late. It's time to end this." The train gets closer, Connor holds his victim beside the tracks, pulling him away just in time as the hunk of metal passes. My brother turns to Harrison. "Call Violet and get the girls to meet us where we discussed."

"What do you mean?" I snap, annoyed at being left out of an earlier conversation.

"Samantha needs to see this for herself," Connor replies.

"No, she doesn't." My words are hard and acidic. I don't attempt to hide my disagreement.

"Yes, she does. She must know this bastard is finished and has paid for what he did."

"You've changed your tune. A matter of days ago, you wanted her to quit her job due to danger, but today, you're inviting her to dispose of a body."

My brother's eyes focus on me, and we stare at one another. There's a new hardness on his features, an unrelenting hatred I've never seen before.

"Maybe I've accepted she's much stronger than I gave her credit for." He strides by me, and Hunter grabs for our victim, wrapping him in a blanket that seems to appear from nowhere. I limp after my brother, completely forgetting my crutches from the earlier room.

"Connor, are you sure about this? This will change her." He stops then turns to face me.

"She changed the moment we fell in love with her," he says simply, then walks away.

***

Deserted Warehouse, River Thames

After Connor left the underground tunnels, he pulled the car to the gray door, and we bundled Hastings into the back. The blanket covering him soaked through with blood quickly; we needed to leave fast. Once in the car, he passed out. Hunter called his right-hand man, Greyson, to come and clean the scene.

Now, the four of us and Hastings are standing at the river's edge, waiting for Samantha to arrive. She needs to see for herself that the bastard who hurt her is gone for good. I want her to know we sought revenge on her behalf, but she deserves to have a choice whether to be involved in his execution. Her being at peace with her past is my priority. Closure is part of that. Offering her all of the options is what is best for her.

The warehouse has been abandoned for a long time and is now owned by Hunter. He has big plans to renovate and build housing here in years to come once the surrounding area is developed, which is underway. The space is dark and eery, with hardly a sound beyond an odd owl hoot. A trash can clatters to the ground startling us, and a fox scurries across the asphalt.

Headlights appear from behind the building, and I see my sister's little black Mazda MX-5 come around the corner.

"What the fuck is she doing here?" Harrison mutters, annoyed by the unexpected arrival of his wife.

"And, of course, she had to bring the go-kart," I add. Harrison grunts. The change in his expression tells me he is furious.

"She'll be child-free, so she likes to use her sporty wheels. Makes her feel less mum-like," he says under his breath. Harrison bought my sister the car as a present when she gave birth to my niece. He said it was her adult toy to use when she was off mum-duty. "This isn't exactly what I had in mind for childless days out."

As they get closer, Violet and Samantha come into view. She grinds to a halt ten meters away, slamming the brakes hard enough that they screech. Harrison shakes his head, then strides toward his wife as she climbs out of the car.

"Vi, light movements. You don't need to stamp on the brake pedal. And what the fuck are you doing here?" She beams at him as she closes the door, then skips toward him before throwing her arms around his neck. He takes her in his arms naturally. "Thank God you're good at things other than driving. Maybe you need more lessons." She giggles but doesn't respond. Even with his grumpiness, she looks so fucking happy.

"Why are you here?" he repeats.

"To support my friend, and I didn't want to be left out of the fun." She rises on tiptoe and kisses his lips. He visibly thaws in front of me. My sister has him on a leash; the man would do anything for her.

"You hate this stuff," he counters. She looks up at him with wide eyes, then shakes her long dark hair down her back.

"Sam said you were taking out the trash. Well, I'm here to ensure you do a good enough job. Is that him?" Her focus moves to Hastings, her face pinching in disgust as she takes in his bloodied appearance.

Sam appears from the passenger seat. She walks over cautiously. I watch her eyes move around, taking in the situation before her. She comes to my side, and I pass my arm around her waist. "Are you okay, Trouble?" I ask. She mumbles positively, but I'm not convinced this was Connor's best idea.

"Sam," my brother calls to her, then waves for her to go to him standing next to Hastings, who's lying on the ground barely breathing. I release her. As she reaches him, he takes both her hands and pulls her close, then places a soft kiss on her lips. "I told you we would get justice." She looks from him to Hastings on the floor, then to me.

"I want to be part of this," she says, her voice clear. The request is deliberate. "What can I do? I need to be part of it."

Although I knew it was an option, I'm surprised by her immediate request but bizarrely proud that she wants to take some ownership of what we've done tonight. My girl wants to be part of the sentencing we've passed on our convict, whether the means are legal or otherwise.

"You can help us bury him," Connor tells her.

The ready-to-mix concrete is prepared. Hunter pulls Hastings to his feet, and Harrison stands behind him, keeping him steady. One leg at a time, Connor places one of Hastings's feet into the waiting plastic buckets then passes a shovel to Sam. "Fill them up," he tells her, and she lifts some wet concrete from the ground then slides it into the bucket. Hastings focuses on her and leers; she ignores him.

We all stand and watch as the concrete sets fast around his feet. I hobble over, pull a hankerchief from my pocket, then pass it to Sam. Without any need of instruction, she takes it and stuffs it in his mouth. His eyes bug in surprise, and she flicks a strand of blonde hair over her shoulder.

"Goodbye, Jasper," she says sweetly before turning and walking away. Violet runs over to embrace her friend. The two women pull back and stare at one another.

"Have you seen what you needed to see?" my sister asks, and Samantha nods. "Good, then let's go." Violet looks at us all standing in a circle with a man ready to be thrown in the river. "You boys clean up," she says. "Us girls are going to celebrate."

"Violet Waite," Harrison growls. "Go straight home. I want you to be there when I return." She blinks at him then cocks her head to the side. He bristles at her defiance. "You shouldn't fucking be here."

"No, I *should* be here. I am supporting my friend, and we are going for a drink," she replies sharply. She takes a step toward the waiting car.

"Do you not think you'd be better returning to The Level?" Connor suggests to Sam as she turns away. "We can all celebrate later. Together."

"Perhaps we should just go back to The Level." She turns to Violet, who narrows her eyes, annoyed. Samantha laughs, then looks between us all.

"Fine," Violet says. "We will head off and meet you there."

We watch the two women climb into the little sports car and drive off.

"Do you think they'll be going where we told them to?" I ask.

"Not a fucking chance," Harrison responds, then pulls his phone from his pocket. "Luckily, I have systems to keep control of my argumentative wife."

CHAPTER TWENTY-SIX

The City of London

Samantha

Violet weaves her compact car through the labyrinth of London streets. The clock strikes one, yet the roads are still teeming with life. Drunken partygoers' laughter and off-key singing fill the air as they stumble along the pavement. My friend remains focused, her eyes fixed on the road as if she's on a mission.

"Where are we going?"

She glances in my direction and smiles. "Out," she replies.

"Out where? We told them we would head back."

"For some fun, but first, we need to lose them." Her eyes flick up to the rearview mirror, and I glance over my shoulder. A black car I haven't seen before sits behind us, following a matter of meters away. Two men sit in the front, both dressed in dark suits.

"Who are they?" I ask, a tad anxious that we're being followed by men we don't know.

"Security," she tells me. "Harry thinks I don't know that he has me followed when I go out by myself. Men can be so dumb sometimes, no matter how clever they are. I want to go out, drink, and have girly fun tonight."

"Tonight?" I giggle. "Vi, it's tomorrow already." She shrugs, unruffled by my observation.

"I don't care. London never sleeps. We're having a girl's night out. We're celebrating that bastard who hurt you being at the bottom of the Thames."

My chest strains with her direct assessment, and the uncertainty that I've been burying resurfaces. Tonight, I was involved in someone's murder. Someone who had hurt me. And terrifyingly, it hadn't crossed my mind to object when I heard what was happening. Hell, I *wanted* to be involved.

"Are you comfortable with all this?" I ask. She seems completely at ease with our current situation.

"All what?"

"This," I say, raising my hands. "Your life, what just happened at the docks, the fact your husband pays men to follow you."

She giggles sweetly and shakes her head. "My life is the one I must live if I want to be with the man I love."

Her words are simple and honest, a perfect summary. Harrison's career and lifestyle are interwoven with the criminal world, both on the right and wrong sides of the law. He couldn't have one without the other, and she couldn't have him without accepting that.

"It's a decision you'll need to make too," she says, concerned eyes holding mine for a beat. "You need to ask yourself whether you can be with a man who lives his life in danger. Because, Sam, that's exactly what our men do. They walk a fine line every day. They create enemies not only for themselves but also for their families. You need to ask yourself if that's something you can live with." She pauses, smirks, then adds, "Whichever of my brothers you end up with."

I ignore the jibe, not wanting to discuss my current romantic predicament with my two boyfriends' little sister, who's never shy about venting her opinion on anything. My mind returns to the scene I witnessed at the warehouse parking lot. How both Russell and Connor were there to seek vengeance on my behalf. I felt love from both, not one, and my heart split in two as I moved between them, unsure how to show both I care equally. Picking a favorite seems impossible, sorting this damn mess into a viable outcome more so.

"Anyway," Violet says, interrupting my thoughts. "We have celebrating to do. There's an underground car park a few minutes away with six different exits onto the street. I say we dump the car and run."

"Will you not get in trouble with Harry for ducking past your security?" I question.

She lifts a hand and fans her face dramatically. "I hope so," she replies with a cheeky smile. "Because angry make-up sex is so much better than any other kind."

"You're terrible," I mutter but laugh. "Okay, I'll follow your lead. Let's ditch these idiots and find a bottle of vodka."

Violet swings into a small basement car park, the simple red and white barrier lifting to allow us entry. She floors the accelerator and aims for the furthest corner of the parking lot before coming to a screeching halt in a free space. We grab our bags, jump out of the car, and run to the nearest exit as the black car following us comes through the barrier.

There are about twenty steps to jump up before we step out onto a busy pedestrianized street filled with bars. Hundreds of people mill about in groups, talking and drinking. Violet grabs my hand and pulls me toward a tiny, dank pub that sits between two modern ones with vibrant signs and huge glass windows.

She pushes open the old wooden door, and we step into a small traditional pub decorated in dark wood and faded checked material. A handful of men sit at the bar, and in the corner near the back of the room is a square pine table with two matching chairs.

"I'll get the drinks. You sit down," she says, signaling to the free table. "They won't look for us in here."

A few minutes pass before my friend joins me, placing two tall glasses filled with clear liquid, ice cubes, and fruit before me. She collapses in the chair beside me, then lifts her drink offering in my direction. I lift mine, and we chink them together.

"Thank you," I tell her, and she cocks her head to one side.

"For what?" she asks, a genuine look of confusion on her face.

"For walking into that clothes shop last year and falling into my life. Meeting you has changed so much for me." She smiles, a genuine smile filled with love and admiration. "I don't know how I will ever repay you.

"Sam," she says, placing her glass back on the table then taking my hand. Her soft fingers squeeze mine. "You saved my life. Your friendship means the world to me. All I ask is you stay in my world and..." She giggles, as Violet does when she's due to say something naughty. "Make one, or better, *both* of my brothers happy."

"Oh, let's not talk about that," I mumble, and she laughs.

"So what do you want to do then?" I shrug, being quite happy sitting in her company, hiding from security guards, and sipping whatever fruity concoction is in my glass. "I have an idea."

"What?" I ask, mildly concerned by the look in her eyes.

"How do you feel about getting pierced?"

***

Raven's Tattoo and Piercings, London

Violet huffs dramatically as the shop owner, who is actually called Raven, explains again why she won't pierce her vaginal clit hood within three months of giving birth.

301

"You need to give yourself time to fully recover…" Raven's eyes flick to Violet's I.D. in her hand. "Mrs. Waite. I am sorry I can't help you at this time." My friend pouts, sticking one painted red lip beyond the other. It makes me chuckle; she can be so juvenile at times. It shows how young she truly is, and exactly how sheltered her upbringing has been.

"Well, you'll just have to get one, Sam," she says, turning to face me. "You get it done now, and I'll come back in a few weeks."

"I'm not getting pierced on my own!" I narrow my eyes, and she glares right back. "You brought me here because *you* wanted to be pierced down there."

"If you're not breastfeeding, Mrs. Waite, I could offer you a tattoo," Raven attempts to move Violet's focus from my privates to herself again. "That would be perfectly safe. Maybe your daughter's name and date of birth? A small symbol? Or a combination of the three."

"Oh, I like that idea. No, I'm not feeding," Violet responds, her frown turning upwards. "Okay, I'll get a tattoo, and Sam will have the hood piercing." I wince at the thought of the pain. I'm sensitive enough down there without someone sticking a needle through my hood, but the benefits do sound intriguing. And I did half-commit to having the procedure done alongside my friend. So, I guess I'll be walking out of here sporting jewelry on my bits.

Violet lies face down on the tattoo artist's bed. She squeals again as the needle pricks her skin. My friend decided to get her daughter's name and date of birth imprinted on her lower back.

"I'm glad you didn't pick a more sensitive area, Mrs. Waite," Raven says as she flashes me an amused smile. "The lower back is low to moderate on the pain scale when getting a tattoo."

"Low to moderate? I very much doubt that. My skin feels like you're ripping it from my body." I laugh out loud, and my friend's annoyed eyes move to me. She glares. "What are you laughing at?"

"The fact you are such a drama queen and act like a petulant teenager. I love you, Violet, but, oh my, sometimes I feel sorry for your husband."

"And I deserve your sympathy," Harrison's voice interrupts us. I look up, and he's walking into the room, closely followed by Connor, with Russell limping behind. "She causes me nothing but fucking headaches."

Russell laughs, jovial and lighthearted. I love to hear him happy. He can be so broody and melancholy, but when he's joyous, it takes my breath away.

"I think Trouble is planning similar issues for my brother and me. What do you think, bro?" He taps Connor on the shoulder, whose eyes haven't left my body since they walked in. They stand tall at the entrance, dominating the space and demanding everyone in the room's attention. Owners here to collect their possessions; we wouldn't get out of here without them even if we made a run for it. Which is unlikely, with Violet's position and my recent treatment, which I never want to repeat. The pain was unbearable as the artist pushed the needed through my most sensitive skin.

"On that, I have to agree with you. Samantha is nothing but fucking trouble," Connor mutters. My heart skips as the same endearment his brother uses leaves his lips. A rebellious part of me loves the fact I don't make their lives easy. It's exciting that even with our challenges, they fight for me.

"Are you nearly finished?" Harrison asks the artist, who's sitting with her needle still poised and her jaw hanging open. She gapes at the three gorgeous men in her doorway dressed as if ready for court.

"Ten minutes, maybe," she stutters. "I need to finish this, then pad her up."

"Take your time. I don't want my wife with permanent errors." His tone is hard, but I can sense a hint of sarcasm underneath.

"So," Russell interrupts, "what did you get, Trouble?" I glance at him, and my cheeks heat. I know what I had done barely three hours ago. The nip between my legs is fierce, and I can't wait to get home to take some painkillers. It's safe to say I do not want the sensation of a needle being slid through my private areas again.

"Oh, she had her clit hood pierced," Violet announces to everyone in the room, and the whole place goes silent. "It's meant to make sexual experiences more intense. I wanted mine done, but it's not long enough since Evie's birth. So jealous."

My friend mumbles under her breath as Harrison walks to the front of the table and crouches before her.

"Patience, Vi," he says, laying a hand over hers that is lying flat on the bed. "We can always play with the original model before you're ready for the upgrade."

"I know, and I love it. But I wanted..." She trails off as he squeezes her fingers and drops a kiss on her forehead.

"And you can, just not now." He stands again. "But Mrs. Waite, you're in so much fucking trouble tonight. It's almost five in the morning and you're face down on someone else's bed."

"I was hoping you were going to say that," she whispers. "How did you find me?"

"Do you really think I would let you run around London with no way to track you down?"

They stare at one another, so many unspoken words passing between them. Harrison and Violet have an understanding as a couple I yearn for, and in my heart believe I am developing with both the men in my life.

"You track me?" she hisses. It's obvious from the smirk on her lips that her annoyance is completely faked. She probably already knew or at least suspected as much. Us "losing" her security detail was all a game in Violet's mind.

"Vi, I would microchip you if I thought it would make you safer. But, alas, I merely air-tagged your phone."

"You had your privates pierced?" Connor says, stunned, interrupting my viewing. I square my shoulders and look him straight in the eye.

"My vaginal clit hood, actually. The bead will sit on my clit and increase the sensation as I fuck." We gaze at one another, and I'm unsure if his expression is excitement, disgust, or awe. "It should be beneficial for both parties."

"That's fucking awesome, Trouble," Russell butts in. When I look at him, he is grinning from ear to ear. Connor glances at his brother and then back to me, increasing the tension in the room. I'm not sure which man looks more ready to pin me down and find out if what I am telling them is true.

"How soon can we test it out?" Connor asks.

I blink at him, surprised by his open question and him looking for more information in front of everyone in here.

"It is up to the client," Raven begins, taking the opportunity to insert some professional experience. "It's important only to do as much as you feel ready for and to follow the instructions I gave you." She focuses on me. Her expression stern. "No matter how impulsive you or your partner is, please don't do anything that doesn't feel right. But normally, within four to eight weeks, you'll be fully healed."

"Excellent," Russell exclaims, clapping his hands together like a seal. "Just in time for this bastard thing to come off." He gestures to his cast, and I shake my head at his idiocy.

"Yeah, but I'm fit and able right now," his brother responds. "I'll get to try out its effectiveness first." Raven looks from me to both men and back to me, her lips quip into a small smile. Her eyes dance with amusement, and unable to stop herself, she grins.

"If I'm reading the room correctly," she says. "You, girl, have won the lottery. Fucking enjoy it."

After Violet's artwork is completed, Raven covers the design with the pad and Harrison helps his wife from the bed. She takes hold of his hand, and he leads her from the room. Connor steps toward Raven, who is sliding the latex gloves from her fingers. He holds out a hand in her direction.

"Thank you for taking care of my sister and her friend," he says as they shake. "Have you been paid for your services?"

"Not yet," Raven tells him, and he pulls a wad of cash from his back pocket. "It's seven hundred pounds." Without counting he hands her a bundle of notes.

"That should cover it," he says before moving to my side and sliding an arm around my waist. "Let's go." He leads me from the tattoo shop and out onto the street. Harrison is sitting in the driver's seat of Connor's jeep with Violet in the passenger side. Connor opens the rear door, then takes my hand to help me step into the vehicle. He climbs in behind me.

A few minutes later, Russell climbs in the opposite side and lays his crutches on the floor. Both men take a hand each, interlocking their fingers with mine. I sit in the back of my boyfriend's car, holding the hands of two men I am completely devoted to.

CHAPTER
TWENTY-SEVEN

———◆○◆———

Russell's Penthouse, The
Level

Samantha

"Connor was really pissed at you earlier," Russell says as we sit on his sofa watching nothing in particular. When we arrived back at The Level at seven in the morning, everyone was too wired to sleep. Connor has an early case today, so he went back to his apartment to freshen up and head into the office early. He's due in court in a matter of hours.

Russell and I came up here to relax. It's been blissful wrapped around him, chatting about nothing important. We've covered everything from our latest favorite television series to the type of music we like.

"Why?" I ask him, surprised that it was Connor who was annoyed. "You're the psycho control freak. I would have expected it to be you losing your cool."

He chuckles, then places warm lips on my forehead. "I have no concerns regarding your ability to keep yourself alive. I would even go as far as to say I trust you to keep my sister on this earth, too. Though she can be a bit ditsy." His grip tightens on my shoulders. "Not many women would be able to knee a mafia boss in the nuts and live to tell the tale."

"You know about that?" I stammer, warmth coating my cheeks. No doubt they'll have turned tomato-red. That early morning altercation has run through my mind more times than I care to admit, the feeling of being both proud of standing up for myself but also idiotic for taking such a risk with a man like Hunter. He could end my life in a heartbeat if he wanted to.

"Hell yes," he replies, his face beaming. "I wish I'd been there to see it. Hunter Devane being brought to his knees in the middle of a parking garage by a nurse."

"It was epic," I agree. "But perhaps not my best moment."

"You impressed Damon and Greyson. They couldn't believe he let you walk away." He takes a breath, his chest rising and falling before he speaks. "However, I must admit that you impress me every time I see you. You really are remarkable, Trouble." His lips drop to mine, and he kisses me gently. The gesture is slow and intimate; it's everything a kiss between two people who care about each other should be. I turn toward him, then wince with the pain from my new piercing. "Are you sore?" he asks softly.

"A little." His hand comes to my cheek, and we kiss again, this time deeper, our tongues dancing together as we enjoy the connection. "You be careful with her," he whispers. "I want my pussy in perfect condition when I get this damn thing off this leg." The word "my" causes every ounce of independence to evaporate from my body. These men wanting me, loving me even, feels so fucking good.

"We can do other things before then," I tell him. Partly for him but mostly for me. Not being able to investigate the sexual part of our relationship is beyond frustrating. My need for him to touch me is growing by the minute. "You having a cast doesn't need to stop us having sex."

"No, Trouble, I've thought about this. When I get to take you for the first time, I want to be in full working order. No restrictions. It's a matter of weeks. I've been patient and won't allow my enthusiasm to ruin what we've been waiting for."

"I'm not sure I can wait." My words are needy leaving my mouth. I twist a little more up onto my knees to face him. His strong fingers move to my hair, wrapping around the strands and pulling my lips to his once more. "We've been wanting this since..." I don't complete the sentence, unsure when our relationship morphed from a distant yearning to the all-consuming need we have now.

"Since that night I picked you up from work and didn't bring you straight home. Also the night you told me to stop contacting you." My gaze moves over his shoulder. I focus on a painting on the far wall of the room. It's an image, almost erotic, of two people in a passionate embrace. Painted in muted tones, it's hard to decide whether they're clothed or not. "It's okay," he consoles. "I know why you did."

"I was trying to do the right thing. I never wanted to hurt Connor."

"Neither did I, but sometimes two people can't be kept apart. And I think you agree with me that this feels so damn right for us." He tugs at the strand of hair that hangs loosely by my cheek and twists it around his finger. His thumb strokes the soft surface, pulling gently then releasing the curl. "Do you agree, Trouble? This feels right."

"Yes," I admit. "Yes, it does, but..." I stop speaking again, uncertain whether to tell him what I want to. The truth that could be the end of my time with both brothers.

"But what?" he prompts. His eyes are soft, softer than I've ever seen them. The edges of the lips that have kissed me gently and whispered encouragingly tonight turn up once more.

"When I'm with Connor," I say, before taking a steadying breath. "It feels right too."

"I would hope so," he replies, surprising me with his lack of jealousy. He chuckles before explaining. "You're not a woman to waste people's time, Trouble. You're direct, honest, and independent. I don't see you keeping one of us around to massage your ego."

"I would never do that!"

"I know. That's why Connor and I trust you to explore what's on offer and make the best decision for you. For everyone. Who you see yourself creating a life with."

"I don't want to hurt anyone," I whisper, my voice pained as my gaze drops to my fingers, which are twisting together nervously. "That was never my intention."

"No, but that outcome is inevitable. Because I tell you now, neither my brother nor I are willing to give you up without a fight. As far as I'm concerned, Trouble, you're already mine." He places one strong finger beneath my chin, forcing my eyes upwards and back to his. "I won't give you up, Trouble. What we have is forever, whether you know that now or not. In time, you'll come to realize that you've always been mine. From the first minute I laid eyes on you in the boardroom last September, there was no doubt we would end up here."

"I never wanted to see you again," I tell him, and he smiles. "You were an arsehole."

"But you couldn't resist once I unleashed my relentless charm."

"Something like that." I roll my eyes dramatically, and his hand snaps to my face. He squeezes my cheeks between strong fingers. We stare at one another, the brewing sexual tension we've been trying to ignore heightening again. He grins, his eyes bright and full of life.

"Do you know the best thing about your new addition, Trouble?" I give him a curious look, confused by his change of direction. "Your new jewelry," he confirms.

"I have no idea what is going to come out of that gorgeous mouth of yours," I murmur, my face still held fast in his hand. He smiles again. Fuck, he's beautiful when he smiles.

On first meeting Russell and over the following months, I doubted he ever smiled, but now it seems a much more regular occurrence, and I love the fact they're aimed at me.

"You and I will be healing simultaneously and back to full working order together." He pulls me closer, his warm breath tickles my lips as he talks. "And I promise you this, Trouble. When I do fuck you, you will never forget it. It will remain in your memories forever. Part of me will be with you until the end of time. You'll be marked as mine."

***

Connor's Apartment

My phone buzzed at one in the afternoon when Connor let me know he was on his way home from the office. Russell had fallen asleep on the sofa, and I took the opportunity to leave without any objection.

Once I extricated myself from his arms, I found a light blanket stored in a hallway cupboard. I pulled the fine material over his large frame as he snored gently, lost in whatever dream he was having. Every so often, long eyelashes fluttered as if he was going to wake before falling back into a steady comfortable rhythm of sleep.

Now, I'm sitting in Connor's apartment, waiting for his return. The transition from one man's house to the other's was strangely comfortable. It didn't feel odd moving between them. They're both important to my sanity. My happiness.

With my legs curled beneath me, I'm pretending to read a Stephen King novel I found on his shelves. It's the one I've seen forever about the deadly clown, though I've never read the book or watched the movie. The small snippets I've consumed were enough to tell me I would hate the horror it offered. The idea that something otherworldly is out there waiting to hurt people is unsettling. I've seen enough evil in the real world to do me a lifetime.

The front door opens, and Connor appears. He's dressed in a smart gray suit with a fine black checked pattern. His jacket is open, exposing the crisp white shirt beneath. He pulls the hem from the waistband of his trousers as he walks toward me, then unbuttons two more buttons at his chest. I lay the book open on the sofa beside me, face up.

"Hey," he says before bending to kiss me. "I've missed you."

"I've missed you too." I reach up and ruffle his perfectly styled hair. He closes his eyes momentarily under my touch then takes my wrist, turns it slowly, and places his lips on my skin.

"I've missed you more," he whispers. "Are you enjoying the book?" His focus moves to the literature I was pretending to read, lying disposed of.

"It's okay, a bit tame for me." He smiles naughtily. "But I wanted to see why you thought it was so good, why you own every book this man has written in multiple copies." To one side of the living area is a huge bookcase filled with Connor's favorite reading material.

"Because he's a legend," he tells me. " And I like to collect legendary items." He raises an eyebrow, then smirks. "Both living and inanimate. I'm extremely pleased with the latest addition to my collection of favorite things."

"And what would that be?"

"You." I laugh out loud. "I think I know what the problem is and perhaps why you can't appreciate the words of Mr. King as much as I do." I narrow my eyes, and his glint with mischief. He's going to tease me, it's as clear as day on his face. "It's hard to read a book when it's upside down." I look at the open book lying beside me, the words the wrong way up. I shrug, then bite my lip.

He slides the jacket from his shoulders before folding it neatly and placing it over the back of the sofa. Strong fingers move to the remaining buttons on his shirt, and he undoes them one by one. The shirt falls open, and he releases the cuffs. The white material hits the floor.

"Maybe I should start on this," I suggest, signaling to the book. I pick it up, opening the pages wider. "I really need to find out what I am missing out on, especially now I can understand the words."

Pretending to have my eyes fixed on the ink, I sneak glances as Connor removes his shoes, trousers, and socks. He sits down beside me in only a pair of snug dark boxers, close enough that the hairs on my arms stand on end.

"Don't break the spine," he mutters. "I like to keep my collectables pristine."

"Oops," I say, bending the book wider. The perfect surface strains, and an audible crack sounds. "What are you going to do about it?"

His eyes darken, his stunning mouth twisting, amused by my naughtiness. "Punish you."

"I'm a little tender," I caution, needing to ensure he knows full intercourse is off-limits.

"Your pussy may be, but this mouth of yours looks in perfect working order." Without any warning, Connor stands, turning to face me. He plucks the book from my fingers then throws it onto the floor. "You've damaged a signed first of my favorite novel ever." My heart sinks. I never even thought of looking at the title page. Not being a reader, it never crossed my mind it could be signed or a first . "You're coming with me."

He scoops me from my seat, then throws me over his shoulder. I wriggle to ensure no pressure goes on my sensitive area. Bent double across his body, he carries me easily through to the bedroom. I kick and squeal, then a strong hand connects directly with my ass.

"Quiet," he growls, and the hilarity spills from my lips, my laughter uncontrollable.

"Don't make me laugh," I tell him. "My poor clit can't stand the vibration."

When we arrive at the bedroom, he lowers me onto the perfectly smooth sheets. I lie looking up at him, standing before me practically naked apart from his underwear. He reaches for the shorts I'm wearing and slides them down my legs. I'm bare beneath, wanting to limit the friction against my new piercing. Dark eyes stare down at the silver bar decorating my privates.

"Wow," he mutters as his cock hardens in his boxers. It strains against the material, desperate to be free.

"You like it?" I ask, flashing him a sexy smile, then bend my knees and drop them as wide as comfortable with my new decoration.

"Like? I fucking love it. I can't wait to leverage some orgasms from this newly improved clit of yours."

"Leverage? What kind of description is that?"

"When you leverage something, it means you use it to maximum advantage. And I plan to use every part of you to mine." He crawls onto the bed beside me, lying on his side, propped up on his elbow. "So, if your pussy is off-limits, what can I fuck tonight?"

"I'm sure you'll come up with a solution."

He leans down, taking my mouth with his, strong and dominant. Deft fingers trail over the skin at my throat then move over the cropped tank top I'm wearing. My nipples bud below the fabric, straining as my arousal heightens. The familiar sensation of excitement swirls between my legs. My pussy didn't get the memo that tonight is all about him.

"Move to the edge of the bed," he orders. "On your back with your head over the edge. I'm going to fuck this pretty mouth of yours. Hard."

I move into position, my neck straining back a fraction. He stands in front of me, pulling his boxers down his legs and then kicking them to the side. His cock is hard and heavy, throbbing to be used and hanging at my eye level. I push the straps of my tank top down my body to expose my breasts. Connor loves to play with my tits and I know as he fucks my mouth, he'll appreciate watching them jiggle to the rhythm.

"Open," he orders.

"Yes, sir," I respond, then open my lips wide. He steps closer, placing the tip of his cock in my mouth.

"Close and suck the tip." I do as I'm told and start sucking. His hips push forward, causing more thick cock to slide into my mouth. I suck harder. "Good girl," he praises. "Show me how well you can suck my dick. How much you want me to shoot my load for you."

He withdraws a fraction and I snap my hands up around his thighs, holding him to me. Strong fingers pinch my left nipple and squeeze. I yelp with unexpected discomfort. He pulls his cock out. I blink up at him, and he smiles down.

"This is what's going to happen," he says firmly. "I'm going to fuck your mouth, my mouth to use. You'll lie there and take it. I'll shoot my load over your skin. You'll be covered in me, smell of me, and have no doubt who fucked you and *will* be fucking you for years to come."

"Connor," I mumble, surprised by his directness. The look in his eyes leaves no room for debate. Connor is here to lay claim to me tonight. In his eyes, I'm his and always will be.

"In here, while you and I are fucking," he snaps back, "I'm sir. Do you understand? Don't question me. Don't defy me. Take me. All of me. Everything I'm willing to give you."

"Yes, sir."

"Good girl, now open that fucking mouth so I can fill you with my cock."

My mouth drops open again, and he slides his full length inside. I balk at the unexpected movement, but he withdraws immediately and then re-enters, giving me more time to adjust. My lips wrap around him while my hands still hold his thighs, pulling him to me with all my might.

At first his pace is slow—he enters and withdraws fully with each stroke. I close my eyes, allowing myself to get lost in the moment, enjoying the fact that this man is finding pleasure in using me as he is. The tip of his cock hits the back of my throat, and his fingers move to my breasts. He plays with the soft flesh of my nipples, tugging and teasing as he thrusts.

"Your tits are fucking incredible," he says, his voice deep and animalistic. "I'm going to cover them in my cum. I want to shower you in me, so I smell myself on you all fucking day."

My eyes open and I look up. His are closed, he's completely lost in the moment. His hips work, pushing his rock-hard cock forward, the speed increasing with each stroke. I tighten my grip on him, moving my hands upwards nearer his ass, digging my nails into firm flesh.

With my eyes wide, I watch him struggling to control his orgasm. His face tells me he's close. The quickening of his movements more so. His hands grab my breasts tighter; delicious pain surges through me, an intense pleasure somewhere between pleasure and agony. He groans loudly, pausing his movement then withdrawing his cock from my mouth.

His cum hits the skin of my chest, the warm salty liquid running pleasurably over my throat. The sound emanating from him deepens as he releases himself. His smell invades my nostrils, and I revel in his peak. Him fucking my body makes him so happy, I can see it for myself. And knowing that feels so damn good.

"Fuck, you're amazing," he whispers, his voice breaking. "Even with an out-of-bounds pussy, I can't control myself around you." He turns and walks away toward the bathroom, returning seconds later with a towel. I lie still with my head hanging off the bed, smiling up at him. His cum drips from me to the floor. After dropping to his knees beside my head, he starts to clean the remnants of himself from my skin. "This, what we have, could keep me alive forever. Sam, never leave me. I need you."

"We're special, Connor," I tell him, taken aback by his honesty and his declaration of need.

"Not just special," he murmurs, stunning dark eyes locking onto mine. "You're the elixir of my life. Without you, I'm nothing but a shell."

CHAPTER TWENTY-EIGHT

---•◦•---

Connor's Apartment, The Level

Connor

My alarm rings loudly, my phone vibrating madly on my bedside table. Samantha groans. She's undoubtedly as annoyed by the infuriating noise as I am. I'm wrapped around her, my hand securely on her stomach, holding her close as she faces away from me.

"Morning," I whisper, kissing her shoulder.

"Urgh, what time is it?" She pulls the duvet over her head.

"Six. You start work in an hour and a half. How are you feeling?"

"Sore," she admits, and I chuckle. "This piercing thing perhaps wasn't the best idea."

"Once you're healed, it will be so damn worth it though." My lips move to her neck, and I pull her closer against my abs. She pushes her ass onto my already hard dick, then wiggles gently. "Oh, you're a fucking tease."

"Always," she whispers back sexily. "And that's all you're getting. I need to get up." Dramatically, she pulls the duvet from her face then throws it down the bed, exposing us both. As she moves to leave, I hold on tighter so we remain connected. Warm skin touches skin, nothing between us. "Connor, let me get up."

"No."

"I won't ask again..." she warns, and it only makes me flex my fingers on her flesh. In my mind, I'm asserting my dominance, though deep down I know she's the one in charge.

"And if I don't comply, what will you do? You're mine. You're in my arms. You're under my complete control." I can't see her face, but I imagine the naughty smile on her lips. "What could you threaten me with that would make me give this up? My dick between your ass cheeks is exactly how every morning should begin."

"If you don't do as you're told, I'll withhold sexual favors for a week," she suggests.

"You would never be able to cope without my sexual favors."

She giggles. It's both sweet and sexy. My favorite sound in the whole fucking world. Samantha happy means I'm happy. When I feel like this, all the other complications in my life become completely irrelevant. This woman is the other half of me—of that, I have no doubt.

"I am one hundred percent certain my patience is better than yours," she tells me. "You couldn't keep your hands to yourself for an hour, never mind any longer. You, Mr. Chase, have no self-control."

"You're probably right," I agree, keeping her firmly in my arms. "And before you ask, I'm unwilling to test your theory. It would be better to accept I can't control my hands when it comes to your body."

The alarm sounds again, this time louder. It's a setting I added to my phone after being late to the office multiple times since Samantha entered my life. My schedule is constantly adapting and changing these days to suit hers. If the opportunity arises to have time together, I'll move heaven and earth to make it happen. With her is the only place I want to be, however she'll have me.

"Can you not phone in sick?" I ask her, already knowing the answer would be no.

"No," she says, her jovial mood disappearing. "We have that kidney transplant today. The one with the unwilling donor."

I attempt to stop the conversation before it begins. "You're speculating. There's no evidence she is unwilling or by any means being coerced." Samantha was disappointed when we refused to intervene in the upcoming transplant operation at the hospital. It was difficult explaining to her that sometimes we have to let situations we don't like but are aware of play out in order to gain information or, ultimately, evidence.

"I'm right," she says firmly, moving again. This time I release her, and she shuffles off the edge of the bed. "That girl was in Dr. Rivera's office for all the wrong reasons. I know a frightened person when I see one. She was terrified." She turns to face me, standing at the side of my bed stark naked. Fine-boned hands fall on her hips. "But for her to agree to give part of herself to save a man she doesn't know makes me wonder what she's running from or trying to pay off."

"Still speculation," I mutter, propping myself up on my elbow. "But what you suggest would make a decent crime novel. Maybe you should plot it out." She picks up a pillow then launches it at me. When I remove it from my face, all I can see are her pert buttcheeks stalking off in the direction of my en-suite.

"Fucking lawyers," she shouts over her shoulder. "Stick your speculation up your ass."

I flop onto my back and lie looking up at the ceiling.

My cock remains solid beneath the duvet. I will my mind to think of anything but Samantha. We don't have the time this morning to get carried away with sex, and there's a conversation I need to have with her before she leaves. With the situation she's walking into today and what she's lived through the past forty-eight hours, I need to ensure she's okay, that the crazy turn of events at the abandoned warehouse hasn't affected her more than she realizes.

Ten minutes later, Samantha reappears with a soft white towel wrapped around her torso, a matching one covering her hair. Long, slender legs cross the room back toward the bed. Her blue eyes flick to me, then to the floor.

"Are you okay?" I ask. She shrugs but doesn't look at me as she sits down on the bed. "Talk to me; a lot has happened in the past few days."

"You can say that again..." Her voice trails off, the confident, self-assured woman fading. "We killed a man." The statement is blunt. Samantha's directness is a quality I love. She doesn't sugarcoat information to make it sting less. "Jasper is dead."

"He won't be the last man I kill or order to be disposed of," I tell her, just as frank. "Men have died by mine or my friend's hands before. But I truly believe every bastard deserved it. What he did to you deserved to be punished. His actions triggered his fate, not your vengeance."

"You and I both know that's untrue. My need for revenge poured the concrete into those buckets. I did that knowing full well he would be dumped in the River Thames." She pauses, glances at me, then returns to looking at her feet. Her pearly white teeth sink into soft pink lips. "And I was happy about it."

"How can I help? What do you want to know?" I ask her. I've spent enough time with Samantha to know when she's holding back. When she's desperate to ask a question but is unsure how to.

"Who put him into the river? And was he alive?"

I stare at the back of her head, but she doesn't turn around. Moving beside her, I swing my legs out of the bed so we sit side by side.

"He was alive and awake. He was fully aware of what was happening and how it would end." I keep my explanation clear and concise. She asked a direct question and deserves honesty in return. "Russ and I put him in together." Her head snaps around, wide eyes fixing on my face.

"How did Russ manage that with a cast on?"

"Hunter helped me maneuver him to the edge, but Russ and I lowered him in. He saw the pair of us as he sank. We both executed the bastard on your behalf. We delivered his punishment together. Can you be with a man like that? Like us?" A familiar nervousness bubbles in my stomach. It appears every time I consider Samantha and my future.

"A man who would kill for me?" she asks.

"Yes. Could you be with a man like that?"

"I don't think I could live without him. The darkness in you both is mirrored in me. I enjoyed seeing Jasper's pain, and I want to inflict the same again. I want to make people pay who hurt others."

I look at this beautiful woman I consider to be mine and wonder how much her life has changed since she met my family. Would this part of her have ever surfaced if it wasn't for us? And are the hardened lines and thirst for revenge a good thing in her mind?

To me, she's perfect. These changes only make her even more desirable. With each day, my reliance on her grows, and I've never felt more connected to anyone in my life.

***

Samantha

Varley Medical

The elevator doors slide open, and I walk out onto the fourth floor of Varley Medical. My fingers rise to my lanyard, securely hanging around my neck, in search of comfort. Today, I would rather be anywhere but here. The uneasy feeling in my stomach has grown since I left The Level. With every step I took toward work, the more certain I became that something will go terribly wrong today.

After trying to convince Russell to interfere in the upcoming transplant today and him refusing, I tried to convince Connor that he could somehow delay the process. Neither of them were willing to step in without more evidence. Russell wasn't even willing to contact Dr. Rivera, who thinks the world of him, to ask any questions.

"I don't want to open conversation with her," he told me. "The last thing I want is to encourage any sort of communication between us."

"But—" I challenged, and for once he silenced me with a look.

"No more discussions on the subject. Go to work, keep quiet, and learn what you can. Don't put yourself in danger, and don't ask questions that promote dangerous answers." His shrewd eyes held mine. When I looked away, he growled for me to return to his stare. "I trust you, Trouble. But I don't have faith in anyone else in that hospital. If what we believe is happening there is true, anyone could be involved. Keep your head down and mouth shut. We'll intervene when necessary."

"The girl, though, what if she's innocent?" I continued, desperate for him to see my point of view. "If she's vulnerable and they are taking advantage of her, I can't stand by and watch that happen."

"You must!" He'd lost control a little then, a glimpse of the unhinged man who followed me for months reappearing briefly. Russell has been so calm since his accident in so many ways; his emotional outburst was a surprise. He took my hands in his, holding them to his chest. "You, Trouble, are the most important fucking thing in my life. You have to put your own safety first. As I said, I trust you to be sensible. Prove me wrong, and I'll lock you up in this penthouse and never let you out without supervision." I smile to myself as I relive our conversation.

When I reach the reception desk, Bryan clears his throat, causing me to look up. He smirks, then returns to focusing on his computer screen.

"Good morning," I say. "Why do I think you have something cheeky to say?"

"Me?" he replies without as much as a glance. "I would never tease."

"Bullshit. Go on, spit it out."

His blue eyes move back to mine and widen. He cocks his head to one side and smiles wide. "Whose bed were you in when you got out of the elevator?" he asks. "Casanova or his brother's? I'd love some details if you were willing to tell, because someone was fucking you as you walked across this floor. That face of yours was lit up like a Christmas tree."

"A lady never tells." I wink at him, turn on my heel, and go to walk off.

"Spoilsport," he mutters. "And there was me thinking we're friends."

I retrace my steps, then place my hands on his desk before leaning forward. He rises a fraction from his seat closer to my lips. "I'll tell you a secret," I say, my voice low and conspiratorial. He leans in closer, his breathing quickening with excitement as he thinks I am going to divulge some big, juicy secret. "Connor likes cream in his coffee, but Russell prefers it black. Both of them love a cookie in the morning."

"Fuck's sake, Sam. Unless cookie is a code word for blow job or anal, then I am deeply disappointed in your lack of transparency."

I shrug unruffled by his complaint, and he throws himself back down in the chair. "As I said, a lady doesn't tell."

"You're no fucking lady," he mutters. "You're fucking two of the most gorgeous, eligible men in London. That's greedy, and ladies are not greedy."

"You're just jealous."

"Totally," he agrees with a small smile. "But allow me to wallow in my self pity. Your life gets more exciting as mine gets more complex."

"What's happened now?" I ask him. Between Bryan's kids and his ex, there's always drama.

"I received a letter advising me that the witch will be reducing her child support payments due to her unemployed status." He stops typing and drops his head into his hands. "I'm not sure how I'm going to survive, Sam. I can barely make ends meet as it is."

"But she pays next to nothing!" I squeal, infuriated for him. "There must be a way we can fight this. She's married to a billionaire!"

"Fighting costs money, and money is one thing I don't have."

"Bryan..." I trail off, not knowing what to say but my mind whirling with possibilities of how I can help.

"It's okay," he says. "You can't fix my situation any more than I can. Just talking to you helps. Thanks for being my personal agony aunt." I laugh, but deep down my heart breaks for him. Bryan is one of my favorite people; he's one of the only joyous things in this damn hospital. "Anyway, you better be getting on. The dragon will arrive soon, and we don't want her to find you standing around talking to me." With a salute, I turn and walk off toward the staffroom to prepare for my shift.

My morning rounds are relatively quiet. As I visit each patient to wash and change them, I enjoy the basic interaction. Both the transplant giver and receiver's rooms are empty, however. The early hour of the operation is a surprise; normally, Dr. Rivera doesn't operate until eleven in the morning.

As I reenter the reception area to quiz Bryan, the doctor herself comes screaming down the hallway. She blasts into the waiting area in her scrubs, pulling the latex gloves from her fingers. There are no patients yet; only Bryan and I are in the room.

Bryan jumps from his seat, running to her and grabbing her shoulders. Tears stream down her face, and she drops to her knees. Unsure what's happening, I stand and gape at the scene in front of me as she crumbles before my eyes.

"What is wrong, doctor?" Bryan asks, his voice surprisingly firm but kind.

"She's dead," she wails in answer. Bryan's glance flicks to me then to the back to the crazed woman in his arms.

"The patient?"

"I need to leave. I need to get out of here." She pulls herself from his grasp. He steps toward her, but she holds up her hands defensively. "Don't touch me!" Her eyes blaze, and she drops the rubber gloves on the floor.

"Doctor, if you lost a patient..."

"Not a patient," she hisses. "A lifeline, and now the clock is ticking down for me too."

Without giving either of us the chance to ask any further questions, she turns and runs for the back staircase. Bryan turns to me.

"I'll go to the operating theater and see what's happening," I tell him.

"And I'll try to calm her down." He takes off in the direction Dr. Rivera took.

When I reach the operating room, I find the remaining surgical staff tidying up the dead body of the donor patient. The young woman lies on the table, cold, gray and gone. Everyone in the room looks shellshocked, and seem to be going about their business on autopilot.

"What happened?" I ask, as I push open the door. Four sets of eyes turn to me, but no one answers. "When did the doctor leave?"

One older nurse walks over and stands directly under my nose. She's short but lifts her chin defiantly before speaking.

"As soon as that trace line went flat, that treacherous bitch ran," she spits. I blink at her, stunned by her venom. "Doctors don't run when a patient dies; they act professionally and do their duty of telling the family. They take responsibility if any mistakes have been made."

"You think there was a mistake?"

Her face twists in displeasure with the question. I focus on her, trying to push her to say more. After a few seconds she relents, sighing and rubbing her forehead before answering. "That girl was no more suitable to be a donor than a child is. She was weak and malnourished. The operation should never have gone ahead."

"And yet Dr. Rivera signed off on the operation?" I ask to confirm what I already know, but I want to hear from the senior nurse's lips.

"Yes, she signs off on every surgery in this department. Whatever she's involved in, it's bad. And judging by her actions, her career is over. Something despicable happened today in that operating theater, and I feel sick from being made part of it."

Chapter Twenty-Nine

<hr />

The Level Boardroom

June 2023

Russell

"Is there still no sign of Josephine Rivera?" I ask again for what must be the hundredth time in the past few weeks since she disappeared.

"I told you," Damon says, "the doctor and her husband have gone off the grid. None of my old contacts have turned up anything. After she ran from the hospital that day, they cleared their house and literally disappeared into thin air." My friend raises an eyebrow, which only encourages my defiance of his explanation.

"People don't just vanish."

"No, they *choose* to disappear or are taken care of. The question we should really be asking is why?" Damon straightens his shoulders and leans back in his chair.

My friend reappeared from Scotland with his daughter and the woman who stitched him back together only days ago. It took three months of groveling for him to win Emma over after he smashed her heart to pieces, but it's heartwarming to see their family together finally. They'll now have their happy ending, all three of them.

Harrison and Connor are sitting, chatting quietly between themselves. Their voices raise a fraction as their debate becomes more heated. Hunter stands, then walks over to the squabbling men, laying a hand on each of their shoulders.

"Now, now, boys," he says. "What would the two most mellow men in the room be arguing about that the rest of us don't know?"

"Him," Connor spits, wagging a finger in Harrison's direction. "Him having information and not telling the rest of us."

"I didn't keep any information from you. I was doing my due diligence, ensuring all my facts were correct." He straightens his shoulders and shoots my brother a look that offers no argument. "It's called being a professional."

"No, it's being an arsehole. Here we all are, searching for that bitch of a doctor and her husband, and you've bloody found them."

"I didn't say I found them. I said I know where the money came from. There's quite a difference. Emma wanted to double-check her findings before telling you all," Harrison says, his tone relaxed.

"Emma did?" Damon interjects, his attention grabbed by the mention of his girlfriend's name.

"Do you know any other Emmas I work with?"

Damon bristles, clearly annoyed by the obvious fact Harrison pointed out. "I wasn't aware she had been working."

The two men stare at one another. They've had plenty of similar disagreements since Emma started at our law firm last year. She's still in training but proving extremely useful within our business. She has a sharp eye for discrepancies in documentation and tracking down the truth when something doesn't feel right.

After her split from Damon in January, it was Harrison who arranged for a six-month contract on a small cottage up in Scotland for her. He told her to go away and take some time to herself to regroup and focus on what she wants in the future. It doesn't surprise me that she's been working for him directly but under the radar. Sometimes, I think she would be a better detective than a lawyer, but having the skills of both makes her invaluable.

"Well, she has," Harrison tells him. "Emma has been trawling through Josephine Rivera's finances. Did you know their house was being foreclosed on last October?" he asks, turning to me.

I shrug. "No, why would I? My relationship with Josie is ad hoc, especially since she returned to her husband." The information doesn't surprise me; her husband has a reputation for bouncing between wealth and bankruptcy proceedings.

"Ah, right."

"Waite, you're really beginning to piss me off," Hunter grumbles. "Stop being so fucking dramatic and tell us what Emma found out." He pulls his trusty knife from his waistband and spins it between his fingers. "Who can I make into a piece of artwork?"

Harrison stands, then walks over to the window. He looks down at the city below. The sun is beginning to set, and the orange glow of evening shines behind the already-illuminated buildings.

"Before the bank could foreclose on the Rivera house, they miraculously came into enough money to clear the debt. The payment came from Varley Medical Funding Inc., a direct payment into the Riveras' personal joint account."

"Why would a medical funding group pay a doctor directly?" I say, frustrated with how slowly Harrison is parting with information. "If it were research, surely the funds would be deposited directly into whatever organization's account."

"You would think so. Emma did some digging on Varley Medical Funding, assuming it was attached to the main hospital. It turns out there's very little connecting the two businesses beyond one sole director on the board.

"Emma has been through every bit of paperwork she can find on the business. Apart from the payment to the Riveras, it seems Varley Medical Funding has supported very few causes. A few small-scale cancer research initiatives and a nationwide program into dementia in local communities. "

"And do we know what initiative the payment to the Rivera's was meant to fund?" I ask, perplexed by the random evidence of goodness knows what.

"Nothing more than the description line on the bank payment. Rivera Organ Study. The payment came from a bank in Bermuda that's well known for protecting customer data. There are no details of such a study listed anywhere we can find," Harrison says.

"So, what are we thinking?" Connor asks. "That the payment to cover the house is actually a loan. How much was it?" Strangely, no one asked what should have been an obvious question before now.

"One-point-five million pounds."

"What? Is their house worth that?" I stammer, stunned by the amount.

"According to my property guy, no. The house is valued at one-point-two million. Two payments were made from the Rivera's account within twenty-four hours of the large deposit."

"Let me guess," Damon says. "One to the bank and the other to an untraceable destination."

"Bingo," Harrison confirms. "The house was not only in arrears but also in negative equity. Clearing the debt to the bank cost just under one-point-four million. Sadly for the Riveras, they bought when property prices were high and have remortgaged multiple times during various financial disputes and, of course, their divorce."

"People are insane," Hunter mutters. "Marriage is for idiots. To get divorced then remarry the same mug is certifiable."

"Devane, you *are* married," Damon points out, and Hunter shrugs his shoulders. "You and Harrison are currently the only two married men here."

"Only on paper. It's all for show. I've not seen her in years. Isabella does her thing, and I do mine."

"You mean she told you to fuck off," Connor suggests, and Hunter glares at him.

"The feeling was mutual."

"Do you think you'll get married again?" I ask Damon before I can stop myself. I immediately regret it. My friend's eyes come to me, but instead of anger, there's only confusion.

"In all honesty, I don't know. I've only just got Emma back, and with my track record, I'm praying I don't fuck it up again. Marriage isn't off the table, but it won't be soon." His answer is simple and straightforward: he honestly doesn't know. "I don't even know if she would want to. We've never discussed it. She's home. That's all that matters. Annie has her mother back." His use of the word "mother" doesn't go unnoticed, but no one comments and every man in the room relaxes a fraction. Damon finally accepts the truth that Emma has always been his daughter's mother.

"Anyway, as happy as I am for Damon and Emma, can we get back to the task in hand?" Connor says. "Is the Riveras' house still in their name? It's been sitting empty since they disappeared."

After the couple vanished, Hunter's men have been keeping tabs on the house they seemed so desperate to keep. To obtain a huge payment of money from an unknown source to allow you to pay your mortgage off and then abandon the house indicates they've run for their lives or are being held somewhere. If the funds received were a loan... My mind starts whirling with possibilities.

"After the house debt was cleared, were any regular outgoing payments made?" I question, and everyone focuses on me. "If the payment was actually a loan, perhaps we're missing the repayments."

"Nothing beyond the usual living costs covered by Dr. Rivera's wages have left that account since the large deposit. And there's been no movement beyond direct debits since they disappeared."

"Do we know who owns this funding company?" Connor asks.

"This is where it gets interesting," Harrison says. "The sole director is named Maeve Carlisle. When Emma tracked her down, it turned out she was an eighty-year-old single lady living in Manchester with no knowledge of the company. She said her son Den had her sign some paperwork a while ago but didn't know what it was for. It was for her security, was all he would tell her."

"And do we know where we can track Den down?" Hunter asks.

"No, sadly, Maeve relies on him contacting her. He told her he has no phone. She gave us a basic description of dark hair and blue eyes. She couldn't even provide a photo. Emma looked at the old lady's finances; she lives on her pension plus a monthly payment from a private fund, again in Bermuda. She could find no trace of any living relatives or, in fact, a son called Den." Harrison sighs before continuing. "The only true connection we can find is that Maeve attends a club for dementia sufferers, which is one of the programs funded by Varley Medical Funding."

"So let me get this straight," I say, needing to summarize the nonsense spoken in the boardroom today. "The Riveras obtained money to clear their debts plus extra from what seems to be a dubious medical funding organization. The sole director of said company doesn't know of its existence. She's in her eighties and signed paperwork that she had no understanding of on the say-so of a son who doesn't seem to exist. And she attends a memory loss clinic of some kind funded by the organization she supposedly owns."

"In a nutshell, yes." Harrison rolls his shoulders, unruffled by the bizarre situation he just described. "He usually contacts her by phone. Checking the phone records, I see regular weekly calls from a US mobile phone but located in London. It's a burner, so there are no customer details.

"I told her he was due to receive some maturing investments, but we had lost his contact details. We asked Maeve to alert us if Den contacted her. As a reminder, I left a note on the pad next to her handset on the table in her house. She seems to be able to read still, though is quite confused when talking. If this man is a scammer, which he clearly is, the lure of money should bring him out of the woodwork."

"Maybe, but he is also fucking dangerous," I say, uncertain. "This all seems such a damn mess with no real resolution. I've finished studying the hospital paperwork from transplants completed over the past year, but there's a lot of missing documentation. I doubt we'll ever truly know who received which organs and what operations were completely lawful. Most of it could be passed off as incompetence and poor administration. Even the poor woman who died on the table's documents have gone. The system had a *bug*, apparently."

"A bug my arse. Has Samantha heard anything at the hospital?" Hunter asks. "Medical staff love to gossip, especially during their breaks."

"How would you know?" Connor challenges.

"You see it on those medical drama shows all the time. Staff room antics."

"They also all sleep with each other. You can't assume real life from fiction," I tell him.

He responds with a grin. "Maybe Samantha would get to have some fun with doctors if you two didn't keep her tied to your beds," he replies cheekily, and I narrow my eyes as Connor straightens, ready to argue.

Hunter still can't get over us both dating the same girl. He would be extremely disappointed to learn I haven't even slept with her yet. However, that will soon change as my cast comes off tomorrow. The idea of finally being able to have her is both exciting and terrifying. A monumental day for her and myself but also the start of the clock ticking down on one of her relationships.

"Sam has switched departments since the doctor left. She's been removed from her old team and placed in day units. She can continue her training and be home every night. Her degree has been delayed for twelve months until we find a suitable safe placement." Connor puffs out his chest, proud of what he negotiated with the board of directors. "She's not allowed to speak to anyone from Floor Four until every staff member has been fully investigated and cleared of any wrongdoing."

"Not that either of you is controlling," Damon chimes in with an eye roll. "Where are the other staff?"

"At home on full pay until this is all put to bed."

"What about the reception guy? Bryan, was it?" Harrison questions.

"Samantha keeps wanting to talk to him. She says he has enough issues at home without losing her friendship. I've arranged for his cell to be blocked from contacting her," I say.

"If he's in as a poor position financially and mentally as Trouble tells us, he would be the ideal sidekick for Dr. Rivera to utilize to push this whole scam through. Desperation makes good people do crazy things."

"And Sam agreed not to contact him?" Harrison's tone conveys skepticism.

"She knows what the right thing to do is. We've told her not to take risks with her safety." I look to my brother, who nods in agreement. "Neither of us will stand for her pigheadedness, or her being responsible for her own demise. But Bryan is off-limits until we are satisfied that he isn't a threat."

"Fair enough," Hunter says with a shrug. "But I don't for one minute believe that little ball of fire will do anything because you two tell her to." He laughs out loud. "I mean, come on, she's managed to get you both to agree to share."

"Fuck off," Connor snaps. My eyes move to my brother, his expression furious. "It won't be like this forever. The arrangement stands only until she decides."

"Decides what?" Hunter shoots back. "Whose dick feels better? Wake up, boys—this woman has you both over a barrel, and you're letting her run the show. It's time to man up."

"She'll pick," I say bluntly. "When the time is right."

"And when is that?" he continues, clearly having the bit between his teeth. "When she's bored of both and moves onto the next guy? I wouldn't stand for it."

"That's why you're alone with a wife that hates your guts," my brother tells him. "Because you're too frightened to fucking try and possibly get hurt."

Hunter moves so fast that we barely see it, then his blade sits at Connor's throat. He leans down so the two men are nose to nose. Damon goes to rise, but Hunter stops him in his tracks with a glance.

"Remember who you work for," he snarls at my brother. "Always treat the man in charge with respect."

"I work with you, not for you," Connor snaps back. "And do what you want to me with that knife of yours. It will be nothing compared to the pain if I lose her."

"You're pathetic." Hunter releases him and steps back.

"No, I'm aware. And I know exactly who I want and what will make me happy. I hope one day you come to that realization, too."

"Back to the hospital," Harrison says. His voice is firm, wanting to defuse the tense situation. "I'm not sure that we can right every wrong."

"If we can bring those at the head of it to justice," Damon pronounces, "we will have done our job."

"This isn't a job." Hunter opens his arms wide. "This is a calling. Righting wrongs is exactly what we are all meant to be doing. Taking down the bad guys one by one."

"By breaking the law," Connor points out, clearly keen to continue to provoke the most dangerous man in London.

Hunter waves his comment away. Thankfully, he's no longer looking for violence.

"Laws were made to be broken. Morals need to stand forever." He puffs out his chest dramatically and grins. "And we, my friends, always stand up for what is morally right."

"You tell yourself that," I say, shaking my head.

"I do, and I will." Hunter turns and walks toward the private elevator. "And I sleep like a baby every fucking night," he calls over his shoulder as he leaves.

CHAPTER THIRTY

---◆◆◆---

Russell's Penthouse, The Level

Russell

When I return to my apartment, the smell of freshly cooked food hits me hard as I enter. I step into my home and make my way directly to the kitchen, but instead of finding Mrs. D as I expect, it's Samantha behind the stovetop.

"You hungry?" she asks with a smile. "A free man's food will always taste better than an incarcerated one."

"Slight dramatization, Trouble. My leg was in a cast. I wasn't locked up." I limp over to her, my foot still swollen and the relief of freedom still throbbing. "I can't believe it took so long to get this damn thing off." My arms slide around her middle as I stand behind her, bend, and lean my chin on her shoulder.

"Well, if you won't heal as the doctors tell you to, then you need the medical intervention for longer." She giggles softly as I blow on her neck before placing my lips on her skin.

"Are you saying I was badly behaved?"

"Always, but I like it," she whispers, keeping her eyes fixed on what I assume is chili in the pot she is stirring. "Being a good boy wouldn't suit you."

"You like bad boys, Trouble?"

"I'm with you, aren't I?"

"And what about my brother? Is he good or bad?" She freezes in my arms, her anxiousness about discussing the situation clear. "It's okay; there are no secrets. It's alright to mention you and him in front of me. I'm well aware of the situation."

"Connor isn't too keen to talk about you." Once again, she falls silent, and I sense her mood dipping from jovial to melancholy. It would be easy to think, as Hunter does, that Samantha has all the perks of her current romantic setup, but I know she's really struggling with the conflict. Both the ongoing one between my brother and myself, and also one within her.

"That's not surprising. He's always been the more sensitive of the two of us. Even though he started all this with his suggestion, I believe he struggles most." She turns in my arms, blinking up at me with wide eyes. "I've thought a lot about walking away, leaving you both to be happy. Perhaps that would be best before we take things any further."

"Where did you come from?" she asks, her voice quiet.

"Who?"

"This man here." Five fine fingers with bright red nails drop to my chest and spread over my heart. "The sane and considerate one. The man who thinks of putting others before himself. Where is the unhinged, possessive lunatic I met?"

"He's still here, but he's fallen for a girl whose happiness is the most important thing in his world. He's learned to control his darkness so others aren't hurt by his actions."

"Could you really let me go? After waiting all this time, could you allow me to walk away and create a life only with Connor?" she asks. We hold each other's gaze, lost in the words of the question asked. Before I can answer, she does.

"Because I can't. Even if it's only once, I need this to happen. I need you to make love to me." She rises up on tiptoe, kissing me softly. When she pulls back, tears run down her cheeks. "Why does this feel like the beginning of the end?"

"Because it is," I say, my heart breaking. "We're all moving closer to a conclusion with each day that passes, even though we don't know the outcome."

I should tell her about the agreement Connor and I made before taking her to bed, but I want no more distractions or difficult conversations. Despite knowing I should walk away and allow the two people I love most to be happy, I'll be selfish one last time. She will be partly mine for a short while, but I accept he'll always be her first choice. She was his first, after all.

What started as a competition became a lifeline to my soul. Samantha has shown me I can love and be loved in return. But she was never mine to keep, and I know that now. My mother told me as a small boy to enjoy each moment as we are never guaranteed tomorrow. That advice means more today than it ever will. My moments with Samantha will be cherished long after my fingertips leave her skin.

"Come with me," I say. "Switch this all off, and come spend time with me."

She turns to remove the pot from the stovetop then twists the dial to zero. I take her fingers before leading her onto the outdoor terrace beyond the glass sliding doors. We weave slowly through the pots laid out across the space, me walking stiffly a fraction in front and her following behind.

As we round the corner, my infinity pool comes into view. It's pristine, crystal clear water glinting under the warm summer sun.

We come to a stop at the edge of the pool, and I turn to face her. She smiles softly up at me, her cheeks highlighted with a soft pink glow. "Do you know how often I've thought about bringing you out here, Trouble?" I say.

"I would assume a lot."

"Every fucking day since I met you I've pictured you up here, strutting around in a tiny bikini while I lay back and watch."

"I don't have a bikini here." The words are simple but filled with sexual innuendo. "I'll need to go home and get one."

"If you think I'm letting you leave this penthouse now..." I step forward so our bodies connect. Her soft breasts give way to my chest, and I wrap my arms around her, spreading my fingers across her ass. "You're going nowhere, Trouble, until I'm done with you."

"Done doing what?" she replies cheekily.

"Filling you full of me, so I drip from that sweet pussy of yours." My dirty words don't appear to affect her. She rolls her eyes then shrugs, the upward movement of her shoulders jiggling her breasts a little.

"You've never seen my pussy." She bites her lip, knowing she's pushing my buttons. "How do you know she's sweet?"

"Because every part of you I've tasted so far is honey, and I have no doubt you will be the most delicious thing I've ever eaten."

In the corner of my terrace is a large daybed draped with white satin. I take her hand once more and lead her across the remaining distance. We stop at the end of the bed, and when I turn back to her again, she eyes me warily. Uncertainty stabs in my chest for a second. This feels like the last time we can walk away and not change our relationship irrevocably. Although the past months have been filled with sweet kisses and talk of what we want to happen, now we're here, I need to be sure she wants this too.

I can't ignore the reality that after she leaves me, if her relationship with my brother progresses to marriage and forever, the fact will remain that I fell in love with my sister-in-law. I slept with her and tried to build a future together that was never mine to have. My conscience rears its unfamiliar head again. I've second-guessed myself more since meeting Samantha than I have during my whole life.

She brings out a part of me I both love and hate, a man who yearns for love with a woman who loves him too. The joy of normal family life. A man who constantly questions what's right and who puts others before himself. It's not what I ever saw myself being or becoming. The asshole is making way for the gentleman, but the man coming forward knows he's going to get hurt. That fact isn't enough to stop him craving the love he shouldn't have.

"Are you sure you want to do this, Trouble?" I ask. She drops her eyes to the floor, and I place a finger under her chin to lift them back to meet mine. "Because say no now, and I'll stand down. I'll take you back to Connor, kiss you goodbye, and we can forget this happened."

"I could never forget," she mumbles.

"We can try. My brother deserves happiness, and so do you; this is a complication none of us need." I drop my hand away and step back. My sanity, for once, surfaces. Her hands snap forward, grabbing my arms, and her fingers lock tight to my skin.

"No," she hisses. "You promised. You promised that once you had the cast removed, we would take things further. Why put the time into getting to know me? Why look out for me if you planned to walk away. Was it all the fun of the chase? And now that you have me here, in your home, willing to sleep with you, have I lost your interest?"

"You could never lose my interest, Trouble," I reply simply. "I've thought about this day more times than I wish to admit."

"Well, fucking stop thinking about it and start living it."

"But..."

"No more buts, what ifs, or excuses. I'm standing here in front of you saying yes. Take my word as the truth and enjoy me. We need this, both of us."

"It's all so fucked up," I mutter, glancing over the city rooftops.

"Someone was always going to get hurt," she challenges.

"From the moment I decided to allow my infatuation to take me to Guilty Pleasures, yes, I made sure someone was going to get hurt."

"That's not what I meant," she whispers angrily.

"Maybe not, but it's the truth." I close my eyes, turning my face upward and allowing the soft summer rays to warm my skin. My head tells me that no matter her argument, I need to take her hand and lead her to my brother's apartment. I must remove her from my life before I take this final step. But my soul knows that no matter how reformed I feel, this is one experience I'm not willing to give up.

When I reopen my eyes, I find her standing, still holding my arms, but with tears on her cheeks. She sniffles softly.

"Don't give up on me," she says sadly.

"Letting you go isn't giving up on you. It's giving you freedom. It's protecting my heart and yours. It is protecting you from making a choice." She doesn't respond, but her fingers loosen a fraction. I will her to hold on, to show me that she doesn't agree. For once, I'm looking to be led. "The last thing I want to be is more pain in your life."

"That result is inevitable." Unable to stomach her hurt or my own, I do what I knew I always would. I pull my arms from her grip, then take her face in my palms. "Don't do this," she mumbles against my lips.

"I don't think I could walk away now if my life depended on it," I growl, then take her mouth with mine. We kiss, but it's not sweet, slow, or sensual like most of our precious moments. Our lips collide, our tongues roaming together, wanting more with each taste. Her arms wrap around my neck as I lock mine around her middle, holding her soft body close enough that I feel every inch of her. "You, Trouble, are the most beautiful woman ever created. No one will ever convince me otherwise."

"I told you I didn't believe you," she replies against my lips. Her warm breath touching my skin.

"Didn't believe what?"

"That gentle isn't a word in your vocabulary." I still as she repeats back how I described myself a matter of months ago. "You, Russell Chase, in your own warped and crazy way, are one of the sweetest men I have ever known. And I've fallen for you."

The shoestring straps of the mint cotton summer dress she wears sit on her shoulders. I slide a single finger beneath one and pull it down onto her arm, then repeat with the second strap. The dress is loose-fitting and drapes from her breasts in swathes of fabric. It hides her curves but emits a feminine glow that is oh-so-fucking appealing.

My hand moves to her throat, my fingers wrapping around the back of her neck while my thumb strokes her windpipe. Her skin is sensitive beneath my touch; with each caress, she shivers. I kiss her again, this time more gently, taking a moment to enjoy her taste. My hand glides down over her shoulder, skimming her skin as our tongues dance.

Finding her straps again with each hand, I encourage the garment downward. The material falls to the floor and lies in a pool at her feet, exposing plump breasts with perfectly erect nipples. She stands before me in only a small white thong after slipping her feet from her sandals.

Crouching, I move to her panties, pinching the lace between my fingers and sliding them down her body. She steps out of them, and I collect her discarded clothes from the floor, folding each item and laying it on the bed. She watches my every move with eyes I could get lost in for days.

We don't speak as I unbutton my white shirt, remove it from my body and carefully place it next to her clothes. My trousers, socks, and boxers go the same way until we are left standing naked in front of one another. Even though I've seen her in next to nothing dancing and practically naked under my brother's touch, she's more beautiful than I remember this close. Part of me wants to stand here and stare, enjoy the view as long she will allow me.

Her focus drops to my cock, which hangs heavy and hard between my legs, already throbbing with the need for her attention. My eyes follow hers as she looks up and flushes red, the glorious color coating her skin from her cheeks to her breasts.

"Come," I say, holding out a hand. She takes it and we walk side by side to my pool. Five small steps take us down into the beautifully warm water; it's deep enough to cover my body to the top of my chest. Samantha, being shorter, is covered to her neck. I take her in my arms and lift her up onto my waist. My cock rests against her pussy as we make our away across the pool to the edge. The water laps around us as we move, creating small waves. The glass wall with its chrome railing looks out over the city, buzzing beneath the evening sun.

"What if someone sees us?" she says, suddenly aware of our surroundings.

"Do you care?" I ask her.

"I'm not sure I do." She giggles, that fucking sound that speaks directly to my soul. My cock hardens to the breaking point as my heart swells with her happiness. I never believed the saying that you'll just know when you meet the one person you're meant to be with. As I watched my friends fall in love, I never truly thought that time would come for me. It burns that this love won't continue beyond a few months now that we're here at this point.

I push her up against the glass, her legs around my abs and my fingers in her hair. "That ass of yours will look so fucking sexy right now on view to the world. I can imagine your cheeks spreading over the glass." I move my hand down to her breast, cupping her gently then squeezing. My fingers go to her nipple and twist, caressing the bud between my fingertips. She groans. "You like that, Trouble?"

"Uh huh," she mumbles, her voice barely audible. I move to her second nipple, repeating the gentle encouragement for them to stand tall until I'm looking down at two perfectly aroused nipples on soft, plump breasts. They breach the water, and I lower my lips to exposed flesh, scattering kisses over the mounds. Wrapping one arm beneath her ass, the other moves lower, and I step back a fraction to allow my fingers access between her legs.

"Keep those legs wide, Trouble," I whisper, splaying my palm over her pussy. I enjoy being able to touch where I've most desperately wanted to for months. We stand together, me holding her most intimately and her playing with my hair. She grins at me unexpectedly, and I laugh in surprise. "What's so funny?" She shakes her head, then looks away. "Trouble, tell me."

"Of all the ways I imagined my first time with you being..." She chuckles again. "In your pool, in front of the city, was never where I imagined."

"I am a man of surprises."

"I learn that every day," she says, then kisses my lips. "You just become more perfect." It's my turn to laugh then, and I bury my face in her neck.

"Of all the things I've been called in my life, perfect has never been one them."

"You're the perfect blend of passion, love, and insanity for me."

A single finger finds her clit, and I push her piercing gently. "I love this. My own personal fuck button. One touch and that body of yours stands to attention," I whisper in her ear. She flutters under my touch. It is so fucking sexy.

Slowly, I circle the spot, and her legs flex around me as the sensation begins to build. She rests her head on my shoulder as I work without haste, her body tensing and relaxing as the familiar build of a woman's orgasm begins. I slide my finger inside, adding a second immediately as her slick walls encase my digits. I pump, and her body sucks me in, holding fast. I place my thumb on the bar over her clit as I move my fingers. She groans again, this time deeper, more needy.

"My girl is ready," I whisper." Does she want our long-awaited first time?"

"I've always been ready. Take me."

I don't need a second request, immediately removing my hand from her legs and grabbing an ass cheek in each palm. My cock lines up at her entrance, and I push forward carefully. She's fucking tight. I need to thrust my hips to encourage her to open for me.

"Come on, Trouble, let me in." I push again, her body giving way more but still resisting. Her pussy vibrates around me, the sensation intense. "Oh, Trouble, I can feel that pussy of yours wanting to come. Have patience, baby girl. Let me work you for a little while." I stop moving, and she flexes her hips in impatience.

"Please, Russ," she whimpers.

"Enjoy it, Trouble. Close those pretty eyes and feel me, what it feels like to have a man obsessed with you inside." I kiss her shoulder. "Let that pretty pussy of yours hold me." I rock my hips slowly, and my cock throbs for me to move harder. Wait, I will myself. I want this moment to last until the end of time. With each small stroke, she tightens more and it's fucking ecstasy.

"I'll always hold you," she whispers, and the joy of the moment breaks.

"Don't make a promise you can't keep."

"I have every intention of keeping my promises."

Needing to move on from the heartache her words trigger, I move faster, thrusting forward hard. Her fingers grab my hair, pulling my head back as I move. She takes my mouth hard, her tongue diving deep. It feels like she's marking me as I claim her with my cock.

"Come for me, Russ," she says, her breath catching on each word. "Fill me up like a good boy so there will be part of you in me for longer. Show me I'm your girl."

I slam her hard against the glass, pushing my dick as deep as it can go. She screams as her body erupts, her pussy clamping tight, demanding I give her what she wants. My cock jerks on her command, and I empty myself fully, the relief of finally having enjoyed her the way I wanted mixed with sadness. I stay inside her as long as I possibly can in an attempt to burn this amazing feeling into my mind, so it will be forever remembered.

I carry her over toward the daybed, stepping out of the water with her wrapped around my body. I lay her down, then grab a blanket from the stack folded by the side of the bed before joining her and covering us both.

We lie beside one another, breathing in unison, unspeaking. When I glance over, she's smiling, her eyes fixed on the white canopy above. My heart sinks; I know I need to have the conversation my brother and I agreed would happen. The one we discussed would take place as soon as Samantha and I took the step to being sexual.

"Trouble," I say softly

"Uh-huh."

"We need to talk. Now we've had sex, we need to discuss what this means for us all." She rolls onto her side and then props herself up on her elbow. Her expression changes from relaxed to uncertain.

"What is there to talk about?" she asks, a quiver in her tone. "We were always going to have sex."

"Today, like you said, marks the beginning of the end." I attempt to keep my tone calm but even I sense the nerves in my voice.

"Stop speaking in riddles, Russ. Fucking tell me what you're on about." She scowls, annoyed by my evasive words.

"Connor and I agreed once your and my relationship progressed to this stage that..." I stop speaking, my concerns getting the better of me. She's going to be furious we made this decision without her, but both my brother and I needed a plan, a boundary as to when we would be released from this love triangle. We needed to know it would end and that one of us would win.

"You mean when we had sex," she states.

"Yes. We agreed that would start a clock on when you were to choose." Her features fall in horror. Pain flashes in her eyes, betrayal staring me in the face.

"You never thought to discuss this with me?" Her pitch is high and her words rapid.

"We agreed this was best, and that it would allow both relationships to progress as naturally as possible," I attempt to explain, but the look she gives me tells me that it's not accepted. "You were always going to have to choose, Trouble. Neither Connor nor I have said differently."

She rolls onto her back and stares blankly up at the canopy again. There's no smile or warm feeling now. "How long do I have?" she says sullenly, all the fun of what we shared evaporating with each syllable.

CHASE

"Three months. You have ninety days to decide which of us you want to keep."

Chapter Thirty-One

The Estate, Buckinghamshire

September 2023

Samantha

Sitting at the dressing table in my hotel suite, I watch the second hand on my new Omega tick around the gold face. I hold my wrist to the light and watch the tiny diamonds around the edge twinkle. It's a stunning piece of jewelry, and I was taken aback when Connor presented it to me earlier today.

The arrangements to celebrate my turning twenty-eight had been complex. My request to spend the day with both my boyfriends fell on deaf ears. There had been huge debates over who would get to spend more time with me and, more importantly, whose bed I would be in that night. Eventually, I devised my own solution with the help of their sister—spend it with neither of them. It hadn't gone down well.

Last night, I insisted on staying at my own apartment. Mia was surprised to see me, as I'm rarely home anymore. My nights are spent split between the penthouse and floor fifty-seven of The Level. There's rarely a reason to be in my own bed.

But knowing I needed to choose between them in a matter of weeks, it felt important to get some space. My actions needed to not give either man the wrong idea or make anyone think I had already made a decision. Because I haven't. Right now, I have no idea who or *if* I'll pick anyone.

Earlier today, I agreed to meet Russell and Connor at a small coffee shop in Canary Wharf. The place is stuck in the 1950s, with wood-paneled walls and cabinets filled with cakes. The two men looked completely out of place in their designer suits, sitting on red leather-effect chairs surrounded by tradesmen in their boilersuits. But you get the best carrot cake in town here, and it was my birthday, so they had to do as I requested. Their Earl Grey tea and Scottish shortbread would have to wait.

With a few days booked off work, Violet and I had plans to go out to celebrate. At two in the afternoon, I was dressed for a night on the town. My overnight bag was already packed at my feet for our subsequent hotel night and spa the next day to recover from what, no doubt, would be terrible hangovers. I was meeting my friend immediately after leaving her brothers.

As I entered, two sets of dark eyes turned to me. They both widened when I smoothed the fitted black bodycon dress I wore. The sun still warmed the air as summer turned toward autumn, but my short denim jacket provided a little extra protection as I made eye contact with them.

Both men stood on my approach. Russell placed his hand on my hip then leaned down to kiss my cheek, and Connor repeated the action on the opposite side. I smiled at them, loving having them both there with me. It was a situation I don't get to enjoy often. Since our countdown began, their incessant peacocking has become worse. I feel like a pawn in the center of a game that's been played for decades to decide which brother is most successful.

Once we were all seated, each of them placed a small box on the table wrapped in oodles of silk ribbon. My eyes moved between the eerily similar items, one in pink and the other black and red. Russell pushed the darker box toward me and signaled for the waitress's attention.

She tottered over in her high heels, her deep red pinafore perfectly in place. Long black hair was piled on top of her head, secured with a huge gold clasp. She smiled broadly, exposing yellowed teeth smattered with tomato-red lipstick.

"What can I get you, boys?" she asked, standing between them and jutting one hip to the side, almost connecting with Russell's shoulder. Her breasts extended beyond her thin frame as if beacons in the night.

"Do you have any herbal infusions?" Connor said, his usual calm and collected self. I snorted, and my hand shot to my nose in a sad attempt to hide my amusement.

"Infused with what exactly?" the woman responded, the expression on her face highlighting her genuine perplexion.

"Ginger, hibiscus, or verbena, perhaps?" he ventured.

"Sorry, posh boy," she said with a smile. "I can infuse normal tea with sugar and milk if you like."

"That will have to do," he muttered as her attention moved to his older brother, who flashed her a sexy smile. I narrowed my eyes, but he didn't look at me, so I kicked him under the table, hard. He ignored that too.

"I'll take the same. Tea with milk and sugar. Any way you like to make it." His eyes focused on the pin badge strategically placed on her chest. "Gloria," he added. She all but glowed with the use of her name. "I love a cup of well-made tea. And a woman that can make it is invaluable to a hard-working man."

"You've not done a hard day's work in your life. Don't be such a sexist bastard," I snapped at him, and he turned to me. His face lit up with delight. Fucking Russell knows how to rile me up in more ways than one. "Women were not put on this earth to make your fucking tea."

"Perhaps not, but it's a bloody good quality to have."

"I'll make your tea any day," Gloria interrupted, handing him a folded piece of paper I just watched her pull from her bra. "Call me." She turned and strode off toward the counter, swinging her hips exaggeratedly as she left. Russell handed the paper to Connor without looking at it.

"Here you go, bro, her number. Gloria will suck your dick once Trouble chooses me. Don't say I never look out for you."

Connor moved so fast, I didn't see it happening, nor did Russell. He pulled his brother to his feet, holding him by his pristine shirt collar. Russell being slightly taller meant Connor had to raise himself up a fraction to look in his eye.

"Fuck off," he hissed, and the two men glared at one another. The café that had been relaxed a moment ago, as people ate their greasy food and sipped cups of hot coffee, fell silent, and all gazes landed on us. Gloria stalked over once again.

"Tell your brothers to behave themselves," she yapped in my direction.

"Don't speak to our girl like that," Russell growled, and the two men glowered at her. She wilted under their stares. My brain misfired as I computed what he called me. "Our girl." Two small words that meant the world leaving his lips.

"If you have an issue, Gloria," Connor added, "you shout at us, not our lady."

Connor's elevated description of my status didn't go unnoticed by his brother, who narrowed his eyes but kept his mouth closed for once. I stood and placed a hand on each of their arms.

"Sit," I said firmly.

"Are they dogs?" Gloria muttered, clearly unable to keep her catty comments at bay. "Will they roll over, too?"

"If I tickle their tummies, possibly." Her eyes bugged then moved between the men before landing back on my face. "No, I'm not their sister. And I suggest if you want your café kept in one piece, you don't aggravate the situation further. Please get our drinks, Gloria. You two, sit down." All three adults did as I suggested, and I sat in my chair feeling much more powerful. My men turned to me and beamed.

"You're hot when you're in control, Trouble," Russell said.

"Totally," Connor agreed. "You shot her down in flames. It really is quite attractive." He leaned forward and extended a hand, his deft fingers skimming my cheek. "A woman in charge has its benefits."

"Completely. I mean, it's nice to be a leader, but when you're getting told what to do, fuck, it feels good," Russell announced, and his brother nodded. They glanced at one another, grinned, and bumped knuckles. My jaw dropped open in shock at the playful interaction after they nearly wrestled in the center of the café.

"Well, one woman anyway," Connor said. "And it's her birthday, so we should focus on that." Two sets of dark eyes held mine, and my heart skipped.

"Open my present," Russell prompted, gesturing at the unopened box. Gloria reappeared and placed three mugs of milky tea on the surface. I never even ordered a drink. Obviously, she was too flustered after my revelation of two boyfriends.

As I unwrapped the red ribbon, Connor lifted his mug. His eyes screwed up instantly as the liquid hit his lips, and he slammed it back on the table.

"Don't bother," Connor told his brother. "It's vile, no better than dishwater." Russell eyed his own tea warily but left it untouched on his brother's advice. I rolled my eyes at the pair of them.

"Not everything has to cost a fortune to be good," I said as I stripped back the black paper to reveal a black leather box with the word Rolex embossed across it in gold lettering.

"You've got to be fucking kidding me," Connor muttered. My eyes flicked to him then his brother before returning to the box with the brand name I know so well from the high-end shops I walk past. In years gone by, I would stand peering in the window at a jeweler with my nose almost pressed to the glass, hoping one day the beautiful sparkling items would be mine. I cracked open the lid.

Inside, I found the most stunning ladies' watch I had ever seen. The bracelet was made of what I thought was steel, and the Roman numerals blinking back were highlighted by diamonds. But the star of the show was the face; it was the most stunning shade of rose pink that glistened under the light as matching steel hands with a single diamond on the end ticked softly.

"Do you like it?" Russell asked.

"It's beautiful," I stammered. He reached for the box and extracted the watch from its red cushion before wrapping it around my bare wrist. "It's too much."

"Nothing is too much for you, Trouble. A woman as beautiful as you deserves to be dressed in only the best accessories to heighten her shine." Russell focused on his brother. "Your turn."

"You're an arsehole," Connor grumbled, pushing his box in my direction.

"That information isn't new or unexpected. Arsehole is a name I'm comfortable with." Russell shrugged, sat back in his chair, and crossed his arms as if he had just won a battle.

I bristled, annoyed by his manners. Yes, today, he was being an asshole, and I would be sure to tell him later.

"Sorry, Sam," Connor said, and I glanced at him, the softer man I've come to love appearing. "I'll take it back." I slowly removed the paper and ribbon from his gift only to find a box similar to the one Russell had given me, but this time, the word Omega decorated the lid. "You don't need two designer watches." This time, Connor leaned back and ran a hand through his hair.

When I opened this box, a gold watch encrusted with a ring of diamonds around the face sat on heavy blue velvet. I audibly gasped, then took the item from its resting place before wrapping it around my free wrist. I sat in the middle of the two men I love with all my heart, wearing the dazzling jewelry gifted to me, stunned into silence.

Gloria chose this moment to skip across and ask if we wanted any more drinks. Her focus landed on the empty boxes and then my wrists. Her jaw dropped as her eyes popped from her head.

"Oh my fucking God," she stammered. "You have over fifty thousand pounds on your wrists." I glanced up at her, taken aback by both her knowledge and audacity to point out the value. "Which one gave you the gold one?" She flicked a finger between the boys but didn't actually acknowledge them. I gaped at her, mute. "Well, whichever one it was, fuck him first as a thank you. He spent a good ten thousand more." With that revelation, she spun on her heel and skipped back to her station the way she came.

The tension at the table reappeared with force, but before anyone could make any further comment, our time together was interrupted again. Violet rushed into the café with Harrison hot on her heels this time. She stopped at my chair, bent down, and grabbed me into a bear hug.

"Happy birthday!" she squealed. "Let's go!" My enthusiastic friend took my hands and started pulling me to my feet. "Come on, Sam. There's wine to drink and music to dance to."

"It's only half past two in the afternoon," I told her with a giggle.

"I'm a mother. I still want to be in bed by eleven, so let's make the most of the day." I shook my head but rose to stand. Harrison stood behind her and opened his hands in defeat. When his wife wants something to happen, it usually does. Russell and Connor joined us as I collected the boxes from the table. "Oh, nice watch," Violet cooed. "Wait, two nice watches."

"Yes, both Russell and Connor gave me a watch."

My two men moved beside me, one on each arm, as their little sister glared at them. She crossed her arms over her chest, and her left foot started to tap furiously on the floor, the silver sandal she was wearing clinking off the tiles. Harrison walked to her side and wrapped his arm around her waist before whispering in her ear. She shrugged him off, and he held his hands up before raising his eyebrows in our direction.

"Russ," she said sternly. "Did you know Connor bought Sam a watch?"

"Yes," he replied petulantly. "It's none of your business, Violet. Stay out of it." She took two steps forward and prodded at his chest with a slim finger.

"You're a dickhead," she told him.

"That seems to be the general opinion."

"Well, it's the right one. Come on, Sam," she said with a sigh, then took my hand, pulling me from her brothers' arms. "We're going." She led me across the café and out onto the street with Harrison following behind and not so much as a backward glance.

***

"Wow!" I said as Harrison pulled up in front of the huge sandstone mansion. "This is incredible."

"It really is something, isn't it," Violet gushed. "Harry and I love coming here, don't we?" Harrison climbed out of the driver's seat and opened our doors as we stepped out onto the perfectly white gravel. He took his wife in his arms and kissed her softly.

"I love going anywhere with you, Vi," he said.

"How many rooms does it have?" I asked, my eyes roaming over the array of windows and doors.

To get here, we drove through a mile of immaculate gardens, where every flower and bush looked exactly like they did in old movies set in English manor houses. I half expected Lords and Ladies dressed in Georgian attire to be wandering around the paths.

"There are no rooms, only suites," Violet corrected me, and I rolled my eyes at her husband, who smiled. Even though my friend has pretty much always had access to a lot of money, even when her life was complicated, her husband knew true poverty in his childhood. It makes him more realistic regarding life, something Violet will hopefully never have the pain of experiencing.

A man dressed in a grey suit with a long jacket and wearing a cap appeared from nowhere and began emptying our bags from the car. Violet grabbed my hand and led me up the stairs toward where it was signposted reception. An older woman in a fitted black dress stepped out from behind a table and walked across holding out her hand.

"Mrs. Waite," she said. "We are delighted to have you back at The Estate." She took my friend's hand and then mine to shake warmly. "Let me show you both to your suites. Do follow me."

"Thank you, Katrina," Violet gushed as if the woman was a lifelong friend. We both followed behind her as she led us through magnificent rooms decorated with exquisite furniture and artwork before climbing a staircase to the upper floor. We stopped outside two doors marked "The Shakespeare Suite" and "The Keats Suite."

"Our best suites, Mrs. Waite. Please decide between yourself and Mrs. Chase who would prefer which room," Katrina said, and I balked, then scowled at my friend. Fuck sake, here she goes again, marrying me off to one of her brothers against my will. If she weren't so loveable, I would wring her neck.

Katrina turned to me and beamed. "Congratulations on your recent marriage, Mrs. Chase. We will be sure to make your stay exceedingly special." With that, she turned and walked off.

Violet pushed open the Shakespeare door first, and I followed her inside. The suite extended for what seemed like room after room. There was a living room, bedroom, bathroom, and relaxing area, all decorated in elegant cream and gold.

"Why did you tell her I was married?" I hissed, and my friend smiled.

"We might get some treats. Places like this love to keep their customers happy."

"Is this not a treat enough?" I opened my arms wide, and she giggled.

"Relax, Sam. Enjoy the rest from keeping my brothers from killing each other."

"Who did you tell her I was married to?" I asked, suddenly realizing the added complication of the fake information.

"I didn't specify. Maybe if someone asks you, whoever you pick may be your answer to who you want to spend the rest of your life with." I stare at her, stunned by the flippant comment. "Anyway, I'm going to unpack. Your bag is over there." She gestures to my overnight bag, which is magically already sitting on the bed. "I'll meet you in the bar in twenty minutes."

I stood in the most luxurious hotel room I'd ever been in and watched her leave with the truth in her words stabbing at my heart. Soon, I will need to choose between them, and I don't know how.

Unable to help myself, I take photos of the view from my window and of the room, then send them off to Bryan.

> Guess where I am.

Since everything happened at the hospital, I've been sending him the odd message so he knows he still has my support. Russell and Connor would be furious if they knew, but he's my friend and I know he wouldn't be part of the criminal ongoings within the department. His reply comes instantly, a simple thumbs up. Since then, any conversation has felt one-sided.

> I am here if you need me. Much love my friend.

I type back, and he replies again, this time with a heart. I smile to myself.

> Things will get better.

They need to. Because Sam, I'm not sure my family can cope with much more.

CHAPTER THIRTY-TWO

―――――◆○◆――――――

The Estate, Buckinghamshire

Connor

"This doesn't feel right," I mutter to Russell and Harrison as they watch the girls enjoy a jacuzzi in the hotel spa. "Do you not think they'll figure out there are no other guests here?"

"I doubt it with the volume of champagne being drunk," Harrison replies, and Russell punches his arm. "Vi will be asleep by eight o'clock at this rate."

There's a knock at the door, and an elderly man dressed in the clothes of a butler steps into the room. "Good evening, gentlemen. Would any of you like a drink?" he asks.

"Another round of beers, please," Harrison says, his eyes never leaving his wife. Somehow, he convinced the hotel manager to give us access to an office next to the spa with one-way glass. We've been somewhere on the grounds since our ladies arrived at the hotel three hours ago, just in case anything goes amiss, which is unlikely since we booked out the whole damn place.

"Do you not think you're slightly overprotective?" Russell suggests to him, and Harrison glares back.

"This coming from a man who stalked his brother's girlfriend to get her to notice him." My brother's mouth falls open. "No, Violet could find trouble in an empty room. So being here means I know she's safe, and I wouldn't sleep at home anyway without her."

"Sam said they weren't using the spa today," I continue, trying to divert a disagreement. I was only made aware of their arrangement to follow the girls minutes before Russell and I left the café.

"I paid the receptionist one hundred pounds to convince them otherwise," Russell says. "It was too good an opportunity to see Trouble strutting around in her bikini." My focus moves to the girls having the time of their lives, laughing and joking together, completely unaware of our presence.

"I wish we could hear what they're saying," Russell grumbles.

"Maybe we can." Harrison cracks open a small window, and the sound of excited female voices floats toward us.

"This isn't good," I mutter, and the men scowl at me.

"Shut up! If we can hear them, they'll hear us," Harrison whispers, annoyed.

The bubbles stop, and our girls groan dramatically before standing up. Samantha looks incredible in a bright pink bikini scattered with crystals. When she turns to step out of the tub, her pert ass cheeks jiggle merrily on either side of the tiny string. My cock stirs in my trousers in hope. Once out, they wrap themselves in fluffy white towels while pushing their feet into matching slippers.

"Where do you think everyone is?" Samantha asks my sister. "It seems very quiet for a hotel." Violet purses her lips and taps them with a finger before answering.

"Maybe we are the only booking," she suggests, completely unfazed by the random situation. I'm never sure my sister will live or has lived, for that matter, in the real world. As much as I love her and her fierce loyalty to us all, she'll always live slightly above the clouds. She's oblivious to the reality around her, but with Harry by her side, I don't think that is a bad place to be. "So, what do you want to do next?"

"How about a massage, ladies?" a male voice interrupts their conversation, and they both turn in the direction of the question. When I follow their gaze, two men walk over, dressed from head to toe in white. One signals to two massage beds set up at the poolside. "I'm Thomas, and this is Francois. We would be delighted to help you relax here at The Estate."

Violet squeals and claps her hands together, bouncing up and down on the spot. Samantha's lips twist into an amused smile at her friend's antics.

"Oh, I love massages!"

"That won't be happening," Harrison growls under his breath.

"You booked the fucking hotel," I tell him. "With a spa. Was a massage not an obvious perk of the trip?"

"Yeah, but not from those two boneheads." He signals to the masseurs with an angry finger. "No man other than me touches my wife."

Our girls stroll toward the beds and quickly remove their towels before lying face down. The three of us watch on as the two men, younger than any of us, step towards our women.

"Not a fucking chance in hell," Russell says, starting to remove his shoes and socks.

"What the hell are you doing?"

"Going to massage her my fucking self."

Harrison follows suit and begins to remove his shoes. Feeling like I have no other option, I remove my own. Once our feet are bare, we take off our suit jackets and throw them over the back of the chairs we sit on. Russell heads for the door. He unbuttons his shirt sleeves as he walks, turning them up to expose his forearms.

When we reach the massage tables, all of us are prepared to pleasure our women, not that I think either will be pleased by our unannounced arrival.

The two masseurs stand beside a unit, pouring oil into a small container and lighting candles. The girls still lie face down, chatting between themselves. "You don't think they would book the whole place?" Samantha asks Violet. "It doesn't seem a cheap deal kind of place." My sister laughs out loud then snorts, the same way she has done since we were kids.

"I wouldn't put it past them," she replies once she has control of her hilarity. "Our men aren't exactly normal. As far as we know, there are no other guests, which makes me think we're the only booking tonight."

"Yes, the whole place has been booked for a private event. Were you unaware?" one man says over his shoulder. "You're the only guests we have today."

"Controlling arseholes," Violet mutters. "I knew it. When I see Harry, I'll—"

"You'll what? Suck his dick a little harder as punishment" Both girls chuckle, and their bodies vibrate softly against the white sheets.

"Probably. I can never be angry with him," my sister admits. "He's my kind of perfect. All dominant and possessive, but as soft as butter underneath." Harrison smiles, biting his lip to stop himself from chuckling. "God, I love him."

The men turn toward the tables but catch sight of us standing in the shadows to their side. Russell shakes his head before stepping forward and covering his lips with a finger. Harrison and I pluck the oils from their hands. Russell signals for them to leave. When they don't, he pulls a small handgun from his waistband and motions again for them to go. *Well, we won't ever be welcome back at this hotel.* The masseurs scurry away like scalded cats. We all smirk at one another. Pathetic.

Harrison moves immediately to my sister, unspeaking. He coats his hands in oil and places them on her back, kneading softly. She moans with pleasure immediately. Russell and I look at each other. He shrugs and then dips his hands in the oil I'm holding before moving to Sam. Not wanting to lose out, I do the same.

We take a side each, placing one hand on her skin. She wriggles beneath our touch, making herself more comfortable on the bed. Our hands glide simultaneously over her shoulders, down her back, stopping just above her ass. My brother glances over, raising his eyebrows as if seeking permission to continue. I nod. Samantha groans softly, her eyes still firmly closed.

We are all settled in the moment, enjoying the peace and calm. Our ladies are relaxed and pampered, although unaware it's us, until Violet's voice sounds angrily from the bed.

"Harry, what the fuck are you doing here?" she shouts, and he steps back as she pushes herself up to sit. Samantha's head snaps around, and she hesitates as she clocks my brother and me. "I'd know that bloody big toe anywhere." My eyes flick to the face hole Harrison is standing above.

"If you think I'm letting another man touch you, Vi, you don't know me well enough. I don't fucking share." He steps forward and takes her face between his hands. "You're all fucking mine. I don't share," he repeats before glancing at us standing at the next bed. "No offense."

"None taken," I reply, holding my hands up as he passes her a towel.

"Get up. We are going to bed," he tells her. His eyes are fixed on my sister, the unwavering love for her since they were teenagers burning strong. Harrison has always looked at her the same way, with pure, unadulterated want.

"Why?" she asks, and he laughs before kissing her softly.

"Because I want to put a baby in you tonight, and I would rather not do that in front of your brothers." She flushes red, then we all watch as he lifts her into his arms and carries her from the spa.

Samantha pushes herself up and fixes her bikini top. She looks from Russell to me, then back again. "What do you boys want to do then? As you've interrupted my girly evening," she says, cocking her head to the side. "Violet has abandoned me, and you two have been playing stalker." I wince at her description. "As you're both here, we may as well—"

"I want to eat," I tell her. She bites her lip.

"Are you hungry?"

"Always."

"Shall we all go to my room?" she suggests. Russell extends a hand to help her from the bed, but I stand where I am and avert my eyes. A few moments pass without anyone speaking. She sighs softly, and the mood dips. "As you're both now in crazy stalker mode, I have no doubt you know which room I'm in. When you sort it out, you know where I am." Russell and I watch her walk away, her bare feet padding softly on the cool floor. Once she's out of sight, I turn to my brother. He glares back at me.

"What?" I say, confused by his anger.

"Could we both not have gone upstairs with her, rather than putting a dampener on everything?" he says.

"I don't want to watch you have sex with my girl," I growl.

"She isn't your girl. She's our girl. You need to get used to that fact." He straightens his shoulders and puffs out his chest. "Watching her with someone else can be quite a turn-on. You get to focus on her expressions and the way her body reacts. I learned a lot about how to pleasure her from you."

I see red, and my fist connects with his jaw instantly. So much of this fucked up situation makes me hate not only myself but him. Most days, I regret giving her the green light to investigate their relationship; it burns every damn day. I pull a coin from my pocket.

"That was a compliment, you idiot." He rubs at his jaw. I've hit my brother more since meeting Samantha than I have in my whole life. She brings out a possessiveness I've never felt before. It's almost uncontrollable.

"Heads or tails," I ask him.

"What, you're seriously going to toss a coin to see who goes first?"

"Got a better idea?" He shakes his head. "Well, shut up and choose."

***

Samantha

As I apply my makeup in the mirror, a soft green candle flickers in its glass vase. The aroma of jasmine fills the air. Typically, this essential part of putting yourself together isn't located over the dressing table where it would make perfect sense. No, I can only see my reflection in a full-length mirror located on a random wall with no outlet nearby. Why do even the most luxurious hotels get this simple requirement wrong? All I want to do is sit down and do my hair and makeup, but poor design makes it difficult.

Sitting on the floor, I survey myself in the glass and thread mascara through my lashes. The long black strands extend before my eyes, highlighting the blue beneath. Once again, I look to the door, willing it to open and both of my men to walk through. I left the latch off so nothing would cause them to falter if they decided to visit.

Time passes insanely slow, the large wall clock ticking each second at what feels like half-time. Once my makeup has been applied for the third time, I push up to stand and look at myself again. Walking back from the spa, I debated what would be suitable to wear this evening, unsure who would be coming to visit. I never expected either of them to be here.

I didn't want to make any assumptions, but also wanted to leave every avenue open to be explored. I opted for a simple, black lace pajama set of a tank and shorts that cut high, exposing the bottom of my ass cheeks. Either of them would appreciate that.

Worrying that neither man will appear, I begin to pace around the most stunning hotel room I've ever stayed in. I'm on my fifth lap when the door opens, and Russell walks in, holding a bottle of champagne in one hand and two flutes in the other.

"Impatient, Trouble?" he says, closing the door with his foot. My heart sinks in my chest when I realize Connor must have left without seeing me. "Sorry, Connor and I had some business to sort first."

"What kind of business?"

"A game of luck, and the winner got you." His mouth moves into a small smile, but there's a sadness in his eyes. "He still isn't ready to see you with someone else. But I think in time..."

"I doubt it," I say, moving to sit on the bed. He walks over, lowers down beside me, and places the two glasses on the side table before opening the bottle of fizz. I watch as he masterfully pours two glasses with one hand while holding me to his side. He passes me one, then collects his own, angling it in my direction. We tap them together and take a sip.

"To our girl," he toasts, and I blink at him. "My brother will come up and see you later."

"*Our* girl?"

"Yes, Trouble. You're not only mine but his. And for now, until this is all over, you're ours. Know that we'll both protect you with our lives." His words are firm, direct, and honest. The truth behind them burns bright, and tonight is the safest I've ever felt. "We both love you, Trouble. And I know no matter what you decide, that's a fact that will never change. You will be ours whether we physically have you or not."

I lift my glass to my lips again and drink deep, draining it. Russell's eyes roam over my body, starting at my lips then moving down to my breasts which strain against the dark silk fabric.

"I love your pajamas," he tells me, a single finger skimming over the material at my chest. "The perfect blend of pretty but damn sexy. How easy is my access?"

"You'll need to investigate that yourself," I tease, standing then deliberately strutting to the opposite side of the room and putting my glass on the farthest unit from the bed. His focus never leaves my body—I feel it on my skin every step. I turn back to face him and drop my hands onto my hips.

Russell remains on the bed. He watches me with hungry eyes, then his fingers move to the top button of his shirt. He unbuttons each one, pulls the hem from his trousers, and stands. My stomach flips, awed by his sheer size. My mouth dries as he unclips each cufflink, places them on the bedside table, and shrugs out of his shirt. He throws it onto the floor like trash.

My gaze runs over his torso; fuck, he looks incredible. The leather belt from his hips slides free. He holds it across his middle and snaps it hard. The sound crackles, and my pussy clenches immediately. The dangerous man who stalked me for months is in this room tonight. Still holding the belt, he raises an eyebrow.

"Come here, Trouble," he orders. Without hesitation, I walk over, stopping less than a meter from him. His eyes flick to a bottle of massage oil. "Pick it up." I swallow, the sexual tension in the room high. When I don't move instantly, he cracks the belt in his hands again. The leather snaps deliciously in the air. "Pick. It. Up." I reach for the bottle and hold it at my chest with two hands.

"Open the cap and squirt." He smirks on the word "squirt." "Fuck, Trouble, I can't wait to watch that pussy of yours squirt all over my face." The pussy in question throbs with the dirty image of me sitting astride his face as he licks deep and my juices run into his mouth. "Squirt some of that oil into your palms and come here." I do as he says, rubbing my hands together then stepping toward him. "Now, place those pretty fingers on my skin and oil me up."

Starting at his shoulders, I set a palm on each side of his neck then trail my hands downward. My fingers spread across his chest, the bumps of his nipples in the center of each hand. The oil slicks over his skin, creating a shimmer under the dim lamplight. I glimpse up, and it's clear he's undressing me with his eyes.

"Keep going," he orders, and my hands obey. They move over every inch of his torso, enjoying every indentation and bump.

Occasionally, my fingers skim the waistband of his trousers. The bulge of his cock tells me he's loving this as much as I am. He turns under my fingers, and I repeat the process with his back, the hard muscles beneath my fingertips solid and tense. Once every inch of him is covered, he spins back to face me, still holding the belt.

I watch in awe as he moves the leather into one hand then unbuttons his trousers with the other. He slips off his shoes, sliding the material down his legs and removing his socks at the same time. The items join his discarded shirt. He cocks his head to one side and smiles boldly.

"Take off my boxers." I reach for them and pull the silk down his legs. He kicks them to the side as his cock hangs, fully erect and demanding. "On your knees and suck." Every word is filled with authority. Unhappy with my hesitation, he retakes the belt in both hands, cracks it, then hooks it around my waist and pulls me hard against him. He leans down. "I said kneel, Trouble. Suck. My. Cock." His lips drop to mine briefly, then retract. My knees buckle, and I'm left at eye level with the tip of his dick.

My tongue darts between my lips, excited as the leather touches the back of my head. He applies a little pressure, encouraging me forward. I open, taking his cock in my mouth. His hips flex, pushing deeper as he maintains pressure on the strap. He holds me to him, and I close my lips around his thick cock. My hands move to his thighs and he pauses.

"Do you want me to stop?" he asks, and I mumble an indistinguishable "No," my mouth full of dick.

"Good," he groans, starting to move again. The belt holds me steady as he thrusts, his momentum building fast. With my eyes closed, I take him, loving the sensation of hard cock sliding over my tongue. I hold his thighs tighter, digging my nails into his flesh, encouraging him to go deeper. He pushes forward hard, and the tip hits the back of my throat. "Fuck," he yells as salty cum explodes in my mouth. It coats my tastebuds as his cock leaves my mouth. When withdrawn, I smile up at him and lick my lips.

"Yummy," I murmur, lifting a single finger to my mouth and sucking deep.

"Fucking come here," he growls.

"Is that all you ever say?" I tease. "Come here?" He ignores the jibe and moves to lie on the deep red rug in the center of the room.

"What about the bed?" I ask, confused.

"Later. Come here and sit on my face." I giggle at his use of the phrase again but do as he asks. He lies staring up at me as I remove my pajamas. He taps his lips once I'm naked. I step over his head and stand above him. Strong fingers wrap around my ankles. "Sit, Trouble. Or I'll do more with that belt than hold my dick down your throat." I lower myself onto my knees, one leg on either side of his face, my emotions a mixture of lust and excitement.

Greedy hands roam over my body, taking a tit in each grasp. He squeezes gently as his tongue explores my entrance, running over my already wet flesh. He sucks greedily, and I wriggle, enjoying the increasing buzz in my belly and between my legs. His tongue finds my clit. He plays with the sweet spot, circling and then flicking my piercing slowly and deliberately. It taps my most sensitive nerves, and my pussy contracts hard then relaxes, each sensation stronger as I build toward orgasm. He knows when he plays with that silver bar it drives me wild. Every so often, his tongue wanders back to my entrance, sweeping over my skin and lapping up my juice as it prepares my body for his cock.

"I want you to come all over my face, Trouble," he says. "I'm going to play with this jewelry of yours until you squirt that sweet nectar down my throat. You drank me down, now I want yours." His hands drop to my ass, wrapping around my waist as his fingertips dent my skin, holding tight. Keeping his word, he works my clit. The movements becoming shorter and faster. My pussy clenches, my knees trying to close for relief from the building orgasm, but his head blocks their passage. Every part of me vibrates with the upcoming hit of pure fucking pleasure, my brain terrified of the power but desperate for the intense sensation.

"Shit," I mumble, throwing my head back. He tightens his grip, pulling me harder onto his mouth. The pressure in my body has been leveling up by the second as my orgasm screams to the surface, the walls of my pussy desperately searching for a cock to jerk dry. My breaking point nears as he works, one hundred percent focused on his goal. His tongue moves faster, all my muscles vibrating with the need to let go.

"Come on, Trouble. Give me the best fucking drink of my life," he orders from between my legs. My body strains hard in sheer ecstasy as he sweeps my clit again, moving the steel bar rapidly, greedy for me to give him what he desires. Every nerve in my body contracts as it releases, my juices pouring from me. He sucks greedily on my lips, then his tongue sweeps across every surface he can reach. I try to move, but his hands hold me fast to his lips, not ready to let me go. "I'm not done. Sit. I want more."

Without giving me a moment to compose myself, his hands trail back up my body to my breasts. He massages them gently. When I glance down, his eyes are closed and his focus has returned to my clit. The buzz begins to build again immediately. It's not long before a fresh wave of my cum streams over his face as sheer fucking joy scatters over my skin. When I glance over my shoulder, one of Russell's hands has disappeared from my breast in exchange for stroking his dick. He pulls himself hard, and I watch as cum spurts over his abs. He groans with relief, and spots of the salty delicacy smatter my ass.

"Fuck, Trouble. You're simply delicious," he says, wiggling his face from between my legs. I rise then walk over to the bed, climbing onto all fours in the center. He stands, picks up his trousers, pulls his phone from his pocket, and presses a button. I stare at him, bemused, as he wipes himself down and begins to redress.

"Um..." I stammer. "Aren't you forgetting something?" He buttons up his trousers, his feet still bare, and mischievous eyes fall on me, still naked on my hands and knees.

"What?"

"Well, is my current position not a hint?" I mutter, sitting back on my heels. My breasts swing with the movement, and his eyes drop, then return to hold my gaze.

"Is that greedy little cunt of yours not satisfied?" he asks, and fresh arousal snaps in my belly. I narrow my eyes. He chuckles. "No, Trouble. I'm not fucking you tonight. My brother is." He walks toward me, leans down, and drops a kiss on my lips. Without speaking, he turns, still barefoot, and walks toward the door as Connor pushes it open.

"I got a message," he says as he locks eyes with his brother.

"Yeah, brother," Russell responds. "Our girl is owed a massage and a good fucking. It's on your to-do list tonight."

"I am more than happy to oblige." His fingers lift to his shirt buttons, and he begins to undress as Russell disappears. "Lie on your front," he tells me, his eyes widening as he drinks me in, naked on all fours. "Let's start with the massage."

CHAPTER THIRTY-THREE

Unknown Location

September 2023

Connor

Darkness. Close, confined blackness I can't move in. I wiggle a finger on my left hand, and it connects with what appears to be wood. Lying on my back with my arms at my sides, it feels as though I'm in a coffin. I try to lift my head, but a rope around my neck holds me fast. More restraints secure my body to the solid surface I lie on. I feel them across my shoulders, arms, stomach, legs, and ankles. It's cold. Chill seeps into my skin from every direction. It's then I realize I'm naked, nothing but a thin sheet covers my body.

As I become more aware of my surroundings, the biting sensation of the bindings against my skin heightens as the rough material rubs. I try to move my arms, but they're held fast at my sides. The way I'm secured ensures I don't have an inch of movement. Looking up, I can only see black. It could be merely air, but my sense tells me there's a lid on whatever contraption holds me. For all intents and purposes, it *could* be a coffin.

Silence stretches out around me. I hear nothing. There's no hum or hint of where I could be. Lying in an unknown place, naked and surrounded by fuck knows what is the most vulnerable I have ever felt in my life. All the abuse and dangerous situations I've endured pale in comparison to the situation I'm living right now, the sheer knowledge that someone else has the control and I can do nothing about it to save myself. Their identity and intentions are a mystery. I'm at their mercy.

The last thing I remember is having a shitty day. My client, who'd appeared in court on fraud charges, was sent away for over a decade. Losing doesn't come naturally, and I've been reliving the case since the verdict was announced.

Not wanting to return to my apartment in a foul mood, I walked around Canary Wharf before going home. Samantha would be waiting for me, and the last thing I wanted was for our evening together to start badly. My remaining time with her is precious, and I'm determined not to ruin a moment of it or unnecessarily risk the relationship we have created together.

The day is approaching when she'll decide between Russell and me. The last few months have been as difficult as they have been enjoyable. However, if my current predicament is anything to go by, I may not live to learn the final verdict. The thought is horrifying, but I can't focus on where I am right now or I'll start screaming. I can feel the panic rise in my throat, but I force it down with a few deep breaths and thoughts of Sam. Fuck it. If I have to be depressed to think about her, I'd rather that than contemplating this torture.

At the hotel only days ago, Russell and I wanted Sam to feel more secure as we lived the final days in our love triangle, and I think we did. As Russell left Samantha's room at the hotel, our shoulders bumped briefly.

"Enjoy," he whispered under his breath. "She's fucking divine." An unexpected joy with his positivity bubbled in my chest. I buried it before it could be appreciated.

After Russell won the coin toss in the spa, it was agreed that he would see Sam first——our girl, as he keeps calling her. The endearment feels as right as it does wrong. Attempting to draw some boundaries at the last minute, I requested he didn't fuck her. Penetrate her anyway. The idea of me being where he'd been is still hard to accept, even though I'm fully aware she has sex with us both. He agreed easily, to my surprise.

When I arrived at her room, she was naked on all fours on the bed. Her eyes snapped up to mine as I pushed open the door. Her jaw dropped, and I took pleasure in her shock. Yeah, baby, you didn't expect to see me? I wondered if Russell had told her I was coming or not. She scrambled to her feet as the door closed, then practically ran into my arms, throwing her hands around my waist.

"You're here," she whispered fiercely against my chest. I pushed her back slightly and placed a finger under her chin, encouraging her gaze upwards.

"I would never give up a chance to be with you. You're my everything." I'd kissed her softly. "Let's get you cleaned up." I took her fingers and led her toward the bathroom. I undressed myself as we walked, so by the time we reached the doorway, I was naked too.

Stepping into the chic space, with its all-white tiles and highly polished chrome, I turned on the huge shower. Hot water spilled from the head, and we both moved under the stream. I squirted creamy shower gel into my hands from the silver bottle attached to the wall and ran my hands over her skin.

"I love you, Sam," I told her beneath the water, unsure if she could hear me and part for me not wanting her to. "I'll do anything for you to be mine, but I need you to smell of me when I'm with you. Not him." She stood as I washed her body and hair. Once done, I switched off the water and wrapped her in a towel before leading her to the dressing table in the room.

She sat on the black velvet stool as I used her bright pink brush to comb out her hair. With no mirror, I couldn't see her expressions, but I enjoyed every damn moment of touching her as she sat there, breathing softly beneath me. It took an age to complete the process of brushing and then drying her blonde locks, but I had no intention of rushing. I planned to relish her fully.

"I owe you a massage," I said, my voice soft.

We moved to the bed. Both of us were naked as she lay face down on the duvet, which was still made apart from the wrinkles where she had been on all fours. I plucked the bottle of massage oil from the side table and then moved to straddle her, placing one knee on each side of her waist.

Lowering myself, I allowed my balls to rest on her plump ass as my cock hardened against her skin. I squirted a dollop of oil into my palms before placing the bottle on the duvet. My slick hands moved to her shoulders, my fingers wrapping around the curves. Slowly, I ran my palms over her body. Enjoying her softness beneath my touch. Each part of her I caressed using circular motions, and every so often my hand dropping down her side to feel the swell of her breasts against the mattress.

"Make love to me," she whispered, her tone needy.

"We have all night," I soothed, continuing to touch her. "Turn over."

I raised myself slightly as she turned between my thighs. My palms migrated to her neck, connecting with her skin again. As I looked at her, she stared straight back with wide eyes, never taking her focus off me as I massaged her body. When I reached her breasts, I twisted each nipple simultaneously, and she moaned mesmerizingly on command. It was the most delicious sound of a woman wanting her man, and fuck, I needed every part of her. I needed to be inside her.

Once done with the massage, we slipped beneath the sheets together. "Make love to me," she whispered again, almost inaudibly. "I need to know you want me." I'd risen up on my elbow, turning to face her. My hand splayed across her stomach.

"Want you? I'd fucking die for you."

"Then show me." She opened her legs, and my fingers trailed between them. I played with her piercing, the tip of one finger circled her clit the way I knew she loved. When I pushed the whole thing inside, slick walls wrapped around it, ready for me to slide my cock home. "Push my body," she challenged. "Fill me like you never have before." I pressed my lips to hers. We kissed, then her hands moved to my hair, pulling the strands in her fingers.

"What do you want?" I asked her, and she raised her knees.

"As many fingers as you can fit. Don't be scared," she cooed when I gaped at her momentarily. "Two more. Be a good boy, and open me up for that cock of yours." I slid two more fingers inside her, and her pussy encased all three easily. I pumped, and she raised her eyebrow. "Are you brave enough to add another?" she asked.

"I don't want to hurt you."

"You won't, I can take it." I inserted my smallest finger, and her body arched off the bed. She groaned with pleasure, and her body rewarded me with sweet juice over my fingers. I withdrew my hand and licked each one clean, then pulled the covers from her body. She looked fucking edible, legs wide and pussy swollen, ready for taking.

I slid on top of her, lining up at her entrance and pushing forward. Wet walls clamped onto my cock, and I didn't hesitate in driving her into the mattress hard. My hips moved fast, wanting to put my own claim on the woman in my arms—show her like she wanted me to.

Her tits bobbed beautifully as she wrapped her legs around my waist. I rode her hard and fast, with one hand on either side of her head. My eyes trawled over every part I could see.

"Open your fucking eyes," I growled as I came close to my peak. "Open them, and watch me take what will always be mine."

"And what is that?" she goaded, and I slammed again.

"You. *You* have always been mine. You're my girl."

The sound of a door slamming closed surprises me, and my eyes fly open again, but all that I am looking at is darkness as before. I chastise myself once again for my stupidity in ending up here.

On my walk from the office earlier, I had turned down by the river, a familiar route I'd taken hundreds of times before. Ahead, a group of three men in suits stood in a circle. They looked like every other businessman who works in the financial district. The material was perfectly pressed, their shoes shined, and each held a leather briefcase in one hand. As I strolled past them, the man closest turned to catch my eye.

"Excuse me, mate," he said. The phrase was surprising and not the normal greeting I would expect from a professional in the city. "You don't happen to know where the Saltire building is?" I stopped, facing him, and he smiled.

"We have a meeting in ten minutes," another man from the opposite side of the group said, causing me to turn and stand in the gathering with them. "And this fuckwit..." He gestured to the younger man next to him, who looked uncomfortable to be there. "Never brought the address."

"It's the other side of the river," I told him. "You can catch a water taxi over there." I gestured to the passenger boats sitting at the small dock a matter of meters away. "You'll need to be quick if you want to make it within ten minutes."

The man who initially stopped me shrugged. He looked to be in his mid-forties, tall with graying black hair and sharp features. "Our boss is happy to wait for a positive outcome, Mr. Chase," he said as the sensation of cool metal touched my skin beneath my suit jacket and through my shirt. "Connor, isn't it?"

"Who's asking?"

"No one. I'm only the messenger and wanted to ensure I collected the correct package." His eyes flicked to a dark SUV sitting at the curb, someone already in the driver's seat. "This is what's going to happen. You will come with us for a short ride. Walk calmly to that car and get in the rear. No arguments."

"And if I don't?"

"I'll put a bullet in you right here and drag you," he said menacingly. I had no doubt he would by his tone. "You're not a stupid man. You know you're outnumbered. Our boss merely wants to discuss some business with you. Shall we go?"

I stepped toward the car in answer. He walked at my side while the others followed behind. I could sense the tension as we made our way over the pavement. My captor opened the rear passenger door, and I climbed in.

"My girlfriend is expecting me. She'll sound the alarm when I don't return."

"Oh yes, the little blonde you share with your brother," he mutters. "Peculiar situation. A real man would never share a bit of skirt."

"It works for us," I replied blandly, not rising to the bait.

"Pass me your phone. Both of them." He held out his hand, waiting for me to drop them into his palm. His knowledge was disconcerting; I took my personal phone from my pocket, then collected the emergency phone from its hiding place in my suit jacket.

He turned to his younger accomplice. "Take these," he said. "And place them together somewhere believable. No doubt both can be tracked, so go to a bar or something. I believe our friend here lost a big case today. Him drowning his sorrows won't be a surprise."

"Yes, sir," he responded before scurrying off back toward the bustling area of Canary Wharf.

"Now, strap yourself in, Mr. Chase. You're in for an eventful day," the man in charge advised, then slammed the door closed. On my other side, another brute sat bursting out of his suit. In his hand was a small syringe; he turned around in his fingers before removing the cover from the needle.

403

"What is that?" I hissed, and he grinned.

"Oblivion," he told me, waving it around. "Now, hold still. It's time to go to sleep." I pulled at the door handle, but not surprisingly, it was locked. I took a swing at him, the back of my hand colliding with his face, then I heard the click of a safety being removed from a gun.

"Stop," the first man growled. "Take the sedative, or I'll sedate you permanently." He was turned in the passenger seat, his gun pointed at my forehead. I stopped struggling as the sharp metal pricked my skin, and everything went black.

Now, lying in the pitch black with no idea what is happening, I curse myself for not fighting. The sound of metal sliding against metal cuts through the silence. My instinct is to try to run, but it's impossible in my current position. Instead, I lie like a sheep awaiting slaughter, wondering who the fuck is out there.

The creak of old rusted hinges as a door opens scrapes against what could be stone. Multiple people's booted footsteps can be heard, but among them is the distinct click of high heels. It's hard to distinguish how many people are in the room as they move around in what feels like a haphazard manner.

Suddenly, light hits my face as whatever covers me is lifted from above. I screw my eyes closed, the unexpected brightness uncomfortable. Slowly, I reopen them to be met with blank air and only see a single strip light above. The ceiling of the room is covered in old, worn polystyrene tiles. They're yellowed with age, and most have gauges on the surface. My captor's face appears above me, and he smiles down nastily.

"Good morning, Mr. Chase. I hope you had a good sleep."
He reaches in and begins to untie my bindings.

"Where the fuck am I?" I snarl.

"All in good time." As he unties the final rope, I push myself
up to sit. The pathetic sheet falls from my chest, and I pull it up
around me. "Don't worry, you've not got anything we haven't
seen before."

It turns out that I am, in fact, lying in a coffin. Dark wood
surrounds me, and an involuntary shiver scatters over my skin
with the realization. I appear to be in the center of a derelict
operating theater. The walls are now only tattered paintwork
and fallen cement. Around the edge, there are still metal units
housing boxes of equipment. Most of it looks ancient, however,
a few more modern items sit to one side.

The men who stopped me by the river stand around the
space. Each looks to be guarding a door. But to one side, I
notice a familiar face—one I'm unhappy to see. Dr. Josephine
Rivera doesn't look at me. She focuses firmly on the floor while
shuffling nervously from foot to foot. I open my mouth to ask
a multitude of questions when more footsteps can be heard
approaching, along with a strange squeak.

All attention in the room moves to the double swing doors
where the doctor stands. The left hand door opens, and a
dark-haired man walks in then steps to one side, holding it
wide. A moment later, a wheelchair appears; an older, frail man
sits bent over in the seat with another gigantic brute pushing

him into the room. It takes me a moment to process who they are—two men I most definitely never planned to see again.

"Get up," my captor snarls, pulling at my arm. I climb out of the coffin, landing on the floor and wrapping the sheet around my waist before approaching the wheelchair. A security guard appears on either side of me, ready to intervene if I decide to attack. Instead, I stare at the old man I have known all my life, a man who was meant to protect me but never did. Old, withered eyes rise up and meet mine.

"Hello, boy," my father says. "It's good to see you."

"The feeling isn't mutual."

"Oh, I'm not happy to see you in the sense of catching up, but rather because of what you'll be doing for me. You're about to give your old man the ultimate gift."

"I'll give you fuck all."

He laughs before spluttering violently. His companion moves over and rubs the old man's back, then looks up, locking his stare with mine. In this moment I hate him as much as I hate my father.

"Do you really think you have a choice?" Aiden Marley replies with a smirk.

I step forward, wanting to take a swing at him. The two guards beside me grab an arm each and hold me steady. Marley looks no different from when I saw him earlier this year when he escaped at Harrison and Violet's failed wedding. He'd absconded abroad and, the last I heard, was living the high life on his criminal funds.

My father, however, has been incarcerated since his capture. The two men worked together without our knowledge for years. Aiden was the man Violet ran away with at eighteen; he's also who my father agreed to give his daughter to in return for his loyalty.

"When did you get out?" I ask my father, and his lips thin to a nasty smile.

"Who said I was released? The benefit of having a terminal illness, son, is they allow you hospital visits. All I needed was a few loyal men to ensure my escape. This man," he boasts, signaling to Aiden, "is more loyal to me than any of my bastard children. He's ensured that I've been kept comfortable and could escape when the time was right. It's more than any of you did..."

I look down at the decrepit waste of a man before me. His skin is withered and yellow. In less than a year, he's transformed from a strong and dangerous enemy into someone barely able to stand. But in his eyes, the vile look is still there, the twinkle of enjoyment in other people's pain.

"No doubt you're wondering why you are here," he says casually. He wriggles in his chair as if wanting to rise. Aiden goes to his side, taking his elbow and supporting his fragile frame. My father rises, wobbling unsteadily from foot to foot. He moves closer so we are almost nose to nose. The stale smell of unwashed teeth hits my nostrils, and my stomach clenches. "You're going to save my life." The words are blunt and direct. A grin spreads on his sunken face, and I narrow my eyes.

"Never," I whispered angrily. "You'll have to kill me before I ever save you."

"That's exactly what I intend to do, son. A life for a life. I need a liver; you're the perfect man to supply it." Aiden supports my father as he lowers down into his wheelchair again. The old man coughs once more, wrinkled hands moving slowly to his mouth before saliva spews out onto his lap. "And as for your brother, the knowledge that he didn't save his baby brother will be sweet revenge. Russell always saw himself as the hero, albeit a deranged one."

"It's been a sudden diagnosis," Aiden says, taking up the conversation. I stand silently, listening to him. "Your father has an unusual AB blood type that you and your brother share. It seemed the sensible course of action to locate a donor from the family. Biological sons are the best course of action."

"Liver donation can come from a living donor," the doctor says meekly, her voice pathetic and barely audible. "We only need to use part of his liver."

"I want fucking all of it!" my father snaps. "This little jackass took everything from me, him and his band of vigilante bastards. My home, my businesses, and my freedom. He will repay me with his life."

"I owe you nothing," I hiss, furious with the curveball before me. Of all the people I expected to open my eyes to once the light reentered the room, my father and Aiden Marley were the last men I ever expected to see.

"Perhaps you owe me less than your brother," he concedes. "Or that treacherous whore of a sister you have. But the doctor requested that we claim the donation from you and not your brother. It seems my little surgeon has a soft spot for him. Her pathetic feelings saved his life but ended yours."

I look at Dr. Rivera, and she skulks back to the corner of the room she was hiding in before.

"He hates you," I tell her. "You're nothing to him." Her face twists, but she doesn't respond, only looks back blankly. All color has drained from her face, and she appears completely exhausted.

"Doctor," Aiden says firmly. "Please advise the patient of the timeline. In other words, how long he has left on this earth." His focus flicks to me. "I'll enjoy watching you die."

The doctor gasps at the crude statement and visibly takes a breath before speaking. "I have a few tests to carry out, but we plan to operate tomorrow evening. I have a colleague on stand-by to perform the removal, and I will transplant the organ myself."

"Excellent, do you hear that, boss?" Aiden chortles, grabbing my father's shoulder. The two men smile at each other, and the finality of it all becomes more clear. "Tomorrow, your death sentence will end."

"Thank you, my boy," he replies. "You are the son I should have had."

The doctor clears her throat and refocuses their attention. She straightens her shoulders, a false confidence in her eyes.

"And after this," she says firmly to Aiden, "my debt is clear. You'll leave me alone and return my husband." I glance at her, confused by the statement.

"Yes," Aiden agrees. "Once you've saved this man's life, I'll write off any debt owed. You can go back to your regular life, and I'll return that pathetic cretin of a man to you. With all his organs intact."

She visibly relaxes before my eyes, and another piece of the puzzle falls into place. Not only has the doctor been carrying out illegal surgery to repay debts, but she's also trying to save her husband.

"What should we do with him?" a brute asks, gesturing to me.

"Put him back in the box," my father advises. "That's where he'll be ending his day tomorrow anyway. He may as well get comfortable."

CHAPTER THIRTY-FOUR

Connor's Apartment, The Level

Samantha

Connor is never late getting home without telling me. We were meant to leave for dinner an hour ago. I glance at my phone lodged in my grasp again, and my palms sweat as my nerves rise. Something is wrong. I know it.

Tonight, Connor has booked a table for us at a new Italian restaurant I've been dying to try out. It's not his usual high-end type place with slick design and gold fixtures. This place was created to look old with red and white checkered tablecloths, dark wood-paneled walls, and green wine bottles stuffed with melting candles. When I walked past it the other day, I was taken right back to being a child when my mother would take us to our local pizza place on my birthday. Normally, only one of my chosen friends and I would celebrate with my family. Money was tight, but I loved that meal every damn year. It's a childhood memory I cherish. Connor should be reliving that time with me tonight, but he's not here, and I'm worried.

Our night at The Estate was hot and unexpected. It was breathtaking that I got to share my body with both of them in the same beautiful space. Those hours spent being cherished were some of the happiest of my life. I can't visualize moving on from one of them. The idea of losing the love of either of them breaks my heart. At this moment, I can't imagine existing without both men.

Russell met us in the breakfast room the following morning. He was at a table set for three with highly shined cutlery and dazzling plates. Freshly-squeezed orange juice was being poured into glasses by a waitress dressed in a stereotypical black uniform with a white lace pinafore. He smiled up at her, and my jealousy bit in my chest. I don't like him smiling at anyone but me.

Holding his brother's hand, I mentally chastised myself for the absurdity of my feelings. Here I was with two men, both gorgeous, eligible, and obsessed with me, and I was jealous of him flashing a staff member a smile. When did I become so entitled to his affection? I was only in my position because these men cared for me, and sometimes I wondered why.

Connor pulled out my chair, and I sat. Russell leaned across, placing a warm palm on my knee beneath the white tablecloth. His hand traveled upwards under my skirt to sit on my thigh, and he flexed his fingers against my already hot skin.

"Morning, Trouble," he said, his voice low as Connor settled in the final seat. "Did you sleep well?"

"I did, thanks," I replied, my lips pulling up at the sides a little. "Worn out?"

"Something like that."

"Orgasms have that effect on a lady," he said with a smirk. His use of the plural form didn't go unnoticed, and his brother's eyes lifted then narrowed. "All that tension takes its toll on that delectable body of yours, I'd imagine from what I saw." He shuffled his chair closer, bending forward more and placing his lips at my ear. "I can still taste you, Trouble. You were fucking beautiful last night."

Connor pulled his phone from his pocket and started scrolling the screen. His finger slid across the glass. I don't know if the action was for show or if he was attempting to keep himself busy. The waitress reappeared behind him.

"Coffee or tea?" she asked.

"Coffee, please," we replied in unison.

"Sugar and milk are on the table." She filled each white cup then walked away. I stood and began making the three drinks. Two sets of eyes watched me prepare their individual cups to their liking. My nipples budded beneath my bra as the intensity of having both men staring as if I were their last meal hit home.

413

Fuck, that is what I want.

Both of them.

Am I greedy? Maybe.

But it's as essential as the air I breathe.

"Thanks," Connor said, lifting his drink and sipping. Russell acknowledged me with a wink and brushed my panties with his fingers. His brother took my hand closest to him, linking our fingers and laying them on the table. I giggled to myself, and they both gave me a look that requested a reason for the random noise. I shook my head and bit my lip, trying to contain more chuckles.

Their treatment of me at breakfast was so apt considering their personalities. The way they handled my body, both of them with love and care, but differently. Connor held my hand and pulled out my chair. Russell grabbed my leg and his fingers strayed to my pussy. If every morning could be like that, it would be perfect.

"Did you have a good night?" Russell asked his brother. A familiar annoyance flashed in Connor's eyes. I know he buries his head in the sand most of the time with our situation.

"I always have a good night with Sam. She's the perfect teddy bear." Russell bristled, pissed by the reminder I assume, that Connor slept in my bed while he had a different suite. This time, Connor leaned in, his breath tickling my flesh. "I'm glad you didn't put your pajamas back on. You feel so much better in my arms naked."

"Stop it," I hissed. "Both of you. Last night was special; don't ruin a perfect experience."

"It won't be happening again," Connor mumbled. His eyes moved between Russell and me, the expression unreadable beyond the obvious struggle.

"What won't be?" My chest ached, saddened by his words.

"What we did last night. When I'm with you, I want you all to myself. All fucking night. I don't believe I'm a man built to share what's his."

"I don't know," Russell said, pushing back in his seat. "I could get used to tag-teaming. Maybe it's something to consider? You take one end, and I'll fuck the other. I don't really have a preference as long as her hole is wet."

"No." Connor stood. His chair crashed backward, smashing against the tiles. He placed his hands on the table, gripping the fabric. "Once, Russell. Once for her. Never again. That's what we agreed. I told you I would do this once." His eyes streamed with hurt and confusion, and they flitted to me. I wilted under his unusually stern expression.

"It's not as if we were all together," Russell countered. "You had your privacy."

"But I knew you had been there. Sam, you need to choose," he said. "If it's not me, then break my heart before I fall for you more." He stepped back and started walking away, then paused and looked over his shoulder. "Not that I think I could love you more than I do now. I've loved you since the beginning, and it's grown daily. The thought of losing you destroys me. It's been my greatest fear since I knew you wanted him, probably before you knew yourself. I would hate to live the reality."

Since that morning I've stayed at home. I haven't seen either of them, needing time to consider what I would do. Tonight was meant to be my time to connect with Connor and hash things out, though I have no idea what that conversation will look like. My head tells me that perhaps the kindest thing I can do is walk away from both of them. My heart screams for me to sort out a solution that suits us all.

Right now, no permanent arrangement seems possible. Perhaps finding love with two men was too good to be true. It's not as wonderful as the romance books predict it will be. With the wrong people involved, what could be a heavenly situation for some turns into nothing more than a love triangle that will break all our hearts.

Nine o'clock flashes on the digital clock in the kitchen, and I call Connor's number again. It rings out. Deciding I have no other choice, I leave his apartment and head for the penthouse. I know Russell is home. He messaged me earlier to say I could meet him later if I wasn't satisfied with my on-rota boyfriend. I'd rolled my eyes at my phone and not replied. He sent me a dick pic ten minutes later. What an idiot, but he made me laugh.

Outside the elevator, I swipe the black key-card over the pad. Russell's free access to his home had been a monumental step for both of us. The doors glide open, and the cabin rises the short distance, one floor up.

I find Russell sprawled on his sofa, watching his immense television. In his lap is a bowl of chips. He stuffs a handful into his mouth then lifts the beer in his hand to wash the food down. Wearing only his boxers, he looks like a college student still in the first throws of independence. His eyes flick over as I walk across his living room, and his mouth twists with amusement.

"Bored already, Trouble?" he asks. "If I'd known you would visit, I would have made myself presentable."

"It's Connor," I say. He immediately sits up, switches off the television, and turns to face me. He focuses on my face with intense eyes.

"What's happened?" His tone is sharp and tense.

"He's not come home." Russell shrugs, then throws himself back on his sofa, unconcerned. "He was meant to be back hours ago."

"Connor lost a case today. A big one. If the firm weren't partly his, I'd probably fire him." Russell swigs his drink again. "Get yourself a beer and come sit down. No doubt he'll call you when he arrives."

"He's not answering his phone," I continue, ignoring his complete lack of alarm. "He always answers."

"Maybe you, but he's quite happy to ignore my calls. Seriously, Trouble, he'll be walking around Canary Wharf to clear his head. Connor likes to beat himself up when things go wrong. I did tell him the guy was cooked; the evidence against him was watertight." He switches on the television again, and a reality show on a desert island flashes up on the screen. He flicks to another channel.

"If you won't help me..." I turn on my heel and stalk off toward the elevator. "I'll go get someone who will."

I don't reach the doors before he's behind me, strong arms wrapped around my middle. His sheer force stops me in my tracks. Sharp teeth skim my neck before sinking softly into my skin. One hand spreads over my stomach, then lowers so his fingers sit just above my clit.

"Okay," he says. With one hand, he keeps me from moving. In the other, his mobile appears from heaven knows where. He drops it in front of us both so we can see the screen.

On the last page, a small red app sits alone with a simple "T" in the center of the icon in black. He taps it, and a map of London opens. A few little blue dots are scattered over the streets. Most are marking what is clearly The Level. I glance up at him, but he doesn't look at me.

"Is that what I think it is?"

"Depends what you think it is." His thumb taps the search bar, and he types "Co." The name Connor pops up. The map immediately zones into an area close to the river known for bars and restaurants. "See, I told you, he'd be drowning his sorrows."

"Do you have me tracked?" I ask him, knowing damn fine the answer is yes.

"You? No. Your phone, however..."

"Controlling unhinged arsehole," I mutter, wriggling from his grasp.

"Not just me. This app has five user logins," he tells me with a deep chuckle. "You'll always be safe with me, Trouble. I'll always know where you are." He runs his fingers across my lower back. I will my body not to respond, but like the treacherous bitch she is, my nipples pop hard.

"Not if I leave my phone at home," I jibe. He spins me to face him, holding my arms by my sides. My neck cranes as my chin rises to look at his darkened face.

"Deliberately leave your phone at home, and I'll install a tracker in your arm. Fucking men like us will bring you enemies. Being loved by men like us can be a death sentence." He cocks his head, astute but slight wild eyes running over my face. "I told you before. No matter what happens, you're now ours."

"What bar is that?" I ask him, signaling to the phone crammed next to my skin with my eyes. He takes the bait and releases me, his attention moving back to where his brother is. Possessive idiot.

"I don't know or care. A shitty one. Come to bed. Connor's loss will be my gain. Why should our girl lose out tonight because he's had a bad day?" There it is again, that phrase: *our girl*. Russell uses it more and more, and it gives me a tentative hope that we could sort out some arrangement. If only Connor would compromise, too.

"No, I'm going to find him. Something has happened." I pull my remaining arm from his grasp. "Stay here and jerk off, or come with me and help."

He rolls his eyes, then turns and walks off in the direction of his bedroom.

"Where are you going?" I call to his retreating back.

"To get some fucking clothes on. What does it look like?" I watch as he strides away, his tight ass gorgeous in the silk. "Sometimes I wonder who's fucking in charge here." When he returns, he slides his arm around my waist before leading me to the elevator. We step in, but he looks furious at the inconvenience and doesn't speak.

"Do you want the answer to that question?"

"Which one?"

"Who is in charge?" He scowls and I step forward, placing one foot between his. "I am, Russ, because I could hold out a hell of a lot longer than you. Amenable men are much more enticing to pleasure than arseholes."

"I would love to pleasure your arsehole," he tells me.

***

Russell

The Union Jack Bar, London

The temptation to lift her onto my waist, hit the stop button, and fuck Trouble to hell and back in that elevator had been hard to contain. But she also questioned my ability to hold out, and as hard as it was, I didn't want to prove her right within five minutes.

So now we're standing beside a back street tavern that's heaving with drunkards on a Friday evening. They spill out onto the streets, staggering around as if it were the early morning hours already. Sam, unfazed, weaves through the crowd toward the bar; I follow her like a puppy dog.

The bartender is tall and dressed in a grimy white T-shirt with jeans. His blonde hair is slicked back as if it hasn't been washed for days or a whole tub of hair gel was emptied on it this morning. Perhaps both are true. His mouth widens when he spots Sam at the bar, exposing yellow teeth and raw red gums.

"Hello, sweetheart," he drawls, spit oozing between his cracked lips. I step up beside her, and he glances at me. "Brought yer rottweiler with you, doll?"

"Show some respect for your patrons," I growl.

"My pub, my rules. And yer no a customer if you've no paid. Take yer fancy suit and fuck off."

Sam glances up at me and shakes her head before focusing back on the cunt behind the worktop. "Sorry about my friend," she says, her voice meek. Her tone is nothing like I've heard from her before. The use of the word friend as a descriptor pisses me off too. I squeeze her hip, and she nips the skin on the outside of my hand between razor-sharp nails. "We were hoping you could help us. Check the phone app, Russ."

"He's here," I say, looking around the chaos, but my brother is nowhere to be seen.

"Our friend has gone walk about. His 'find my phone' app says he's here. Have you seen him?" She pulls her own mobile out and shows the guy a photo of Connor and her in front of the London Eye. I wonder if she has any pictures of the two of us on her phone that she flashes at people. "He had bad news at work, and we want to ensure he's okay."

"Guys like that don't come in here, sweetheart. Look around." He gestures with his hand at his clientele. "But feel free to check, as long as you buy a drink."

I drop a fifty-pound note on the counter. "No drinks required," I say. "Come on, Trouble. This is good for locating someone within ten meters. He can't be far." We follow the little blue dot that marks Connor's position; it brings us to the bathroom doors. We both stare at the dark wood with the tattered yellowed signs designating men and women. "You look in yours, and I'll do mine."

I step through the door, pushing on the gold finger plate, and my hand sticks to the surface. On entering the bathroom I immediately wash my hands.

"Connor," I say loudly. "Where are you, bro?" I half expect to find him passed out in a stall. A few minutes later, Sam appears behind me. "This is the gents," I tell her.

"I've been in worse," she replies, then starts kicking each cubicle door open. "He's not here."

"But his phone must be," I mutter, now genuinely concerned about where the fuck he is. Sam is ripping the lids off the toilet cisterns one by one. Within seconds, she holds up two handsets, both of which I recognize as my brothers.

"Shit," I say, stunned that we haven't found him and panicking at what the outcome of our little search could mean. We have more enemies than I care to admit. My brother missing and his phones stashed can only mean something bad is happening. "I'll call the others."

Samantha walks over and passes me the two mobiles. Her face tells me she's terrified. I place my hand on her cheek in an attempt to manage her building fear, but the next words from her lips are like a punch to the gut.

"I can't lose him," she whispers, choked with emotion. "I love him."

CHAPTER THIRTY-FIVE

The Level Boardroom

Russell

The boardroom is buzzing with a mixture of adrenaline, fear, and vengeance. No one sits—every person here is standing or moving around impatiently as we search for my brother, my best friend on this earth. The man who has stood by me through thick and thin, from our days of being beaten by our father until now, when *we're* the men distributing the retribution.

Damon and Hunter are standing by the large screen running through the CCTV footage from near the bar where Connor's phones were found. With so many people, it's hard to zone in on anyone in particular. According to the tracker, Connor left the office at 5:24 p.m., and his phones were placed in the toilet cistern seventy-two minutes later. So, somewhere between 5:24 p.m. and 6:36 p.m., he was waylaid.

Harrison and Emma are watching a second screen, this one nearer the river, where Connor's phone paused for a while before being taken to the pub. If someone snatched him, it most likely happened there.

"Have you found anything?" Damon asks. He walks up behind his new partner and trails his fingers across her shoulders. She glances up at him, her eyes concerned.

"Not yet," she replies.

"Ma-ma," the voice of a small child calls, and their daughter, Annie, wanders over to her, arms wide from where Samantha and Violet were taking care of the two children. Evie, my niece, crawls around the floor, grabbing the legs of furniture and people's feet.

"There's my girl," Emma coos, lifting Annie onto her knee before returning to look at the screen.

"There," Hunter shouts, pointing at the video. He gestures to a man walking through the crowd fast, dressed smartly and clearly out of place. "That's the bastard."

"How do you know?" Sam asks as she walks up to stand beside him. She stares intently as they replay the video, then zooms in on the man's face. Her eyes screw up, focusing in on the grainy footage. "He just looks like a normal guy."

"I know a nasty bastard when I see one, and someone who is working under instruction," he tells her. "I've taken many off the streets. That isn't a man going to the pub for an after-work beer. Do you think your old friends in the force could run facial recognition on that, McKinney?"

Damon looks up on hearing his name from being crouched beside Emma. "Sure, it's not as if I've asked too many favors already." He rolls his eyes, but his mobile is already at his ear.

My sister comes to my side as I pace up and down the windows that look out to the city below. "Where is he?" I mumble, and Violet slips her hand into mine. "Fuck, we can't lose him." She squeezes my palm, but the devastation is written all over her features. She's losing hope alongside me. Our family has lost so much and taken dozens of blows; the chances of us coming out of another attack with us all unscathed are minuscule.

"Russ, look at this," Harrison calls, and we move to his shoulder. He focuses the screen on a group of businessmen standing in a circle. Another man in a suit with a briefcase joins them. "That's him. That's Connor," he says. "Come on, where did you go? And why the fuck did you stop?"

Samantha appears on my opposite side. She grips my hand. I stand and watch my brother disappear from view, my sister on one side and the woman I love on the other. Just then, a phone beeps. Samantha pulls her handset from her back pocket.

"It's Bryan," she whispers, her voice cracking. "He's sent a..."

"What did he say?" I snap, plucking the phone from her fingers. Samantha mentioned recently that Bryan has been less available. She wasn't meant to be talking to him at all. My brother and I weren't amused when she ignored our instruction to cut contact.

They used to talk a lot at work and by message, but she hasn't heard from him as often lately. A lot of the time her communication is being left on "read" with no response. She put it down to his complex family situation and having more important shit to worry about. To me, this is all too coincidental not to be connected. I didn't like him anyway.

"Nothing."

When I look at the message, there are no words, only a map location pin. I click the link, which zooms into an address outside the city. Flipping to street view, the screen shows an old sandstone building with black gates chained closed. The property information box shows co-ordinates rather than any address.

"Where is that?" I mutter.

Harrison appears behind us with his daughter, whom he collected from the floor moments ago. He passes her to Violet, then reaches for the screen in my hands. His eyes widen a fraction as he looks at the information.

"Fuck, I know where that is," he says, his words sullen. "I remember it, but I wish I didn't."

"What is it? Where is it? We need to go." He places a hand on my arm as the girls retake and tighten their grip on my fingers. Both panic and adrenaline burst in my veins; we have an address where Connor could be. What is everyone waiting for?

"Corvendale Sick Asylum," he says, bringing me up short. I've heard the horror stories of the patients who stayed there. The ones who survived, anyway. "It's closed down, but it's the abandoned mental health hospital. I used to have to visit my mother there when she was unwell before she died." My friend lost his mother as a child brutally before he met us. He was eight years old. He visibly shivers at the thought. "It's an evil place. Why there?"

"I don't care. Let's go and get Connor," I say, moving for the door. The girls still hold my hands. I try to pull them away, but they hold on tight.

"Wait," Damon interrupts. "Don't jump the gun. What if this is a trap? Why this hospital? We need to know what we're walking into. What if this Bryan guy is part of all this?"

"No," Sam says firmly. "Bryan wouldn't do anything to risk his kids. He's trying to help. He's my friend. I trust him."

"He could be being threatened," Damon counters. "You've not known him that long. There are too many connections between the hospital and Connor going missing. This guy pops up every time."

"Whatever is going on, we need to go and find out," I snap, pulling my hands away and striding to the exit. "I'll be in the garage in ten minutes; whoever is coming, meet me there. We can make a plan on the way." As I slam the door closed, I hear Hunter's voice carry across the room.

"Yes, boys! Let's go bleed some arseholes of their last breath."

***

Corvendale Sick Asylum, London

CHASE

"It's like a fucking family day out," I mutter as we all sit in cars parked opposite the old hospital. It took two vehicles to get us all here as everyone insisted on coming.

"Women with guns are sexy, and can't believe we have one on the team," Hunter says over the speaker. Damon and him are in the large SUV behind. Harrison and Violet sit in my back seat while Sam is beside me. Emma stayed at home to look after the children.

"I wasn't staying at the boardroom waiting to hear what the fuck was going on," Samantha tells me. "I told you, I can fire a gun." She taps the handgun strapped to her thigh below the shorts she is wearing. "Champion shooter at my Girl Scouts camp, four years running."

"There is a big difference between a static target and a man trying to kill you. I wish you had stayed back, Trouble." She glances at me blankly, then returns to staring straight ahead. "I couldn't survive if you get hurt because of all this."

"We'll stay in the car as discussed. Won't we, Sam?" Violet pipes up from the rear seat. "The gun is purely for our protection when you all go inside and save Connor." The tone of my sister's voice indicates she doesn't believe Sam will sit in her seat either. One hint of her needing to get involved, and she'll be bursting into the center of the fiasco, gun poised. "Isn't that right, Samantha? We will stay here," Violet prompts, and her friend mumbles something that resembles agreement.

"*You* will stay in the car, Vi," Harrison adds. I glance around and see that he's handing her a can of pepper spray. "If you

429

put yourself in danger, you won't sit down for a week. It isn't our enemy you'll have to worry about." She flushes a soft pink, but her eyes dance with happiness. The pair of them can be insufferable when they get all gooey over each other.

"Does that promise go for me too, Waite? I bet you're handy with a belt," Hunter interjects. It's easy to forget he's there listening.

Damon doesn't speak. Undoubtedly, he will be brooding over everything that could go wrong today.

Harrison completely ignores the comment, unflustered; he leans across and kisses Violet's cheek.

"I love you," he whispers.

"You too," she says, turning to him and planting a kiss on his lips. She pulls back, pauses, then takes his hand and places it on her stomach. Tears fill her eyes instantly, and my friend's respond by popping wide. "Come back safe...for your family."

Harrison's jaw drops a fraction as he searches her face, his mind running so fast I can almost hear it. "Fuck, Vi. Are you? Are we?" he stutters.

"Yes, baby. You're going to be a daddy again." Her hand lifts to his cheek, and he closes his eyes. I know Harrison has been desperate for Violet to get pregnant. Even though he treats Evie as his own child, they've both been keen to add to their family. "You need to come home for our children," she tells him fiercely.

"I will." He leans in and kisses her again; Samantha and I turn away to give them as much privacy as we can in the car. It hits hard that the older we get, and as more people enter our lives, the stakes get higher each time we face danger. Every day, our lives grow, but with that, so does what we can lose.

Samantha reaches for my hand, our fingers interlinking. She sits them on my knee. We both look out of the windshield our minds whirling with what may happen in the coming minutes and hours. Since she told me she loved Connor, I've flitted between determination to bring him back, hurt, and jealousy. I wonder if she would feel the same if it were me who was missing; would my removal make her want me more?

"How do we know he's in there?" she asks me, and I shrug.

"We don't. We have to hope that the location tag was to help us find him. If not, and we're jumping to the wrong conclusions, it could all be for nothing." I lift a hand and wipe my brow. I've never been more terrified than I am now. My brother's life depends on me, on us, on our friends, and we have no idea who the actual enemy is or what his disappearance is really connected to.

"I love you," she whispers, and I turn to face her. "Come back for me, and bring your brother too. We all need each other."

I lean forward, my forehead pressing against hers. Closing my eyes, I allow a tear to roll down my cheek. I've never felt more vulnerable than I do now in all aspects of my life. My heart, head, and future could be blown to pieces depending on how this plays out. "I love you too, Trouble. I'll bring him back for you. Remember, if you see anything, sound the horn and I'll come for you."

Without waiting for her response, I push open the door and step out into the street. My friends appear from their respective seats.

The old hospital is located in a poor area of the city surrounded by rundown apartment blocks. No one is on the streets. Cars are scattered around, a lot with tires too flat to drive. Every other property seems to have an old sofa in the garden as trash cans decorate the flowerbeds.

"This place is as terrifying as it ever was. The screams, fuck—I swear I can still hear them." Harrison shudders, his focus fixed on our target. "Do you think they'll be waiting for us?" he asks as we cross the road and reach the huge black iron gates marking the entrance.

"If they're here, whoever they are, I have no doubt they will be," Damon says. He stops as we step through the gates, touching the heavy chain clearly cut with bolt cutters.

We all pause beside him, looking up at the huge sandstone building. The old blue signs directing patients to various parts of the building still hang on the damp walls. Every window appears to be boarded up. Broken glass lies across the entrance. We pull our guns from our belts and make our way across the carnage to the front door.

"Clear," Hunter advises as we move inside the building. The wooden boards ripped from the front doors are lying discarded on the floor.

"What are we looking for?" Harrison muses as all our eyes scan the space.

"Any sign of life," I say as a car horn blasts in the distance. I spin to face it just in time to see a brute lifting his weapon in my direction. A second man appears beside him; then I feel eyes on my back.

"We've been waiting for you," the first man says. "You certainly took your time. That poor brother of yours will think you don't love him." I look over the men's shoulders to where Violet and Samantha are. There's no movement around them, and I feel a little relief. During our drive over, we planned not to hide our arrival; sometimes, you must be brazen to find out what's truly going on. Today, what we need is to find out exactly what the fuck this is all about.

"Hello, boys," Hunter says, his face splitting into a wide smile. He spins his gun on his finger and slides it back into his belt. "How lovely for you to come and greet us."

"Give us your guns," the man barks, and Hunter shakes his head. The asshole wiggles his weapon in the mafia don's direction. "Gun. Now."

"Do you know who I am?" Hunter asks him, straightening to his full height and not looking in the least concerned that we are outnumbered or surrounded. The henchman blinks as if confused by the question. "Have you heard of Hunter Devane?"

"You're not him," a second man scoffs. "Hunter Devane is the most feared man in London. He wouldn't just walk in here. He wouldn't be that stupid." I roll my eyes as Hunter puffs his chest out. His slim frame gives people the wrong idea of how deadly he can be. "You couldn't skin a banana. Devane can skin a man alive in minutes."

"I appreciate the sentiment," Hunter says. "But it would take longer than a few minutes to flay a whole body; perhaps a hand I could complete in the two-minute time period." His hands move to his hips, and he bares his teeth once again. The men surrounding us look at one another, bemused by the strange character holding court.

"Bullshit!" the second man says, waving away Hunter's claims. "You're nothing but a lowlife idiot. Head of the Irish Mafia, my ass. Maybe you should be checking in here, mate."

Hunter moves fast; his knife lodges directly in the bastard's eye. He wails, grasping at his face. The men behind us pounce forward. One grabs my arms and pulls them behind my back. Hunter spins, swinging a second blade from side to side.

"Who's next?" he asks with a laugh. "Does anyone else want to question my identity?"

"I'll shoot," the first man stammers. "I'll kill you." Hunter glances over his shoulder. The man stabbed through the eye falls to the ground on his back. Hunter walks up and pulls the knife from the wound. The man groans like an animal whose life is seeping from its body.

I realize that Harrison and Damon are nowhere to be seen. They've gone, as planned, taking advantage of the distraction. If we ran into trouble, we were to split up. Hunter was to stay with me. He loves facing up to an enemy.

"I'll shoot," the bastard says again.

"I dare you," Hunter responds. "It will be the quickest way to die. Take me out, and my family will seek revenge on you one person you love at a time. You would have written yours *and* their death sentences." He raises an eyebrow. "Is that a risk you're willing to take?" Everyone falls silent. The men with the guns look at each other, completely lost at how to deal with the situation. "Let go of my friend and take us to your boss," Hunter barks. "We need to know what the fuck's going on."

One man nods to the other, and my arms fall free. I shrug to release the tension. Two men walk ahead of us into the building, another following behind.

"Find the other two," the man in charge says. I hope Damon and Harrison manage to find something before being caught. Not knowing what we're walking into, having them free could save all our lives. "Bring them all to the theater." My ears perk up at the word theater, confused about where that could be. We follow the men through the maze of corridors with cracked plaster and smears of God knows what.

After walking what feels like an age, we come across a room in the very center of the building that looks to be renovated. As we step through the doors, I'm met with the pungent smell of bleach. The lights are on, and the white room is lit up bright. More men appear, grabbing Hunter and my arms again then training a gun on each of our foreheads.

"Search them," the chief goon orders. "Remove all their weapons. Check everywhere; it wouldn't surprise me if that lunatic had a blade lodged up his arse." He signals to Hunter, who grins.

"Give me a thrill and check for yourself," he says with a wink.

Our weapons are pulled from their hiding places and thrown into a pile at the boss's feet. They find every gun and knife strapped to us, hidden from view—even the small blades lodged in the sole of Hunter's shoes. We can only hope they haven't found Damon and Harrison yet.

"What is this place?" I ask the men, once their search is complete.

"Your viewing area," one man replies, then the doors slam closed, and I hear the bolt slide over.

"Fuck, they've locked us in," I snap, running to the exit and pulling lamely on the handle.

"Chase, forget that and come here. We've found him." Hunter walks to the other side of the room, a large window facing further into the building. I join him to look through the glass, but I see nothing like I could have predicted.

Connor is lying on a hospital bed in the center, a drip attached to his hand and a monitor blinking beside him. A door opens on the other side, and Josephine Rivera walks in. I lift a hand and bang on the glass. Her eyes pop up momentarily, then she returns to tending to my brother's arm.

"Josie," I shout, hammering the divider again. She keeps her eyes fixed on Connor. "Fuck, we need to get in there." I scan our cell looking for anything to smash the glass, but it's empty. Just then, the doors we entered through open once more and two of the men who brought us here step through.

"Follow us," they say in unison, raising their guns and gesturing for us to exit into the corridor. They direct us down the murky passageway, then through a door on the left into another pristine hospital room.

It takes me a moment to process who the man in the bed is, my mind struggling to connect the seemingly unconnected dots. My father lifts his head and attempts a smile. Happiness never suited him. He's old and worn, a sliver of the man I saw earlier this year.

"Hello, son," he croaks. "I am so glad you could join us for the monumental day." The man standing beside him steps forward and smiles. I recognize him too. Aiden "Fucking" Marley, the bastard who broke my sister's heart and made her life hell. Of all the people in the world, these two are the ones with who I have the most unfinished business.

"You mean the day you die, Father," I snarl, and he laughs.

"It won't be me who is dying. That's your brother's role in all this. It's quite ironic that one of the arseholes who ruined my life will also save it." His focus moves to double swinging doors held open by large rocks, my brother lies silent in the next room. "I suppose you are wondering what this is all about." He barely lifts his hands before letting them drop back down. His body screams of death and mortality. The man is clinging to life.

"Allow me," Aiden begins. He places a fist over his mouth and clears his throat. "Your father was diagnosed with liver failure not long ago, and we needed to find a replacement liver as soon as possible. Luckily, a small business opportunity I operated made this all possible, and his hospital appointments made his escape relatively easy to execute. It's amazing what having the right people on hand can do in a complicated situation." He walks around as he speaks, enjoying all the attention being on him. Hunter, plainly bored, leans back against the wall. Aiden stops to glare at him.

"Continue," Hunter says, glancing up. "This truly is an interesting story. I had forgotten what a good storyteller you are, Marley. Do keep going before I fall to fucking sleep."

"This man," Aiden says, gesturing to my father, "I owe him the world, and I would do anything to save him. My business dealings on British soil grew to surpass my U.S. assets only because of his connections and support. Finding him a liver and avenging against those who wronged him was inevitable."

"Why the fuck are we here?" I demand, and my father laughs. His whole body vibrates before he coughs violently.

"Is it not obvious, boy? Or are you still the dense piece of shit you always were? This is revenge, plain and simple. I survive, and you get to watch it happen. And the bonus is you getting to watch your brother die." Marley touches my father's shoulder, a gesture filled with empathy I've never seen from either of them.

"You've always felt responsible for him, Russell. And I know Connor dying because you failed to save him will be the best punishment for you. Your death would be too kind. Initially, I was taken with the idea of your liver, but then I think of your teenage years. It probably doesn't have long left itself."

"Touch him and..." I trail off as the doctor walks in behind them, Bryan by her side. She doesn't look at me. Her gaze is directed at the floor.

"We're ready," she whispers, and I swear a sob escapes her lips. Bryan stands at her side, staring blankly ahead. I look at them, and all I want to do is wring their fucking necks.

Have they both been part of this damn thing since the beginning? Did me using my connections to get Samantha's traineeship throw us all in the firing line, or would this have all happened anyway? It's so twisted, I have no idea. Hunter is still leaning against the wall, now cleaning under his fingernails with a piece of smashed tile he found somewhere, seemingly unperturbed by anything going on.

"Thank you, doctor. Please proceed," Aiden says. He strides over and grabs her arm, pulling her hard against his chest. Nasty eyes stare down, locking on fast. "This is the most important operation of your career. Your team better be ready."

When I glance back over my shoulder, Connor's room is filled with other medical staff, maybe a dozen. They have pulled back his sheets, and a tray of implements has been wheeled into the room. I recognize one doctor as one named Winslow from Harbridges Medical Center in Mayfair; his picture and name had been shared in The Level months ago when all this came to light.

Josephine turns away, moving to leave.

"What the hell did you do, Josie?" I snarl, and she stops dead.

"Saved my husband," she whispers, her voice devastated. "I'm sorry." With that, she walks away toward Connor, closing the doors behind her.

"Well, son," my father says, diverting my attention to him. "It's time to say goodbye to your brother. Today, he saves my life, but in doing so, he loses his own. And I know for a fact, Russell, the knowledge you couldn't stop it will eat you alive from the inside."

I step forward and he wags a wrinkled finger. "You were always a conundrum. Violent and hot-headed, but fiercely loyal to your siblings. If they knew how many beatings you took for them as children, they would never feel as though they could re-pay their debt. I've never met another man so selfish but selfless at the same time."

The person I've been suppressing for years comes forward. All my days pushing the anger down burst through; all I see is blood red. I look from my father to Marley, two men who take joy in hurting those around them in any way they can.

"You can't be saved if you're already dead," I snarl, lunging forward. Hunter comes to my side, pushing Aiden backward as I grab for my father. An unseen blow knocks me sideways. I stagger, then fall to the floor, and one of the henchmen throws himself on top of me; heavy hands pummel my face. I grasp for his throat, trying to stop him. I hear the wails of men. When I look up, Hunter has grabbed a scalpel from the prepared medical tray and is slicing at his opponents wildly. But there's only one of him and many of them.

A gunshot rings out, but I have no idea where it came from. Frantically, I kick and push my assailant. I reach on impulse for the hidden gun in my waistband; it's gone, of course. So I grab the next best thing, a small stool, and slam it against his face. His expression goes blank, then he falls to the side. When I clamber to my feet, the chaos continues. I grab the man's gun.

Hunter fights off Aiden plus another henchman. My father attempts to move off his bed away from the danger, but his old body doesn't comply. He's left sitting like a duck waiting to be shot.

I glance into Connor's room. Damon is pinning what looks like a doctor to the wall while Harrison points his weapon at Josephine Rivera. The other medics are pushing each other out of the door. Damon raises his gun and fires again. Everyone stops.

"Sew him back up," Harrison growls to the doctor. I realize then that they have already started operating. The familiar blue sheet poised across my brother's abdomen with spotlights focused on his stomach.

Connor sleeps peacefully amongst the fray, completely unaware he's been cut open. I pray we aren't too late. Damon says something I can't hear, and the doctor moves to Connor's side.

With everyone else occupied, I walk over to my father. I lift my hand to my lip, and it comes away red. He grins up nastily.

"That will bruise in the morning, boy," he says. "You have surprised me with your spirit. If you weren't such a disappointment as a son, I'd almost be proud of you. There's certainly part of me in your blood."

I take my gun, holding it high and bringing it down hard on his cheek. His head snatches sideways, but he laughs.

"You don't even deserve the freedom of death. I hope you burn in hell," I tell him.

"Hell is where I've always been, boy. My life was spent surrounded by idiots." Once again, I raise my weapon; this time, my father is staring down the barrel. I look around, and it's clear we've won. "You could never kill me," my father goads. "Deep down, you've always known you owe me. I created you; without me, you would never exist."

I glare at the man who gave me life, a man who should have made me feel safe, and I want to pull the trigger. But the child in me yearns not to. I want him gone, but not by my hand. I hate him, but my family means everything to me, even if I don't show it. Harrison reappears with a line of medical staff, Bryan walking at the back. A smaller group of medics continue to work on my brother under Damon's command, the dividing doors now closed again. Through the glass panes, I can see Connor has been connected to a heart monitor, and the consistent spike of the line brings me a little relief.

Aiden's eyes land on Harry, and he smirks. "Oh, Harrison Waite, how is Violet?" he asks him. "Is she missing me? Is she still a stupid little bitch with a nice cunt? I hope she appreciates my nod to her in all of this. Varley Medical." He laughs hard, the sound on the verge of hysteria before placing his hands on his knees and bending from the waist. "Varley and Marley, who'd of thought eh? Sometimes, the obvious clues are in plain sight."

"Not for you," Harrison responds deadpan, lifting his gun and shooting Aiden perfectly between the eyes. "You'll never think a vile thought again." He drops the weapon, turning to walk away. "I'm off to get my wife. Do what you want with that fuckwit." My father wails as Marley's body falls to the floor. His old, tired eyes close tight as his last line of defense falls.

Hunter lines each person up against the wall and begins asking them their names and reasons for being there. Damon appears and pulls a pad and pen from an inside pocket. You can remove him from the police force, but he'll always be a copper.

"They're starting to sew him up, but they are scrubbing back up to minimize risk," he tells me as a way of explanation. "I told that bitch of a doctor he better not die or she'll be up on a murder charge." I nod, then return to focus on my father.

"So, son, what's it to be?" he asks, his voice quiet as he looks at Marley bleeding out on the floor. "I'm beaten. You win."

"No one wins, Father. That's where you always got it wrong. When there's pain and death, most of the time, we all lose."

The other men in the room are distracted by processing the people apprehended. Damon begins to escort them from the room.

"You have an option, and we could both still come out on top," my father says.

"And what would that be?" I ask him.

"Release the doctor, let her operate. Your brother will pass away painlessly, and you'll get the piece of skirt all to yourself. You'll be a hero for catching the dangerous organ thief, Aiden Marley. You'll bring to an end a crime circuit no one knew was operating." He grins. "And you can reward yourself with a fuck with your own tart. You won't even have to share."

"And what's in it for you?" I reply, attempting to bury my disgust behind fake calm. My mind immediately plays the scenario of Samantha's devastation that we didn't save my brother. The pain on her face breaks my heart in my imagination, and I am damn sure it will happen in reality. I will not allow my father to hurt her more than he already has.

"I'll take my new liver and disappear from your life. All I need is the doctor and a few of the staff."

"No. I'm not the same man you are, and I won't make a deal with an evil bastard like you."

I don't see the approach, but then a bullet passes through my father's skull. He instantly flops forward. Dead. When I look up, Bryan stands to one side, arms straight in front of him like a zombie. To his side is Samantha, her finger over his on the trigger. I look between them, perplexed. My girl encourages the gun from her friend's fingers; she places it down on the floor.

"Trouble, what the fuck did you do?" I stammer. She walks over and throws her arms around my neck.

"For once," she whispers, "someone was saving *you*."

CHAPTER THIRTY-SIX

The Level Boardroom

Samantha

Russell holds my hand as we take the elevator down to the lower floor. We step out to find Connor waiting for us. He's dressed casually in his gray sweats, as he has been since we brought him home from the hospital a week ago.

"Could you not put a fucking suit on?" Russell says angrily as his brother takes me in his arms and kisses my forehead briefly. "You're milking this patient shit."

"I have the best nurse," he replies, squeezing me close. "Her bed baths are awesome. There are a lot of extras to be enjoyed. I especially like..."

I place my finger on his lips and shake my head. He grins back, and then his eyes flick to his brother. Russell is standing, arms folded across his chest, emitting a silent growl.

"Don't aggravate him," I tell Connor. "He's had a complex morning."

"Oh, do tell me, what could have gone so wrong?" Connor, who seems to have found a passion for being a nuisance since being told to stay home and recover from the delirium he suffered due to the anesthetic and the botched surgery, rearranges his face into one of nonchalance.

"You know damn fine," Russell snarls. "I'll be taking my key card off you."

Connor shrugs, unconcerned. When Russell was at the office late yesterday, he snuck up to the penthouse and set various traps around the place. As his brother carried out his morning routine today, he was met with many inconveniences. "What the fuck did you put in my shampoo?" Russell holds out his hands, which are stained with streaks of red.

"Fabric dye," Connor says bluntly, and Russell's mouth drops open. "My research concluded that it would stain your hands but wash straight out of your hair. I thought the results would be comical, but overall more manageable."

"Manageable!"

"Well, yeah, you tend to always wear something with pockets." He rummages in his sweatpants and pulls out a piece of folded-up paper. "Here, I printed this off the internet. Seemingly, lemon juice helps."

"Great, so now I'll have patchy red hands and smell like fucking toilet bleach. Come on, Trouble. Everyone is waiting." He stalks off toward the door of the boardroom, Connor and myself wandering behind. Russell pushes the door hard. It swings open and bounces off the wall.

"Be fucking careful," Harrison yells, and when we enter the room, I see him standing at the table, hands on his hips, glaring at my other boyfriend. Russell ignores him then throws himself down on a chair. I wander over to sit beside him, and Connor plops down beside me.

The door swings open again, hammering the same spot it did moments ago. Mrs. D appears with a tray of freshly baked goods in her hands. Harrison drops his face into his hands. "My wall," he mumbles. "I'll need to get it painted again."

"Who's hungry?" Mrs. D says with a huge smile. She looks around the room at us all. "I love the fact you're all here. Where are my girls?" She places the tray on the sideboard as Annie scampers over to her, arms wide. She picks the little girl up and swings her around. Evie, who is sitting on Violet's knee, claps her hands with the older girl's antics.

"We're going to have our hands full with these two, Violet," Emma says, and the two women exchange a knowing look. "Never mind the one in your belly."

"About that..." Everyone falls silent, waiting for news, a nervous energy taking hold. "There are actually two new recruits in my belly."

Hunter jumps to his feet, running over to Harrison and wrapping his arms around his neck. "Well done, my friend," he yells. "Those swimmers of yours are strong!" Harrison laughs but shakes his head at our crazy friend. So dangerous, so deadly, but with the people he loves, one hundred percent present.

"Congratulations," Damon says with a sincere smile.

Violet's eyes move to me and her brothers sitting on the opposite side of the table. She flashes them a wary smile, and they both stand before rounding the furniture and pulling her into a hug. Connor takes Evie into his arms.

"We will be the best uncles we can be," Connor tells her. "To you and your little brothers."

"They might be two more girls. Nothing is guaranteed," his sister warns.

"We have enough girls." Connor's focus moves between Evie and Annie. "Little ones and fully grown, all of whom cause chaos."

"But we wouldn't have it any other way. These ladies won't want for anything," Russell adds, and the three siblings beam at one another. I move to join them, but the boys step away and Violet embraces me.

"I can't believe it," she whispers.

"You deserve all the happiness," I tell her. "When are you due?"

"April, I'm just twelve weeks gone. We found out at our scan yesterday."

"Us girls are going to have the best time getting ready for the new arrivals." My eyes move to Emma. She's new to the group, having only returned after sorting out her relationship with Damon in June. My friendship with Violet is solid, but it's important Emma knows she's part of this homemade family too. "All of us." Emma smiles back, genuine appreciation on her face.

"So, shall we get this wrapped up?" Russell says. "Some of us have places to be."

"Exciting plans?" Hunter asks, watching Russell look from me to Connor and back again. "The three of you?"

"We're celebrating," Connor replies. "Samantha is due some pampering, and we can all be civil for a few hours. Even my brother and I." Russell lifts his hands, turning his palms over, then glares at his brother.

"Perhaps we could have been."

"Chill, we'll pick up some lemon juice for you."

"You didn't just fucking tell me to chill?" Russell snarls as Mrs. D. drops a bottle of lemon juice down in front of him.

"I noticed when you arrived," she tells him, squeezing his shoulder. "That will take those dye stains right off." We all watch as she turns and totters off out of the door.

"That woman really is a miracle on legs," Russell mumbles, squirting the liquid into his hands. Harrison jumps up and collects a towel from the bathroom, dropping it in front of him before returning to his seat.

"So," Harrison says, "before we all go home to celebrate our respective wins, my first will be the fact my wife actually stayed in the car like she was told. I am taking that as an improvement in her behavior." He smiles at Violet, who sticks her tongue out playfully. She had wanted to come with me into the hospital when I heard the gunshot. I demanded she stay, but I won't tell him that. "I can confirm that the police have moved past us regarding last week's issues. Thanks to Damon's contacts in the department, we've been able to remove our names from the case file."

"How did you manage that?" Emma asks him.

"Don't ask," Damon replies. "Put it this way, I've called in every favor ever owed."

"And Bryan?" I ask, my words nervous. Neither Connor nor Russell would tell me anything of his fate. Last week, I had been pulled away within seconds of killing their father. When they asked me why I did it, I told them that when I reached the room, Bryan had been standing with the gun pointed at Edward Chase. On instinct, I'd stepped forward and placed my hand over his; in that moment, I knew we were both protecting people we loved.

"He's been released for now," Harrison says. "I'm moving to have the charges against him dropped due to diminished responsibility. Marley had his son, and he threatened to remove his organs if Bryan didn't help him lure us all to the hospital. I don't believe Bryan was ever involved or being paid for the organ theft at Varley Medical. He's just a hard-working father trying to look after his kids."

"Also," Emma pipes up, and all eyes move to her. It's easy to forget she works at the law firm and probably has a better idea of what is happening than Violet or myself. "His eldest son just turned eighteen, so he can take responsibility for the younger ones if the worst happens. I've managed to negotiate child support payments from their mother as well." She beams, clearly proud of what she achieved. "It's enough to cover all their monthly living costs and have plenty left over. Amazing what a dive into her billionaire boyfriend's finances can achieve."

"Great job, Spitfire," Damon says, leaning over and kissing her softly on the lips. "Watch your back, boys." His eyes flick between the three other lawyers in the room. "My girl will be taking your jobs."

"Suits me," Harrison says. "With three kids in the future to look after, more time at home would be helpful. Maybe I could be retired by forty." Everyone laughs, but deep down I think he could be serious.

"And what about Josie?" Russell asks, and my pesky jealousy appears. Fuck, after everything she did, does he still care?

"She's remanded at HMP, Bronzefield. I did go to visit her, but I can't represent her. It's too close to Bryan's case, though a colleague has agreed to take her on. There's little chance of her walking out of this free." Harrison speaks clearly and precisely, his tone professional. "Sadly for Dr. Rivera, there are just too many complications. Between the loan from Varley, the death of the illegal organ donor, and her operating without authority and knowingly distributing organs, she will spend decades behind bars."

"Why?" I ask after he lists the offenses.

"Why would she go to prison, or why did she do it?"

"Why do it?" I confirm.

"Greed," Russell says quietly beside me. "Josephine always wanted more than she had. She probably got wrapped up in this stage by stage and never thought of the consequences. I'd guess by the time Marley had her husband and was threatening to take his organs, she was too far down the rabbit hole to stop. Sad but true. She deserves to feel the full force of the law for her crimes."

I relax a fraction with his assessment. My man isn't interested in her romantically, and he has never given me any indication he is. I need to let his previous relationship with her go.

"You would be right," Harrison agrees. "This seems to be the case for all the medical staff involved. Big payouts dangled before their noses via Dr. Rivera. Then once they were in, there was no getting out. They will all spend time locked up I think unless they manage to broker a deal. But Rivera and Winslow will end up behind bars as the senior doctors. Both Varley Medical and Harbridges are under investigation by the police and the Care Quality Commission. Anyone connected to the incidents has been removed from the boards or staff as required. Some people end up doing bad things, when to start with all they were trying to do was save themselves and those they love."

"I believe we're all two decisions away from jail," Hunter tells the room. "Decision one is choosing to do wrong. Decision two is doing it."

"So tell me why you aren't in the slammer then?" Damon asks, and Hunter smirks.

"Because I'm really good at decision three."

"What's that?" Connor asks.

"Covering what I did wrong up." The head of the Irish Mafia smiles, stands, and brushes off his jeans. "Anyway, I'll be off. I have some business that needs attending to."

"Are you going to cause me a headache?" Damon says wearily.

"No, this is personal." He bows before turning on his heel and making his way to the elevator.

"Don't leave us in suspense," Russell calls to his back.

"I'm going to tell my wife she isn't getting a divorce." With that, the doors open, and he steps into the elevator, waves goodbye, and leaves.

***

Oxford Street, London

"Any one you want," Connor says again. I nip the price tag of the insanely expensive dress between my fingers. The three of us are in a high-end ladies' clothing boutique, perusing the rails of dresses.

When I walked through the door with my men behind me, the woman behind the counter visibly swooned. Russell had flipped the sign from open to closed and then dropped a pile of one hundred pound notes at the cash desk.

"Personal shopping experience," he told her, and she nodded enthusiastically.

We've been here for thirty minutes, though, and I've not tried anything, terrified I'll rip something with my clumsy fingers or oversized tits. Small zips and my body do not go together.

"This dress costs more than a month of my wages," I hiss.

"Just get in the fucking changing room, Trouble," Russell orders as Connor puts a hand on my waist and encourages me in the direction the sign says. The shop assistant appears a few minutes later with an armful of dresses. Connor grabs the hem of my t-shirt and lifts it upwards. I automatically raise my arms.

"Strip," he says, softly. "We have a lot to try on. And you need to look extra special for tonight."

"Where are we going?" I ask for the thousandth time, but all they'll tell me is that we have plans. The niggling worry that this is the day they want me to choose has bothered me since they told me we were going out. I'm both excited and terrified about the evening ahead with both of them.

"It's a surprise," they say in unison as I wriggle out of my jeans. Connor passes me a soft pink dress.

"No, that's not her," Russell barks before I pull it over my breasts, thrusting a blue option in my hands. This one does a

454

little better as I manage to pull it over my ass before Connor vetos the item.

"They're all beautiful," I say in almost a whine, before taking it back off.

"Not beautiful enough," Connor tells me with a small smile. "But the issue we have is three people here have opinions, and one of them has no taste." He glances at his brother who is talking to the sales assistant animatedly. His hands gesture to parts of his own body as he explains which of my assets he wants to highlight. "My brother is also a breast man, but I have a special affection for that ass of yours. It isn't going to be easy to satisfy both of us."

"And what about what I want?" I ask him, cocking my head to the side and trying to appear serious. They are infuriating but oh-so-fucking cute when they bicker. It gives me a small peek into their life growing up together: brothers who adore each other but can't stand to be the one to lose. Their affection is heartwarming but hilarious.

"Your decision is always the most important one." He speaks softly, his tone gentle as if he is talking to someone he is terrified will run. "We'll both honor whatever choice you make." It's a few simple words laden with so much importance, a clear sign that my time to choose is coming closer. Soon, I must decide between them and I'm not sure I can. "For now, let's enjoy the present," he soothes, leaning in and kissing my cheek before running his fingers through my hair. My heart aches; I can't lose this.

The process of them arguing about what I should wear continues for what feels like days, but it's only fifty minutes. The boys squabble about colors and styles while I try each item on. Every dress is beautiful in its own way, but none of them are truly me. I don't get that glow when I look in the mirror, the one when you just know this is the dress for you.

The sales assistant appears again, this time with a bundle of red silk in her arms. She smiles at me, walking past the two men who barely notice.

"This one," she tells me quietly. "This, my dear, is one hundred percent you."

I slide the slick material over my head. It falls perfectly into place. The neck is a high sweetheart cut, exposing just enough of my breasts to be sexy. Thick straps hold it firmly on my shoulders as the silk skims my curves, finishing above my knees. She passes me matching heels, and I slip them onto my feet then stare at myself in the mirror.

"Wow," I mutter, and the male voices go silent. Russell steps up behind me, slides an arm around my waist, and places a kiss on my neck. We look at one another in the reflection. Connor appears at my opposite shoulder and slips my fingers into his.

"Fuck, our girl is hot," Russell says.

"She's a furnace," his brother agrees. "We'll take it."

***

Guilty Pleasure's Gentlemen's Club

"Where are you taking me?" I ask as Connor and Russell maneuver me between them. The silk mask around my eyes turns everything black. I totter along in the red heels with my silk dress, not knowing where I am going. My heart beats hard in my chest with excitement.

"You'll find out in a minute," Connor says. A moment later, a firm hand wraps around my waist, bringing me to a stop.

"It stinks," I mutter as they remove the obstruction from my eyes, leaving me staring at the rear entrance to Guilty Pleasures. I spin round to gape at the pair of them; my face must be hilarious as they both press their lips together to hide their laughter. "Here, you brought me *here*?"

"This place is the start of our story. It was here you looked after our sister. It was here that brought you to us," Russell says, his voice soft as if speaking to a terrified child. "Come." He takes my hand and starts climbing the rickety old stairs. I glare at his suited back. Connor follows behind.

"I feel you staring at my ass," I hiss over my shoulder. He holds up his hands in mock surrender. "You're both in trouble."

"That makes a change, it's normally you in trouble, Trouble," Russell mutters over his shoulder.

Upon reaching the top, I see that the door is already open. We step through, and the sound of romantic music surprises me. Russell leads us toward the notes, pushing open a door at the source. I immediately recognize the space as one of the private rooms available.

In the center of the room is a table laid for three with perfectly polished silverware. A wine bottle sits in a cooler in the middle. My boys lead me across; Connor pulls out my chair while Russell supports me as I lower myself down.

At my place setting is a small white card with the words "Our Girl" written in thick black calligraphy across the front. I pick it up and gaze at it, my head wanting to know what's inside while my heart is terrified to look. The boys take their seats, and two sets of dark eyes land on me.

"Before you open it," Russell begins, and my heart falls. This is it. This is when they make me choose. Tonight is the final time I'll be with both of them. My heart beats hard in my chest as my nerves rise. "There's something we both want to talk to you about."

"What is it?" I ask, my voice barely audible.

"We want to thank you," Connor says. "Both of us. For making the decision to pull the trigger." I blink at him, stunned by the reference to me killing their father. It's barely been mentioned. I took that as them not wanting to discuss my actions. "Neither of us would have been able to do it. As much as we hate him, and as much as he hurt us, I know I could never have taken his life."

"Are you angry with me?" I look between them, searching both their faces for clues of their true feelings. They both maintain that professional look I've seen them use dozens of times now when trying to appear impassive.

"I was in the beginning," Connor tells me honestly. "The decision for revenge was taken out of our hands. I'm used to being in control." His eyes drop away, his hands on the table, fingers twisting nervously.

"And now?" I prompt and his face lifts, intense eyes meeting mine.

"I am indebted to you for loving me, loving us all enough to remove our deadliest enemy. You making that decision was the greatest gift you could give us."

"Trouble," Russell says, reaching over and touching my elbow. My attention moving to him. "You protected us. You're the heroine in our story. We love you."

We all fall silent, both sets of stunning eyes of the men I love with all my heart watching my face. Looking at them, I promise myself that whatever happens, I will cherish every memory we've created. This is love, pure and simple. Not sensible, not understandable, and doesn't fit snuggly in a box, but it's love all the same and no less real.

"Open it now," Connor encourages, gesturing to the card. Russell, however, sits back, his gaze focused on my face. My body heats from the unexpected conversation and tension within minutes of arriving at the last place I ever expected to return to. "Open it," he says again. "There's nothing to be afraid of."

I peel the flap and remove a small white card from its resting place. My eyes pop wide when I read the inscription.

We've decided, but we have conditions...

I flip it over but the other side is blank.

"What have you decided? What conditions?" I stammer.

Russell reaches forward, taking my hand closest to him, Connor repeats the movement with my other. A waitress appears and places our first course on the table, then fills each of our glasses with white wine. We sit silently until she leaves.

"You don't have to choose," Connor tells me softly. "After everything..." His emotion breaks, and he presses his lips together attempting to contain what sounds like a small sob.

"But you said you could never learn to share long-term."

He gives me a reassuring smile. "Being threatened with having your organs removed kind of makes you reevaluate what's important in life." His hand lifts to my cheek. "I told you from the beginning I would do anything to keep you. I almost lost you through death; I am damn sure I won't lose you through my own pigheaded stupidity."

"And you're okay with this?" I ask, turning to Russell.

"Sure. I kind of like the idea of having days off. You like to work a man hard, Trouble." We all laugh, and the mood lightens. My men are offering me everything I've ever wanted. I'm getting my dream: both of them.

"What are your conditions then?" My eyes move between them, looking for the last piece of the puzzle.

"There's only one," Connor says, his cheeks flushing soft red. "And it's mine."

"And it is a perfectly reasonable one. For this to work, we need to be open when things don't," Russell says supportively.

"But if you ever change your mind..." Connor glares at him in jest, then smiles. "What the fuck have you done with my arsehole brother?"

"He fell in love, grew up, and realized sometimes we have to compromise to be happy," Russell replies, straightening a fraction in his seat. His expression turns serious, every word from his lips chosen with care. "If I have to share the woman I love, there's no other man I would trust with her heart more than you."

"Stop it," I squeal. "You're going to make me cry. That will ruin my makeup, and no doubt splatter my dress." They both chuckle. My curiosity needing to know what the stipulation could be, I ask, "What is your condition?"

"No penetrative group sex," Connor says quietly. "If we're both there, I want it to be all about you. Some parts of a relationship need to be private, and this is one of them for me. And if you want to get married in the future, you marry me."

"That's two stipulations," I tease with a glance at Russell who nods in approval.

"Okay, I have two stipulations," Connor admits. "But Sam, I want to one day call you my legal wife. When the time is right."

"Deal." I squeeze his knuckles, and he relaxes under my touch. "Deal, deal, deal. I want you for so much more than that. Both of you."

"Excellent," Russell shouts jovially, then lifts his glass in the air; we all do the same before clinking them together. "To us." His focus falls on my lips, and he cocks his head to one side. "Eat up, Trouble," he says, sexily. "You'll need your energy for what we have planned next."

Our meal eventually comes to end; the three of us cleared every delicious morsel. Connor stands then moves behind me, and familiar dark silk falls over my eyes. Strong hands take mine, encouraging me to stand. I step away from the table and am lead across the room and through another door. We stop in what I think is the center of a new space, but I can't be sure. I don't even know whose hands I'm holding.

"Do you trust us?" Connor asks.

"Always."

"Lift your hands." The red dress is lifted from my body in one slick movement. Someone takes my right wrist and wraps something soft around it, then repeats the process with my other wrist and each ankle. They secure each binding to something behind me, so I'm left splayed with my arms and legs wide. The mask is removed from my face, and when I blink my eyes open I'm left staring at myself in the mirror.

Connor and Russell have removed their shirts, socks, and shoes. Both of them walk in a circle around me, hungry eyes devouring my body, which is spreadeagled for them attached to a metal frame in the middle of the room. My red lace underwear shimmers in the dim light, interwoven with silver thread.

"Oh, you look fucking good like that, Trouble," Russell growls. It's then I notice what looks like a riding crop in his hand. He snaps the dark object against his palm, and my pussy clenches. "Do you remember when you used to call us the good brother and the bad brother?" I nod, and he smiles darkly. "Tonight, we'll be putting those personas to good use."

Connor walks up in front of me; he stands millimeters away, not touching my skin. "I love you restrained," he whispers. "Is that pretty little mind of yours thinking of all the possibilities? And all you can do is take it. Feel every last touch, every hint of pleasure. We won't let you go until we're sure you are fully satisfied."

I strain against my bindings desperate for contact. Focused on him, I don't notice Russell behind me. The stick bites hard across my ass cheeks as Connor's lips lock with mine. He kisses me deeply as his brother lays another blow to my flesh. My body buzzes hard, caught between two men, one inflicting sharp delicious stings while the other soothes me with a kiss.

Connor's hand lifts to my shoulder, and he runs the back of his fingers slowly over my chest to between my legs. There is the undeniable buzz of a vibrator as the crop comes down again. I can't see Russell, but I can sense him behind me, watching me react to both the pleasure and pain.

I've only just recovered from the sting when Connor touches my clit with the vibrator through my panties. My bar vibrates madly under the toy, and my legs try to snap closed, but they are held wide. He chuckles, then drops a kiss on my top of one breast before slipping a finger between the string at my waist and my skin. He pulls hard and my panties snap free.

Neither of them speak—the time for words is done. We've worked through all the complications of our relationship, and this is their solution. Pleasure me together, but enjoy privacy apart. I can live with that. I will love every damn moment I get with them.

Connor places the buzzing object once again between my legs. It sucks on my clit relentlessly as my orgasm builds. Russell's blow comes down again, but it only heightens the sensation. My stomach twisting in knots, not knowing what they plan to do next. Connor's eyes lock with mine as he gives me no chance of relief. He takes my lips again, increasing the speed of my pleasure with a click. Every nerve in my body stands to attention, ready for him. Ready for them. My body wants to give them what they want: my pleasure.

"Please," I whisper against his lips.

"Please what?" he replies as Russell's hand wraps around my waist from behind, his strong body at my back.

"What's our girl begging for, brother?" Russell asks, his hand sliding down my stomach. His thick fingers stop just above the vibrator that's still working my sweet spot. The walls of my pussy clench again, this time harder. I'm at that insufferable point of needing relief, but not quite there.

"I need to..." A moan escapes my lips as another surge takes hold of my body.

"Look at those tits," Russell says, ignoring my need. His hand retreats back up my stomach. It pauses on my breastbone, then his other fingers take hold of my hair and pull my head backward. He drops a kiss on my neck softly, then I feel his teeth sink into my skin. He sucks hard, and I know that will bruise in the morning. "Marking my territory, Trouble. When you look in the mirror later, you'll see where I've been and think of me."

Just then, my body releases, and I let go. My orgasm runs down my legs as I see fucking stars, my stomach clenching harder than ever. I sag in the bindings, but my men hold me up tall. Connor gives me no time to recover, placing the vibrator on my clit again. His hand trails up the inside of my thigh, then he lifts his finger to his lips and sucks each one clean of my arousal.

"That's a good girl," Russell praises. "Let us see those sweet juices puddle on the floor."

"Our girl has a lot more where that came from," Connor tells him

"Our girl won't be able to walk tomorrow. I think it's time for stage two." Russell releases me; I hear the padded footsteps of bare feet retreat, then return moments later. Connor maintains contact with my clit, and my orgasm builds again. My overstimulated knees buckle as the sensation heightens.

"Hold it," Connor growls, his good brother persona slipping. "Feel every fucking nerve in your body, but don't you dare come until I tell you."

"It's so strong," I pant, my voice cracking as I will my body to obey. It doesn't. My orgasm flows from me again as a big hand lands on my stomach.

"Naughty girl, Trouble. My brother told you to hold it." I feel the sensation of cool wet metal between my ass cheeks. "If our girl can't do as she is told, we'll fill her fucking full." The butt plug slides in smoothly while my pussy vibrates, searching for cock to hold on to. I sense Russell passing something to Connor by my side. The vibrator is removed, and it falls to the floor with a bang.

"I was enjoying that," I mutter as Russell's finger replaces it from behind.

"Slide it inside," Russell says, and Connor lifts a large dildo into view. My eyes pop wide. It's fucking huge. "You can take it, and we want to watch."

"Just because I requested no group penetration doesn't mean we don't want to appreciate what that pussy of yours can do." Connor places the tip at my entrance, sliding the cock in slowly. My walls clamp around it, desperate for attention. He moves it slowly. Russell's hand slides down my leg as he crouches.

"So fucking beautiful, Trouble," he says. "That pussy of yours is pure perfection. She sucks it in so damn well."

Connor keeps the dildo moving; without warning, it starts to vibrate.

"Oh, fucking hell," I wail and he laughs, then leans in, one hand holding the bar above my head. He kisses my lips gently, and his dark eyes close then reopen.

"You wanted both of us. You got both of us," he murmurs against my lips. "Now, Trouble, do you think you can handle us?" Fuck, that's hot. Connor called me Trouble. they are *both* calling me Trouble. "Answer me. Do you think you can handle us?" Another kiss hits, this time deeper, demanding I respond.

"Yes," I pant out. "Yes, I can handle you both."

"Or you'll die of orgasm from trying," he tells me, and the whip bites my skin once more. I smile to myself. Sure as hell, the pair of them are mine.

The winner of the man lottery – me.

***

Thank you!

If you enjoyed Chase, I would appreciate it if you would take the time to leave a rating and review on Amazon, Goodreads, or Bookbub. Reviews are so important to authors. It really does help. Thank you for reading.

Review on Amazon here: https://mybook.to/chasebo ok

***

Bonus Scene

If you're not quite ready to let go of Russell, Connor, and Samantha yet, sign up for my newsletter and receive a bonus scene.

Sign up here: https://BookHip.com/HWBGXJP

Still to come in The Level Series

<u>Greyson's Novella</u>

Part of All Shades of Romance Anthology – Winter 2024

I am delighted to be teaming up with my author friends, Carolina Jax and Mercyann Summers, to bring you the All Shades of Romance Anthology.

<u>Greyson; A Level Series Novella.</u>

Being Hunter Devane's right-hand man always brings added complications for James Greyson. Things become even more challenging when Hunter's niece runs off to Scotland without his consent.

Greyson is ordered to go and bring her home, but Tilly Devane doesn't take orders from anyone, including her uncle, the head of the Irish mafia.

Can he bring her home safely? And more importantly, with her virginity intact?

Preorder: https://mybook.to/allshadesofromance

<u>Hunter; The Level Series #4</u>

The Final Instalment– Spring 2025

In his mid-twenties, Hunter Devane was forced to marry Spanish Mafia Princess Isabella Espinosa. The childhood friends separated after a disastrous wedding night. Since then, they have lived in London, married but barely crossing paths.

Now, two decades on, Isabella is demanding a divorce, but Hunter isn't willing to give up his wife so easily. Just because he has been unable to touch her doesn't mean someone else can.

Isabella is about to find out what being married to Hunter Devane means.

Preorder: https://mybook.to/hunterbook

Acknowledgements

This is book number ten, which is incomprehensible to me. It's hard to believe that in a few years, what started as '*I will try to write a book*'...became this. I have so many people to thank who have helped and supported me along this crazy journey. It grows with every book!

My friend Joann, the person I gave six chapters of a random story that popped into my head, and asked her to read it. Her enthusiasm and feedback are what propelled me to write more.

Shirley who cheered me on for the beginning reading chapters as I went.

Without these two ladies, I most likely would never have gotten beyond a few lines on a Word document.

Jessica, a new friend from across the pond, read my completed manuscript and gave me constructive feedback. Her positivity and reassurance that Loving Dr. Jones was good enough to pursue pushed me to look at publishing my book seriously.

Now, she is a key part of my team and still helping me with developmental editing, copy editing, and proofreading.

Tasha and Tiffany, both took the chance to read my first book as ARC readers. Now, they help me with the BETA process, reading as I write. I feel so lucky to have found amazing cheerleaders and friends.

Lilibet and Lakshmi who were willing to give up their time to be the final eyes on this manuscript. In an attempt to catch those pesky typos. I am still convinced there is a 'typo fairy'.

Mercyann Summers, Carolina Jax, and VH Nicolson our daily chats and brainstorming are one of my favorite things about this journey. We laugh, celebrate, and moan together.

Fiona, my chief hook woman, a new addition to my team for this book. Our never-ending conversation is awesome, and I love the new friendship we've created.

Casey, my awesome PA, who organizes all things ARC/Street team and anything else I ask for!

TL Swan, the woman who inspired me to attempt writing between her amazing books and selfless videos which explained the process of becoming an author.

My fellow Cygnets, a brilliant group of writers in which I have found both friends and mentors.

Extasy Books took the risk on a brand new author and published four of my novels within a year. Thank you for the amazing opportunity and education.

My incredible street and ARC teams, who take time out of their lives to read, share, make content, and talk about my books.

Every person out there who has bought one of my stories, thank you so much. Whether you are a friend, family member, or stranger, I feel so grateful you chose to spend some precious time on my book.

Finally, my long-suffering husband and daughter, Gavin and Talia, who have been living with fictional characters since I woke up one morning and decided to write a book. Their support has been constant and without it, the journey would have been near impossible.

About VR Tennent

VR Tennent writes contemporary fiction for women filled with love, heartbreak, and spice. She never promises a happy ending, but guarantees a rollercoaster of emotion. Her flawed characters will navigate their journeys through life, often making controversial decisions in the process. Be prepared to laugh, cry, and scream in frustration as you read.

In January 2022, she decided to put pen to paper and write a book after joining the writer's group of her favourite author. Five months later she was offered a publishing contract on that very book.

Sign up for my newsletter at www.vrtennent.com

Find me on social media

Facebook: https://m.facebook.com/vrtennentauthor/

Instagram: https://www.instagram.com/vrtennentauthor/

TikTok: https://www.tiktok.com/@vrtennentromanceaut hor

Goodreads: https://www.goodreads.com/author/show/22716361.V_R_Tennent

Bookbub: https://www.bookbub.com/authors/vr-tennent

Also by VR Tennent

Surviving Heartbreak **https://mybook.to/survivingheartb reak**

Rebuilding My Future **https://mybook.to/rebuildingmyfu ture**

***

Guilty Secrets Series

Locked **https://mybook.to/locked**

***

Under The Sun Duet

Discovering Me **https://mybook.to/discoveringme**

Embracing Us **https://mybook.to/embracingus**

***

Wild Blooms Series

Heather and Heartache **https://mybook.to/heatherandhea rtache**